I0653742

The Lotus Blossom

A Novel About Waking Up

D. M. Kenyon

Copyright © 2011 D. M. Kenyon and Thought Locker Media, LLC

All rights reserved.

ISBN: 0984016724

ISBN-13: 9780984016723

Dedication

For my daughter by blood and my daughters by creed:
ride hard,
smell the air as you breathe
and love your guts out.
And for my son, the very model of a man,
warrior, friend and lotus blossom.

Acknowledgments

It is said that no one is ever really more than the sum of the contributions made to them. This is as true about people and books too. To my old friend Dick whose wisdom is all over these pages and to the constellation of masters who took me in as a student instead of throwing me out of their *dojos*, temples and retreats, I would like to extend my deepest gratitude for sharing with me what you have learned.

To Jane who I have watched struggle under the glass ceiling of sexism both blatant and latent and who has risen above it all to become a warrior just the same, thank you for providing the space for me to say what I have to say here and everywhere else.

To my parents I must give special thanks. No man and woman alive have ever worked harder to do right by their children. I can still see the younger version of my father, more boy than man, holding up a fallen leaf and twirling it in his fingers – "have you ever seen anything so perfect?" This is the moment I learned how to see. And to my mother who has said "I love you" in ten thousand ways and showed us all that it is what you give that defines you, I love you back in ten thousand ways and more.

To the Lotus Blossoms, my private book club of one book in many rough editions, thank you so much for taking the time to read, think, share and suggest – Malinda, Dick, Nancy, Alice, Jane, Anne, Beth, Hanna, Annie, Susan, Bianca, Laura, Matt, Mary and Grace.

And to Van, Emma, Maaike and Hanna: this is what I have been trying to say to you all of these years – that I understand now what you were trying to teach me.

Contents

Prologue 1
Chapter One: What's In A Name? 4
Chapter Two: The Art Of Niceness 10
Chapter Three: Past Lives 14
Chapter Four: Lesbian Is Just Another Word For Freedom 24
Chapter Five: The Highway Option 33
Chapter Six: Grasshopper Learns About Floppy Fish 41
Chapter Seven: The Meat Market 50
Chapter Eight: The Vortex 58
Chapter Nine: Is There A Victim In The House? 65
Chapter Ten: Back In The Saddle Again 69
Chapter Eleven: Daddy, Can I Be A Warrior? 74
Chapter Twelve: Learning The Ropes 78
Chapter Thirteen: Flying Lessons 83
Chapter Fourteen: War And Manners 91
Chapter Fifteen: Palden Lhamo 99
Chapter Sixteen: The Very Fine Line Between Heaven and Hell ... 107
Chapter Seventeen: Mu 112
Chapter Eighteen: Born To Be Wild 120
Chapter Nineteen: My Name Is Lhamo 125
Chapter Twenty: Training To Run With Scissors 129
Chapter Twenty-one: Lhamo's Mule 135
Chapter Twenty-two: The Fine Line Revisited 141
Chapter Twenty-three: Face The Music, Then Dance 152
Chapter Twenty-four: The Wild Horse 157
Chapter Twenty-five: Eddie Manta 161
Chapter Twenty-six: Dojo Moan 167
Chapter Twenty-seven: When There Is Nothing Left To Give 177
Chapter Twenty-eight: Daddy's Little Girl Is Gone 184
Chapter Twenty-nine: The Usefulness of Muck 193
Chapter Thirty: Randori 199
Chapter Thirty-one: Learning How To Walk 217
Chapter Thirty-two: War, What Is It Good For? 224
Chapter Thirty-three: All I Want For Christmas Is A Very Sharp Katana... 239
Chapter Thirty-four: You Can't Bring A Llama Into The Dojo, They Spit. 249
Chapter Thirty-five: Give Me Shelter 265
Chapter Thirty-six: The Yidam Who Does Not Blink 281
Chapter Thirty-seven: Puja In The Suburbs 288
Chapter Thirty-eight: The Mystery of Tuesday Nights 294
Chapter Thirty-nine: A Different Kind Of Spring Break 307
Chapter Forty: The Art of Tea 329

Chapter Forty-one: My Sweet, Sweet Buddha-boy 345
Chapter Forty-two: Storm Damage 352
Chapter Forty-three: The Monkey Trap 355
Chapter Forty-four: The Difference Between Loneliness And Solitude 366
Chapter Forty-five: The Lotus Blossom 370
Epilogue: A Meteor Over Kansas 378
About The Author 384
Glossary 386

Prologue

Rinchen says that the Chinese have a custom where they write a prayer on a thin piece of rice paper and light it on fire. As the paper burns down to ash, it rises up into the air and delivers its message to the gods. I guess that's what I am doing now. After everything that I have been through over these past two years, my journal is beat to hell, but surprisingly I am not. I am eighteen years old, more woman than girl, and I have just made camp alone in the mountains of Colorado. The engine of my motorcycle is still warm and it is a comfort to me. Here I sit with a flashlight stuck in my mouth writing in my journal as if I am closing in on the end of it. All this writing is really just an opportunity to think about what things mean, at least, what they mean to me in this moment. And like the prayer on rice paper, I may very well just light this thing on fire when I am done and let it float up into the air to find someone who gives a shit.

Damn, that sounded a bit dark and depressing. It's not how I meant it. It's just that the past is the past even though it seems to take on new meaning every time I find myself actually telling someone about it.

I have been taking the time to rewrite my scribbles and notes into a story. I started out as a gossiping fashionista with a fake tan and a deep concern for my social credit score. Now, everything that's important to me fits on a wicked-fast motorcycle as I am making my way toward the coast. I can fight three grown men at once and can meditate on a ball of light for an hour without seeing a single pink elephant. My, how things have changed.

When I was younger, some of my friends got into diaries, but I was not a fan. I was not going to write my deepest thoughts and secrets in a little pink

1

book with a flimsy lock that my brother and a paperclip could expose to the world. And as for Facebook, well, that is just out of the question. I don't even have a Facebook page anymore. No one tells the truth in social media in the first place -- it's just way too public. And besides, these days I am having a hard time understanding why anyone needs to market their personal life like that just to have a list of virtual friends. It all seems to me to be a part of the hungry ghost realm, as Rinchen calls it. It all seems to be driven by people's need to believe that they are known by somebody somewhere in the world even if it is only by an endless stream of trivia.

Rinchen says that you don't need to let people see every random thought that you have no more than you need to parade down the street in your underwear. He says that throwing yourself willy-nilly at the world in an endless string of babbling text or thirty-four photographs of you and your friends mugging for a cellphone camera is not the record of a life. It is the record of an accident. Not every thought is a keeper. It's the thoughts that you are going to stand behind after experimentation and consideration and the chance to say "maybe not" that is all that the world really needs to know about you.

Recently, I started reading through my journal in what started out as a sappy, sentimental stroll down memory lane. Profound joy and utter disaster have been walking uncomfortably close to me as I have been making my way along the path of my life. Rewriting these old notes-to-self and writing new entries has given me the opportunity to think things through. Like the ancient calligraphy masters, this is my Zen circle. Write it down and be done with it. Light your prayer on fire and let it go.

I find myself talking to an undefined *you* as I write. It is interesting how you talk about yourself almost objectively when you are telling your tale to a hypothetical somebody. It does help me weed out my own bullshit as if someone might actually check into what I am saying here and catch me in a lie. But without my imaginary *you*, my thoughts about these journal entries would probably be drowning in violin music.

Rinchen says that when someone talks about their life, they are always telling a story. He says that no one gives out just the facts. They can't. Everything that happens to you gets interpreted – by you, by the people who were there and the people who heard all about it from Gossipedia at school. The story of your life changes as it passes through your lips and into the ears of others who have their brains tuned to a completely different channel.

The only part of your life story that is truly yours, is the one that you keep to yourself.

No two *Budoka* fight in exactly the same way. No two fights can ever happen in any way other than how they happen at the precise time and in the exact place that they do. A butterfly landing on your shoulder in the middle of a sword cut can make the difference between life and death and the tale that is told about it later. At least, that's what Rinchen says.

A really great guy once told me that it is not the picture that you have on paper at the end of drawing that makes a difference to your mind. It is the act of drawing, of absorbing and considering your experience as you stroke the meaning onto the paper, that truly nourishes being. The scenery, the artist and the art become one, but only for the duration of the strokes. We can't store our lives – not even in art. We must simply live, consider and then let go.

-Lhamo

Chapter One: What's In A Name?

My name is Madison and before I say anything more, I would like to state for the record, that I hate my name. That is, I hate my *given name*. Rinchen calls me *Lhamo* and I like that a whole lot better. What the hell is a *Madison* anyway? Who names their daughter after a street in New York City or the fourth president of the United States? I have friends who have equally screwed up names like Taylor Baynes, Reagan Riley and Carter Wilhelmsen – all of whom are girls, by the way. Now that I think of it, their first names are also the last names of mostly dead presidents. They, like me, were born at a time when the whole surname-inversion fad was all the rage for a new age of mothers who were desperately trying to get motherhood right. Somewhere in our house, stuffed in a box in the basement, is the book of baby names that my mom used to figure out what to call me. My name was not intended to have some deep meaning carefully chosen to guide me into a hereditary legacy like Billy Whimplethorpe whose real name is William Darcy Whimplethorpe III or Sunshine Johansen whose parents did a lot of drugs when they were younger, but at least managed to give their daughter a happy thought for a name. "Madison sounded dignified and sort of chic" was how my mom explained it. As far as I am concerned it has all of the dignity of a strip mall.

Of course, it could be worse. My buddy Ack, whose real name is Acaryanandana Balasubramanium, was old enough to drive before he could even spell his name. At least his given name means something – "son of the teacher". Of course, it is not like this meaning shines any particular light on

4

Ack or his dad, given that Mr. Balasubramanium is the vice president of a chemical company.

My friends have taken to calling me Lhamo after the name that Rinchen always calls me, but they have not missed the opportunity to add their own touch to it. They always spell it L-M-A-O, a play on texting shorthand for "Laughing My Ass Off" -- and always in capital letters. I can live with it. Rinchen says that the double meaning is quite fitting if you think about it. I guess I have not thought about it enough because I am not sure what he means, but at the end of the day, nicknames are given, not taken.

I did not grow up in any place of particular importance. In fact, it seems like the people who make up my suburb of St. Louis have gone out of their way to suck the importance right out of it. My town, if you can call it that, is called Westchester. Rinchen says that it is a desperate name. He says that as people moved farther and farther away from the city in order to get away from poverty, crime and racial minorities they left a trail of wanna-be utopian names like Sunset Hills, Town and Country and Westchester. These names were thought up by real estate developers and marketeers and were made to sound like places that you always wanted to come from. Rinchen says that they were pre-fabricated dreams where all the kids look like they are on TV and where everything is perfect – that is, if you are white, at least loosely Christian and middle class. I guess you could say that Westchester is where the American Dream is supposed to happen. Rinchen says that dream and delusion mean the same thing.

Growing up, it was just where I lived. I thought every place had big yards, no fences and the houses all looked pretty much the same. I thought every neighborhood had a pool and you could ride your bike in the streets because the only time there were cars around was just before school started and when my mom and dad came home from work. I thought everyone had a daddy car and a mommy van. I saw pictures in text books and on TV of poor kids living in ghettos but thought that they all lived on a planet called Guatemala, wherever that was. Rinchen says that I was born into a world of meaninglessness, and not in a good way (although he says that there is a good kind of meaninglessness) and that I was reared to be numb from birth. He calls me and my friends "the walking almost dead". I am starting to see what he means and it is deeply disturbing. I am starting to see it everywhere, in fact, as if I live in a world full of zombies. These aren't the scary kind of zombies that you see in movies; they are more like pathetic gotta-have-a-latte zombies that wander around on a tight schedule pretending that they have a life.

5

Rinchen always said that if I worked at it, I could undo the numbness. He said that this would be liberating – from what, I was not sure. He said that if I could wake myself up, it would be the beginning of a powerful life. I immediately thought of those hokey cartoons that my brother used to watch when he was little with robots making high-minded speeches about heroic ideals. A powerful life – what does that even mean? It sounds like the happy, happy, joy, joy crap they teach us at school or an advertisement for the Army. When he said it, I had this flash of a thought of me behind a machine gun in a helicopter over Afghanistan. Girls get to do that now, you know. I saw it in a recruiting poster at school. My mom talks about being powerful, but she usually describes it as standing up to men at work. That has never struck me as particularly powerful so much as being just a little bit bitchy.

And what is all this talk about happiness that Rinchen always harps about? I can see that my friends at school are not always happy. Some of the more *emo* among them even pretend to be miserable. It seems that they are really just trying to get attention. There are the really odd ones like Nick Thompson. He had this thing about cutting himself which is a particularly stupid way to try to get someone to care about you. He even recorded himself doing it and posted it on YouTube a couple of times. That's just whacked. It is actually pretty gutless if you ask me. If you are going to end it all, make it stick. After a few too many fake suicide attempts, they stop bringing the safety net to the side of the building. If you did not get attention before, the world will positively ignore you after you don't jump - again.

Actually, Nick eventually did make it stick and I am still very freaked out about that.

In Nick's case, he was just trying to be important enough to drag his parents away from their social schedule. My guy friends call Mrs. Thompson one of the "hot moms" or "Mickey the MILF" (her first name is Michelle). She is tall, slender, has well engineered boobs and quite the stunning wardrobe. My dad refers to her as a "trophy wife" and then almost always makes the sad joke that he has his own trophy wife, meaning my mom. As if. Nick's dad is a man's man. He drives a big black SUV, works out every day, is well dressed and, to be perfectly honest, has a great butt. Most people say he is everything a modern man should be: smart, well put together, friendly in that fake "hello, Bob, how's your wife" kind of way. He is the very model of a man and a gaping asshole of a dad.

I think Nick gave up trying to be the apple of his parents' eyes at a pretty early age. They only seem to have eyes for themselves and not necessarily for each other. Instead, he sought proof of his own existence by creating an endless series of emergencies that forced them to run to his rescue, even if they came to deeply resent him for it. Back in the old days, kids with parents like that ran away to join the circus. Unfortunately, these days, you actually have to have skills to be a part of Cirque du Soleil. Who goes to see an ordinary circus anyway when you have the mall and MTV?

Nick eventually settled for blowing his mind on whatever drug he could find floating around the halls of Westchester High. I once overheard his mom telling one of the school secretaries that he was getting better, meaning that he was no longer a complete pain in her ass. He hadn't changed. He was just sedated. He spent most of his time loafing around the house lost in the 10,000 songs on his smart phone. It seemed like he had finally figured out a way to be dead without the pain of actually dying. Ack was friends with him and said that if you could get past all the angry youth stuff, he was a pretty nice guy. He liked to read and knew lots of stories. From time to time, I had thought about getting to know Nick better. He wasn't a horrible guy to anyone. He just seemed to be in a constant and incurable state of pain. But when push came to shove, I always backed off. I just didn't want to get sucked into the Nick vortex. As a consequence, he never made it very high on my list of things to do. My life, at least before I met Rinchen, seemed to be complicated enough without trying to save the whales, if you know what I mean.

In my opinion, all that that self-pitying crap gets you is therapy lessons and the loss of car privileges. At our house, my parents are students of parenting. They have read books to figure out how to raise my brother Tyler and me. Yes, my brother is named after yet another dead president. And by the way, what the hell is that all about? They pay close attention to the psychological impact of every decision they make and every action they take and yet remain utterly oblivious to the fact that turning every moment into psychotherapy totally messes with a kid's mind. Nothing could be more annoying than constantly being asked how you feel about this or that or being coached to express your anger. Dude, I have no trouble expressing my anger. The problem is that other than anger, I am sometimes not sure that I have any other real feelings. Okay, so that's bullshit, but I do spend a fair amount of time on the island of Don't-Give-A-Damn.

My parents don't get it. I am not a science experiment. I mostly just want to be left alone. I will figure this stuff out as I go and, after all, I have Rinchen if I really need to get deep into my own cranium. Most of my friends and I would prefer that our parents simply be resources for the things that we cannot get for ourselves like shelter, transportation and unlimited cellphone service. That is their primary job after all. I think there are even laws that say they have to give us that stuff. I don't recall ever learning in history class that Neanderthals spent a lot of time teaching their kids how to cope with their feelings while hunting wooly mammoths. They more or less stuck a sharp stick in a kid's hand and told him to throw it. And, they probably taught him how to run like hell. I am pretty sure that Neanderthal parents did not give a damn about how little Ugg felt about any of it. Ugg only had to face deadly beasts and learn how to kill and eat them. This is pretty straight forward stuff. I, on the other hand, have to learn how to make it through Mr. Leary's history class while he keeps trying to look down my shirt and how to pass by Rita Montrose in the hall at school without busting her in the face for telling half the school that I had mercy sex with Ack. (I didn't, by the way.)

Rinchen says that parents always worry about how their kids will turn out because of their misgivings about how they turned out. He says that parents look back and see everything that they could have done better and that would have given them more. He calls it the consciousness of woulda, coulda, shoulda. Rinchen says that a cat can waste its entire life chasing its own tail in "order to'". We chase a good education, not for the joy of knowing, but in order to get a good job. We chase a good job, not for the joy of doing, but in order to have a nice house. We chase after potential mates, not for the joy of loving another person, but in order to have access to an object of luscious hotness. A good job, a cool crib, some prime beefcake and, of course, a great set of wheels seem to be everybody's gold standard (your mileage may vary on the beefcake).

Rinchen does have a point, though: humans are creatures of acquisition, pretty much like squirrels. But on the other hand, who goes through life playing for a crappy job, a dumpy apartment, a dorky boyfriend and a bicycle? Rinchen says that we all tend to miss the opportunity for real fulfillment. This has something to do with being. I am not completely sure what he means by "being"; I mean, what is the alternative – not being, like, dead? He is a rather confusing person sometimes (although some would say mystical); like one of those guys in a Kung-Fu movie who always speaks in riddles. He would say that they are only riddles to me because I am still a dumbass. He is a rather blunt guy, but never mean about it. But I am not the one who says that perfectly alive teenagers are "the walking almost dead." He says that *being* should not be confused with simply *existing*. He also says that I will figure this out eventually. He says a lot of things. Sometimes I wonder if he isn't completely full of crap and I am a total moron for listening to him in the first place.

Chapter Two: The Art Of Niceness

Since I was in third grade, I have been friends with Ack Balasubramanium. And I can prove it because I can pronounce his name. Lots of girls are friends with Ack because he is funny, but mostly because he is safe. As we got near the end of high school, Ack came to really resent being considered safe. In fact, it drives him nuts. He always has a date for school dances and they are usually really nice girls – who almost always happen to be in between boyfriends and really just want a reliable escort that isn't going to get drunk and maul them in the parking lot. Ack fits the bill perfectly. He is not at the top of the A-list, but he is not a B-lister for sure; so that makes him acceptable to most girls, at least for event-dating purposes. He has manners like my grandpa. They must have locked him in the cupboard under the stairs for quite a while to get a boy to be so amazingly polite like that.

Ack's parents are from India. Ethnic diversity in Westchester is pretty much limited to the children of highly educated professionals from India, Pakistan, Korea, China and Japan and only in small doses. There are guys like Kwame Johnson who are bussed in from the city with a few other kids. Their lives suck. It takes them two hours to get to school and two hours to get home at night. Kwame and the other kids from the city seem to get along pretty well at school, even though it has to be, for them, like going to school on Mars. The fact is, however, most of the white kids think that the black kids are pretty cool. Their toughness and street cred is assumed even if they are science nerds. Kwame comes to school looking all gangsta and that, but he plays the clarinet in the jazz band. I am pretty sure that most gangsta rappers skipped clarinet lessons. The birth of cool just doesn't look like that anymore. He is actually one of the best musicians in school and a math whiz, too.

Ack, however, despite having jet black hair and medium brown skin, may possibly be the whitest kid in Westchester. He is what every mother out here is shooting for in a son. He is not allowed to wear jeans to school and his shirt is always tucked in. He does his homework first and watches TV last. He is one of the smartest kids in school and always makes the effort to be friendly. The thing that I like best about Ack is that he never really says anything bad about anyone, unless he is really, really pissed. It is like criticism and judgment are just not part of his programming. It is almost weird. If he is hanging out in a group and someone starts dissing on someone else behind their back, Ack almost always finds something nice to say about the victim of the back-stabbing. I don't know how he gets away with it, but he does and because of it, he is one of the best-liked guys in school. The reason I like him so much is because I can absolutely trust him.

Up until recently, Ack had been the guy that I knew the best. When I was younger, he was my personal ambassador to the League of Boys. I could ask him things that I would be too embarrassed to ask even my brother. And dads, well, who the heck can talk to them about anything? Lately, Ack has kind of slowly disappeared from my scene as I get deeper and deeper into my own thing. I sometimes wonder if I haven't been kind of using him, in a way. I think he still really likes me in the more-than-just-friends kind of way and while I really, really love the guy, he just doesn't flip my skirt.

It makes me wonder. Why is it that the hot guys are usually knuckleheads and the sweet, honest guys have missed the bus to gorgeous? And why do I get all hot and bothered by looks and not sweetness? Surely sweetness is so much better for you. Rinchen says that if I ever grow up, gorgeous will lose its power and I will eventually look for kindness and forgiveness as the basis for my love life. Until recently, I hadn't really had that much of a love life, so this has all been a bit theoretical. And yet, I do wonder. When I see all of the pretty people in their beautiful homes who seem to merely tolerate each other rather than actually love each other, it seems to me that nearly everybody gets it wrong. The divorce rate in Westchester is off the hook. Half of my friends are portable kids in a joint custody agreement. The parents that stay married do not seem to be happy and the ones who get divorced seem to be happy by themselves, but turn vicious when they have to think or talk about their ex-spouses. It's a mess.

11

I think that's why the boyfriend-girlfriend thing is becoming increasingly rare. Most of my friends hook-up and do the friends-with-benefits thing. Nobody kids themselves about permanence except for a couple of the Malibu Barbie types. Those girls not only practice codependent relationships with their boyfriends, but they have break-ups that are clearly divorce training. By the time they are on husband number one for real, they will already know how to get the house by a well-planned smear campaign staged on Facebook. When you are in high school, you know that no relationship is going to go the distance, so why formalize it by declaring property rights? And yet, if the right guy comes along, do you really want to be that casual? Of course, the art of hooking up has its advantages in that it seems to reduce the babe-to-bitch and babe-to-prick conversion that happens when someone decides to head on to greener pastures. Maybe. Most guys when they move on still seem to turn into total douchebags.

Rinchen says that guys like Ack will likely have happy marriages once girls figure out that he is the kind of guy to play for. He says that kindness and forgiveness are the real currency of relationships and that sex is just another form of getting high. This may be true, but I would like to get stoned on it a few times before I head off to a life of permanent niceness. (I'm just saying.)

There is one thing, in particular, that Rinchen said about Ack that really caught my attention. According to Rinchen, Ack is very skillful in relationships. Skill? Around school, when they call someone skillful in relationships, what they mean is that the person is either manipulative or good in bed. Rinchen says that Ack does not just fling himself at his friends and splatter himself across his social groups in an accidental pattern of whatever. He pointed out to me once that Ack truly has discipline when he relates to people. He doesn't run his mouth off about any old opinion that comes into his mind. He chooses to say nice things. He works at being polite. He cares about being helpful rather than trying to grab power in a group of people by dissing someone to put them down so he can look big. In fact, the key to Ack's popularity is that he consistently builds people up when he talks about them. He is the one guy that everyone knows will not punk them when they are not looking. While he may seem awkward and does not always like the path to "just friends" that he always winds up on, he refuses to step off of it. It is true, after all, that this is the higher, more difficult road and Ack is who he is by choice and his choices are actually pretty good ones.

Rinchen says that when a person starts living her life on purpose, cultivating her thoughts instead of just blurting out whatever comes to mind and starts building relationships based on compassion, she will no longer leave behind a vapor trail of malicious gossip, hurt feelings and animosity. When such a person starts creating relationships based on real caring rather than choosing friends who improve her social score, then good karma will flower in her footsteps.

Karma. Now there's a million dollar word for you. The more I learn about it, the more I realize that I have been an idiot too often in my life and have wasted a lot of time and effort on foolish things.

Chapter Three: Past Lives

In Westchester, there is a vague, yet accepted method for raising children. Books and therapists have a lot to do with it. My parents say that it was very different when they were kids. Both of my grandmothers were stay-at-home-moms, which in those ancient times were just called "moms". Both of my parents have worked for as long as I can remember, but there are many women in my neighborhood who stay at home with their kids. Most of them seem to fit the same mold. They all have the best kiddie gear, like strollers made out of aircraft aluminum. They all drive vehicles with the best crash ratings and ample cargo space. Most of them talk about how much work it is to raise children and sometimes make it sound like it is harder than coal mining. They complain about their kids driving them nuts in one breath, but then talk about how freaking special they are in the next. Fun fact: almost all of them have babysitters. Some even have full-time babysitters. I have heard my mom comment, with a hint of skepticism, that these babysitters are necessary because stay-at-home-moms need some relief from the rigors of child rearing. Basically, they hire sitters so that they can go hang out with other stay-at-home-moms over lunch or at a day spa. Frankly, it sounds like a scam to me and I have some babysitting credentials. But I suppose that the stay-at-home-mom thing is good work if you can get it. I have noticed that in my house, neither of my parents have a huge appreciation for stay-at-home-moms. My father never says that much about it, but has occasionally implied that he thinks that they are opportunists and my mother seems to be jealous of them. I could be totally making that up, but that's my story and I am sticking to it.

14

I remember being with my mom at a grocery store and meeting one of our neighbors, Mrs. Sheffield, on a Saturday morning. Mrs. Sheffield was pushing a double stroller with two toddlers. She looked incredibly well put together for a dash to the store. My mom was in jeans, a work shirt and no makeup. They chatted briefly. My mom's half of the conversation consisted mostly of obligatory doting on the children. Mrs. Sheffield's half of the conversation was mostly about Mrs. Sheffield and her highly dramatic struggle to raise two small children as if normal people didn't have more than one. The whole conversation seemed like a set up. The well groomed appearance, the massive stroller and the tale of woe all seemed to be well-orchestrated to leave everyone who met Mrs. Sheffield with the same question: how does she do it? As we made our way through the grocery store to find laundry detergent, I overheard my mom wondering out loud, "why does she do it?" Mom said that Mrs. Sheffield reminded her of some of the people she knows at work who always make a big deal about every little thing they do so that it covers up the fact that they spend most of their time surfing the internet shopping for shoes.

Mom went back to work when I was about six months old and despite having a career, she continued to do all of the things expected of a Westchester mom. Both of my parents attended every parent-teacher conference unless one of them was out of town on business. My dad's participation in school conferences, however, was largely a strategy to avoid getting yelled at by my mom. My dad's standard of child well-being has always been based on the principle of no blood, no problem. My mother, on the other hand, was talking to teachers even when there were no conferences scheduled and actually read the notices and bulletins that were sent home from the school in my backpack. Because I took dance lessons all through elementary school and was in cheerleading during middle school, that meant endless transportation logistics for both of my parents, but especially for my mom.

Most of the working moms in Westchester have jobs, but not necessarily careers. A ton of them sell real estate. They engineer their working lives so that they can pick up kids when they need to be picked up and drop off kids when they need to be dropped off. Mr. Edwards, down the street, is a stay-at-home-dad, which in my neighborhood is like being a cross-dresser. I have noticed that the other men in the neighborhood, on the rare occasion that they gather for a party at the pool or something, don't treat Mr. Edwards with that same seriousness as they treat each other. They don't ask his opinion about manly things like golf or professional football. While he is not exactly ignored, he seems to spend most of his time talking about children with the moms. I hear that the guy has actually climbed mountains with ropes and stuff, but because he does not play golf, he is an outcast.

My mom is a master car-pooler. She even sets up spreadsheets that orchestrate five or six other moms into a taxi service with dispatching and logistical routing. When I was really little, we had to ride in car seats and this limited the number of kids that could be hauled in a single vehicle. As we got older, my parents bought my mom a minivan that had room for seven kids. It was practically a school bus. It wasn't until my brother was in middle school and I was in high school that my mom got to have a car again. My dad was against giving up the minivan because he said that it was handy for hauling garden supplies and home repair materials. Mom offered to switch vehicles with him. He drives a fairly large silver car with black leather seats, a killer stereo and a sunroof. Dad, realizing that he was being wedged into the middle of his own double standard, caved in and my mom got herself a convertible.

Before I turned sixteen, I had dreamt about all the places I would drive. My parents were dreaming about the transportation burden that I would be taking off of their shoulders. They could not get me to the license bureau fast enough. Since that day, I have been doing more than my fair share of hauling my brother and his creepy little friends around.

The one thing that parents really care about in Westchester is grades. Reading is a big deal here, especially when you are little. My dad once joked, at least I think it was a joke, that my mom started reading to me when I was still in the womb. How weird is that? There is a casual competition among parents to see whose kid passes the critical development milestones first. The Parenting Olympics categories are: walking, talking in full sentences, potty training and reading. How a child places in any of these events amongst the parental social circle will give parents no small amount of pride, or embarrassment, as the case may be. My brother Tyler was almost disowned. He was not fully potty trained until he was three and half. My parents avoided neighborhood functions for the six months of that era in my brother's life, considering it safe to socialize only after he stopped crapping in his pants.

Rinchen says that kids these days are not really educated so much as they are processed and I totally get what he means by that. Everything centers around standardized tests. Even the text books were designed to help you do well on these tests although you don't really learn anything useful. Rinchen says that is the karma of American education. Parents expect politicians to be responsible for educating their children instead of themselves. Politicians want to keep their jobs so they make promises to raise test scores. They then put pressure on administrators and teachers to abandon actual learning in order to spend the entire year preparing for standardized testing. They even delay standardized tests in my school district if there have been too many snow days as if a couple of days is going to make a difference. The scores at Westchester High are among the best in the state and yet we are still a school of complete dumbasses. But we are certified by the federal government as 100% grade-A beef.

Looking back at it now, my young life was structured primarily to build a résumé so that I could stand out on a written application and make it past the gatekeeper of success. I participated in things. There were ballet lessons when I was in first grade. This gave way to hip-hop dancing by fifth grade because the cool girls did not do ballet. Hip-hop was not allowed in Westchester until the white rapper M2 went legit. I still don't think that the adults here have actually listened to his lyrics. They just heard that he won a bunch of major awards and declared hip-hop safe for Westchester children. My mother was wounded when I told her that I did not want to do ballet any more.

I was a Brownie and then a Girl Scout until that became lame. By middle school, I was cheerleading and playing basketball. My dad hated cheerleading. He said that the proper place for a girl was on the court, not cheering for some guy from the sidelines. My mom was not too hot about cheerleading either and by eighth grade I was pretty much over it. I think it had something to do with the cheer moms who wore cheer team jackets to sporting events as if they were reliving the glory days that most of them never had. I guess back in the olden days only certain girls got to cheer. Some of the cheer moms had made the cut and some had not, but they were making damn sure their daughters made it to the top ... of what, I cannot say. Nowadays, the middle school cheer teams are pretty much open to anyone. The high school team is still picked through tryouts, but the A-list does not do tryouts, so being a cheerleader is not really a status builder anymore.

By my freshman year, I was pretty sure my dad was right. I had no interest in cheering for guys. I had no interest in guys who needed to be cheered for and there were a lot of them. Freshman boys are total dorks – except guys like Ack. He was always just my friend. He moved to Westchester when we were in the third grade. He was very shy in those days, but always polite. It did not take the teachers long to figure out that Ack was a brainiac. He had the highest scores on every test and they even talked about letting him skip a grade for a while there. Ack and I participated in the after-care program at school. Our parents picked us up after work, well actually, my mom picked me up after she got out of work. My dad worked later than my mom did. My mom once told me that this was the burden of being on the *mommy track*. Someone had to take one for the team and that was my mom. Because of my brother and me, she could not always devote the same amount of time to her job that some of her co-workers did and because of this she had not been promoted as frequently as my dad had been.

After-care meant that Ack and I had several hours to do homework and goof around. In third grade, kids are just starting to develop cliques. I did not like hanging out with the girlie-girls who played games where the same alpha-girl got to be the boss. Ack was no athlete, so he did not usually hang with the mini-macho boys who were constantly playing games involving the destruction of the universe. We both liked to play soccer and kick-ball, however, and we always seemed to wind up on the same team.

If truth be told, Ack was my first kiss, but I am not sure it counts because I did not kiss him back. It happened when we were in sixth grade. We were sitting by ourselves at a table supposedly doing homework. Ack was telling me about India and how the young people there did not get to pick who they were going to marry, but rather, their parents do. I thought that this was the stupidest thing that I had ever heard. I remember asking him whether or not his parent were going to pick his wife for him.

"My grandmother says that they are," he said suddenly looking down at his book without really seeing it.

"Will she have to be an Indian girl?"

"I guess she would have to be," he said still off in some foreign distance in his mind, "American families don't do it that way."

"Maybe she will be really cute."

"Maybe she will be a cow," he said in despair.

"Find your own wife here and run away and get married," I said. Ack looked up at me suddenly with a grin of hope and then sunk back in his chair and frowned.

"My parents will never allow it."

"Hey, this is America, when you grow up you don't have to listen to your parents. I think it's a law or something."

Ack smiled again. Before I knew what he was doing he leaned over and kissed me on the cheek. I wasn't sure what to do. I wanted to wipe it off, but I didn't want to hurt his feelings. We had been talking about such a serious subject and I could not bring myself to insult him. And ... I kind of liked it. I gave him a hug in return. "It is going to work out, you'll see."

"I hope so".

"It will, geez, you have years and years to figure this out." From that point on, I was special to Ack. He would defend me on the playground. He would say nice things about me behind my back. He was always there to talk to and always there to help me with homework. And he never liked any of the other guys I hung out with -- ever.

More than once, he would create situations so that he could try to kiss me again, but he was never so forward as to push himself on me even though I could tell that he wanted to. I was the first of a long line of girls that told him that they loved him like a brother. In time, the mere whisper of the word "brother" on the lips of a girl would make him instantly sick to his stomach. It was a source of great irritation for him when we got to high school. He complained about it constantly. And yet, he would never degrade himself to push a girl against her will, nor would he ever talk trash about anyone, even the girls who were using him for a safe date.

By high school, most of my friends were girls and we usually traveled in packs, mostly for our reassurance and sometimes for our protection. I would like to say that it was safer in a pack, but not always. While girls band together publicly, privately they will mercilessly tear each other to pieces with gossip and back-stabbing. This is not just confined to the Malibu Barbies, but pretty much happens with all girls except your BFF. And even then, you cannot be sure. I would love to say that I have never done this to anyone, but before I really thought it through, which is before I met Rinchen, I had slashed many a girlfriend's reputation behind her back. The way this usually happens is by text messaging or Facebook, although Facebook can be a bit too public. And besides, we have all had lectures in school about cyber-bullying so it is generally safer to do it by texting. In the olden days, you had to gather in secret to gossip about your classmates. But in the cellphone era, all it takes is fast thumbs and a Send button and you can get broadcast coverage to the whole school and beyond. Every time a phone vibrates in the halls of Westchester High, someone is getting nailed.

I remember thinking at one point, that it was almost an obligation to participate in Gossipedia at school. After all, we all have the right to know the truth about our classmates and if one says she didn't when she actually did, well it is a matter of truth and justice that everyone be informed. Right? I used to think it was amusing. Who needs reality TV when you have text messaging? If someone really screws up, you can hear the phones throughout the whole school vibrating at once as the scoop rips through the hallways and classrooms at the speed of thumbs. CNN does not have a communications network that is this fast.

Rinchen says that people gossip because they believe it gives them power over others. He says that we put people down so that we can look big. He also says that it is a really sick thing to take pleasure in another person's suffering, let alone cause it. You don't learn this for real until you are the one suffering.

A lot of the gossip at school is about sex. It is funny that in the days of internet porn and sexting that sex is still regulated by the unspoken approval or disapproval of the social order. This can vary from clique to clique. The kids who party the most are typically the loosest about sex. The girls who show up drunk at football games are assumed to be having sex. Oddly enough, however, the guys who show up drunk at football games are usually assumed not to be having sex. The Malibu Barbies are having sex but are denying it. The Five Suspected Lesbians are believed to be having sex with each other which is considered, in the halls of Westchester High, to be something less than real sex. This is because real sex has risk. While I suppose there are diseases you can get from girls having sex with girls, it is not the same risks as when girls have sex with guys. Risk is what makes it real and what makes it newsworthy.

Every year, several girls disappear from school for a week or two and Gossipedia reports that they have just had abortions. These reports almost always come from the girl's best friend who promised that she would never tell a soul. Most of the adults in Westchester oppose abortion religiously, politically and morally unless, of course, it is their daughter who has been knocked up at a party. Some girls never tell their parents and slip downtown to Planned Parenthood, if they can get past the age screening. Ah, but the daughters of parents of true conviction that make the mistake of telling their parents of true conviction that they have created a science experiment have to ride out a pregnancy. Nothing crushes your status at school more than being pregnant. It is social bankruptcy until everyone forgets about it and they never forget about it. You are forever branded as a slut although that can, over time, make you popular with a certain type of guy who is cruising for low hanging fruit. The girls that carry their babies to term usually transfer during their pregnancies, but not always. Baby mammas, however, are not accepted at Westchester High, though having sex certainly is.

This is not a great problem for me. My parents would absolutely freak out if they thought I was having sex, let alone got pregnant. I think about sex a lot, but so far, it has not been worth the risk for me. It is something that I will probably get around to in college. I have been told that having sex is practically part of college degree requirements. At least, that is what everyone says.

During my first two years of high school, I really did not have the guy-thing figured out at all. That was largely because the guys in the first couple of years of high school did not have the guy-thing figured out either. But, over time, it starts to sort itself out. First of all, you figure out that how you look is directly related to how much attention you get from guys. While this should be the first clue that a guy only sees you as a thing, most of us think that the attention we get is proof of some sort of worthiness. Pimples are a huge problem and for that reason nearly all of the girls and many of the guys at my school see a dermatologist. Most kids try to get braces out of the way before high school, but it does not always work out that way. I had mine on until half-way through my sophomore year. That is one thing that Westchester has in abundance – abnormally straight, unnaturally white teeth, just like on TV.

Of course, there is the all-important issue of clothing. I would love to say that this is a mixed bag at my school, but it's not. There are a variety of basic styles from Gangsta to J. Crew that are beyond ridicule. Boys wear their jeans baggy and girls wear their jeans tight. It was not until recently, that I noticed that this is an incredibly one-sided fashion phenomenon. Why are we expected to show off every dimple on our butts, but the guys get to wear denim pajamas? Seriously? I remember spending all day at the mall looking for jeans that "fit" which is girl-code for makes-my-butt-look-awesome. Recently, I have begun to wonder what getting your look just right even means anymore. But you know that you are getting into good fashion choices when you see the guys checking you out. This is a bit weird when you think about it because you really only want the hot guys to check you out and you do not want any attention from the dorks. There is no fashion filter that you can wear that only appeals to the guys you want to have look at you. It is an all or nothing thing. Rinchen says that fashion is sexual bait and that people, especially women, often confuse it for power. We think that because we can give a guy a boner that this is some kind of homage to our goddess-like hotness. Rinchen says that this is kind of like saying that a lamb has some kind of control over a tiger just because it has gotten the tiger's attention. It is pretty stupid when you think about it, but it is amazing how many of the girls I know pray to that goddess. Rinchen says that the person who really gets trapped by fashion is the person wearing it. I am starting to see what he means.

Some of my friends get way into looking good. They spend small fortunes on clothing. They make sure that the quality of their clothing matters in the conversations that they have with their friends at school. After all, if a girl is going to invest in a wardrobe she has to make sure that the other girls are educated enough to know what good taste she has. No one wants to be accused of a fashion offense, so everyone pretty much looks the same. Conformity is a safe space. Of course, part of the problem is that the only real shopping you can do in Westchester is in chain stores. Wearing a sweater that your grandma knitted for you, regardless of how nice it is, looks weird because no one has seen it in a store before or on the internet. As a consequence, it has not been approved by the fashion authorities. It is easier to stick to the safety of accepted national brands. Everyone seems to take great comfort in the fact that the clothes they are wearing have been seen somewhere else, and wherever that place was, it didn't suck. Individuality is risky and, in some cases, social suicide.

The guys all wear their hair just a little scruffy to suggest an image of carefreeness, but not too scruffy so as to suggest that their parents have lost control of them – even if they have. The girls all go for straight hair parted on the side, long, but not too long. If you have naturally curly hair or, worse, frizzy hair, you are required to spend an hour each morning forcing it to conform to the code. You think that you are actually evolving your fashion sense, but what you eventually realize is that you are just trying to stay within the boundaries of normal. Rinchen says that kids are more concerned about acceptance than self-expression. They prefer safety to art. Even when they are supposedly expressing themselves, they are really working off of a script. He says that what you wear when no one is looking says the most about you. This is disturbing. I often hang out in my room in my underwear and I do not even want to begin to guess what that means.

My parents are pretty cool about letting me buy clothes and getting my hair cut. My mom and I used to go shopping together all the time. Lately, I have been losing interest in clothes and she more or less has to drag me to the mall to shop. I have been thinking about getting my hair cut short. None of the girls at school except for a couple of the Five Suspected Lesbians wear their hair short, but long hair is becoming a hassle. I cancelled my tanning salon membership while ago. The tanning bed thing has always been a health risk. I hear that they can give you skin cancer and, worse, there is the chance that you will be lying down in a pool of another customer's juice. Most of my friends are going with the spray-on tans these days. Lately, I have been going with my natural skin color.

My dad says that tanning is a quirk of history. He says that prior to the Industrial Revolution, women wanted their skin to be as pale as possible because it was proof that they were of a class of people who did not have to work in the sun. When everyone moved off the farm and into the cities, only the wealthy spent any time outdoors and tans, as opposed to pasty whiteness, became a status symbol of wealth and leisure. A Victorian woman of any stature would not have been caught dead with a tan. My dad says that the French even used to powder their faces to get as far away from tan as possible. Rinchen says that people are always trying to show off things that they have and that others do not. He says that it makes them feel special and privileged. He also says that in the end everyone dies the same way; everyone becomes the same sort of dust and that understanding what makes us the same is more important than trying to find ways to feel different. I am not sure if I buy all of that, but I think I get what he is saying.

So what was my process? I got pre-schooled like nearly everyone I know. I took dance lessons like girls do. I was taught to use fashion as bait. I became obsessed with my status at school, like everyone does. Years of training and programming went into Madison Albright to teach her how to accessorize and get people to like her. There has to be some reason why our whole society is designed to do this. Rinchen says that people used to make friends with their neighbors because they needed each other. I barely know my neighbors. He says that a few good friends used to be enough. People don't have friends nowadays, they have contacts. He says that being useful and friendly used to be how people kept their friends, but that was hard work and actually required being involved. So nowadays, we just market for them using social media. Rinchen says that most people don't have true friends anymore; you know, the kind of friend that would pull you out of a burning building. Instead, he says we only have customers for our personal brand. I get that every generation does it differently because they have to rise to the occasion of the ever-changing world that they are stepping into. But what exactly am I stepping into? There has to be a reason for all of this, right?

Chapter Four: Lesbian Is Just Another Word For Freedom

Julie Roth has guts. She is the only lesbian that I really know and one of the only openly gay students at Westchester High. She seems older than the rest of us. I guess that happens when you spend more of your time thinking things through.

Julie isn't particularly butch, in fact, she is really pretty. I have heard even Ack say things like, "too bad that she's gay" meaning that he would like to go out with her. It is probably not out of the question for Ack because sex is never an issue when Ack goes out with somebody anyway. I am assuming lesbians have guy friends that they love but don't want to sleep with just like anyone else.

I didn't really appreciate what kind of person Julie really is until after graduation. (This is one of those moments where history is changing as I look back at my diary with older, wiser eyes.) We had government class together and I remember once that the teacher was talking about constitutional rights. Mr. Whaley was asking us what freedoms we actually have and what freedoms we don't have. Everyone says the Mr. Whaley is a closet Communist. He lives in the city with his wife in a loft and wears his hair several inches too long for Westchester. Occasionally, we played a game called "Legal/Not Legal". He always had a few wild scenarios that caught everybody off guard.

"You and five of your friends go down to the Jefferson Memorial, hold hands and dance around the statue of Thomas Jefferson singing *Kumbayah*.

Legal or not legal and tell us why," said Mr. Whaley trying to sound like a game show host.

Adam Kokesh raised his hand, "Legal. Freedom of speech and freedom of assembly."

"How wrong you are, Mr. Kokesh. Organized gatherings at national monuments are considered protests and are illegal without a permit. The government says that it has the right to control free speech and assembly around national monuments to protect those visitors that want to take in the solemn atmosphere of these hallowed sites." As usual, there was a murmur of discontent that made its way around the room not quite reaching the intensity of an uproar. Someone in the back of the room coughed out the word "bullshit".

"Next question, you are passing through security at an airport and a TSA officer singles you out for a pat-down. She has the right to put her hands on your genitals whether you want her to or not. Legal /not legal?"

"Legal," I said not waiting to be called on.

"No points for the girl in the third row!" Transportation Safety Administration agents may not touch you without your permission. If you don't agree to be felt up, you will not get on a plane, but they cannot force a pat-down search unless they have probable cause to believe that you have already broken the law."

"Well, it is the same thing as legal. I mean, who is going to miss a flight just because a federal agent wants to cop a feel?" I replied, trying to sound all edgy and stuff.

"And that, my young Americans, is why they get away with it. Who says anything about this sort of stuff anymore? Back in the 60's ...." Oh crap. Once Mr. Whaley got going about the 60's we were done for. It always led to the "you guys are losing your rights because you are too busy polishing your nails or playing video games" lecture. Back in his day they "stuck it to the man". Mr. Whaley was born in the 70's. What I heard was that his activist credentials only included a couple of protests against global warming when he was in college in the 90's.

The game continued, "legal/not legal: homosexual sex is legal in every state among consenting adults."

"Illegal in some states" blurted out Rita Montrose "and it should be illegal everywhere!" Rita was a Malibu Barbie. She dressed like a slut, but spat out judgment on others like a preacher's wife. She went to church every Sunday with her family. I guess she needed to be forgiven for all of her double standards. You would see her around school with her friends. They were always taking pictures of themselves, usually trying to look like pop stars sticking their asses out and lifting their chests to get the most out of their padded bras. I heard that they had to add an extra file server at Facebook just to hold all of the pictures she had uploaded of herself.

I was sitting next to Julie and she suddenly got this look in her eye like she was going to bitch-slap Rita back to her ancestors. "Gay sex is legal in every state since 2003 after Lawrence v. Texas and somebody needs to pull her tampon out because she stuck it in sideways." Julie had just pulled off a ninja diss and the class burst out laughing.

"Let's watch the language," said Mr. Whaley trying not to smile. "Ms. Roth is correct, homosexual sex was declared a protected liberty by the United States Supreme Court in 2003 in a case called Lawrence v. Texas. Very impressive, Ms. Roth. Wow, a student who has actually read a Supreme Court case. Maybe I am being presumptuous here, I am assuming you have read it."

"Yes, I've read it," said Julie. Her facial expression had gone cold as she continued to stare at Rita.

That is one thing I had in common with Julie Roth. We both seriously disliked Rita Montrose. Rita was the one who had coined the phrase "Five Suspected Lesbians" and tried to stick it on Julie and four other girls like a scarlet letter. Julie was not overly confrontational, but she did not take crap either. I didn't know her very well, but I liked her self-confidence.

I did not have a problem with gays and lesbians. I took the politically correct point of view that "to each her own". It was kind of cool that Julie could have all the sex she wanted and not worry about getting pregnant. But she did have to take a lot of shit for it, mostly behind her back and mostly from chicks like Rita. Most of the guys thought that Julie was kind of hot and the thought of her having sex with a girl was a turn-on for most of them.

A couple of days after Julie whacked Rita in class, I saw her in the lunchroom and decided to ask if I could join her. I guess I was curious and wanted to know more about real, live lesbians. She was a bit surprised when I asked if I could sit with her and her friend Shana, but she seemed equally curious as to why I was suddenly breaking ranks and changing my lunch pattern.

"I have to tell you, I nearly peed my pants when you took on Rita in class the other day."

"Yeah, I am not a big Rita fan," said Julie crunching into an apple. Shana started to smile. She had not been in the class, but the whole school had heard about it. Julie had definitely earned some cred for that one.

I was at a loss as to how to strike up a conversation with a lesbian about how she came to be a lesbian. It seemed like a pretty personal thing to me, but in high school, your sex life, if you have one, is anything but personal. What exactly do you say? "So, I hear you are a lesbian, how is that going for you?" I opted for the indirect approach.

"How did you know about that Supreme Court case?" Julie looked at me trying to assess where I was going with this, but decided to play along.

"Well, my parents are college professors. My mom teaches at the law school at Wash U and, I'm gay, so it is something that concerns me in particular." She was watching my face to see how this was landing for me. I think she was trying to decide if I was sincere or not. After a pause she continued, "I am part of the school's gay and lesbian coalition. It is not much of a coalition, there are all of six of us and two are straight, but we have a group that has been pushing on the school to improve gay-lesbian awareness and fairness. Ever since the court case, the school, like it or not, kind of has to deal with us."

"So that explains all the sensitivity training and stuff that we've been getting from the teachers," I said. I hadn't realized that this was an actual program, *per se*; I just thought it was what schools do.

"Well, some of the teachers talk about it, but not all of them. There are still a whole bunch of homophobes here and don't get me started on the parents. If some of these assholes had their way, people like me would be burnt at the stake."

Homophobe. That was a new word for me. I had to look it up on the internet when I got home. It's funny that Julie just threw that word around as part of her normal vocabulary, but I guess for her it is a very important word and it made sense that she would use it so matter-of-factly. I started to notice that Julie actually talked like she was in college or something. She used big words frequently and was pretty intellectual.

Rinchen says that everybody's mountain is a different height and yet we all have to climb ours just the same. We can complain that our path is longer and steeper than someone else's, but it will not make the journey any easier. Your life is your life and you have to deal with it as it comes. I knew that some kids, not just Rita Montrose, ripped on Julie and the other Five Suspected Lesbians behind their backs. Some of the guys got lewd about it making jokes about how they would like to watch. There was only one gay guy that had come out at my school and a few more who everybody pretty much figured were gay, but were not open about it. I have noticed that our society does not treat gay men the same way as gay women. With women it is considered kind of sexy by both guys and girls, whereas, most straight people think that two men having sex is just gross. What is up with that? For Julie, life is way more serious because she is not doing the normal thing and she has to stand up against a lot of grief. It would make sense that she would have to think some things through more than I would, but it seems to have made her a better person – like being part of an unpopular group has actually made her tougher and smarter. Rinchen would say that all hardships are opportunities. Whoa! I think I just had my first flash of wisdom and it didn't even hurt!

"Do you get a lot of shit?" I asked Julie.

"Not really. Most people are cool about it. The Rita Montroses are fairly rare. But everyone is kind of awkward around you, you know. You can tell that it is not normal for them. A lot of straight people are well intentioned, but still afraid. It is like they are worried that if they think too much about what it is like to be gay that they might actually become gay themselves. I think that, for some of them anyway, it is like standing on the edge of a roof. They are afraid of the drop, but at the same time, it has this eerie attraction to it. Some of the people who hate us the most are the ones who probably go home and watch gay porn on the internet when no one is looking. I might be a little jaded on that point, however." Her smile gave away her sarcasm and she rolled her eyes.

"It seems pretty unfair," I said, "to be hated just because you fall for people of your own sex. I mean, who cares, right?"

"Lots of people care," said Shana.

"But why?" I asked.

"Why do they make women cover their faces in the Arab world and stone them to death if they cheat on their husbands? Why do most of the girls in this school wear their jeans so tight that they can barely walk? Are they comfortable? No. But does it get you noticed? Yes. You need to wake up, sister. Your sexuality is managed by men. Granted it is not as bad as it was, but you do not have the same power to be you that the guys do." Shana was looking at me as she finished talking like I was part of the problem .

"Bullshit! No guy tells me what to do!"

"Really?" she asked sarcastically.

"Really!"

"Do you shave your legs?" Julie asked.

"Yes, all the time. What's that got to do with it?"

"Do you like shaving your legs?"

"Not really. It is a total pain in the ass."

"Then why do you do it?"

"Because, I am a very hairy person and it looks gross if I don't," I said starting to wonder where this was going.

"Why is leg hair gross? And first of all, who told you that it was gross?" Julie asked. She was starting to get a little agitated.

"My mom, I guess; other girls," I said trying to remember how and why I was taught to shave my legs. It was weird, now that she mentioned it. I remember my mom showing me how to do it in eighth grade before a dance. I had become very self-conscious about the hair on my legs. I have dark hair and it really shows up. The boys at school were starting to call me Gorilla-girl behind my back.

"Think really hard Madison, who says that hairy legs are gross? Your mom was just the messenger. Who does it ultimately offend?" Julie was leaning over the table like a lawyer in the heat of cross examination.

"Well, I guess guys don't think it is very attractive."

"DING, DING, DING, DING, DING! MADISON ALBRIGHT YOU'RE OUR GRAND PRIZE WINNER!" Julie shouted waving her hands in the air in mock congratulations. "Shaving our legs is the American version of the burka, you know those slip covers they make Muslim women wear in Afghanistan and places like that."

"But I like the way it looks," I replied trying to defend myself.

"Well, for starters you have been taught to think that way since you were little. You do not see women on the cover of Vogue with hairy legs. And because women wear dresses that show off their legs and men don't, we get to bear the burden of this custom. It has been part of a cultural message that has been pounded into our heads since we were born."

"But I like to shave my fricking legs, damn it! I, me, Madison Albright like to shave and I get to do that if I want!" I was getting feisty. I did not like the suggestion that I was some kind of tool in a plot to please guys with my appearance. I was not a Malibu Barbie. I think for myself, don't I?

Julie softened her tone, "it is not whether you have come to like it or not. Hell, I shave my legs, but my point is that this custom comes from male domination of our society. For centuries, men have said how we will look and how we will behave. They have told us that we cannot have abortions if they rape us. They have told us that we should shave our legs. If a girl wears baggy jeans to school and doesn't show off her ass, she is either a slob or a lesbian. It is like these dipshits are sitting around a bar with a pole on it making us dance for their pleasure – and most of these guys are complete morons. Why do they get to set the cultural tone and tempo of being a woman? The whole system is full of double standards." People were starting to stare at us from all around the lunchroom. I was sure that Gossipedia would report that I was getting lesbian lessons from Julie and Shana, but this was new news to me and I wanted to think it out.

"Hmmm. I see your point," I said finally, "but I am not sure that it is as bad as you say."

"No, it is worse," said Shana. She had been sitting there listening to Julie and nodding in agreement, but now she was stepping back onto her own soapbox.

"Why do you say that?"

"Well, first there have been a lot of strides taken to create gender equality since the 1960s, but people act like it is handled. There is still no Equal Rights Amendment and if you look at TV and the internet, women are still being depicted mostly as bimbos. Sure you see women cops and lawyers on TV, but they always cry and get consoled by some bruiser when they have had a bad day. Have you ever wondered why women cry so much? Is it genetic? I don't' think so. They deliberately teach boys not to cry. It is part of their training. It is not particularly healthy, but they do it. We have had the privilege of being more open with our feelings because little kids and women get to do that while men have to stay tough. We are not taken as seriously, so it is okay if we show our emotions at the drop of a hat. We have been trained to be weak. Worse, we have been trained to think that we are weak. We have been bred to serve a purpose in the heterosexual man's world. Everything around us tells us to be a certain way. It tells us how to dress, how to act, and how to fuck." Shana sat back leering at me as she finished speaking as if to say "take that girlfriend!"

This was turning into a tag-team match. Before I could respond, Julie jumped back into the ring. "You know this is not a lesbian thing, right? This is a *woman* thing. Genetically, we are meant to breed with guys and that is pretty hard to deny. But what does that have to do with our identities as people? What does it have to do with who we are or who and what we love? A lot of the rules were designed to make sure that people kept having sex and babies kept being born. Rules like heterosexual marriage, monogamy, punishment for infidelity --- rules, that, by the way, have been slapped the hardest onto women and not men. It is all part of a social design. It is on purpose. But we live in a time when the species has more than enough new members. Why then, is the pressure to breed still on us as if life depends on it? There is no need to bind us to men to make sure that we squirt out the next generation. Hell, in the middle ages we did not even get a say in who we would marry. We were traded like horses because that is what we were to the men in control – animals for breeding. But you know what, I am more than my vagina!" Julie nearly shouted out this last sentence and now nearly everyone was looking at us.

"Wow." That was my best attempt at a response. That is all that I could think of to say to both of them as I sat there thinking about the debate and growing more than a little concerned that Gossipedia was already reporting Six Suspected Lesbians. I said very little as I dug into my lunch trying to get the conversation to cool down a little so that we could step out of the limelight.

After a few minutes, I decided to step back into it. "Well, I see what you are saying, but I kind of like guys. They are idiots, but they are cute."

Julie laughed, but Shana frowned. Julie leaned back on the bench of the lunch table and said, "You know it is not a matter of whether you like guys or not, or like girls or not. Who you like to cuddle up with is a matter of what makes you feel intimate and loving. The point is *freedom*. The point is that I should not be herded by my culture to go in a certain direction. I should get to choose freely from all of the possibilities. I should not be forced to dress a certain way. I should not be forced to have sex with one gender or another. I should get to say how I get to create myself as a work of art without prejudice. If people do not like what I come up with, that's cool. You can't please everybody. And if what I come up with is harmful to others, then maybe someone has to stop me or get me to think things through. But it is ridiculous, that in this day and age, that we are still being pushed into one thing or the other simply because we still live under an ancient habit of breeding management. For centuries the history of woman has been the history of woman as *thing*. I intend to live my life as a *person*."

I thought about this conversation for days and days. I still think about it now. I used to think that Julie Roth took herself way too seriously, but now that I think of it, I do not think I was taking myself seriously. I realized that I was just following along with the herd, that I had never considered what the real differences between genders were and there were not that many, other than the obvious roles in reproduction. It used to be so automatic. I never heard my parents discuss gender like there was anything to talk about. My parents supported gay rights which is not a universal opinion in Westchester, by any means, although it is becoming less of an issue year by year. My dad would sometimes call something "gay" when he thought it was weak or unworthy. He's got it wrong. It takes balls to be a lesbian, no insult intended. Many parents are still scared that their kids, especially their boys, will grow up to be homosexuals although they don't seem to worry whether or not they will grow up to be assholes.

Julie was right about one thing. There is a lot of pressure to be a thing. You hear it all the time. Even the girls in my school see hot guys as objects, as toys, rather than as people with thoughts and feelings. It is funny, I used to look at people and see their shape and color. I might get turned on or be repulsed depending on my opinion of them. They were like clothes on a rack. This one is cool, this one is not. But after talking to Julie and especially after meeting Rinchen, I started to see people as energy and then, once I figured out what the word meant, I saw them as *beings*. Everyone is complicated. Everyone is a mish-mash of stuff that runs through their thoughts and lands in their action, as Rinchen says. I have noticed that I am starting to get a little pissed off when people talk about other people like they are lawn furniture. I have come to realize how little freedom we really have around others, especially in groups, and why most of us haven't got a clue as to who we really are.

Chapter Five: The Highway Option

In 1492, Columbus sailed the ocean blue and turned right instead of left and learned that there was a whole new world just over the horizon. Expanding your transportation opportunities can do that for a person. Rinchen was the whole new world I discovered when I expanded my transportation opportunities. When I was little, I travelled by foot and by tricycle, but never out of sight of my house. The range of my transportation defined the world I knew. That all changed when I learned how to ride a two-wheeler. Suddenly, my world was a whole lot bigger. I knew Beth Hammerstein from school, but we were only school friends. She lived a half a mile away and that was not within my scope of travel unless our moms organized a play date. But that all changed when I learned to ride a bike. I no longer had to hang around with the kids on my block, some of whom were older and some of whom were younger and all of whom I had been stuck with. With a bike, I had choices. Once Beth's house was within my reach, she became my best friend. I could also ride to the grocery store and buy candy and soda at will, as long as I could come up with the money. In fact, it was the beginning of the essential relationship between transportation and money. But one way or the other, it still meant freedom.

If riding a bike expanded my world, getting my driver's license blew the doors off it. Now, so long as I had the money thing handled, I was hypothetically within striking distance of the entire continental United States. Beth and I used to talk about all the places we were going to go as soon as we had the money. Looking back on it, it is clear to me that having a driver's license was the beginning of my freedom of movement, but also my dependence on cash. I even had to babysit kids I didn't like and work as a lifeguard at the pool just to be able to drive to school. This is how it starts. You learn to drive to be free, but in order to be free, you have to pay for the car and the gas, so you give up all of the time that you were going to use to see the world to make the money to pay for the gas that you now have to burn going to work to get the money to buy gas to go to work…. It does not take long before you are a hamster on a wheel. I think you formally become a slave when you buy a house, or so I am told. In fact, Rinchen says that every time you try to improve your life by getting better clothes, a nicer place to live or a new TV, you wind up deeper in slavery to the point that you give up your freedom entirely. It's like crack.

But if you dare to go into denial about transportation costs, St. Louis is a great place to start a road trip because it is close to everywhere. Chicago is a five hour drive and you can be in Denver or New York in a day. Memphis is four hours by car and Atlanta, eight, if you break a few laws. While we drove around Westchester on our learner's permits with our parents by day, we were texting big travel plans to each other by night. At first, when the blessed moment came and we had real drivers' licenses, freedom looked like driving to the mall and wandering around without having to meet up with our parents. Then it was riding around at night looking for something to do or visiting friends when their parents were out. But eventually, we were back to where we started - boredom.

The biggest problem with being sixteen is that there is nothing to do. Other than going to see movies that will all be on cable in a couple of months anyway, there is nowhere to go. There are only so many hamburgers you can eat in fast food restaurants and they make you fat, so why bother? Westchester is not exactly a cultural Mecca. In fact, there are no restaurants here that are not part of a chain. There is no theatre, not even crappy civic theatre. There are no museums, except for The Museum of Transportation, or clever little shopping venues that are local and unique. It is a Cheez Whiz community, albeit the cheese is Vermont cheddar. Art just doesn't happen in Westchester. I think they made originality against the law.

You can hang out at Starbuck's because coffee is legal at sixteen, but other than sitting their sipping a latte there is nothing shaking. Beth and I would drive through an entire tank of gas listening to the crappy car stereo in the Kid Car, the name for the busted old Toyota that I was allowed to drive, talking about all the cool things that we would not be doing that night. My dad says that in his day, he would sneak into bars at sixteen. The drinking age in those prehistoric times was eighteen. Nowadays, especially in Westchester, no sixteen year old is going to get into a bar. First of all, there are no bars seedy enough in Westchester to disregard the law to that extent. And even if there were, no bar owner would be willing to get caught serving a high school student for fear that he would find himself in the center of a minivan posse of Mothers Against Drunk Driving being protested until he went out of business and just before he was hung from a street sign.

It doesn't really matter. I hate cigarette smoke and I am not a big fan of alcohol -- even less so now that I am training with Rinchen. Bars are really only good for meeting people who have nothing better to do than go to bars although some bars have live music and that can be cool, or so I am told.

In my town …. hmm. Actually this is not a town in the traditional sense, in that there is no Main Street or other center of the community. City Hall is located in an industrial park at the outskirts of the geographical boundaries of Westchester. And now that I think about it, it is not a community either. There are no civic groups to speak of other than those connected to the schools. In fact, now that I think about it even more, most people do not actually spend time with one another. On my street, the lights in the front of the houses are out by 9:00 pm and everyone is hunkered down at the rear of the house in front of a television or a computer. There is an annual pool party in my neighborhood that is usually well attended and where everyone seems to know everyone else even though they have not actually spent time with each other all year. It is kind of creepy, in a way. Despite the lack of any real relationship, all the adults seem to know quite a bit about the others, maybe too much. It is like some sort of familiarity seeps into the brains of the adults of our subdivision while they are sleeping. Maybe they text each other. Who knows?

Of course, I did not notice any of this until a couple of years ago when I met Rinchen. Beth and I had decided to lie to our parents about going to the mall and then headed down the freeway into the city. Most of our friends don't dare to travel past the Inner Belt, the highway that circles St. Louis and the crossing of which takes the "sub" out of "suburban". We have all been to the stadium to see the St. Louis Cardinals play baseball and we have gone on field trips to the zoo and to see the Arch. But that is not where Beth and I were headed.

At that time, we were sort of friends with Megan Laskowitz. Megan, to this day, is slightly mysterious to the point of being cool. People say that she drugs a little and drinks a little more, but she has always struck me as pretty laid back and yet street-wise in her own way. She's pretty much nice to everyone and seems to float outside of the normal cliques. What I like about Megan is that she has her own sense of style that cannot be found in a chain store. A lot of girls wear black leather jackets, but Megan's jacket is made for riding a motorcycle which she drives to school when the weather is good. She always looks like she either wants to kick your ass or make out with you, sometimes both at the same time. And yet, she is easy to talk to, although she never seems to be completely interested in what you have to say. She hangs out mostly with guys even though she seems to care even less about what they have to say. For whatever reason, guys never seem to hit on her even though she is really cute. They seem to be either afraid of her or they respect her -- maybe a little of both. Given that respect is probably outside of the genetic design of the guys at my school, they are probably just scared shitless of her.

Megan had told us that she had been hanging out with a guy in the city and that they liked to meet at a hookah bar on Washington Avenue called Ahab's. If you don't know what a hookah is, Google it. The cool thing about Ahab's is that while they serve candy flavored tobacco, they do not serve alcohol which means that if you are eighteen, you're in and I had heard that they do not card unless you are smoking. To Beth and me, this sounded a heck of a lot better than the mall. Megan told us that she was going to be down there on Friday night, so we told our lies, gassed up the Kid Car and headed toward the Mississippi. We even wore our big girl jeans.

I don't know what it is like in other cities. I have only been to Orlando to go to Disney World, although we did once visit my cousin who lives outside of Chicago. But Washington Avenue is a far cry from Westchester. I think it is pretty cool. There are all sorts of restaurants including sushi bars, a couple of Irish pubs, a number of dance clubs and boutiques. The people that live down there all have tricked-out lofts, hot cars and no kids. They actually seem to know each other and hang out at night. A block off of the avenue is the City Museum that is open late on the weekends and is some guy's monument to an acid trip. There is a school bus mounted to the top of a ten story building hanging off it like it is going to fall and crush everyone waiting to get in. There is a life-sized concrete whale inside and, if you feel like it, you can crawl up its ass. There is nothing like this in Westchester or in all of St. Louis County. In St. Louis, aside from being obsessed with where everyone went to high school, even if you are fifty years old, there is a bright cultural line between city and county. If a city kid says that you are from the county what he really means is that you are a privileged pussy. County kids, whenever they venture into the city, try very hard to conceal the fact that they are from the county. The BMW usually gives them away. Most of my friends are not allowed to go into the city at night, me included, because "there be black people there, arrrgh!" That is perhaps the best part of going downtown. The people are different. They look different. They are relaxed. They are awesome.

When Beth and I got to Ahab's, we saw Megan through the window taking a hit off of the hookah that was placed in the center of a knee-high coffee table. She was the only girl at the table and there were several older-looking guys sitting with her, most of whom were quite hot. They were smooth without that twitchy-macho crap that guys at school always pull when they meet someone new. They were a lot like Megan. As we were walking in, a waiter started to ask for our IDs but before we could start our song and dance about how we left them in the car, Megan said, "It's cool Steve, they're old enough". Steve knew that this was a wad of bull, but did not really care and let us pass. Megan introduced us to the guys at the table and told us to sit down. We were really working it to pretend like we went to hookah bars all the time. The jig was up, however, when Beth tried to take a hit and the cherry flavored smoke had her coughing up a chunk of lung. Everyone had a good laugh. Steve looked like he was about to reconsider the ID check. I passed on taking a hit off of the pipe claiming to have asthma. The smell of the tobacco was rich and woody with a distinct smell of sour cherry; not entirely unpleasant. Ultimately, I was afraid of making an ass of myself like Beth had just done and figured that before I hit off a hookah in public, and especially in front of older hot guys, I should probably practice off-grid on a blunt or something.

At first, we sat there soaking the place in. Megan's friends all wore thick black boots and had leather coats of various colors, but cut tight to the torso with padding in the shoulders and elbows. At their feet, was a collection of motorcycle helmets, some matching their owner's jacket and some not. On our way in, we had passed a row of motorcycles, all of them racing bikes, parked diagonally to the curb in the street. There were way more bikes than people sitting around our table. As I looked around the bar, I could see that many of Ahab's customers were bikers.

While we sat there mostly listening to stories of riding wheelies down the freeway and near misses while passing trucks, I thought to myself that this was quite possibly the coolest thing I had ever done. Everyone in Ahab's looked to be twenty-something and there was a complete absence of the adolescent sexual tension that makes the guys at school act like little boys seeing their first naked boob on the internet. Megan's friends were polite, but seemed to find us nearly as uninteresting as Megan found most people. They made efforts to include us into the conversation even though it was perfectly clear that neither one of us had ever ridden on a motorcycle, let alone driven one.

Eventually, the evening started to wind down and some of the guys were planning on heading to a real bar and knew that we could not go with them. One of the guys, a tall lanky fellow in a black T-shirt with a patch of black hair that fell over his right eye, asked me if I wanted to go for a ride on his motorcycle. His name was Tripp. It was hard to tell, but I got the idea that he may have been the guy Megan said she was meeting. Before I could think about it, Megan said "it's a good night to pop your cherry – you ought to go for a ride". All the guys laughed. This was a challenge and I was too self-conscious to wimp out. We went outside to a rainbow row of crotch rockets. Megan's was school-bus yellow. Tripp's bike was candy-apple red and looked like something out of a science fiction movie. The handle bars were low and the back seat, if you can call it that, was higher than the driver's seat by quite a bit. Tripp gave me a helmet that looked like something off of a spaceship and explained that it was important that my whole face be protected. This started to wig me out. Why was this guy, who looked like he didn't give a damn about anything, suddenly so concerned about crash protection? Megan told me to get on after Tripp was already seated and to hold on tight to his waist. The only other thing I could hear her say over the roar of the bike being revved higher and higher was something about leaning with the bike. I was not sure what that meant, but I soon found out.

Tripp took it easy on me at first. He eased away from the curb where he had parked and rolled out onto the street. But when he saw the next three street lights turn green, he gunned it nearly throwing me off the back of the bike. Within seconds we were ripping it with parking meters popping by like pickets on a fence. I nearly peed my pants. I could feel my fingers digging into Tripp's abs and could feel his body heaving up and down as he was laughing at me for gouging his stomach. Within seconds we had travelled three blocks. The light a block further down turned red and Tripp slowed down but only enough to bank hard to the right and round the corner. Holy crap! Nothing but green lights for blocks and blocks and I suddenly became aware of why they call them crotch rockets. The roar of the engine was deafening. Even though it had been a warm evening, it was suddenly cold. Tripp was practically lying on the gas tank and my hands were being squeezed between cold steel on one side and rock-hard abdominal muscles on the other. Under ordinary circumstances, I would have been more than a little aroused, but the absolute terror that was threatening to weaken my bladder muscles took all of the magic out of the moment.

Another hard banking turn to the right; this time he barely slowed down at all. We leaned so hard to the side that I thought the pavement was going to take my leg off. Within a flash we had cleared the corner and were upright again, this time flying toward the river. As we ran down the avenue toward the football stadium the light ahead turned red. There was no right turn on red here and we had to stop. As we idled at the light, Tripp said, "Are you hanging in there, Little Bit?" Trying to sound like I had not just crapped my pants, I said "Oh Yeah!". Tripp took this as permission to break a land speed record the rest of the way back to Ahab's.

Beth said later that she could hear the roar of the motorcycle all the way along the two mile track that we made around the near-north side. "That's so cool," she squealed with glee. "I am glad you think so," I said with more than just a little trepidation in my voice. But as I swung off the bike, it dawned on me that there was a heck of a lot more to life than what I had been lead to believe.

"She did good," Tripp said to Megan.

"Yeah, well at least your seat is still dry," Megan said with a wry smile, "you must have gone easy on her."

"Oooh, nooo," Tripp said defensively, "I wrung out the rag on that one; 'Little Bit' got a run for her money".

Megan smirked, "Little Bit, huh? Hmmm. Alrighty, then."

I could see, despite Megan's amusement, that she was at least somewhat impressed. From that point on, it seemed like I had become, at least to some degree, a real person to her. In the hallways at school she would acknowledge me coming and going with a wink or wave. I have to say, that I really like being liked by Megan Laskowitz.

Beth had passed on taking a turn on the back of Tripp's motorcycle. Megan and the other guys mounted their bikes and joined Tripp out on the street. I could hear Megan's muffled voice from behind her face shield say, "see you at school" just before she gunned it and ripped down the street at the rear of the a pack. Within seconds they had all swooped around the corner and disappeared from sight, but I could hear them for several minutes more as the whine and roar of the speeding motorcycles faded into the night.

"How fucking cool is that," squealed Beth. "Pretty fucking cool," I responded only partly paying attention to her while the rest of my mind was dashing through the night with my arms wrapped around Tripp's waist. "I really hope that's not her boyfriend" I said, not realizing I was using my outside voice. Beth's eyes suddenly widened and then she said half-mockingly and under her breath, "Alrighty then – Little Bit". The smirk was still on her face half way up the block as we headed to the car.

There had been no place to park on Washington Avenue when we had first arrived, so we had parked on a side street. We had deliberately chosen to park in front of a large shop window that was brightly lit anticipating the darkness and the safety risks when we returned. When I had parked the car, I had paid no attention to the nature of the shop with the bright light in the window. In my excitement to get to Ahab's, I had not given it a thought. As we got closer to the car, I noticed that the light was still shining brightly through the glass. It was not a store. It looked like a gym or some sort of fitness center. There were still people inside. Since this was a night of discovery, on a whim, I decided to walk up to the window and take a look in. That is the first time I saw Rinchen. Or at least, the back of his head.

Chapter Six: Grasshopper Learns About Floppy Fish

He was on the floor, sitting on his shins. His arms were folded in front of him, out of sight from where I was standing. He was perfectly still. At first, I wasn't even sure he was real. You expect a living thing to move at least a little, but he did not. His torso did not expand or contract. It was the extreme stillness that caught my attention. Rinchen says that the moment that I noticed this stillness, was the moment that caused me to step onto the path. If my mind had not been completely lit up by the motorcycle ride, I might not have noticed him at all.

After a short while, he raised his hands straight out in front of him and spreading his arms wide, clapped two loud claps. He placed his hands on the floor in front of him and then bowed. When he raised his head, I could see him take a deep inhale that expanded his chest. His torso contracted ever so slowly and returned to its normal size. With that, he jumped to his feet in a single motion, a feat that seemed unnatural to me then. He wore what looked like a black pleated skirt with a white top. Two guys and a girl in *Karate* suits, I have since come to know this type of clothing as a *gi*, had been sitting off to the right when I had first looked through the window and I had not noticed them until the man in the black skirt headed toward them. They bowed to him. He patted one of them on the shoulder and grinned broadly. Everyone behind the glass seemed to be happy, like they had just woken up from a very refreshing nap. It made me smile. And just as I was standing there admiring their happiness, Rinchen turned and looked right at me. His smile broadened even further and he waved at me to come in.

I don't know why I did not just jump in the car and take off, but I had been riding an insatiable wave of curiosity all night. I grabbed Beth's arm and said, "Come on, let's go in." Beth did not resist my goading her through the door, but seemed to be somewhat confused as to where we were going and why.

Our host greeted us as we passed through the door with, "welcome ladies, what brings you to Byakuren Dojo?" Beth looked puzzled and answered hesitantly as if she had been asked a trick question. "Our car?," she said looking at the man in the skirt like his question had been a trick. I was a bit embarrassed by Beth's subtle disrespect. I did not know what this place was, but it oozed with dignity and I scrambled to put the conversation into a more polite tone. Not being sure exactly how to do that, I mimicked the others in the room and bowed slightly before I spoke. Rinchen acknowledged my gesture by bowing back. Now I had his complete attention.

"What is this place?," I asked.

"It is a martial arts and meditation school. We call it a '*dojo*'."

"You called it something else just a second ago … 'bya'-something."

"Ah yes, 'Byakuren'. That is Japanese for 'white lotus'," the man explained.

"Oh, so you do *Karate* and stuff like that here?"

"The 'stuff like that' part, maybe. We practice *Aikido*, *Kendo*, *Kenjitsu* and there is a sifu who teaches *Tai Chi*, but I am sorry, no *Karate*."

"Oh," I said "I am sorry. I don't really know anything about that kind of stuff."

The man in the black skirt grinned. "Neither do we." The others, whom by now I realized must be his students, started to chuckle. The man kept his gaze straight on me. He was looking at me with an intensity that made me quite uncomfortable, though his smile was oddly reassuring.

I was curious, "so, *Aikido* and *Kendo*, that's fighting, right?"

"Yes, more or less."

"I don't mean to be rude, but why name a fighting school after a flower? Wouldn't it be better for advertising to name it after a dragon or something?" No sooner had I spit out my question than I realized that it sounded rude.

The man in the black skirt smiled and seemed to take no offense at all. "Maybe for some schools, but not this school. The lotus is a symbol for enlightenment and white is the color of purity. While we do learn to deal with physical conflict, the real battle is within ourselves. So that is why it is called "Byakuren" instead of something else." The battle within ourselves thing totally lost me. I had no idea what he was talking about, but he seemed like a very nice man.

After an awkward silence, he said, "Since you are here, I could show you a technique? It might give you an idea of what we do here and, who knows, it might just get you out of trouble someday. It will only take a minute and you will leave knowing more than when you came in. Would you like to try it?"

"Okay," I said moving toward him sheepishly. I felt obligated to indulge him after intruding into his *dojo*.

"Wait!," he snapped suddenly holding his hand up to as if to prevent me from moving into the room. "I lied. We will be teaching you two things this evening, instead of just one. Before you step onto the mat, you must first take off your shoes."

I looked down at my feet and then looked at his feet and saw that they were bare. I slipped off my flats and checking to see if it was now okay to proceed, stepped toward him. Beth kept her shoes on and stayed by the doorway. She was going to let me take this opportunity to make an ass of myself by myself.

"Unlike many martial arts, *Aikido* has no hostility," said the man in the black skirt. While it is certainly a form of combat, there are no offensive moves. If no one is attacking you, *Aikido* is impossible. The idea is to engage aggressive energy and redirect it back at the attacker to thwart him and hopefully teach him that aggression breeds bad *karma*. Do you understand?"

I nodded although I had no idea what *karma* really was. I had heard the term "bad karma" often enough and thought it meant "bad luck", but this did not seem to be what he was talking about.

He continued: "I am going to grab your arms like I am trying to abduct you. We will try without any instruction to let you experiment on your own at first. Do I have your permission to do this?" I was startled by his formality. He had no intention of touching me unless I gave him permission. "Yes, of course," I said. He moved forward and grabbed both of my wrists. His grip was gentle at first, but tightened slowly until I could not move my arms.

"Try to break free," he said.

His strength was nearly frightening. I could barely get my arms to move let alone break free of his grip. Had he been trying to abduct me, I was as good as in the trunk of his car.

"Why can't you get away?," he asked.

"You are too strong."

"Strength has nothing to do with it."

I was confused. This guy was three times my size with forearms that were bigger than my calves.

"When I try to dominate you, I have to focus all of my strength along a single line leading to a single point. Strength must be focused to be strong. It is impossible to be strong in all directions at once. In order to control you, I direct my strength toward your strength and overpower you. I get stronger because as you resist and in so doing you tell me exactly where your strength is. Because I am bigger than you, I win. This is true in all matters of brute force. Bigger and stronger always win. So, you have to change the rules."

This was an intriguing idea. The thought that a teenage girl could change the rules and beat a grown man seemed to me, in that moment, to be most likely impossible and yet he was telling me that this was the whole point of the exercise.

"Notice how you try to fight me by directing your strength straight at my strength. You pit force against force. This is foolish unless you are Wonder Woman and have secret powers that we do not know about."

"Nope, no secret powers, " I said sheepishly. "What do I do?"

"When I push on your arms to pin them down, do not be there when my energy arrives."

"How on earth do I do that?"

"If an intruder were to break into your house to hurt you, what would you do?"

"Run, hide, try to get away, I suppose."

"In other words, you would try to not be there when he came in, right?"

"I guess. I would at least try to hide."

"Hide where?"

"Anywhere."

"Smart girl, so do that now." And with that, he squeezed my wrists and pushed them down toward my thighs . At first, the force was completely overpowering. I noticed that I was doing what he had said that I had done before; I was pushing back straight into his power. I got confused as I tried to do what had told me to. Just exactly how do you not be there or hide when a large man has you by both wrists? I tried to move my arms, but with very little success. And then I got frustrated and gave up and let my arms go limp. Rinchen nearly lost his balance, just ever so slightly. I immediately took advantage of this and suddenly moved my hands behind my back nearly pulling him off his feet, but straight into a bear hug around my waist that in a real fight would have made my situation much worse.

"You are starting to get it." He said. "Try again. This time if I push down, you dodge your hands to left. If I follow left, you dodge to the right. Try to move your hands wherever I am not, but do it quickly before I can catch up to you and... try to stay completely relaxed. Every time you use strength, any strength, you tell me where you are." He pushed down on my wrists again only this time, before he could completely tighten his grip, I moved my hands rapidly away from my thighs spreading his arms wider. I could feel his strength weaken as he tried to get back in control, so I moved my hand again and again as he tried to keep up. I started to see what he was talking about, I could actually feel his strength coming and I could avoid it.

"Good!" , he said. "Let's try one more thing. When I try to dominate your arms, I want you to wiggle them like floppy fish or eels in the water. Do not use any strength. Do not stop and do not let me catch up to where your hands are going. Do not try even to think about your motion, just flop your hands and arms around and we will see what happens."

He grabbed my wrists again and I immediately started flopping my arms around like fish on a dock. He was winning, however; clearly I was doing something wrong.

"Relax your arms almost entirely. *Aikido* does not take strength. In fact, strength can be a bad thing. Don't let me feel where your strength is. If I cannot find it, I cannot dominate it."

I relaxed my arms, but flopped them back and forth rapidly. After a few seconds, I could actually feel him trying to locate my strength through his arms. I kept flopping out of the way and eventually flopped around so rapidly that he could not hold on to my arms at all.

"Excellent!," he said. "Why does this work?"

"I guess it is a mystery," I said trying to sound like I had just found a new religion.

"I don't think so," Rinchen replied. "It is architecture."

"Really?," I said. "I am confused."

"Why is a wall built perfectly vertical?"

"Because it would look goofy if it were crooked." Rinchen chuckled.

"Yes, it would certainly look goofy, but more importantly the weight must be directed in a perfectly straight line downward, brick to brick, in order for the wall to bear its own weight. If a brick is placed partially to one side or the other, the wall will be weak. If too many bricks are out of alignment, the wall will buckle under its own weight. Your body is architecture. Knees and elbows bend only one way. The bones are shaped to translate strength from the earth to all that we touch. Strength needs structure and precise placement. That is why a baby falls down while it is learning to walk. It takes some time to figure out how to get everything lined up to stand and walk. Like the wall, the human body is powerful, but only if its structure is properly aligned. When I was a kid, you could stand on a soda can so long as it was perfectly straight. But, dent it on the side, even just a little bit, and your weight would crush it flat. Soda cans are thinner these days, but it used to be great fun. If you take away my ability to establish a line of power, you take away my ability to dominate you. Every time that you move your hands, I have to recalculate how to realign my strength. The truth is that you can flop your hands quicker than I can make these calculations. For you, as the non-aggressor, your freedom can be found anywhere that my oppression is not. But my oppression must always be directed to a specific place that has the size of a head of a pin. This gives you most of the universe to live in. But for me, as the aggressor, I must put my force in a very precise place. Do you understand?"

"I think so," I said.

"It is easy to avoid the point of a needle, but quite difficult to press two needles point to point. The one seeking to avoid an attack always has the advantage. This is the power of peace."

"I never looked at peace as particularly powerful before," I said.

The man smiled and then asked, "Let me guess, you occasionally argue with your parents, no?"

'Frequently," I said.

"Why do you argue?"

"It is usually because they will not let me do something that I want to do."

"Like me holding down your arms against your will."

"Sort of, but they are not physical about it. I mean, they are not child abusers or anything like that!"

The man laughed. "Of course not, I think we can agree that we are now speaking metaphorically. When your parents do not let you do what you want to do, they are putting pressure on you to keep you from moving in the way that you want, do you see this?"

"Yes."

"Instead of moving along the same line that they are moving, you fight directly against them."

"Yes, because I do not want them to dominate me, I guess."

"No one enjoys being dominated, but what you do is, instead of stepping out of the way or moving in harmony with them, you push directly back against their power. You are trying to fight their domination with domination. You become just as oppressive to them as they are being to you. This is always destructive and foolish. At the end of the day, they are stronger than you, at least for now, and they usually win, right?"

"I see." Suddenly, I could envision every fight I had ever had with my mom. She pushed on me and I pushed straight back. It was a losing battle in every case. "But if you always go along with the force or step out of the way, you will never get what you want," I said with a growing sense of concern.

"What is there to win? Winning is just dominating. That is not any better than being dominated."

"To hell you say!" I said to myself. But his point had landed.

He continued. "Think about this: what does it take for there to be a punch in the nose?".

This was turning into the weirdest conversation that I had ever had. "Someone's fist hitting someone's nose, I guess."

"Exactly, but if you take away the fist or take away the nose, do you still have a fight?"

"No."

"That means that both the owner of the fist and the owner of the nose have power to cause peace. It is only when the fist flies and the face refuses to move, that a punch in the nose is even possible."

"Yes, that makes sense," I said.

"So, the secret is not to resist power with power, but either to move with it and alter its destructive course with your own subtle influence, or step out of its way. This is actually the way of harmonizing all energy, but we will save that discussion for another time. Do you get what I mean here?"

"I think so; but I think it is easier for you because you know *Aikido*."

"You do not have to know *Aikido*, you just have to move your face. The point is, you can stand on your rights while someone throws a punch at your nose and belligerently hold your ground. You do this with your parents. According to you, it will be their fault if the punch lands, but you will be the one with the bloody nose. This is the high cost of meeting force with force or matching righteousness with righteousness. Or, you can simply step out of the way. Peace can be had even in a tornado or in the middle of a battle simply by not standing in the way when an angry fist passes by. Remember, pushing back only guarantees that the strongest power wins. Since no one is always the strongest person in the room, it is better to play by a different set of rules. When you get really good at this, there is a third option."

"What is the third option?," I asked.

"You engage the hostile energy without fighting it, becoming one with it, and redirect it to a peaceful outcome. You basically take over the energy by making it part of your own allowing your clear mind to drive the action instead of the attacker's hostile mind."

"Sounds complicated."

"Complicated to learn because you have to deal with the complications of your own mind, but once you have that worked out, it is actually quite simple and instinctive. It becomes second nature."

It was starting to make sense, if just a little, but it also seemed incredibly difficult. "Thank you," I said. "What's your name?"

"My driver's license says 'Steve Jackson'. These guys call me *Sensei*," nodding toward his students who had taken to sitting on their shins while he was teaching me the floppy fish technique. "But most people call me 'Rinchen'".

"Why Rinchen?"

"That is my *dharma* name and what my master calls me. It has caught on, I guess. My friends say that I don't make a very good Steve."

"What's *dharma*?," I asked.

"Oh, sorry, *dharma* is a Buddhist word that means the natural law or the way of something. Sometimes we use it as kind of a slang term for Buddhism itself, but what we really mean is Buddha-dharma meaning "the way of Buddha". To make a long story short, my dharma name is the name my teacher gave me when I became a Buddhist."

"Does it mean anything in particular?"

"It is the Tibetan word for "precious". My full ordained name is Rinchen Dorje, which, roughly translated, means "precious thunderbolt of truth". My master visits here several times a year and refers to me by that name only. He is pretty rigorous about things like that. Over time, everyone else around me has followed his example. It's a Buddhist thing."

"Oh, so *Aikido* is Buddhist?"

"Not really, it is more technically-speaking a hybrid Shinto tradition although the founder practiced a variation of Shinto that had Buddhist elements. I am, however, a Buddhist of a Tibetan lineage."

"How does that fit with a mostly Shinto martial art?," I asked. I was getting really confused.

Rinchen chuckled. "Normally, it doesn't. Tibetan Buddhists are not big on martial arts as a general rule. You don't see the Dalai Lama carrying a sword or throwing people around, now do you? It was my karma that I met my Buddhist teacher and he happened to be Tibetan. I actually met him in a *dojo*. He came to teach meditation there and I stayed after class and listened. He was the real deal. Since I was a little boy, I had hoped to have a real master and to be his disciple. I got my wish. My teacher really liked the *dojo* and its discipline. He said it reminded him of a monastery. He told me to keep training in *Aikido* and *Kenjitsu*. I even trained in Tai Chi and Shi Gong for a couple of years. He said it would be good for me. He was right. Now that you mention it, it does make me a bit of a mutt, from a training lineage point of view." Rinchen smirked as he contemplated the story that he had just told me.

"Well, I think it's a cool name," I said realizing that we were still a half an hour from home and could not drag in too late or there would be questions. " Well, Mr. Rinchen, we have to get going. Thanks for the *Aikido* lesson."

"It was my pleasure," he said with a bow. "And may I know your name as well?," Rinchen said rather formally.

"Madison."

"Is that your first name or your last name?," he asked looking mildly confused.

"It is my first name and I hate it, but it is what I have to work with. My full name is 'Madison Albright'."

"It is lovely name" said Rinchen as if to console me.

"Yeah, whatever," I said sarcastically, "you are nice to say so."

Rinchen laughed a little. As I turned to find my shoes, he invited me to visit anytime I wanted to. I told him that I would like that just as soon as I could plot another escape from the county. Little did I know, that I would be back in just a few weeks.

Chapter Seven: The Meat Market

When I was in fifth grade, I went to Girl Scout camp for a week down in southern Missouri. In particular, I went to horse camp. When you arrive at horse camp, you are assigned a horse and taught how to feed it and brush the dust out of its coat. You also get to ride your horse, but usually just around the trails that circle the cabins. But if you come from a place that does not have horses, and that would be Westchester, this is big adventure. The trail through the woods emptied into an open field. On the other side of the field were the barns where the horses were kept. We were all told on the very first day that when we came off the trail and started across the field that the horses would see the barn and want to get there as quickly as they could. Apparently, horses do not think that carrying Girl Scouts endlessly around the same trail day after day, year after year, is nearly as fun as the girls think it is. Sure enough, as we got to the field, the horses would start to trot. Some would even break into a canter and had to be reined in. Every year, at least one newbie would cling to her horse's neck in sheer terror as the horse broke into a full gallop toward the barn. I never fully understood how those horses felt until I got to high school. By fifth period on Thursday, my friends and I all started to trot toward the weekend. By the final period on Friday, we were all in a dead run for the parking lot. When Mondays made their lap around the week, we were back to trudging in circles around the school once more.

The tale of our exploits on Washington Avenue was making the rounds at Westchester High. The reviews were coming in and Beth and I were running 84% in the approval ratings. Behind our backs, the Malibu Barbies were calling us sluts for going to the city in the first place and hanging out in a bar in the second place. No one seemed to be adding the distinction "hookah" into the equation. Being on the wrong side of MBs can only improve your rep with everyone else. A couple of girls looking for a way to improve their credit scores asked us if we would take them down to Ahab's the following weekend, but we told them that we were all smoked out for now. There was one perk, however; we made it onto the guest list for Tommy Davidson's party. This was not actually a huge deal, because it was an open party and anyone could come anyway, but we actually got invited by Tommy himself.

Tommy Davidson is not half bad for a jock. He is not a bully and does not seem to have a neurotic need to be a big shot at the expense of the class geek like you see in cheesy teen movies. He is the quarterback of the football team, and definitely popular, but he also likes drama club and was the lead in a couple of school plays. One part of the stereotype in which Tommy totally does fit is that he is hopelessly good looking. The fact that he is not an asshole makes him even better looking. Alas, he has a girlfriend, Annie Vega, and, no, she is not a cheerleader, but she is every mom's version of perfect.

Unlike some of the parties that happen on the weekends, Tommy's parents were not out of town and had actually given him permission to have people over. He lived in the subdivision next to mine where the houses are just a little bit bigger and some, including Tommy's house, have their own pools. Beer and dope were forbidden and Tommy would kick your ass if you tried to smoke as much as a cigarette in his parent's house. But the music was loud and the pool provided at least some entertainment mostly for the guys who gathered around to partake in the meat market. Every girl who thinks that she is hot, and that is quite a few girls at my school, always show up at pool parties with a fresh spray-on tan and the smallest bathing suit that they can get past their mothers. It is not exactly teen porn or anything, but it does kind of remind me of some seriously bad reality TV I have seen. For Tommy and his friends, this is the payoff of having a straight party. Of course, eventually their shirts come off and they are diving into the pool, so in the end, there is some eye-candy for everyone.

A dry and smokeless party normally would not have much pull unless you are a social magnet. But Tommy has the juice for a big turnout. On Saturday night, the crowd arrived early and in force. For a lot of people, this was a starter party that would ultimately wind up at Howell Island where the prohibition on drinking and doping would be lost in the woods.

After spending two hours getting ready at Beth's house, we finally had the right jeans and tops that we could live with. It is amazing to me that before I met Rinchen, I thought I looked different in the mirror every day. Some days my hair would happen and some days I thought that I looked like a walking disaster. It could take an hour to put on my makeup and assure myself that I had put on the right clothes and sometimes I couldn't get it to come together at all. I could never figure out why I was the only one that ever seemed to notice this. Rinchen told me that actually, I always looked pretty much the same every day and that it was not the face in the mirror that was changing, but the mind looking at it. I thought that he was totally crazy when he told me this. "Just look! Can't you see, my hair is totally whacked, I look fat; I am a mess today!" Rinchen said that the mess was in my mind. It's funny. Ever since he told me this, I have noticed that I am looking more and more the same every day. I think it is because my mom and I have started going to a new stylist at Salon Au Tout.

Beth and I got to the party about 8:30 and it was already jumping. There were the usual characters doing the usual things. You could see and smell the clouds of pot smoke rising out of the front windows of a couple of Japanese economy cars tricked out like road racers. There was a girl slipping a pint of schnapps into her purse and popping breath mints oblivious to the fact that breath mints actually enhance the alcohol smell. And then there was Nick Thompson. Mr. and Mrs. America must have been out of town, because he was parked out on the cul-de-sac in his mom's power-chick mobile cranking some speed metal. He looked totally baked, but wide awake at the same time. This was not a good sign.

The house was packed and the patio even more so. Most everyone was nursing a soda in a plastic cup. There were open bags of chips everywhere. Generally speaking, however, everyone was minding their manners and nothing was getting broken although it looked like Mrs. Davidson had made a sweep of the house before hand to remove the breakables. We wandered out to the pool just in time to see half of the football team cannonball into the water simultaneously sending a tsunami splashing in every direction. There was a minor uproar mostly from the girls who either got only half of their hair wet or were wearing light colored tops. The wet tops, of course, had been the whole point of the play.

After about an hour, I heard the unmistakable sound of two crotch rockets pulling up the street. They were revving their motors as if driving the expected speed limit in the subdivision was threatening them into a stall. Within a few minutes, Megan strolled in with her usual body-hugging leather jacket hanging open and her cell phone tucked into the top of her bra. Behind her was one of the guys from Ahab's, I remember thinking that his name was Matt. He saw Beth and me and flipped us a nod of recognition and grabbed Megan's arm bringing us to her attention. She smiled. I beamed. Matt was her boyfriend and not Tripp. Oh lucky day!

Megan eased through the crowd and Matt followed. He was considerably taller than most of the people at the party and had wild, spikey black hair that was way beyond the Leave-It-To-Beaver 'dos that most of the Westchester boys wore. He was handsome though his look was kind of radical. He was definitely muscular, but kind of soft-spoken and had this I-don't-have-to-show-off-because-I-can-kill-you thing going on. Megan squeezed between a couple of guys and gave me a hug which surprised me.

"Qué pasa, Chicas? Is this party any good?," she asked.

"Depends what you came for," I replied.

Matt surveyed the room over the tops of the heads. "Not a beer in town," he said finally.

"Nope, this party is authorized by the master and mistress of the domain," I said not realizing that I must be getting really comfortable with these guys because I was actually being my normal, sarcastic self.

"Then why is everybody here? " Matt asked with the slightest bit of contempt working its way across his face.

"Look out by the pool," I said, suddenly noticing Nick Thompson working his way into the house.

"Cool, chicks and dip," said Matt with a false sense of excitement. "Well, I brought my own." As he said this, he pulled Megan close to him like my dad might suddenly hug my mom and struck a pose meant to look like they were the portrait of the All-American couple. Megan pushed him away, "I brought you, you douche bag." She snickered and turned to look at me tauntingly: "Trippster said to tell Little Bit that he said 'hey'." Beth sprang to life like a lapdog and looked at me with OMG! flashing across her bulging eyes as she attempted to suppress her excitement. She looked like she was about to wet herself. I blushed and tried to act like this was a message from my dad. "Oh really?" I replied losing the battle for nonchalance as a smile forced way too much of itself into my already blushing cheeks. "Alrighty then," said Megan rolling her eyes, suppressing her own grin as she looked back at the crowd. "How do you know Tripp?," I asked figuring that I wasn't fooling anyone at this point. "He's my brother," said Megan turning to stare me down as if to dare me to say anything. Before I could assemble any sense of composure, I blurted out the most urgent, overwhelming thing that there was for me to say: "Oh, shit!"

Megan broke into laughter. She had clearly not seen that coming. Matt started to chuckle and Beth just stood there stunned at what seemed to be a relationship disaster in the making. Megan put her arm around Matt's waist and her head on his chest and looked back at me smiling. "It's cool, Little Bit, it's totally cool." At first there was a wave of relief and then the sudden rush that came with the realization that this totally awesome guy liked me. Holy crap! I may be heading for a boyfriend!

Suddenly, I had a thousand questions. How old is he? Why haven't I seen him around school? Does he have a criminal record? And where did he get those gorgeous abs? And yet, I actually said nothing. The suppressed excitement threatened to give me a brain hemorrhage.

Megan decided to take it easy on me. "Give me your cell number and I will have him call you." Without giving me the chance to respond, Beth blurted out 6-3-6-5-5-5-3-3-5-5. Megan rolled her eyes and entered the number into her phone. This was getting weirder by the minute. With the number safely stored in her phone, Megan looked up at me with what appeared to me to be genuine friendliness. "Tripp and I are actually twins. Our parents are divorced. My dad lives in the city and my mom lives out here." She had tuned in to my need for info. There are certain things that a girl needs to know before she hooks up with a guy. Despite the fact that Tripp was her twin brother, she seemed willing to fulfill her obligations to the Girl Nation by providing me with the essentials and not making me beg for them. "Tripp lives with my dad and goes to Metro, I stay down there on the weekends, but I live with my mom during the week and that is why I go to school out here. Our parents get along okay now, but my mom did not do so well after the divorce so I chose to stay with her. Tripp and I have always been pretty close, it's a twin thing, you know, but ever since the split, give or take the first year of living in different houses, we are pretty much best friends -- at least we are now."

There was more to that story, but there was no need-to-know. The dude profile was invaluable and I sat there listening carefully as she filled me in. She told me that Tripp was actually a really gifted artist and spent a lot of his time drawing. He was also a student of the martial arts and so was Megan. They both trained at Byakuren Dojo.

"Hey, I have been there!," I interjected. "I met this guy Rinchen down there last weekend after Tripp gave me the motorcycle ride. He does *Aikido*. He is a very nice man."

"He is way more than that," said Megan, "but that's a start." Megan was carefully studying my reaction to what she was telling me. "Matt trains there too," she added still watching me intently. It was as if she had seen something in my face that she had not expected; like I might actually have more potential than she had originally thought. "Maybe you should come and check it out. The warrior world could certainly use more women."

Warrior? Wow! Now that's not a chapter in *The Care And Feeding Of Your Suburban Teenager*. I think the warrior thing had slipped by my mother when she was shopping for parenting books on the internet. My dad had once told me to be a tough little tiger once when I was playing tee-ball at the YMCA, but a warrior? The concept of this was so novel, so strange, that it slipped in through the back door of my mind before I had a chance to throw it out as being utterly ridiculous.

In Westchester, it is safe to say that girls are not raised to be warriors. We are, however, well versed in the fairy princess arts. When we are little, we are smothered with cuteness. We are given cute clothes and cute toys and paraded around like live dolls. Looking back at it now, the girls I grew up with strike me a little bit like toy poodles dressed up in poofy dog-dresses with a matching hat. It's cute and ridiculous at the same time. The doctrine of cuteness never goes away. Fashion and appearance are a huge part of the programming. Sure, girls are expected to get good grades and to participate in clubs and organizations. But there is absolutely nothing in the curriculum that is designed to help us cope with conflict and altercation, let alone battle. Combat is un-lady-like.

In fact, in Westchester, not even the boys are really trained to be warriors. Sure, sports are still encouraged for those who have the DNA for physical challenge. Most of the guys that I know are obsessed with computer games and that's not exactly rugby, now is it? I suppose that the odd sports team has some of that competitive, overcome-yourself, take-one-for-the-Gipper mentality. But most of our school sports teams kind of suck. They do all right through their respective regular seasons playing other suburban teams, but when they get into the state tournaments, the city schools eat them alive with the exception, of course, of sports like golf and tennis. I guess they do a better job of warrior training downtown.

The best athletes play in select sports programs that require them to avoid playing for their schools. The extreme elitism of these types of teams are bad enough, but the fact that we teach kids to shun the communal success of their schools for elite personal success is probably all anyone needs to know about select sports to hate them. Heaven forbid if Trey and Heather should get dragged down by a team of public school losers. Talk about being "too cool for school". But this is the sign of the times. Who wants to bring honor and glory to your village high school when you can save the glory for yourself without having to engage in something as communistic as actual community spirit. Most of the people that I know on select sports teams love the sports that they play, but love the status of "select" even better. They are all going to be bankers and lawyers anyway, so why be so serious about this?

I suppose that the select sports system makes for good college application and resume fodder. Westchester High School does not produce many star college athletes, let alone professional athletes. I remember my dad talking to one of the other fathers at one of Tyler's soccer games when we were in elementary school. Tyler was a brainiac, not David Beckham. I remember the two fathers laughing at their sons as they fumbled their way across the field when the man next to my dad turned and said, "It's okay Henry, I tell my kid that I am not interested in him growing up to be an athlete; I am interested in him growing up to *own* athletes." My dad laughed and returned his attention to the awkward struggle on the field and smiled with what appeared to be a sense of satisfaction.

They don't make a Warrior Barbie. While girls are required to be as smart as boys, they are not expected to be aggressive. If you are a boy and confrontational, you're a man; if you are a girl and confrontational, you're a bitch. Although it was worse for my mom, even in my generation there is still the everlasting conversation about being lady-like. My grandma is the high-priestess of that religion. How was my mom ever supposed to get anywhere in her career having been taught to be lady-like when the men with whom she was to work and compete against were trained to have at least a virtual sense of battle. She was trained for a different kind of struggle. To this day, she is a smart multi-tasker who never failed to get me and my brother to school on time and sacrificed hours and hours of her life experience shuffling us kids from one useless activity to another.

My dad once told me that the original Olympics were all about military skills. I am pretty sure that the ancient Greeks did not do synchronized swimming and I am pretty sure there were no cheerleaders. He says that all sports were originally designed to build a sense of competitiveness. Sports is supposed to toughen you up and teach you how to struggle in difficult things so that you can be all you can be in real life. Our generation is losing its interest in a lot of physical sports. Most of the guys at my school are a little nerdy, to be honest about it. This seems to be much more acceptable these days than when my parents were in high school. This is probably because all of those nerdy kids that they used to pick on when they were in school are now their bosses. Take my friend Ack. He is seriously smart, but would hurt himself if he ever tried to play real face-in-the-dirt football. He does not even play the occasional afterschool touch football game although he is pretty good at the virtual version on X-Box.

Wow, when you think about it, you can tell a lot about what is expected of us in the future by the games that our parents encourage us to play. I remember when my brother Tyler got his first X-Box for Christmas. He taught us all, first hand, what crack addiction looked like. He couldn't stop playing. He spent days sitting there like a zombie staring at the TV with a controller in his hands. My parents finally had to limit his playing time, but he cheated when they were not paying attention. His favorite game was one where the character wanders through tunnels and is ambushed by monsters and you have to shoot them with a variety of weapons. I guess you could say that this is the dumbing down of youth by way of an addictive, and useless form of play, but I am not so sure. My dad was watching a TV show on the Discovery Channel a while ago about modern weapons. I don't do guns, but it was still pretty amazing. There were these guys in Germany sitting in front of computers controlling cruise missiles and blowing up people running out of buildings in the Middle East. The controls that they were using looked very similar to my brother's game controller. Maybe modern gaming is still military training. The Greatest Generation may have needed sports and extreme physical conditioning to prepare its youth for the invasion of Normandy, but Generation X-Box needs to have wicked-fast thumb reflexes to push a missile up the tailpipe of a speeding pickup truck full of Taliban militia. Even so, I am pretty sure that even Tyler's 300,000 kills on X-Box do not qualify as warrior training. After all, Tyler is kind of a wimp.

Chapter Eight: The Vortex

I have to say that the prospect of an identity makeover from Madison Albright to warrior-biker-chick seemed to me, as I stood in the crowd in Tommy Davidson's living room, to be an impossibly large leap. First of all, it sounded like it would be really hard and scary. Then there was all the training. I could see myself spending twelve hours a day doing knuckle push-ups and breaking stacks of boards and basically having no other life. It sounded kind of boring. Besides, who needs to be a warrior? It is not like I live in the hood, after all. We don't even lock our doors in my neighborhood let alone worry about our safety. Our police officers are trained to deal with drunken driving and speeding, not drug take-downs although they do conduct the semi-annual dog search of the lockers at school. What are warriors good for and why on earth would I want to be one?

On the other hand, the fact that Megan thought that I had the stuff to do it and was more or less giving me her blessing to date her smoking-hot biker brother was all kinds of flattering and it was going straight to my head. I found the habitual traces of cuteness draining from my personality as I tried to introduce myself to my inner badass - that is, if I actually had one.

Megan and Matt decided to circulate and Beth and I decided to do the same. It would not be too long before the exodus to Howell Island would begin and the real party, free from the oversight of Mr. and Mrs. Davidson, would get underway. Even Tommy would probably wind up out there eventually. As we made our way toward the sliding glass door that lead to the pool, I saw Nick Thompson stumble upon a gaggle of girls. He was really gone. I could see that his inhibitions had taken a holiday and while he barely seemed to know who he was, he was speeding on something and it was making him kind of jumpy. He tried to join the conversation in front of him and when they snubbed him, he moved past the no-fly zone toward the girl closest to him. In a synchronized motion, the whole flock moved away at once. Undeterred, he moved on to the next group of girls. I could see that his behavior was starting to really piss a few of them off and one girl separated from the herd and headed toward Tommy. Nick was about to get reported and Tommy, out of a chivalrous duty to his guest, was going to ask Nick to leave. This was kind of the story of Nick's life as far as I could tell. I felt sorry for him.

I made my way over to where he was standing and started up a conversation with the universal hail: "Hey, Nick, what's happening?". Nick was a little surprised in his animated stupor that a girl was actually choosing to talk to him. "Hey Maddie, you're lookin' good." This was Nick's version of being a player. And by the way, they may have called me Maddie in elementary school, but I spent all of junior high making it perfectly clear that I hated that name and most people had abandoned it. Apparently, Nick didn't get the memo. Of course, I may not have actually talked to Nick since junior high.

Beth was getting irritated that we were in the middle of a raging party at the house of one of the coolest guys in school and we were now conspicuously talking to perhaps our school's biggest loser. Beth is one of those people for whom every moment and every conversation with every person either adds up to or takes away from your social credit score. She is totally tuned into the Dow Jones Industrial Average of Fluctuating Social Gravity. It is not that she is status-hungry; far from it. Her concern is purely defensive. The truth is that everyone at Westchester High is aware that they are constantly being watched and evaluated and that their stock price goes up or down as the circumstances play out. Life offered opportunity enough to make an ass of yourself and you did not need to help it along. The Nick-Thompson-in-Tommy-Davidson's-living-room situation was positively swelling with opportunity for some sort of embarrassment. She was right and I didn't care. Part of this whole warrior thing was about not being afraid, right? My inner badass was trying to find its legs.

Beth whispered into my ear, "Tommy's coming" and I knew what that meant. I had already made up my mind how I would play this out. "Hey, Madison, Beth – are you guys having a good time?" Tommy asked as he casually slipped his arm around Beth's shoulders. It almost seemed like he was marking his territory. He seemed to be intentionally ignoring Nick.

"Awesome," Beth responded. As if it was an afterthought, Tommy nodded at Nick and said, "Hey man, how are you doing?" with a tone so neutral that you could not tell if it was a greeting or a threat. As stoned as Nick was he knew that this was an inquest and not a social nicety. "Cool dude, totally cool," he replied after an awkward hesitation. He looked like a bobble-head doll nodding up and down as if he could not stop the inertia of his chin. He was working very hard to avoid eye-contact. I could see that Tommy was zeroing in to sharpen his cross-examination, so I interrupted, "we are getting ready to hit it, Tommy, are you going to the island later?"

"Yeah, probably, and you?"

"Not sure yet, but maybe we will see you there. Thanks for inviting us tonight, it was awesome."

"Glad you could come. I'll see you later."

Before Tommy could return to grill Nick, I said, "Nick, can you walk us to our car?"

Tommy was confused and maybe a little bit concerned. He had not been getting good reports on Nick and he seemed to think that we might be asking for trouble. For Nick, this was a graceful way out – which, of course, was the whole idea. "Certainly, ladies – see ya, Tommy". Nick's spirits seemed to be suddenly lifted now that a show-down had been avoided.

We made our way through the crowd and caused more than a few heads to turn as the judges noticed that our exit technique included leaving with Nick Thompson. By the time we were ten feet from the house, however, I am sure that most of them had moved on to judging other people at the party. As we were heading out to the street, it was becoming very apparent that Nick was in absolutely no condition to drive. Just as I had thought, I was getting sucked into the Nick vortex.

We had come to the party in the Kid Car and we were cruising on fumes by the time we had parked. Nick lived two miles away in one of the McMansion neighborhoods where they actually have *grounds* instead of *yards*. His house was actually way-cool. You had to pass through a fence of trees that secluded the house from the rest of the neighborhood. There was a big circle drive that passed under a portico that you could actually park your car under so that if it was raining you would not get wet making your way inside. Of course, if you were a member of the family, you could just park in the four car garage connected to the back of the house.

I threw the car keys to Beth and handed her a ten dollar bill. "You are going to have to stop and get gas. I am going to drive Nick home, pick me up there." I could see that Beth really, really did not like this idea. Anyone could see, however, that it would be a worse idea to let Nick drive. Nick, of course, was not resisting his newly found designated driver in the least. "Are you sure?" Beth said sending me a "hell no!" emergency eye telegraph through the Girl-Net. "It's not far, just get your ass in gear and I will meet you there." She headed for my car but did not take her eyes off of me the entire way. I turned to Nick and said, "give me the keys."

I slid into the leather seat of Mrs. Thompson car, and started the engine. The car rumbled to life. Whoa! I had pressed the gas pedal just a little too far and the car roared and then settled down to a purr. This was no mommy-van, but it had an automatic transmission, so we were good to go. Nick crawled into the passenger seat and immediately pushed the button to turn on the stereo. An angry tantrum of thrashing speed metal immediately pounded the cockpit of the car from all directions. It was so loud that it sent me into a panic. I urgently pecked at the down-volume button and turned the music down so low that you could hardly hear it. "Holy crap, Nick! Do you think you can hear that?" I asked sarcastically. After adjusting the volume to a more humane level, I eased the car away from the curb wondering if my dad's insurance covered me and how many years of allowance and babysitting earnings it would take to pay for even the slightest scratch on this beast.

We had not even gotten to the end of the block when things took a quick turn toward Creepy Town. Nick was bobbing his head to the music trying to act aloof but kept looking me up and down stopping at uncomfortable intervals to stare at my chest. I tried to start a deliberately meaningless conversation, but was at a complete loss as to what to say. What exactly do you talk about with a guy like Nick anyway? "Dude, saw you slash yourself on YouTube, awesome!" I settled on "this is a really nice car." That seemed to be enough. Nick kept bobbing his head and checking me out and then replied, "yeah, I basically stole it. I am not supposed to drive it, but my parents went to Vegas for the weekend and, well, screw them." Alrighty then. I thought of Megan. She wouldn't be afraid, so I wasn't going to be either.

The trip through Westchester was uncomfortably long and I must have hit a record number of red lights. Nick did not seem to mind that it was taking forever to make it to his neighborhood. He kept bobbing to the music and scanning me up and down. Finally, we came to the entrance of his subdivision. It had big stone lions on both sides of the entry street . The houses in Nick's neighborhood were humongous and while they had large yards that were bigger than soccer fields, they were of only limited use for child's play, however, because of the arrangement of flower beds and carefully selected trees and shrubbery that went way beyond the ordinary Westchester Feng Sui. Most of the houses were only partially visible from the street. I turned into his driveway and drove past the wall of tall, thin trees. I had no intention of pulling the car into the garage nor was I going to step foot into his house. Things were getting weirder by the minute. I decided that I was parking the car in front, throwing him the keys and heading down the driveway hoping that Beth was not too far behind me.

As soon as I stopped the car, Nicked popped open his door and got out. I was suddenly relieved. I had been having flashes of him trying to groove on me while we were inside the parked car. The outside seemed to be so much safer. As I got out of the car, he had casually walked around and was now holding the door for me. When he closed it, he held out his hand for the keys without saying a word. "This is going well," I thought to myself. As I placed the keys in his hand, he suddenly grabbed my wrist with one hand and the back of my neck with the other and slammed my face down onto the hood of the car.

The impact of the warm metal on my cheek shot a sharp pain through my face. I panicked. He had me bent over the front of the car making it impossible for me to stand up straight and he was trying to get my arm behind my back. Still in shock, he succeeded. The pain in my shoulder was excruciating. I started to scream, "stop it, stop it, what the fuck are you doing?" When I felt his fingertips slide down the crack of my butt, trying to yank my jeans down, I knew exactly what he was doing. I freaked out.

Rinchen says that there are moments of crisis that are so profound that you step beyond fear. You almost forget what might happen to you and you become purely focused. I tried to lift my chest off the hood of the car with all my might, but you don't have much strength when you are bent over like that and every time I tried, Nick kept pushing my wrist higher and higher up my back until the pain in my shoulder was absolutely unbearable. Rinchen says that pain takes the fight out of an attacker and as I found myself sucking on the hood, Nick had given up trying to pull off my jeans from behind and was moving his hand around the front of my hips to unbutton them. I pressed my waist against the fender of the car to try to stop his hand from reaching the top button and then without knowing exactly why I was doing it, I started rocking side to side, raising and lowering my torso off of the car hood, if only an inch or two and flailing about like a floppy fish.

I could feel Nicks hands struggling to keep the pressure on my wrist behind my back as he frantically searched for the waist button on the front of my jeans. With every wiggle and flop he kept having more and more trouble maintaining his grip and I could feel his strength pushing this way and then the other, trying to regain control. Faster and faster I flailed until I felt him lose his grip on my wrist altogether and with a sudden burst of energy I pushed him backward with both legs literally using my butt as a battering ram. I could feel him stumble backward as I swung around and started slapping and clawing at his face. As I attacked him, the scene started to impress itself upon my mind. I was shocked to see that he already had his jeans down around his knees. The sudden realization that I was much closer to being raped than I had thought ignited me into an uncontrollable rage. With one hand trying to pull his pants up so that he could regain full use of his legs for balance and with his other hand trying to protect his face from my fingernails, he kept losing his balance and staggering backward. He suddenly stood up, his face stiff with an anger of his own, but before he could get his pants up, I kicked him as hard as I could, smack in the balls.

I kicked him so hard that I felt a sharp pain in my foot. It sounded like I had knocked the wind out of him. He doubled over and dropped to one knee and I kicked him again, this time across the bridge of his nose. And this time, I was sure that I had broken my foot. Blood started pouring across his face as he lay on the driveway rocking back and forth and groaning with both hands clasped over his groin. It was a pathetic sight. He never did get his jeans pulled up.

I wanted to jump on top of him and rip his ears off with my teeth. "Who's the bitch now, you little shit!" I stood over him screaming, "you fucking bastard! What is wrong with you? You fucking shit bag!" Between each shout I kicked him again and again, but my foot was starting to throb and I could barely stand up. Eventually, I couldn't kick him any more at all because my injured foot couldn't take the pain and I needed my good foot for balance. As I struggled to prop myself up on one leg, I saw the headlights of the Kid Car coming up the driveway. There was a sudden burst of acceleration as the headlights illuminated the scene followed by a screech of the brakes. The car was still rocking backward from the stop as Beth jumped out.

"Oh my god, oh my god, oh my god!" she screeched as she raced toward me. Tears were running down her eyes by the time she had crossed the thirty feet to where I stood over Nick's bleeding face still shouting at him, "you asshole! The next time you slash yourself, get it right you fucking moron!" My mind was completely consumed with hate. I realized later that rapist and victim had unexpectedly traded places.

As Beth tried to put her arm around me, we both nearly toppled over. She looked down and saw that I was not putting any pressure on my right foot. "Are you hurt?" she asked. "Not as bad as that motherfucker," I growled. I could not calm down. I wanted to kill him. I just wanted to kill.

Beth's voice started to shake, "we gotta get out of here. We have got to get out of here NOW!" Nick's groaning was becoming less audible and he seemed to be trying to rock onto one knee. As he did, Beth kicked him over and he fell onto his back. I hobbled to the car with Beth's arm wrapped around me. As I started to take in what had just happened, I wanted to cry, but I was not going to let Nick have the satisfaction. My anger was fading rapidly as I took my mind off of Nick and I tried to focus on keeping myself together. I have to say that Beth's arm wrapped across my shoulders as she helped me to the car began to feel like shelter.

Say what you will about Beth. She may have bought into the whole Westchester thing, but she had my back as she whisked me to the passenger seat of the Kid Car like a Secret Service agent. I closed my eyes and could hear her running around the car to get into the driver's side. She wasn't shaking anymore; she was focused and on a mission. She backed the car up like a stunt driver, jammed it into drive and gunned it, hurtling us through a row of well-groomed shrubs that made up the center of the circle drive. She had us out of there like a bat out of hell. Within minutes, I was home.

Rinchen says that you know your friends by their willingness to risk themselves for you. A year later, after I had joined the *dojo* and the visions started, I remember a dream that I had. I was lying on the ground. I was wearing one of those black pleated skirts that Rinchen wears. My white *gi* was soaked in blood, not all of it mine. At my head, stood Megan, dressed the same as me, holding a Japanese sword in both hands and keeping a ferocious lookout toward the East. To one side stood Matt, dressed the same, sword drawn and surveying the North. Tripp was there too, like the others, he was armed and watching to the South. And guarding the West was Beth, dressed like a warrior, sword drawn, keeping careful lookout as I lay helplessly on the ground. I remember thinking that one might become weak by circumstances, but with friends like that, I would never be vulnerable. Even now, after all this time, Beth has never been interested in joining the *dojo*. But in my mind, she is a warrior in her own way.

Chapter Nine: Is There A Victim In The House?

When your best friend helps carry you into the house after a near-rape experience, you do not exactly slip into your jammies and wander off to bed. As much as I like to think that my parents are goofy dorks, we were not home two minutes when my mother, with no sight or sound to alert her but her own intuition, was running down the stairs in her night gown not knowing and yet knowing that something was horribly wrong. It took a few minutes longer for my dad to come downstairs as a series of telepathic alarms seemed to ring through the house in the minds of one family member after another. Even Tyler staggered into the kitchen to find out what was the matter.

I had been holding my own as I slid onto a stool at the kitchen counter – that is, until my mom came into the room. I don't know what it is about seeing your mom in a moment, or in this case, just after a moment of crisis that turns you into a babbling, sobbing little girl, but the sight of her marching into the kitchen and the look of complete alarm on her face had me pouring tears into her nightgown before I could even tell her what had happened. There was no hurry. I was safe now. I seemed to be in one piece. To her this could be almost anything. No, not just anything. My mom knows me too well. I do not fall completely apart like this over just anything.

Beth actually had to start telling the story. She told my mom how I had tried to save Nick from being embarrassed and had offered to drive him home. She could not tell her much about the attack or me kicking the shit of the little creep which might have made my mom, and by now my dad, feel some relief.

In the first round of the telling of it, they only heard of the departure from the party and of me limping away from a trashed attacker on the ground.

Eventually, I filled them in on the details. You can tell when a situation has crossed the border between bad and holy-shit-serious. My parents were not freaking out. They were sullen and paying close attention to me. My dad picked up the phone and dialed 911. There was no debating this. There was only one way this was going down.

By the time the police came to the house it was midnight. Thank god, they simply pulled into the driveway. There were no lights or sirens. By now, I was not all that crazy about having the whole world know what had happened. A female officer was there and took my statement and interviewed Beth as well. The questioning got very graphic. The officer asked me if Nick and I had ever dated or had ever had sex. I had told her that I barely knew the guy, but she must have asked me about the sex thing at least four times. Then there were the questions about whether or not I had been drinking or doing drugs. I was starting to get pissed off. Most of the questions seemed to be about my behavior and not the guy who had tried to rape me. The unmistakable implication of the questions suggested that I might have lead Nick on or had consented to have sex with him on the hood of his mother's car in the middle of the driveway. Maybe I had changed my mind about having sex with him so that he was justified in slamming my face onto the hood of the car. Jesus!

My dad sat next to me as the officer asked her questions and let the humiliation go to the third round of *are-you-really-a-slut*. But when the officer came in for yet another pass, he cut her off. "Officer, this is getting ridiculous. This girl was nearly raped tonight and you are treating her like she tried to rape him. You have heard the facts, you know what happened. So now it is time for you to go do your job. Find this punk and arrest him!"

The officer looked a bit irritated, but my dad stared her down. Finally, she said, "Mr. Albright, we see a lot of this kind of thing, and it is usually not as clear cut as it seems."

That was it! My dad nearly blew his top, but he immediately constrained himself. "Well, officer, in this case it is perfectly clear cut and you will stop treating my daughter like she is being investigated for prostitution. Have I made myself clear?" That certainly wiped the look of superiority right off of Officer Friendly's face. "We are done here," he snapped at the officer. "I will discuss the matter with Captain Johnson in the morning; he's a golf buddy of mine and I am pretty damn sure he is not going to approve of the continuous humiliation of a young girl who was nearly raped by a guy that everyone knows is a creep."

Between the sudden realization that my dad was friends with her boss and that this seemingly mild mannered suburban man was about to go completely mental on her, the officer closed her notebook and headed for the door. "I am sorry if I angered you, Mr. Albright, I know that this is a very difficult situation." My dad was seething by now. "First, there is no 'if' you angered me -- your insensitive and disgusting suggestions have pissed me off beyond all limit. Second, this is not a difficult situation at all. A well-known local psychopath tried to rape my daughter. You have the facts, now go and arrest him before I go looking for him myself. How hard can that be?"

The officer appeared to realize that her continued presence was only going to make my dad even angrier. She simply said, "I am sorry. We will be in touch. Good night". With that she closed the door behind her and high-tailed it out of our neighborhood.

Most kids love their parents in their own way. For most of my teenage years, I mostly saw my dad as lovable but hopeless. He could even be hilarious when he struggled to try to create some type of relationship with me. But there were moments when he was truly my hero. I thought it was super-sweet that he had a florist deliver flowers to me the day after I passed my driver's test. I never knew that a driver's tests was an occasion for flowers, but it was cool just the same. I think he was trying to say that he noticed that I was growing up and that maybe I was starting to slip away. Maybe I am reading too much into it. But my dad had, in no uncertain terms, just stood up for me and then some. He was ready to fight the world for me. I had seen him mad before, but never like this. Rinchen says that hate is insanity, but an angry man fighting for what he holds dear is not motivated by hate but compassionate wrath. Wrath, with the right intention, is compassion on steroids. You never really know what you mean to your father until you see him fight for you. I really love him, you know, and I am not sure that I will ever take him for granted again.

There was no way that I was going to sleep that night. Beth had not said anything to her parents about what had happened, but instead had merely called them to tell them that she was going to sleep over. This was pretty much "situation normal" on the weekends. I kind of wanted to be left alone, but at the same time, I really wanted people I trusted to be near me and on guard. I dozed a bit on the couch, but it was a long night.

In the morning, I couldn't eat and I was starting to drive myself crazy with all of the replays of the events of the previous evening that kept running through my mind. I wanted distraction, but I didn't have the energy to do much of anything. I tried to watch TV, but as I flipped through the channels it seemed like every scene that flashed across the screen was either annoying or stressful. I finally gave up and clicked it off. I decided to check my email and was utterly shocked to see one from Nick. I did not say a word to Beth or my parents about it and I spent an hour pacing around deciding what to do with the thing.

Curiosity finally got the best of me and I decided to open it. As the text screen popped up, it was mostly blank. There was no message other than a hyperlink to a YouTube video. I wanted to throw up. It was one thing to have to read what this jerk had to say, but it was quite another to have to actually hear and see him again knowing that his message had already been broadcast to 194 countries. I had come this far, so I reasoned that I had to stuff in my guts and click the link. The first frame of the video popped onto the screen. I suddenly felt even more nauseous than before. This had been a horrible mistake. There, in the still, opening frame shot of the yet-to-be-played video was the underside of a forearm and the corner of a razor blade poking into the skin just below the wrist. I didn't need to play it to know what it showed. The edge of the razor blade was pointed toward the elbow; the cut would run along the arm and not across the wrist. A cross-cut would have been a plea for help. This cut was Nick's way of cleaning up his mess or telling me to fuck off in the most memorable way possible. I grabbed for the waste basket next to my desk and hurled.

Chapter Ten: Back In The Saddle Again

When I look back at the weeks that followed, it seems that they almost didn't happen. It was like I had gone into a coma or something. But if I make myself remember, those days were unbearably long and tedious. I couldn't sleep much and would drag through the daylight well into the night until I finally passed out from exhaustion. I couldn't eat much. I didn't feel like talking. My foot hurt. The doctor said that I had a tarsal fracture, whatever that is, and I had to wear a black nylon boot that allowed me to walk on my heel, but I could not bend my ankle. It was uncomfortable to focus on any one thing for even a short period of time. It was like my mind would start to settle down and the thoughts of the attack and Nick committing suicide would flood in to my mind and I would cry for hours without being able to stop. It was best to just keep my mind darting from thought to thought, object to object, to try to keep myself under control.

The story of what had happened raced through school although for the first week and a half, I wasn't there to hear any of it. Beth filled me in on the aftermath, in small, carefully selected episodes. Some of it had made the news. YouTube blocked Nick's video. One of my teachers, Mrs. Chavez, organized a solidarity vigil for me. I didn't go. Everyone thought it was because I was too strung out, but it was really because I thought the whole thing was hokey. I was told that nearly the whole school showed up even Tommy Davidson and Megan. Some people made jokes about it, especially about Nick. Julie Roth's girlfriend, Shana, started a militant campaign against date rape.

My parents made me see a therapist. She wanted to set me up with a lifetime of sessions and tried to coax out my suppressed anger. She was clueless. I had no suppressed anger. I had spent it all on Nick Thompson's nuts. And if there had been anything left, he wiped it all away when he settled his account with the razor blade. I think that I was mostly really, really sad, but so sad that I was mostly numb. Beth eventually got around to telling me that the video was fairly short. He cuts open the vein or artery in his arm and it bleeds like crazy. She said that you could hear him say, "I am sorry Maddie" several times in the background. It gets cut off shortly after that as he scrambles around to save the file and post it before he dropped dead.

I couldn't bring myself to hate him. I felt sorry for him and that made me mad at myself. It became apparent that this was very confusing, like riding a roller coaster of emotions up and down. I kept thinking about Tripp, but I could not get myself to feel interested in a boy, even a hot boy, at the moment. The thought of sex, while still hypothetical for me, had been one of my favorite things to think about before the attack, now made me a little sick to my stomach.

After a week, I decided that nothing had really happened other than a fight. I had not been raped. I had kicked his ass. Where was the real down side in this other than I should have had the right to be left alone? It should have never happened. But it did. I started to get annoyed at my own whiny, wimpy attitude about the whole thing. I had faced a crisis and fought my way out of it. I decided to go back to school.

My parents and the therapist all protested that it was way too soon, but I was going crazy sitting at home and I really needed something to do to occupy my time. I knew that I could not duck out on the lines of people in the hallway that would stare at me, or the buzz of the gossip or even the odd idiot that would have something to say about it to my face. But after ten days of soaking in this juice, I had had enough.

I didn't even get my car locked in the parking lot before it started. People were surprised to see me. Most tried to be polite and pretend that they did not know my story, or at least the version that they heard in the halls of the school. That's a lot to try to hide. They don't have a manners class at Westchester High that teaches the proper way to treat a girl who has been nearly raped and beat the shit out of her attacker who ultimately kills himself. Hallmark doesn't make a greeting card for that either.

As I walked into the building, the flow of students seemed to derail as I walked by. I started to think that I had made a mistake. Maybe it was too soon. And then I saw Megan walking down the hall with her motorcycle helmet dangling from her hand. She was not at a loss for how to deal with me at all. I was grateful. She walked in a straight line, barely slowing down and flung her arms around me and hugged me hard. "Damn, Little Bit, I have been worried shitless about you," she said softly in my ear. She didn't let go and I didn't either. It was the first time I had truly felt good in days and days.

Eventually, she held me at arm's length and looked into my eyes. There was nothing but pure concern in hers.

"What a mind-fuck," she said.

"You don't even know," I replied.

The bell was about to ring so we agreed to meet up for lunch. Somehow knowing that I was back in orbit around Megan and what little I knew of her world was deeply reassuring. As I headed off for class, it seemed suddenly easier to face what was surely coming from the herd of people that I mostly didn't care about and a few that I did.

From the time of the fight forward, things around me looked different. I had noticed this at home, but I really noticed it at school. I walked into History class and Mr. Leary smiled at me with what looked like a sense of sadness and compassion. From that day on, he never once tried to look down my shirt. It was as if that kind of thing wasn't harmless anymore.

I ran into Beth after history class. She knew I was coming back to school but had had a doctor's appointment in the morning and couldn't be there when I got there. She came up from behind me in the hall and slipped her hand around my arm and escorted me the rest of the way to class asking, "how ya holding up?" I told her that I was fine although I almost decked her when she took ahold of my arm from behind like that. She was suddenly embarrassed. "I am sooo, sorry!" She was nearly in tears. "Don't worry about it. I was glad to see it was you." The relief on her face spread out into a smile.

In between classes, I stopped at my locker and as I turned around to head down the hall, I saw Ack just standing there looking at me. His face was pursed up into a crumpled frown that looked like he was trying really hard not to cry. He didn't move. He just stared at me like that with a face full of sadness. I walked up to him and hugged him hard and kissed him on his ear.

"Oh Maddie, I have been so worried about you" he said. I could feel a warm tear from his eye roll down the side of my neck.

"I'm okay, really I am."

"What a horrible thing. What a horrible guy."

"No Ack, he wasn't horrible. He was just really fucked up." Ack pushed back from me so that he could see my face. I had surprised him with my remark. He searched my eyes and then started to smile. He was probably the only person in my world at that moment that understood.

"I am proud of you," he said hugging me again.

"Walk me to class," I said taking his hand.

As we passed through the hallways, I lost all sense of the other kids fumbling with their lockers and making their way to the next period. I was back in third grade with my friend Ack and it was a deep comfort to me.

After what seemed to be days, I finally made it to lunch. I really wanted to see Megan, but I really did not want to face the mob. She was waiting for me by the door to the cafeteria. It was a relief to have someone to talk to while we made our way through the lunch line. For starters, it gave me something to look at other than the entire school staring at me. We got our lunches "to go" and headed outside to sit in the grass on the football field.

The warm St. Louis weather lingers well into the first months of the school year. Sitting in the grass, the warm sun was tempered by a much welcomed breeze. My junior year had gotten off to one hell of a start. It was hard to believe that this had happened in Westchester. Nothing this traumatic ever happens in Westchester, or if it does, no one ever talks about it. Things were changing quickly. Suddenly, everything seemed so serious. Beth and Ack were no long simply childhood friends; they were witnesses to something quite outside of the comfort culture of Westchester. The fight with Nick was so radically different from the world that I had always known that it seemed to have propelled me into an entirely different future. The horizon was changing. New and mysterious people were emerging out of nowhere into my life as if they were answering some kind of summons. As I sat there in the grass with Megan, it felt like the center of the earth had moved and the two of us were now sitting on it.

Megan didn't ask me what happened. She didn't have to. I took her through the play by play anyway. When I got to the part about using the floppy fish technique that Rinchen had taught me, she smiled, but she still did not say a thing. When I got to the part where I kicked Nick in the balls, she broke her silence and said, "That's my girl." I told her everything. I told her about getting the email with the link to the video and how the police officer had basically accused me of causing the attack and how my dad had taken her to task. I told her how Beth had even gotten a shot in too and how she had taken me home and watched over me. "She's a good egg," Megan said.

"Yes she is," I agreed.

When the story was all told out, we just sat there staring into the deepening blue sky and let the breeze dance across our faces. After a while she looked at me and said, "I really want you to join the *dojo*." I sat there thinking about it and then she added, "please". It struck me as odd that this would be so important to her. I had no idea why this was the case, but I wasn't going to question it. "Let me talk to my parents. They are not saying 'no' too me lately."

"Alrighty then," she said with a nod.

"Alrighty then," I said mimicking her gesture.

Chapter Eleven: Daddy, Can I Be A Warrior?

Six weeks passed before I was able to get rid of the big black boot that was helping me heal from a what turned out to be a hairline fracture of a tarsal bone. It was two weeks more before I thought it safe enough to raise the subject of *Aikido* lessons with my dad. He was not crazy about my plan to join the *dojo*. On the one hand, he thought that self-defense training might be good for me in light of recent events, but he was totally not into me going down to the city by myself. The therapist that I was now refusing to see had told my parents that martial arts training might be therapeutic and give me a sense of power. Didn't anyone get the memo that I won that fight? I did not plead or beg. I simply told my dad that I needed to do this without much explanation. It is amazing what you get to do when your parents are taking you seriously. He ultimately caved in when I told him that Megan, her brother and her boyfriend all trained at the *dojo* and that I would never be downtown by myself. I left out the part about the motorcycles.

The day after I told Megan that I was joining the *dojo*, she showed up at school with a large bag. "This is for you," she said proudly - "its underwear". I opened the bag and instead of finding a pair of granny panties or a thong, there was a brand new, pure white *gi* in the bag.

"I thought you said that this was underwear?"

"I did and it is," she replied. I was confused.

"A *gi* in ancient Japan was an undergarment. A *hakama*, that's the black skirt that the senior students and *Sensei* wear, are considered actual clothes. Beginners have to train in their undies so that the master can see their posture and foot movements. Clothing would conceal those things preventing the teacher from being able to make corrections. After your third test, you get to wear a skirt." Megan's use of the slang reference "skirt" instead of calling it by its proper name made me suddenly aware that she was probably pretty far down the *Aikido* road.

I poked around the bag and was about to thank her when I noticed that the *gi* seemed to be incomplete. "Aren't these things supposed to have a belt?" I asked, trying not to sound ungrateful.

"Oh, yeah," said Megan and plunged her hand into the pocket of her biking jacket and pulled out a ratty, graying rag of a belt. I examined the belt that was coiled up in her hand. It looked like someone had used it as a napkin and band aid and god knows what else. I wasn't even sure I wanted to touch it. "Maybe, I'll just get a new one," I said cautiously.

"Oh no, you don't want to do that. It is a long standing tradition that when a *sempai*, a senior student, brings a *kohai*, a junior student, into a *dojo* that the *sempai*, that would be me, gives the *kohai*, that would be you, her old belt. This belt has never been cleaned. It has the sweat and the blood that I have shed in the process of earning my next belt. By giving this to you, I am not only giving you something that I hold very dear, but I am also giving you a piece of me in the hope that it will help you. This is the bond between a *sempai* and a *kohai*. You will become my responsibility in the *dojo* and I will not fail you."

Wow, I did not see that coming. Megan was worried about failing me? Why was a senior student worried about the newbie? Wasn't it supposed to be the other way around?

"In the *dojo*, seniors have the responsibility to make sure that junior students learn the ropes correctly. If you screw up, *Sensei* is not going to say a lot about it to you, but I am going to get a face full. Rank is not a privilege, it's a responsibility." As Megan said this, she seemed to be searching my eyes for some sign of comprehension. If I had been nervous before, I was now officially petrified. What if I suck at this? It would be bad enough to embarrass myself, but now, as I am learning a little bit more about the system, I would be embarrassing *her*.

This was a lot to think about. I was touched by the deep meaning that Megan attributed to her gift. I was completely new to the *dojo* world, but to see this devil-may-care sort of girl be so serious and formal about a tattered rag of a belt was making an impression. It suddenly dawned on me that in my new world, this was important and I needed to honor it if for no better reason than to avoid making an ass of myself.

"You wore the hell out of this thing," I said as I accepted Megan's gift.

"Not just me," she said. "This belt was given to me by my brother when he got his brown belt which he got about a year before me. So, he gave this one to me. Before that it belonged to our father."

"This belonged to your *father*? Why in the heck are you giving it to me then?"

"It's tradition. It has a lot of good karma trained into it and besides, my father gave me the belt that I wear now."

"I thought that your teacher was supposed to give you your belt, although I guess, the fact that you are giving me this one proves me wrong."

"A white belt does not come from your teacher. For most people, it comes from the store where you buy your first *gi*. Unless you are brought into the *dojo* by a *sempai*, it has no special meaning other than it holds your *gi* closed. Your sweat and your blood become the meaning of your belt. When you are promoted, you are given a new belt of a different color to indicate your rank. Only your teacher can do that."

I was confused. "But I thought you said that your father gave you your current belt."

"That's right, he did."

"I don't get it."

Megan started to smile. "Duh ... Sensei Rinchen *is my father*."

"You're kidding me!"

"Nope."

"But he told me that his last name was Jackson."

"It is ... and so is my brother's. My last name was Jackson too, until my mom and dad got divorced. I was pretty pissed at my dad for divorcing my mom. When my mom moved to the county she took back her maiden name. At that time, I guess you could say I was on my mom's side and asked to change my name to Laskowitz too. My dad wasn't going to fight me over it. He said that I could call myself, Penelope Snigglefritz if I wanted to, but I would still be his daughter. I didn't speak to him for almost a year. That is why I am a year behind Tripp in rank. Eventually, I figured out that my dad was still my dad and that he had his reasons for doing what he did. Like I told you, I still live with my mom during the week. She really doesn't have anyone else. Changing my name back to Jackson would have been a hassle and would have hurt my mom's feelings. Besides, everyone knows me as Megan Laskowitz now. But I know whose daughter I am."

Megan seemed to be at ease with her story – and with her dad for that matter. I got the sense that this inner peace had been won only after quite a struggle. So, Rinchen is her dad and Tripp is her brother. Well, alrighty, then.

Chapter Twelve: Learning The Ropes

Joining a *dojo*, at least one like Byakuren, is a little bit like joining the Marines. You come in off the street in jeans and the first thing you do is put on a uniform. You might wander around the halls of school texting your friends perfectly oblivious to your surroundings, but in the *dojo* not only do you not text or talk on the phone; you have to turn the thing off for the entire time you are there. From the moment you step through the door until the moment you leave, there is a rule for everything.

On the day of my first class, I had gotten to the *dojo* early and Megan gave me the tour. It took at least a half an hour just to explain how the shrine and the seating arrangements worked, let alone the short lesson on manners. I could not believe how uptight this place was. You couldn't scratch your butt in the *dojo* without having to follow some rule about it. (Megan says, however, that you never scratch yourself or pick your nose in front of your teacher, nor do you ever show him the soles of your feet or use curse words in his presence or refer to him by another name other than *"Sensei"*, that is, if he is the *head* teacher, otherwise you call her *sempai,* that is if she is a senior student who is teaching and you never disrespect a fellow student or lose your temper or fold your *gi* incorrectly after class or ....) Remembering it all was going to be hard enough. Doing it all seemed impossible.

My first class was on a Monday night. She said that at first, I should only train about two or three times a week. According to her, it takes time to build up your body to handle the rigors of training. She said that she and Matt train at least five days a week and that Tripp trains twice a day, every day. Whoa!

That certainly explained the abs. I thought that I was in pretty good shape and before class I was figuring that I would take classes when Megan and Matt took classes. As I was driving home after class, however, I could barely press the gas and brake pedals because my legs hurt so bad. I changed my plan. Maybe I would start with two classes a week and work my way up to three.

The *dojo* has a small foyer from which visitors can watch class and parents can wait for their kids. There are no children allowed in the *dojo* during the evening training. There is only one kids' class during the week and two on the weekends. Kids' classes are for anyone under twelve. The adult beginners' class starts at 7:00 pm every night of the week and the advanced class starts at 8:30. Senior students are expected to attend both classes. They basically use the beginner class as a warm-up. Seriously advanced students stay after the advanced class. Megan says that's when you learn the really cool stuff.

In the summer, there is an open morning class outside near a stream in Forest Park. "Open" means that if you can get there, you can train. Megan said that you can tell who the real *Aikidoka* are by who shows up in the morning. It starts at 6:30 am and goes until 7:30. There is no mat. Everyone trains in bare feet and if you take a dive, there is only the ground to break your fall.

This is nothing like training in the *dojo*. There, the floor is covered with a large, white canvas that feels like it is stretched over some kind of foam. It doesn't squish much under your feet, but when you fall down, it is not concrete. The mat is encircled by a wooden frame and you never, ever step over the frame onto the mat with your shoes on. Megan told me that the Japanese used to believe that the dirt that collected on your shoes carried demons and would come into your house if you did not leave your shoes outside. She mentioned that this was probably an early form of sanitary practice that was not so much about demons as it was about disease. In those days, I suppose people saw them as the same thing.

In the center of the training area there is an alcove built into the wall. This is called a *tokonoma*. Megan explained that a *tokonoma* by itself is not a shrine though it is a special place in a room. In Japan, she said that you see them in tea houses and they usually have calligraphy or some type of art displayed in them. At the *dojo*, they built a *tokonoma* to house the shrine, called the *kamidana*. This is a small frame with a shelf in front of it. There is a picture of the founder of *Aikido*, Morehei Ueshiba, in the center of the frame. I didn't notice at first, but the frame is built to look like a house, in a way. It has a little shingled roof that juts out over the top of the frame. This makes it look like a building rather than a picture frame. On the shelf, students keep a bowl of fresh water and a bowl of rice. Sometimes they stick a couple of sticks of incense in the rice and occasionally it burns during class. I have already come to love the smell of *dojo* incense.

On the floor of the *tokonoma*, there is a rack with two swords in it. There are other items arranged around the swords kind of like how you might arrange a coffee table or a mantle over the fireplace. These are either offerings to the protective deities of the *dojo* or are sacred items used to focus the thoughts of practitioners. The floor space in front of the *tokonoma* is the place where the most important person in the room sits. By tradition, the most important person, even if she is a guest, sits with her back to the *tokonoma*. This place is called the *kamiza*, or the "top seat.". The Japanese are obsessed with rank, not just in *dojos*, but in every place that two or more people might meet. Rank is just one more way in which the warrior organizes her existence.

The locations in the *dojo* are never designated by relative directions like left or right because this would only lead to confusion. After all, whose left or right would be the starting point? It turns out that there is a similar problem aboard a ship. If a crew member is at the bow of a ship and says, "holy crap, there is a big shark over on the right!" and he is looking back at you at the stern, does he mean his right or your right? Even in the days of Christopher Columbus they solved this problem by using non-relative directions. Starboard is to the right of the ship if you are at the rear looking forward. Port is to the left. The front is the bow and the back is the stern. In this way, the captain can always get the crew to move to the correct part of the ship without creating chaos. "Ensign Jones, get your butt up to the starboard bow" can mean only one thing. These names create clarity and order.

Megan said that the floor space at the front of the *dojo* has a similar organization. The front, the space closest to the *tokonoma*, is the *shomen* (pronounced "show-men") or "head". Because it is the head, it is the place of the *kamiza*, or, as I mentioned, the top seat.

If there is a head, then there has to be a base. The spot at the back of the training space furthest from the *tokonoma* is called the shimoza. Students sit in order of rank across the *dojo* mat. If more than one row is required, then a second row is formed toward the shimoza, or behind the first row, and is populated with lower ranking students. The seating arrangement is strictly dictated by rank and it is considered incredibly rude to sit in the wrong place. Knowing where you fit into the pecking order is part of your training and part of developing an awareness for order and organization. If you are standing at the back of the training area facing the *tokonoma*, then the space on the right is called the *joseki* . This is where the seniors sit with the most senior student sitting the furthest to the right. The order of rank descends from the *joseki* side of the *dojo* to the *shimoseki* side. When you walk into any *dojo* and see the students formally seated, immediately you can tell the bad asses from the newbies. This is a good thing to know because, first, you do not want to piss off a badass and, second, you can easily identify who has more experience and can help you.

Megan says that it is important that when you bow to someone of higher rank that you make sure that your head is lower than theirs. This is a sign of respect and respect is something that you never forget to show. She said that when you are a beginner, bad manners are expected because you do not know what you are doing. In fact, she said fresh meat is not even considered to be capable of bad manners because they have not yet learned what manners are. Bad manners only occur when you know better. In the *dojo* world, ignorance is perfectly acceptable, so much so that no one sees it as offensive or even something to be forgiven. But ignorance is something that you are absolutely expected to overcome. A senior with bad manners is either neglectful or intentionally rude. Neglect, unlike ignorance, is considered sloppy and unskillful and is never overlooked and never appreciated. Megan says that neglect, in some ways, is even worse than intentionally being rude. She also said that rudeness in a *dojo* is a really bad idea. It is the quickest way to get your ass beaten to a pulp and have everyone shun you. I guess there is even a ranking system for bad behavior: rudeness is unforgiveable; neglectfulness is highly annoying; ignorance is merely something to work on.

We had been chatting in the foyer after my orientation tour when her father and brother arrived. Rinchen seemed happy to see me. "Ahh, it's true! Miss Madison, I heard that you were going to be joining us and I am very pleased to see that this is so." Rinchen' s verbal formality seemed odd to me. As far as I could tell, he was all white-guy. There was no trace of Asian anything in him. And yet he behaved and spoke like Jackie Chan or some of the other Asian martial arts guys you see in the movies. It is not like he had a fake accent or anything, but he always bowed before he spoke. His language was always formal and eloquent. The emotions that seemed to radiate so easily out of his face were somehow singular and undistorted by any trace of complexity. Rinchen was a man who was always under control and yet not fake in the least. Everything about him was on purpose.

Come to think of it, Megan was a lot like that too, in her own way. At first, I saw her as this confident, awesome chick, but eventually started to notice that she wasn't like the other girls at school at all. She wasn't one big accidental personality. She didn't have spontaneous and unedited outbursts of emotion to draw attention to herself. She was the opposite of theatrical. And yet, when she had hugged me the day that I had returned to school, she was intensely loving. There was no sense of self-control or any noticeable attempt to suppress her feelings. How could a person be both things at the same time? How can you be totally on purpose and totally spontaneous at the same time? She was well thought-out and this was the source of her cool.

Chapter Thirteen: Flying Lessons

The *gi* was crisp and scratchy on my skin as I pulled it on in the dressing room. It was too big and I looked like I was wearing my dad's pajamas. Megan told me that it would shrink after I had washed it a few times and that once I had trained for a few months, it would be as soft as cloth diaper. She had warned me before I got there to wear a sports bra because new gis do not like to stay closed at the top. And then came the moment that I had to put on my belt which Megan had told me was actually called an obi.

I watched Megan wrap her brown belt around her waist twice, slide one end behind the concentric wraps, flip the loose ends, one over the other, and pull both ends hard. It took her only a few seconds to do this and you could tell by the way that she hardly paid attention to the process that she had made this knot hundreds of times. Because of her rank, Megan also wore a hakama. This required considerably more weaving of straps and tying of knots, but when she was done, there was this perfect bow resting gracefully in the center of the pleats that ran down the front. The knot looked a little bit like Colonel Sanders' neck tie. "If you do it right, your *gi* never comes loose no matter what they do to you out there," she said. This statement was a bit daunting on two levels: one, was I ever going to get it right, and two, just exactly what were they going to do to me out there?

Every new student comes into a *dojo* worried about looking foolish and trying to conceal their newbieness. This is a purely pointless exercise. The unavoidable fact was that I was new. I did not know what I was doing and there was no way to hide this. As Megan finished tying, tugging and straightening her apparel, she turned to see how I was doing and had to suppress the sudden burst of laughter that disappeared as quickly as it had come on. *Gi* pants are pretty straight forward and not unlike my pajama bottoms at home. There is a draw string that you pull to tighten the waistband and you tie it off with a bow knot like you would use to tie a shoe. The top, however, is designed to have one flap fold over the other creating a V-neck. There are small straps inside that are meant to be tied together to keep the top closed. I had tied the wrong straps together and the *gi* bowed open as if I was planning to store a basketball in it. I had wrapped the belt around my waist and tied it in the first knot that occurred to me. I felt like I was in kindergarten and had just made a mess of the art supplies. We had not even made it to the mat and already I needed to be rescued.

Megan untied the inner straps of the *gi* and neatly pulled the left flap over the right. "If you ever walk onto the mat with the right flap over the left, everyone will think you are dead and run away from you," she said smiling. Apparently, in the samurai days, you always wore the left flap of your *gi* and *kimono* on top. When you died, they reversed the flap so that if you saw your body from the mind of death, you would know that you were dead. While this is not taken terribly seriously in modern times, even so, no one ever, ever wears the right flap over left – ever.

After a quick lesson on the secret of the inner straps and another on how to tie the belt, Megan got suddenly quite serious. "Your *obi* is your life," she said. "It is the record of your time here, but it is also who you are now. If it is sloppy, you are sloppy. If it falls off, then you have fallen apart. We are going to train hard, but you are expected to keep your obi, your *gi* and yourself in proper order at all times. It will eventually become second nature to you." She was looking me straight in the eye and searching for some confirmation of understanding. I nodded. "When we step out of the dressing room, bow to the *kamidana* before stepping onto the mat, then find a place to start stretching out. When you hear Tripp clap his hands that means that class is about to begin. He will be leading the warm up. Run to your spot. By the way, your spot is to the far left of the line, at the farthest part of the *shimoseki*. You are the newest, so you are last. You won't be for long. While this is not a place of rank, it is a place of respect and everyone knows that you are new and everyone on their life will make an effort to help you learn. Do you got it?"

I nodded again.

"Alrighty, then – let's do this."

Megan started for the door of the dressing room that opened into the main training area. "And by the way, do not be afraid of mistakes, that is what you are here for. Mistakes are what teach us. They tell us where to train. Better to go down in a blazing screw-up than to stand there frozen in the ice of fear. Are you ready?"

I wasn't, but we stepped out of the dressing room anyway, bowed to the *kamidana* and stepped onto the mat.

The canvas felt cold on my feet when I first stepped onto it. There were about twenty other students quietly engaged in stretching and warming up. Some were doing the familiar hurdler's stride stretch. Others were running a few steps and diving through the air and then suddenly tucking into a roll along the outside of one arm. Once they had made a full rotation, they bounced off the mat onto their feet. They looked like circus tumblers. It was amazing. Many of the students were my age but there were some that were my parent's age and even they were doing diving rolls. I could not visualize either my mom or my dad doing something like this.

After a few minutes, I heard a very loud double clap. Tripp, dressed like Megan, was standing at the corner of the mat with his hands folded in front of him. He somehow looked older and much more dignified in his *gi* and hakama. His face was expressionless as he watched the students scurrying around to form a single line across the *dojo* mat. Everyone sat in *seiza* (pronounced "say-zah"), on their shins with their backs perfectly straight and their hands perched on their thighs. They sat there motionless, as if someone had just pulled the plug on their brains. I copied them the best I could. My knees almost immediately started to ache. When the room was finally perfectly still, Tripp bowed to the *kamidana* walked briskly behind the row of students to step forward toward the *kamiza* from *shimoseki*. This turned out to be no random gesture. Only the master teacher, the *sensei*, enters the front of the class from *joseki* . This, I have learned, is his right because he has the highest rank. Everyone else, out of respect, steps up from the *shimoseki* side. Tripp took his place at the *kamiza* and faced the *tokonoma*. With a motion of his hand that looked like a *Karate* chop, he slapped the billowing cloth of his *hakama* as he sat in *seiza* like the rest of us. For a minute or two he sat silently with his hands cupped in front of him with his thumbs touching so that his hands formed a circle. I could see his lungs inflate and hear the slow exhale as he seemed to be drifting off into some sort of trance. And then, without warning (well, actually everyone else in the room seemed to see it coming) he bowed to the *kamidana* as everyone in the room did the same. In a flash he spun around on the floor without getting up and was bowing to the students and they were bowing to him. There was a sudden outburst – "*onegaishimasu*" (pronounced "ana-gyshee-mas") and within seconds the entire student body was on its feet performing the precise stretching exercise that Tripp was doing. No one spoke except Tripp who counted the repetitions in Japanese –"*ichi, ni, sang, shi, go* …." You could hear that the entire *dojo* was not only stretching together, but they were breathing together – all except me. I was panting like a dog.

After about ten minutes of some of the most painful stretches that I could have possibly imagined, Tripp clapped twice again and everyone raced to the *shimoseki* end of the mat and formed a line along the edge. The first four students took a step forward and forming a vertical circle with their arms in front of them, fell forward and rolling over the arm-circle as if it were a wheel. As their feet came up over their heads and found their way back to the mat, the students pushed their legs upward finishing the motion exactly as they had started – on their feet. They repeated this five or six times until they had crossed over to the other side of the mat. I was in the last line and was thinking to myself, "hell no". Megan had done the exercise in the first wave with lightning speed and had immediately circled around the mat and was trotting back to help me. As I tried to mimic the arm positions that I had seen the others use. She corrected me and then made me drop to one knee. "You will tear every ligament in your shoulder if you try to do this from standing today, *kohai*," she said without the slightest trace of familiarity. It was amazing how she could turn off her friendliness like that. It was like she was instructing a complete stranger.

My first attempt at a roll was a disaster. I had had a couple of years of gymnastics classes so I was not completely in the dark about tumbling, but this was something entirely different. At first, I fell over myself in an awkward summersault that caused me to do a butt-plant that made a loud thud. The object was to roll down the outside of my arm, but it did not seem like I could hold up my entire body weight. Megan showed me how to raise my arm with my elbow over my head and placing my ear on my shoulder. You did this by placing the palm of one hand on to back of the other hand and lifting your elbow to form a circle. This created a big wheel out of my arms, but as I rolled over it, my shoulder could not bear the weight and the whole structure collapsed. As I came crashing into a heap on the floor, I was getting frustrated. Everyone else was doing this so easily. "You have to exhale at the exact moment that you need the extra strength in your arm. You need to literally breathe the air out of your arm and roll over your breath," Megan said in all earnestness. What the hell was she talking about? How do you breathe out of your arm? Here I was, five foot eight and one hundred and twenty-five pounds (okay, give or take) and I was supposed to hold all this upside down on a ball of breath?

Megan demonstrated. She took a deep breath that I am sure she exaggerated for my benefit. As she lifted her legs to rise off of the one knee she had been kneeling on, her head ducked down and the wheel started to roll. Just as she was about to put pressure on the outer edge of the top arm, I could hear her exhale in a rather forceful way simultaneously pushing herself over the wheel of arms quickly so as to get past the weak point as fast as she could. "The faster you go, the easier it is," she said as she popped up from the roll. "If you say so," I replied focusing on my next attempt and trying to mimic what I had just seen her do. I got half way through the roll, but I was too slow; my shoulder collapsed and I crashed on the floor again. I started to crawl out of the pile I had made out of myself when I saw a second set of feet -- a man's feet. As my eyes followed the pleated lines of the *hakama* upward I saw that they were connected to Tripp. I am quite sure I blushed.

It is really hard to try to impress a guy, especially a hopelessly gorgeous guy with brilliant green eyes and the body of a god, a guy that you have been thinking about for weeks on end, by falling on your ass like a sack of potatoes. Sitting on the floor like a grandma who has just fallen and broken her hip is not really what I had in mind when the warm-up started. In my vision of things, I was going to step on the mat and expose a hidden talent that no one knew I had and knock Tripp to his knees with desire as I unleashed my savage hotness. "Try again," he said with the same detachment that Megan had just shown me. I got onto one knee, made the wheel with my arms and started to lift my hips with my legs while ducking my head as I had seen Megan do. But just as I was reaching the point of irreversible ass-to-head inversion, I felt two very strong hands squeeze my hips and suddenly my body was nearly weightless as I rolled over my arm and landed sitting up.

"Did you feel that?" Tripp asked. For a second, I was not sure what he was talking about because I certainly did feel that! My hips were still tingling as I was scrambling to regain my composure. No boy, man or even my gynecologist had ever taken hold of me like that, and certainly not for the purpose of flipping me on my butt. As the fog in my mind cleared, however, I realized, this was not what he was talking about. "That is all the pressure you should ever feel on your arm. What you are really doing is just using your arm to find the floor so that you know where it is. The work gets done with your legs and you literally jump over your arm. There should never be more than a few pounds of pressure." I organized myself on one knee once again and formed the wheel with my arms. This time, as I fell forward, I pushed my legs upward causing my body to fly over my arms without putting hardly any pressure on them. It was an awesome feeling, like being weightless for a second. I could barely feel the floor. This increased the speed of the roll causing my feet to circle round faster than I had expected. When I felt the floor come around to touch my feet, I pushed hard and the momentum of the circular motion was suddenly redirected into a straight line and shot me up into the air and onto my feet. Suddenly, I was quite excited, "I did it!" Tripp nodded slightly and said in a tone of utter indifference, "alrighty then, welcome to class." And with that, he turned and walked back to the line of students waiting to roll back to the other end of the *dojo* – only this time, they would be rolling backwards.

Tripp took a moment to explain to all of the students as if they had never heard it before that the rolling exercise was called *ukemi* practice. *Ukemi* (pronounced "oo-kem-ee"), he said, was the art of falling down and that every *Aikidoka* had to learn how to fall before she could learn how to throw someone. "*Ukemi*, is the art of keeping yourself safe no matter what someone tries to do to you," he said looking straight at me. "We normally think that if someone is trying to punch us, grab us or hit us with a stick that we have to either take the strike or block it, but we don't. In *Aikido* we never block anything. Instead, we learn to move with the strike or roll away from it and return immediately to our feet. We can take our attacker with us as we roll or twist his own motion in an infinite variety of directions that often leaves him on the ground with us standing over him. But there is no way to safely practice *Aikido* until you have learned how to fly."

Learn how to fly? That sounded a bit dramatic to me. I was soon proven wrong about that too.

Tripp clapped his hands twice and everyone reformed the lines along the edge of the mat. He called a student in a shiny new white belt to the center of the mat. Instructed only by a nod, the student dropped to his knees on the matt and held himself up on all fours. Tripp then nodded to the other students and they formed a single-file line. The seniors always went first in any line and with Tripp instructing the class, that meant that Megan would go first. She began to trot toward the student in the middle of the room. When she reached him, she casually fell over him rolling on one arm and landing on her feet almost effortlessly. The next student did the same until the line had come to the end and I was standing there getting ready to kill myself by attempting to roll over this poor fellow that I was most surely going to flatten.

As I started to trot toward the human hurdle, Tripp stopped me, "no, no, you walk." This was actually a relief. Rolling from one knee was hard enough, but to roll over an obstacle from standing was a whole other adventure in holy-crap! This time, no one came to my aid. As I tried to figure out the timing of my steps and was about to mimic the diving motion that everyone else had done, Tripp once again interrupted: "stop when you get to the hurdle, bend over and using the technique that we showed you, simply fall over the hurdle thrusting your butt up toward the ceiling. It is exactly what you have already done." Taking this on faith, I walked up to the teenage obstacle who was trying to suppress a grin and after a moment of thinking way too much about it, I bent over until I started to fall and thrust myself up and over my circle of arms. It was not pretty, but it worked. And I was a little pleased with myself as I rose to my feet and realized that no one was laughing at me.

Tripp nodded again and a second student ran out to the center of the mat and got on all fours hip-to-hip with the first student. With another nod to the line, the seniors, starting with Megan, broke into a trot and as they approached the newly formed row of human obstacles, dove forward in the air like Superman ducking their heads as they cleared the distance and, each in turn, snapping themselves into a rapid roll that had them almost instantaneously back on their feet. This was getting serious. Soon, I was the lone student on my side of the mat and I started to trot toward the hurdle. Tripp let me cross about half the distances before shouting "stop!" He smiled at me and said, "Not today Miss Madison, not today. But it is good that you are willing to try." He seemed to be more than pleased that I was willing to kamikaze myself over the students hunched over in the center of the mat. I was suddenly a little irritated that he had cut me off, but by the time I got to the other side of the mat, I was actually relieved.

Once again, Tripp nodded and another white belt stepped out to the center of the mat and extended the hurdle. It was starting to look like the row of cars that they line up at one of those monster truck rallies to be jumped and probably crushed for the amusement of the crowd. As I saw Megan take off, I wondered how far this was going to go. Her timing was perfect. She flew through the air over the row of students. She was still using only one arm to roll. She sprung to here feet in a single fluid motion and kept running to the opposite wall as if she had just performed a barrel roll in a jet that barely impaired her flight. The students in the line moved forward as each took their turn. You could see as the line worked its way down to the lower ranks that a little bit of fear started to show on the sweaty faces. A guy, a little younger than me, balked. Tripp made him make the attempt off to one side and not directly over the row of students. It was a good thing too, because he would have dove straight into the ribs of third student. With one more nod, the same young fellow circled back around the mat and took his place as yet another human hurdle. Now there were four and they started to pack closer together. They also changed their posture. Instead of standing on all fours, they were now crouched as low as they could get and were covering their heads with their hands. No one seemed to be particularly concerned about this except for the guy on the far side of the row of bodies.

Megan took a breath, like she was smelling the air, which by now was starting to carry the odor of sweat. She inhaled deeply and darted for the row of students. There was an audible thump as she left the ground and with her arms stretched out in front of her as she flew at least four feet over the crouching students, she landed in a perfect roll. The force of her own circular motion was suddenly redirected into a straight line as she shot nearly straight up off the floor and landed on her feet. Now, she was just showing off. All of the students in *hakamas* cleared the obstacle with ease and so did several of the white belts. The exercise continued until there were seven students crouched in the center of the mat.

Only the skirts remained in the line. I was added to the row of bodies, tucked in the middle, presumably where it was safe should someone crash. I could feel the breeze and hear the flutter of the *hakamas* as they sailed over my back. I could feel the thump on the mat and then the patter of feet trying to brake before hitting the wall on the other side. With seven students in the row, the hurdle was now over ten feet long. Every senior did it twice for good measure including Tripp. They really did know how to fly.

There was the sound of the double clap of hands and everyone scrambled to their place in line. The seniors quickly adjusted their clothing so that as they sat on their shins in *seiza* they looked as tidy as when they first stepped onto the mat. Tripp bowed to the students as they bowed back to him. He then rose suddenly and scurried around the *shimoseki* end of the line, walking briskly behind the seated students and taking his place as the most senior student. Everyone was perfectly quiet. You could hear the breathing being brought under control. Rinchen was coming.

Chapter Fourteen: War And Manners

Like his son, Sensei Rinchen stepped onto a corner of the mat and took his time to organize his breathing and to stare thoughtfully into the shrine. The word "*sensei*" technically means "born before", but is used to describe someone who has walked on a path before you. Generally speaking, a martial arts student can have only one *sensei* in that she can only follow one teacher at a time. Other teachers might be treated with great respect, but only your teacher is *sensei*. I have come to learn that in the west this custom deviates from the original tradition. For example, when you meet your teacher's teacher, many in our country will call that teacher "*sensei*" as well. Fun fact: the word *sensei* is not limited to use in *dojos*. A teacher of *Ikebana*, the art of flower arranging or Shodo, the art of calligraphy, might also be called *sensei*.

Rinchen bowed to the *kamidana* and then walked with deliberation behind the students around the *shimoseki* end of the line and stepped up to the front of the class and sat in *seiza* facing the shrine. At that time, this was not particularly noteworthy, but later it made no sense to me at all. He was, after all, the master instructor of Byakuren Dojo. Why would he take his place at the head of the class from the lowest ranking end of the line? A month or two into my training, I asked Megan why her father did this. She said that it was out of respect for his own teacher who is still living. She said that while Rinchen pays for the *dojo* and runs it like a business, he has given it to his teacher and considers his master the one entitled to enter from *joseki* . She said that no teacher worth his salt actually ever steps up to the *kamiza* of a *dojo* from *joseki* unless there are no other living members in his lineage that outrank him. And

91

even then, the best teachers still refuse to make this gesture, holding this honor in memorium for their deceased teachers or other lineage ancestors. It was amazing to me the amount of meaning that can be put into simply stepping to the head of the class. What is really impressive is the amount of thought that goes into each gesture. This gives new meaning to doing something *on purpose*.

Until I started to train at the *dojo,* I had not realized what a bunch of barbarians we are. My dad always holds the door open for other people, not just women. I once told him that I thought that this was incredibly old fashioned and he debated the point stating that he was just trying to be polite. He does other things that are equally out of date. He always takes his hat off when he is indoors and won't even eat at a fast food restaurant with as much as a baseball cap on. At the table he always serves himself last and is first to take on the after-dinner chores. I once asked him about these things and he said that compared to his parents, he behaved like a pig. He pointed out that when you take off your hat for someone you are taking a moment, however brief, to show respect. It is a tiny gesture that speaks of kindness and thoughtfulness. He says it is a lost art. My dad pointed out that even the smallest gesture of respect can interrupt the ordinary thoughtlessness of the people around you and make them feel appreciated. Rinchen makes people think a lot. Nowadays, most people are talking on a cell phone as they plow through doors. You see people wearing hats even in nice restaurants. It is not just a loss of manners, it is the loss of awareness of others that is the real damage done.

In my world, people are only vaguely aware that there are even other people around them. You see guys and girls texting as they walk, talking on the phone, bumping into each other without even an acknowledgement that they just nearly mowed someone over. At school, kids can navigate the entire hallway system without ever taking their eyes off of their cellphones and never knowing who they are walking past. Megan says that people are more dog than human. She is not being arrogant when she says this. In fact, it seems to make her sad.

When Rinchen began to sit down in front of the *tokonoma,* he made the same slap at his *hakama* as Tripp did. Megan told me later that this folds the extra material of the *hakama* behind the legs and makes it easier to sit in *seiza* without the material binding across the thighs. It is amazing to me that someone would be so organized as to remember to straighten their clothes before each and every time they sit down. He bowed to the shrine and then lit up the room with two loud cracks of his palms clapping together in unison with his students. I would come to see this ritual performed day after day. It is a Shinto tradition. The first clap represents one's action and the second is its echo returning in the form of its consequence. Everything has a consequence. In our media-soaked consciousness we may not notice. Our minds flutter about chasing songs we hear on the radio or pictures we saw on YouTube. We are almost never paying attention to what is right in front of us. We hurt people without even knowing, like stepping on ants on the sidewalk. Everything has a consequence; it is just that most of ours are not planned out. Rinchen says that we are mostly accidental beings staggering our way through accidental lives. He also says that you should always be kind to grocery clerks, because how you treat them will influence the next ten people in line. A single moment of rudeness, intended or not, can cause someone to go home and slap their kid. Who has a mind that can pay attention to all of this?

What I have learned in my own short time in the *dojo* is that training rigorously with attention to every tiny detail teaches you to be precise and to see the details of the world around you. Your mind will not clear itself by itself. It must be trained like a wild horse must be broken. Most of my friends are far too lazy to take on something like this. They are too preoccupied by their own amusement to ever want to see the world as it really is. It cuts into their X-Box time and, I have to admit, it is not necessary if all you want to do in life is slide along. But watching Tripp fly over seven crouched bodies makes me realize that people are capable of so much more than what they believe. While it may not be necessary to become a super-samurai, I am becoming very curious to know what the world looks like through the eyes of someone with serious wisdom and skills. Only a person who has trained and learned gets to know what a master knows and gets to see what a master sees. Food tastes so much better to an accomplished chef. No dull mind will ever get to know the thrill of taste like a master chef does. Twinkies are made for the masses. And for most, it is enough. There are great secrets reserved for the few who are willing to sweat and claw their way up the mountain. Even now, though I do not know half of what my *dojo* friends know, I am hungry for it. I want to learn how to fly with them.

My dad once heard me singing in the car to a tune by Aerosmith. He was surprised that I knew the words to the song. He said that he had taken his first date to an Aerosmith concert. In an attempt to show me that he was not a total dork, he bought tickets to see Aerosmith when they came to town. The concert was being promoted by a video game company that used Aerosmith music in a fake guitar-playing game. It should be noted for the record that going to a rock concert with your dad has no possibility of awesomeness. It seemed important to him, so I went with him. When we got there, my dad was really disappointed. Half of the crowd was a bunch of fat geezers with gray hair and the other half were ten year old boys who only knew the band by the video game music. This was certainly not my vision of a rock-out and I am pretty sure it was not what my dad remembered it being. We actually left early. There was one part of the concert, however, that I really liked. Joe Perry, the lead guitarist, had a guitar duel with a digital version of himself that was shown on a big-screen TV. The digital Joe was recorded, but the real Joe was live. Real Joe kicks ass. By the end of the duel, Real Joe played so hard that Digital Joe exploded. The crowd went wild. After taking a bow, Real Joe stepped up to the mike and said," video games ain't playing shit. You want to rock, learn how to play for real." I couldn't believe he was dissing his own sponsor like that, but he was right. Video guitar is the idiot's version of a jam. You may think you are feeling what Joe Perry is feeling but video guitar is to music what a dog humping your leg is to sex. There is only one real way to rock whether it be music, sports, art, cooking or *Aikido*, and it takes practice.

Of course, as Rinchen started my first class, I was more confused than anything else. You have to start somewhere. It took months before the real Aiki-addiction took a hold of me. After he did the traditional double clap, Rinchen turned to face his students and bowed deeply putting his face almost on the floor. As his students returned his bow nearly chanting *"onegeishemas."* *"Onegeishemas"* is an expression of thanks for what you are hoping to be given. You are basically thanking your comrades for what they are about to do for you before they do anything. It is exceedingly polite. Even on my first day, I was learning that an enormous amount of *Aikido* practice was etiquette training.

Several weeks later, I asked Rinchen why we had to be so formal in the *dojo* and if all of the anal retentive rules were really necessary. He pointed out that in ancient Japan, just like Medieval Europe, culture was held together by force and necessity. It was a very dangerous place. He said that resources were scarce and the competition for them was ferocious. In order to create some sense of organization in a world where the wrong facial expression could get you killed, the Japanese refined their manners to a well-practiced ritual that kept order. They took the refinement of etiquette to such a high level of awareness and effort that they broke through the barriers of consciousness itself. Etiquette, like many other arts in ancient Japan, became a way to gain enlightenment.

I had never thought about it that way before, but Rinchen said that the more dangerous a culture is, the more important manners are. He noted that gang bangers actually have more rules and customs regarding behavior than the average suburbanite. Why? Because on the street if you do not control the aggression and anger of those around you with some system of behavior, you can start a war. Even just nodding to a guy while you are walking past him on the sidewalk can send a little message of peace: "it's cool man, I got no problem with you."

In the middle class world, etiquette is disappearing because threat is disappearing. Looking at someone the wrong way in the hall at Westchester High School might make you the subject of an evil text message, but it is not going to result in you getting jumped. This is hardly a duel over honor. In fact, because we live in such relative affluence, honor, like etiquette, is disappearing too. This is why people road rage and abuse cashiers or customer service representatives in India. Where is the down side to it? It is not like Haji is going to go Ninja on you and slip into your house and kill you and your family while you sleep because you were being a dick on the phone. We live in a world where the consequences of our actions have been dumbed-down because the importance of our actions have been dumbed-down.

Rinchen said that in the days when resources were scarce, alliances had to be made and kept. These friendships were a matter of life and death. As a consequence, the culture set about to train people to keep their word no matter what. Promises were extremely important. Keeping your word, even if it meant defending a friend and dying for her, was an ideal that everyone admired because everyone needed to depend on honor. Of course, from what little I have read about the samurai, they were a bunch of lying bastards at times and treachery was their favorite pastime. Rinchen says that while there were exceptions, most members of the classes that could afford to spend time cultivating manners had exceptional self-control. The samurai are known for this.

Before Rinchen started the first exercise, he bowed to me specifically and said that he was delighted that I had come to join the *dojo*. He then said to the group, "as you know, we have a long standing rule here that you must report all fights to your *sensei*. Your teacher needs to know about altercations to make sure that his students are not using their skill to harm people and that there are no erroneous attitudes being developed here on this mat. Furthermore, we learn from every fight. They are opportunities to study our tactics and techniques. Most of all, I simply want to know that you are safe. Does anyone have anything to report?"

Certainly, he could not have been directing his statement to me. I sat there motionless waiting to hear if anyone else had beat the crap out of a would-be rapist. After a silence, Rinchen turned toward me and said, "I know that this may be uncomfortable for you and you may discuss this with me privately, if you would prefer, but do you have anything to add to this conversation?" Suddenly, everyone in the line strained to stare at me from the corner of their eyes, but did not dare move their faces to look directly at me. Everyone, that is, except Tripp and Megan.

"Yes, *Sensei*," I said clearing my throat. "A couple of months ago I was attacked by a guy from my school. He got ahold of my arm and neck and pinned me face-down on the hood of a car and then tried to remove my pants." I was surprised how matter-of-fact the story sounded to me now, in this place. "Using a technique that you taught me, I believe you called it 'the floppy fish technique', I was able to get him off of me. I then kicked him in the groin and several times in the face until he was unable to hurt me anymore." Protocol or not, by this point everyone in the line had turned their heads and were staring at me in utter disbelief, except, of course, Tripp and Megan.

"What were the extent of the injuries, if any?" I wasn't sure what he meant; Nick's or mine? I had to think about this for a minute and while I did, I could see the blood once again pouring across Nick's face. I could hear his groaning as he rocked back and forth on the ground holding his nuts. "I am not sure how bad the attacker's injuries were. He could not stand up when last I saw him. His face was covered in blood and he was only partially conscious. As for me, I broke my foot." You could hear the communal exhale of the students as their eyes opened wide to take in the scene that was being described to them. I could tell that I had gone from rookie to warrior in a single class.

"Is that all of the damage that happened?"

"No," I said looking down at the mat.

"What else?"

"The attacker, his name was Nick, killed himself later that night." There was a gasp that spread down line.

"And what is your condition now?" Before posing this question, Rinchen had seemed to be merely asking questions to which he already knew the answers. This one was different. This time he was really asking because he did not seem to know what I would say.

"I am fine."

"You realize that there is no state of mind called 'fine', right?" Now he was staring at me with his eyebrows raised and he looked kind of fierce.

"I am okay. I feel good. What else is there to say?"

"A fight like that leaves very deep scars and yet it is true that life goes on. But we must not put these things out of our mind for too long. It can cause us to harden our hearts and become indifferent to suffering – our own and the suffering of others." I could see his point. Ever since the attack, I had tried not to think about Nick or his parents. I pushed it out of my mind. But hearing Rinchen's warning suddenly made me realize that I had been pushing a lot of things out of my mind. I had stopped hanging out with my friends except for Megan and Beth. I never went to parties and only went to the mall with mom. I had started to get very annoyed by certain people, especially the girls at school who picked on everybody behind their backs or the guys who tried to bully younger students. Until Rinchen had mentioned it, I had not realized that I was becoming rather hard especially toward anyone who was trying to force something on someone else.

Turning to the rest of his students, Rinchen continued: "this young woman saved herself from extreme danger with a single technique that she learned in about five minutes. This is hardly ordinary. People with years and years of training confronted with similar circumstances are stricken with fear and, being unable to act, come to severe harm. Do not think that because she produced this extraordinary result that you can do the same. This is one of the many reasons why we train – to have our minds and bodies prepared to deal with whatever comes our way." With that he turned back toward me and bowed and said, "I am very sorry that this happened to you. I know that this has been quite disturbing for you and that you will not likely forget it for the rest of your days. By the same token, however, we are all delighted that you are here in one piece and have decided to join us." He smiled, and I thought for a moment that I could see the slightest trace of tears in his eyes. I returned his bow.

Rinchen popped to his feet like I had seen him do the very first night that I met him. He called Tripp to the *kamiza*. He held out his arm and Tripp grabbed it. Within a split second Tripp was upside down and then landed on the floor with a BANG. They repeated the technique. BANG! Each time, Tripp popped back up to his feet as if he hadn't just fallen six feet and landed flat on his back. On the third demonstration, I noticed why the landing was so loud. Tripp was slapping the mat just before he landed on his back. Later, I was told that this was called a "break-fall". Slapping the ground just before hitting it softens the landing. In a violent exchange this can really save your ass. I noticed as class progressed that the woosh of the throw and the BANG of the landing becomes a kind of rhythm in the *dojo*. It grows on you after a while and eventually becomes the heartbeat of the place; always there, but only noticeable if you listen for it.

I couldn't even roll yet. I could not believe that I would ever be able to do what Tripp and Megan could do. Rinchen ended his demonstration and the students divided up into pairs to practice what we had just been shown. Megan gently nudged a white belt out of the way to ensure that I would do the exercise with her. She took it easy on me. I did not have to do the break-fall, even though she did when it was my turn to try to throw her. My attempts to roll out the throws that Megan was gently inflicting on me were feeble. It was awkward, but with each exchange, I came to see a little bit of beauty in it. *Aikido* could be graceful and yet it was war.

Chapter Fifteen: Palden Lhamo

Eventually class came to an end. Rinchen, in honor of having a new student, combined the beginner and advanced classes into one really long, incredibly painful ordeal – for my benefit. Just before class ended, the students formed their line and sat on their shins in meditation for several minutes as their breathing returned to the regular, controlled rhythm that was synchronized to the point of being slightly creepy. Rinchen had his back to us and was facing the kamidana with his arms fully extended in front of him. CLAP! CLAP! The action and its echo. He bowed to the kamidana and the picture of the founder of *Aikido* who is fondly referred to as "*O Sensei*". This, I was told, translates to "great teacher". He spun on his knee, just as Tripp had done to face and then bow to his students. As if in one voice, Rinchen and the students bowed and in an emphatic tone of voice nearly shouted "*domo arigato gozaimasu*!" – a very formal way of saying, "thank you". The students sat at attention while their teacher rose and walked to the shimoseki side of the line and passed behind them. Only after he had stepped off the mat entirely did anyone move. Then, each in turn, while remaining in seiza, the students bowed to one another and thanked each and every person on the mat. Many of the students raced over to thank me first as a gesture of welcome and made it clear to me that I was now part of them.

As I walked off the mat, I noticed that no one turned their back on the *kamidana* as they departed. Instead, they stepped backward until they reached the edge of the mat and then bowed before stepping off the mat altogether to head toward the dressing rooms. I followed their custom. It would eventually become my habit.

I was a sweaty mess when I got to the dressing room. My hair, that I had pulled back into a ponytail before class, was wet and my *gi* was soaked. Megan, on the other hand, was merely perspiring and the moisture on her skin looked more like dew than the torrents of saltwater that were racing down my neck. She was flushed and yet quite relaxed. Quickly she removed her *hakama* and her *gi* and pulled on her jeans and a tie-died V-neck T-shirt. We had left our shoes by the door. She told me to get changed and bring my *gi* to the mat and she would show me how to fold it. This, she said, was a must-do after-class ritual. We stepped out of the dressing room and I watched her bow to the *kamidana* before stepping back onto the mat. "Wow! They even bow before folding laundry," I thought to myself. Not being one to break the sacred rules, I bowed as well.

Folding a *gi* is a relatively straight-forward matter. The top is placed on the floor and the sleeves are folded in back pretty much like you would fold any shirt (that is, unless you have a mom like mine that does it for you). The pants are placed on the *gi* top and the whole thing is folded into one tidy bundle with the *obi* tied around it just like when you tie it around your waist. It is actually pretty handy in that it turns the whole thing into a package with a handle and can be tossed in the trunk of your car and forgotten. When you undo the bundle, the *gi* is unwrinkled and ready to go, although, if you leave it in the trunk of your car for too long it gets a bit ripe.

The *hakama* is an entirely different matter altogether. This gets meticulously folded to preserve the pleats and is folded into a bundle about the size of the *gi* with the straps woven into an intricate knot on top. It will stay intact despite considerable jostling in a *do-gi* bag (the *dojo* version of a gym bag) or, of course, in the trunk of your car. When you unfold it, every crease is straight and there is not a wrinkle to be found. Megan says that the ancient Japanese did not bother to iron their clothes, they simply folded them. When she said this I suddenly thought of the piles and piles of clothes on the floor of my bedroom at home. The entire heap of it was wrinkled like crepe paper. I often pulled various items from the pile and hauled them off to the laundry room to iron them. That's actually a lie. Most of the time, I just threw on whatever and went to school looking like I had slept in my clothes. But when I needed to look presentable, ironing was always involved. It never occurred to me that it was actually much less work to fold my clothes and put them away in the first place. Hmmm. I think my mom was Japanese in a former life.

After class, several of the students were milling around the foyer of the *dojo* as if they were waiting for something. Rinchen had changed out of his *gi* and *hakama* and was in his street clothes. The students all thanked him as he made his way to the foyer bowing as he passed. As I stepped into the foyer area he turned and asked, "Well, how was it?"

"Pretty cool, but I can see I have a lot of work to do."

"Give yourself time. There is no hurry. *Aikido* is best learned over a lifetime." He grinned and bowed.

"Thank you, *Sensei*," I said, returning an even deeper bow.

Suddenly, the tone of the conversation turned serious. Rinchen looked at me as if he was trying to make up his mind about something. Finally he said, "You have a wrathful nature like Palden Lhamo. We must be sure that it remains focused on wrathful compassion. Yes, yes, Lhamo, indeed." He smiled as if he had come to a conclusion and stepped out the front door.

I had no idea what he was talking about. Even Tripp and Megan seemed a bit mystified by his parting remarks.

"We are heading down the street for some sushi, do you want to come?" Tripp asked. The cool distance that he had maintained on the mat was gone. I was on his radar, I could tell, and I liked it. My legs were mush, but I was not going to miss this opportunity. I turned to look at Megan.

"Don't worry, Little Bit, I am coming too. You don't lose the chaperone until the second date," she said smirking at her twin brother. She shot him a look that caused him to sober up as if to say "this is my friend – don't fuck this up." I was still hanging on the word date. Awesome!

We walked a few blocks down Washington Avenue to a slightly dumpy sushi joint. There were two in the vicinity, but I was abruptly informed that only Terried Sake House would do. As we walked in, I noticed that despite the hour, it was pretty busy. The place had plain plank floors and plank counters along the sushi cooler. There were only a few tables and only one that could seat the six of us that had made the trek to get an after-ass-beating nosh. This table was piled high with chopsticks in paper envelopes, and the small dishes that they put the wasabi in. I soon discovered that this was a ruse. An older Japanese lady appeared from around the sushi cooler and quickly cleared the supplies off the table and we all sat down. Apparently, she had been expecting us and this was her way of saving the table.

I was beat, but excited. The combination of fatigue and being with Tripp again was a rush of mixed feelings somewhere between *Yippee!* and *holy-shit-tired*. Three other students had tagged along. An older guy named Bob was oddly out of place, generationally speaking, but everyone seemed to be quite familiar with him. Tracy, was several years older than me. She was what they called a "dirty white belt", meaning that she had been around the *dojo* for a while. She was taller than me and had reddish hair. If you looked at her closely, she was actually quite beautiful in a spunky but I-can-kill-you sort of way. I had noticed her out on the mat and had even trained with her during a couple of the exercises. She seemed to know her stuff. She was with a guy about her age who was or was not her boyfriend. His name was Sam but everyone, for whatever reason, called him "Thor." Well, actually the origins of his nickname were obvious. Thor was absolutely ripped. Megan eventually mentioned that he was a body builder. Oh, yes he was! He had long curly blond hair that hung down to his shoulders. He was the spitting image of a Greek god and more modest than his name suggested. In fact, he was a bit on the shy side.

The sushi lady brought six glasses of cold water and two pitchers for backup. Everyone began slugging water except for Tripp and Megan. When I asked why she wasn't thirsty, Megan said that she was, but that drinking water that is too cold too soon after practice was bad for the internal organs. Tripp had actually fished the ice cubes out of his glass and was sipping his water with considerable reserve. It was funny to me that even in something as simple as drinking water, these twins were disciplined. They had to be thirsty because I was parched and had annihilated my organs with three glasses of the icy cold water before I even knew it was bad for me. But they, the two coolest people I knew, did not even seem to be tempted by this most innocent form of refreshment.

We ordered some food. Bob, the old guy who everybody referred to as Old Bob, told me that he had trained in *Aikido* two decades ago when he was younger and was coming back to it after being away from it for a long time. He was divorced and had been looking for something to do in his spare time. He had been in the army and had served in the Gulf War. He did not say much about his war experience other than he had seen a lot of dead guys and that it was very hot in Iraq. He said that he was sorry to hear about my altercation with Nick. When he said this, he looked at me with the same sadness in his eyes that my dad had the night that Beth had brought me home after the attack. He did not seem to be particularly desperate or weird. He was simply along for the ride to grab some food after his workout. Megan said that occasionally her dad would come out with them after class and that Bob and Rinchen were very good friends. I realized that I had never had a group of friends that included anyone that was not my own age. Megan said that I should get used to it because the *dojo* crowd was not particularly choosy about its members so long as they could take a beating and maintain their honor. Now there was a word that you do not hear much at Westchester High – honor. I remember thinking in that moment that I was not entirely sure that I knew what it meant. It is not normally a girl word. Of course, these days, it has practically dropped out of everyone's vocabulary.

I was starving and it showed. Both Tripp and Megan watched me wolf down an entire tuna roll before I looked up to see that they were both watching me with considerable amusement. "What? Your parents don't feed you?" asked Megan. Tripp started to chuckle. "Damn, Little Bit, I think you've gnawed the ends off of your chop sticks." he said taking my hand and pretending to inspect the utensils for damage. I was immediately embarrassed. Megan, sensing that she had just called me out in front of the man I might eventually be in love with, backtracked. "Toughen up, Buttercup! If you really are the incarnation of Palden Lhamo, then you will have to learn to take a joke."

There was that name again. Palden Lhamo. I made a mental note to go home and Google it and then realized that I had no idea how to spell it.

"What does that mean, Palden Lhamo?" I asked looking around the table for some sign that someone knew the answer to my question. I was surprised by the reaction of the group. They all seemed to be very well aware of what this name meant, but did not seem to have the slightest interest in telling me. Tripp looked at Megan and they had a moment of twin-telepathy that, in time, I would come to find very disturbing. Then Tripp spoke.

"Did Megan tell you that our dad is a Tibetan Buddhist? Actually, Megan and I are too."

"Yes, she said that he considers himself a bit of a spiritual mutt because he mish-mashes *Aikido* and Buddhism and other things together." Tripp snickered and then nodded his head in agreement.

"In Tibetan Buddhism and, in fact, in most of Buddhism, there are deities; we call them '*yidams*' and they can be both loving and wrathful. They are all compassionate, but one type is the kind that brings you milk and cookies when you are dying of starvation and the other type kicks your ass down the street to force you to give up your egotistical bullshit. Both are trying to help you, but the methods are rather … diverse." Tripp searched my eyes to see how this lesson in Eastern mysticism was landing. "These deities are not believed to be gods like in the Christian and Jewish worlds, but rather they are objects of mental training, that is why they are called '*yidams*'. This is a Tibetan word that literally means 'tight mind'. In other words, we use *yidams* as objects of mental focus. They are both real and not real, for lack of a better way to explain it. Mostly, they are used as strong training methods. *Yidams* have various qualities that are meditated upon and hopefully become part of the meditator's psyche. Palden Lhamo is a *yidam* and she is very, very wrathful."

"What do you mean by very, very wrathful?"

"Well, let me put it this way, the Tibetans believe that they are protected by another *yidam* called "*Mahakala*". This guy is no one to be trifled with. Palden Lhamo is his female consort or better half, if you will. They sometimes call Palden Lhamo 'the Victorious One who turns back enemies'. They say she killed her own son because he was plotting to destroy Buddhism. She used his skin as a saddle for her mule. She is ferocious and protective and 100% serious about protecting Buddhists and Buddhism. She is what angels look like when they are really, really pissed off."

"So what you are telling me is that your dad thinks that I am some kind of over-protective demon? Wow, remind me to thank him, will you?" I was suddenly very annoyed. Yes, I kicked the crap out of a wanna-be rapist, but I was no demon.

Tripp, smiled and shook his head. "I know it's confusing. My dad did not call you a "demon" -- far from it. You have to understand that we hold *yidams* to be manifestations of the many aspects of the Buddha. You could even say that Palden Lhamo is a female Buddha. She seeks the same thing that all Buddhists seek – enlightenment for all and the end to suffering for the entire world. It's just that her methods are a bit severe, that's all. You don't mess with Palden Lhamo."

Okay, well that sounded better. I still had no idea what he was talking about, but at least I wasn't a demon in his father's mind. Maybe I still had a chance with this guy.

Megan could see that this was not going very well. "Ordinarily, we are not supposed to talk about this stuff with non-Buddhists, especially the part about wrathful *yidams*. It leaves people with the entirely wrong impression about Tibetan Buddhism, Palden Lhamo and the whole enlightenment thing. On the other hand, my dad kind of dropped this thing on you tonight out of the blue and I think we both feel like you are owed some kind of explanation. His comment indicates that he thinks of you in the highest terms, but that he is also concerned for you at the same time."

"What is he so concerned about?"

"There is a very fine line between wrathful compassion and being an asshole. Even the most advanced Buddhist practitioners struggle with it. Wrathful compassion is considered very advanced practice and is not taught to everybody. Not everybody can handle it. On the wrong side of wrath is hate and hate is the ultimate mind killer. Step over that line and you are no longer a force for the benefit of all sentient beings, but rather you are the destroyer of sentient beings – some purely evil shit."

I swallowed hard. My mind flew back to the circle drive in front of Nick's house. I could feel the little pills of skin rolled up under my fingernails while I clawed his face. I suddenly could feel once again my extreme hate, my uncontrollable desire to tear him to shreds, to be beat him to a pulp. It was furious. It was unstoppable. It was unrestrained evil. I was not trying to protect myself the entire time. I was trying to destroy him. Sitting there at the table, the whole scene played out in front of me. There had not been an ounce of compassion for that desperately confused boy – not even when he had been defeated and was lying helplessly on the ground. I wanted him in hell and I was willing to take him there myself.

I burst into tears.

"Oh shit," Megan said rushing to put her arm around me and staring at Tripp as if my upset was all his fault. Tripp was devastated. He reached across the table to put his arm around my neck. "I am so sorry, Little Bit, I am so, so sorry. I should have kept my damn mouth shut. Please, Little Bit, forgive me. You do not need to worry about all this Buddhist stuff. It's just mythology anyway." I could feel the intense concern of the twins surround me like being loved in stereo. I was so happy to be with them, but suddenly so ashamed of what I had become that night, if only temporarily, when I stood over Nick kicking him in the face. Megan held me tight and kissed me on the top of my head but I couldn't stop crying.

While I am sure that everyone in the Terried Sake House was gawking at me, no one at the table made any attempt to apologize to anyone or even try to get me to be quiet. Even Old Bob took my hand and held it gently as if by doing so he might give me some of his strength. If this had been the lunch room at school, my friends, with the possible exception of Ack, would have been scattering to get away from such an embarrassing public scene or would have been smothering me with shushes trying to get me to calm down. Apparently, it is well within the warrior code to cry in public. This warrior thing was going to take a lot to figure out.

My new found *dojo* brothers and sisters did not budge. They sat there holding me and saying very little as if they were committed to simply being my witnesses as I descended into the bowels of hell through my memory of Nick. Eventually, I was all cried out. Tripp held out a napkin so that I could dry my eyes. Some first date! But it did not seem to be time wasted for him. I could see that he was sorry to his bones that he had upset me. I think that this was the moment when I started to fall in love with him. Rinchen says that we find our true friends in those moments in our lives when our backs are to the wall and we are out of options. You know these friends because they come to us in times of need, even if we have tried to conceal our plight, and they willingly step into the ugliness of our lives because who they are cannot not stand for you standing alone.

Chapter Sixteen: The Very Fine Line Between Heaven and Hell

One of the great things about *dojo* life is all of the stories that your teachers tell you, or at least, my teacher tells me. Rinchen had gotten the news about the *sake* house meltdown and seemed to be almost penitent when I saw him a couple of days later. My muscles were still sore, but there had been no reason to put off more pain. Megan had told me that if you train diligently, the pain goes away quicker. I was all for that. And besides, I wanted to see if I could make it through another evening with Tripp without falling to pieces.

When I got to the *dojo* for my second class ever, Rinchen was already there and dressed for training. I was early. Megan and Tripp had not gotten there yet. There were only a couple of students on the mat and they were busy sweeping which is yet another custom that is performed before every class. I went to the dressing room and put on my gi. I was pretty sure I had most of the inner straps right, but my *obi* knot did not look entirely correct. I bowed and stepped out on the mat and looked for another broom so that I could help with the sweeping. It is funny that I automatically clean the *dojo* these days with a sense of diligence and pride, but I still can't seem to do anything with my room at home.

Rinchen called me into the small office that was next to the men's dressing room. He asked me to sit down with his usual formality. He studied my face for a moment or two with a smile on his. Having someone look deep into your mind was becoming less creepy by the day. Finally, he spoke. "The kids tell me that you were quite upset by my comparison of you to Palden Lhamo," he said. I could hear the apology in the tone of his voice.

"Not at all," I replied smiling at him with appreciation for his concern. "I actually think I get it."

"How so?"

"The night of my fight with Nick, I started out with the best intentions. I wanted to help him. I felt sorry for him. I was a little worried that something might happen, but it was more important to me that I help him anyway."

Rinchen's smile widened while making an effort to listen even more closely than he usually did.

"But when he grabbed me," I continued, "and once it dawned on me what was really happening, all that 'milk of human kindness' stuff went right out the window. I wanted to kill him. No, I wanted to completely wipe him off the face of the earth."

Rinchen didn't say a word. He was there to listen, a skill that he is particularly good at.

"I really hurt that guy. I mean, I messed him up. I have never done that to anyone before. I have never even been in a girl fight. If I hadn't broken my foot, I may very well have killed him. I suppose it would not have mattered. He died anyway."

"It would have mattered," said Rinchen softly.

"Who was that chick? I mean, I have never been mad like that before. I couldn't stop."

"We all have that in us. Usually it leaks out in small doses with the occasional road rage because we are rarely in dire situations where we let it rip."

"But did I have to let it rip?"

"At the time, yes, you did," Rinchen said as his smile disappeared. His eyes continued to dig deep into me. "What else did you have?"

"Well, there was that spiffy floppy fish technique you taught me," I snickered.

"That's not really a technique. We only show that to visitors to demonstrate the concept of harmonizing energy. It is really a party trick."

"Well, it is a party trick that saved me."

"Your ability to overcome your fear and step into the moment saved you. When disaster reared its ugly head, you opened your eyes and did what you had to do. You can second guess this for the rest of your life, but it is already in the past. "

"But it still haunts me."

"That's a good thing."

"Good thing? How on earth is that a good thing?"

"Well first of all, you now know what you are made of. This gives you a lot to work with because this kind of insight and power can be refined if you know that it exists. Second, you have personally been to hell. You know what it looks like and you know that you do not want anyone to have to live there. You would be amazed at how many people have no clue about this kind of thing. And third, you survived. Not only did you survive, but you prevailed and this apparently has been a pivotal moment in your life. It is one of several critical moments that caused you to step onto the path, although we will probably still have to see about that."

I had to give all of this some thought. For the most part, I understood what he was saying, but what did he mean about having been to hell and knowing that I do not want anyone to live there? "What do you mean when you say that I now know that I don't want anyone to live in hell – who does?"

Rinchen chuckled and then asked, "Where do you think the hell of this situation existed?"

"Well, at the time, it existed on Nick Thompson's driveway."

Rinchen shook his head and said, "No, in fact hell was not on that driveway. The driveway was just a driveway. And by the way, Nick may not have followed you into hell. You may very well have gone there by yourself. Megan says that he actually apologized to you before he killed himself, is that true?" I nodded slowly. The mere thought of Nick slashing his arm made me intensely sad.

"Let me tell you a story that might clarify this for you." Rinchen straightened up in his chair and then leaned forward placing his elbows on his knees and began telling his tale.

In the days of the samurai, there was a very well respected Buddhist monk who was the abbot of a local monastery. One day he was visited by a famous samurai swordsman. The abbot was practicing his calligraphy when the samurai was brought into the room and did not look at or even acknowledge his guest. After a moment the samurai grew impatient and spoke to the abbot despite the fact that the latter was focused intensely on his calligraphy.

"Reverend Abbot," said the samurai, "I have come to ask you to teach me a most important thing. I have been in many battles and have killed many men, but I have been told that hell is much worse than battle.

I was wondering if you could teach me about the true nature of hell and while you are at it, perhaps you could teach me about the true nature of heaven as well."

The abbot did not look up nor interrupt his calligraphy, but did address the samurai: "dear sir, I believe you have come to the wrong place, for I am not nearly a good enough teacher to bestow such an enlightened lesson on a complete jackass like you. You are far too stupid and crude to even begin to comprehend such a teaching and quite frankly it would be an utter waste of my time."

This enraged the samurai. In those days, no one, not even an abbot , dared to say such insulting things to a member of the samurai class. By law, he was well within his rights to strike the abbot dead and he rose to his feet to do just that. The samurai drew his sword and held it over his head and screamed at the top his lungs, "you are a dead man, you insulting dog!"

But before the samurai could strike, the abbot calmly looked up at him and smiled and said, "That my friend would be the true nature of hell." The samurai was dumbfounded and more than just a little embarrassed. He had nearly struck a reverend abbot dead even though his only crime was to bestow a marvelous teaching on him. The samurai sheathed his sword and fell to his knees on the floor daring not to raise his eyes to this most revered teacher. "My dear abbot! Oh, my dear abbot! I am so ashamed! I nearly killed you for no reason at all other than my own foolish anger. Please, please, please, forgive me!"

The abbot smiled again and put down his brush. "That, my friend, would be the true nature of heaven," he said, "Would you like some tea?"

Rinchen is a great story teller. As he told the tale of the abbot and the samurai he acted out the parts and added dramatic tones to his voice for emphasis. "Do you understand now?" he asked smiling.

"Yes," I said. "When I went to hell that night, I went alone."

"Probably."

"I started in heaven and wound up in hell."

"Yes, you did."

"But what else could I have done? How do you avoid hell in a situation like that?"

"You don't, necessarily. Sometimes what there is to do is go to hell."

"Wow, I am not exactly feeling the joy here , *Sensei.*"

"Who said that there has to be joy? Sometimes what there is to do is to get sick and die. Sometimes it is to kill yourself. It is the state of mind in which you embrace the inevitable facts of life that makes the difference. Even a man falling to his death off a steep cliff can be happy, provided that he has the clarity and strength of mind to make it so. That night went the only way that it could go given who you were at the time, who he was at the time and the entire web of events that unfolded as they did. In life, the thing that happens is the only thing that *can* happen given all the circumstances. There is no alternative past. There is no alternative present, although we have some small measure of influence on the future through our choices. But even in that there is no guarantee. Since we cannot change our circumstances, we have to change our minds."

I sat there silently mulling over what he was saying to me. It sounded entirely logical, but yet I was still a bit mystified by it all. This was going to take some time to think through.

"There is one more thing to think about," Rinchen said interrupting my train of thought. "If this attack were to happen tomorrow, it would not turn out the same way. The circumstances have changed. You have changed. You now know about hell. And that knowledge is very useful, Lhamo."

The addition of that name, that frightful name, to the end of his remark startled me. When I looked up at him he was smiling kindly. He patted me on the knee and said, "We had better get out there." And with that, he stood up and stepped out of the office and onto the mat, bowing before he crossed the frame.

Chapter Seventeen: Mu

After the first two or three weeks of pain, recovery and more pain, I was starting to actually enjoy *Aikido* class. I was still losing my breath during ukemi practice, but the rolls were getting easier. Basic *Aikido* is divided into five essential categories of techniques. The first one is called *"ikkyo"*, or first technique and is a category of moves that are designed to take away an attacker's balance. The next group called *'nikkyo"*, or second technique, and is based on the principles of joint locking. I have heard that the Chinese have cooler names for their techniques like "flying *mu-shoo* dragon fly technique" and that sort of thing, but the Japanese are apparently not that dramatic. Rinchen teaches these techniques in numerical order *ikkyo*, *nikkyo*, *sankkyo*, *yankyo* and *gokyo*. When he gets to the end of the list, he starts it over again. Every time you return to a technique, you see it in more and more detail. Over time, these sets of movements, that at first look like you are just throwing people on the ground, become an intricate dance of footwork and motion. Sometimes, it is more like ballet than fighting.

Aikido literally means "the way of harmonizing energy" – sort of. The name is actually three words. *Ai* – means harmony. *Ki* is the word for essential energy, like the energy that lets you walk or causes you to grow from a child to an adult. *Ki* is also the energy that causes you to heal when you are sick or hurt. *Do* (pronounced "doe") is a hard word to translate into English because we do not have an equivalent word. Literally translated it means "the way". The Chinese say, *"Tao"*. This is one of those little bitty words with gigantic meaning. When the Japanese or Chinese use the term "the way", they are not talking about the route to the post office. They are talking about a way or path to ultimate awareness. This is not a path in the general direction of ultimate awareness, but rather an actual tested process that causes a person to realize the fully enlightened state of mind. In fact, the name for a Japanese art such as *Aikido* will not contain the word do in it unless at least one of the practitioners of the art has obtained full mental awakening through its practice. It is said that *O Sensei*, Morehei Ueshiba, reached enlightenment through the practice of *Aikido* making it a do art.

There are lots of do arts in Japan. I have been told that *O Sensei* used to say that "there are many paths to the top of Mount Fuji, but only one summit." There are martial arts like *Karate* which is formally called *Karate-do*, and there's *Judo* and *Kendo*, but there is also *Chado* (the way of tea and hospitality) and Shodo (the way of calligraphy). Even the study of floral arrangement can lead to enlightenment. All of these arts are considered to contain virtually the same mental processes which are based on paying attention in the extreme.

The way of the sword, or *Kendo* as it is called in Japanese, predates most of the other martial arts, but they all evolved around the sword as a weapon and a threat. *Karate-do* was developed in Okinawa so that farmers could fight swordsmen with their bare hands or by using simple farm implements. *Judo*, was developed to take away a swordsman's sword in close combat. *Kyudo*, the art of archery, was practiced as much by monks in monasteries as it was by samurai. The monks used it to train themselves to develop awareness of everything while thinking of nothing. This is where the whole martial art thing gets very tricky. There are two states of mind that we are taught to develop. At first it seems like you are trying to do two opposite things at once. The first state of mind is called *zanshin*. Directly translated this means "lingering mind". There is some debate about exactly what this is, at least in the West, but basically it is a type of awareness that is created by letting your mind take in or linger with everything around you. This is hard to do because when you try to pay attention to things for an extended period of time, your mind starts to wander instead of lingering. *zanshin* can be interrupted when your favorite song pops into your head or you hear something that causes your mind to jump like a little dog as it chases the sound and forgets about everything else. I used to think that my teachers and my parents were just harping on me about not paying attention, but after a month in the *dojo*, it was very clear to me that on my best day, I was tuned in for only about ten minutes out of a day.

Rinchen calls *zanshin* training, "taming the wild horse." We spend about ten minute out of every class practicing it. First, you get your breath organized.

This was another news flash for me. I always thought breathing was just breathing, but I have since learned that this is not so. Most people breathe through their mouths and basically pant like dogs. This uses only the top part of your lung. Your body, however, was designed to breathe through your nose. In fact, your nose, and especially your boogers are designed to act like a filter for the air going into your lungs. Who knew that a booger had such a useful purpose? By breathing through your nose, you remove dust from the air you breathe so that it is clean. Breathing through your nose also warms the air to your body temperature before it hits your lungs. I am not exactly sure what this is supposed to do for you, but it is a good thing. It is also important to take in an entire lung full of air instead of breathing rapidly using only the top of your lungs. A whole breath forces air deep into the tissue of your lungs, pushing oxygen into your blood more efficiently. Also when your lungs are full, the core of your body has no squishy, empty space in it and can be compressed making all of your muscles momentarily much stronger than normal. In fact, we learn to compress and exhale our breath as we do techniques and rolls to give us little bursts of power when they are needed most.

Once your breathing is under control, you relax your mind, but do not let it sink into sleep. This is not terribly hard for me because I am kind of hyper anyway. My problem is distraction. In the beginning, my mind would chase after any sound or fragment of thought. To try to focus our minds, we concentrate on our breathing. We listen to it and feel it going in and going out. This is much harder to do than you think, especially if you have been listening to your car stereo blasting on your way to the *dojo*. If a song gets stuck in your mind, it will drive you nuts trying to get it out. The idea is, ultimately, to let your mind sort of hang out with the things that are actually around you. You eventually hear the individual cars on the street or the rustle of clothing as someone moves. There is a whole intense world happening when you turn down the volume knob on your brain.

Rinchen says that over months and months of meditation, your brain will actually change shape. He says this is because of something called neuroplasticity which is basically a fancy word to say that your brain always changes based on what part of it you use the most. Rinchen says that there are scientific studies involving CAT scans and MRIs that show that meditators have brains that are different from ordinary people. I have started to meditate even at home and it is kind of cool. It really calms me down even though I am starting to get highly annoyed when I am not meditating because of all the distraction around me. I never noticed before how much static there is in my world. There is the mindless chatter of the radio and TV, and people talking just to hear their own voices. Even music is starting to bug me.

The other type of mind training is called *"mushin"*. *Mushin* is so foreign to Western thinking that we do not even have words to describe its basic concept, let alone define it. The word *mu* has no English translation. The idea of *mu* is sort of like nothingness, but without being an oblivious void. I am not all that sure of what it really means. Rinchen explained it this way: *mu* doesn't mean "empty" as in "nothing there" as much as it means "empty of meaning". He says that our minds do not comprehend the essence of reality naturally, but instead we interpret everything around us through our intellect. We know that the sky is blue because we were told what blue is and have tagged that name onto the experience of things that we say are blue. He says there is no blue except in our interpretation of what we see. I don't really get it, but he seems to be pretty serious about this. To demonstrate his point he once held up a glass of water and said, "What is this?"

Someone said, "A glass of water."

"Why?"

"Because that's what it is," came the reply.

"Not if I use it as a paperweight. You gave this a name based on what you thought it does, not because of what it is."

"Ahh, I see," said the student. "Okay, so what word should we use?"

"Whatever word describes it's true nature," Rinchen replied.

"General thingy-ma-bob, then," said that student. Everybody chuckled.

"That's better than calling it a 'glass of water'. But are you sure it is a thing?"

"Of course it's a thing, I am looking it. It is not an illusion."

"Are you sure?" Rinchen asked baiting the student to take the next logical step. Everyone in the room was pretty sure that this question was a trap.

"Well, if it is not a thing, then what is it?"

"The better question is: is it at all?"

"What, you are trying to say it's not there?"

"No, I am trying to say that 'it' is not an 'is'." Everyone sat there silently trying to image how something could be right in front of your eyes, but not exist at the same time.

"Well, how are you going to prove that?" said the student with more than a little skepticism in his voice.

"We could try physics. I am told that physicists would say that this glass is made of atoms and that atoms are made up of subatomic particles. I have it on good authority that these particles in an atom are very far apart from each other relatively speaking. In other words, if you had an atom the size of this room, the part of the atom that was actually made up of particles would be the size of a fleck of dust. Atoms are mostly empty space." Rinchen surveyed the room to see if everyone was still following his conversation. He had lost only one or two by this point. He continued: "and exactly what are these particles made of? Many Buddhists call matter "frozen light" and this is turning out to be true as science catches up to what we have known for 2,500 years. Someday, science will get past the superstition of physicality altogether, but for now this is what we have to work with. The point is that these particles will eventually be found out to be energy and energy is not anything other the propensity for motion. But if a particle is a little wad of energy and energy is not anything but a propensity to move, then what is moving? The answer is: nothing! No-thing."

"If this is so," said the student, "then why does it hurt when you get punched in the nose?"

"Does it hurt?"

"The last time it happened to me, it hurt like crazy."

"What is pain?"

"The achy throbbing sensation running through my face after I have been punched in the nose," came the reply.

"No, that is a thought. When you get hit, an electric impulse moves from the nerves in your face to your brain. This impulse is then interpreted as pain if you were hit hard enough. If you are just picking your nose, there is no pain at all even though the same nerves are firing impulses to the brain. There may even be damage to the tissue, but it is the wiring system setting off the alarm that makes you think you have pain. In fact, some trauma is so severe that you do not feel it all. If the nerves get severed, there is no pain even though there is incredible damage. I have been told that if someone cuts off your head in one quick stroke it doesn't hurt at all, but there has been no one left alive from this experience to tell us for sure." Everyone chuckled, but then after further thought about it, decided that it was not that funny. "My point is that you live in a world of interpretation. You see objects that are made up of energy, but interpret them as solid matter. You know things by names, not by essences. Your mind is painting your reality on what is by nature a blank canvas. Behind all of this creative thinking is mu."

The response to this lesson was mixed. Some nodded as if they understood. Others, like me, mostly frowned and looked confused. Then Rinchen added one last comment: "the problem is that you have to get past the web of interpretive thought that you are constantly generating just to have some experience of mu. If you can't turn off the matrix, you cannot know that I am telling you the truth."

One thing was clear to me; if I was ever going to have any experience of mushin, I was going to have to turn off an endless sea of random crap that was forever floating through my mind. My mind was like a can of soda – a constant fizzing of pictures, sounds and feelings. It was at this point that I realized that my mind was a total mess.

Megan once told me that for advanced meditators, *zanshin* and *mushin* ultimately became one in the same state of mind. The mind would linger to take in what was happening, but would not make it mean anything. She said that this made you a complete bad ass. When you get to that place, you are snatching flies out of the air with chopsticks.

It is said that in ancient Japan, the head honcho called the "*Shogun*" hired a family by the name of Yagu to be the sword teachers for his household because they were simply the best sword teachers around. Over the years, the Yagus got even better and developed a method called "life-giving sword". This actually makes sense down the road, but for now I should say that a whole lot of people got killed by these life-giving swords.

Eventually, the Yagu family began to notice as they studied their art that swordsmen moved in patterns of energy. They figured out that it was possible for a swordsman to blend his energy with the energy of his attacker, even if the other guy was raging with hostility. This gave the harmonizer the ability to control *all* of the energy of the fight. They went even further. They learned that a guy holding a sword or a stick was actually at a disadvantage in a fight because his hands have to be in a specific place at a specific time. In other words, the guy with the sword has to hold onto it or have it taken from him and stuck in highly inconvenient places. A person who only wants a peaceful outcome has no such limitation. His hands don't have to hold onto anything in particular and are free to move wherever they are most useful. This gave the peaceful man freedom to blend with whatever the man with the destructive agenda throws at him. By blending with this furious and destructive force, the peaceful man can remain gentle, or not so gentle, and redirect the hateful force even turning it on itself causing self-destruction. This realization was the birth of *Aikido*.

Despite its peaceful reputation, *Aikido* is *Budo* (pronounced "boo-doe"). *Budo* literally means "the way of war", but this notion of war is completely foreign to Western thinking. In our culture, we think of war as a purely destructive thing. We say things like "war is hell". To the ancient Japanese, it was a proven way to reach the ultimate state of consciousness. I know these things because I have been looking up all this stuff on Wikipedia and, of course, Rinchen and my *sempai* are downloading things into my brain nearly every day. I haven't figured out the whole war-as-a-path-to-enlightenment thing, but I am working on it.

In our culture we think that pain is bad and we go to great lengths to avoid it. We think that destruction is bad and we go to great lengths to avoid it too. Most of all, we think death is bad and we go way out of our way to avoid it. In Westchester, you see the avoidance of pain and death everywhere. There are rich old ladies who have had the skin on their faces stretched way too tight by so many facelifts that they can barely move their collagen injected lips. On TV, we are told that getting old is a disease. Rinchen says that if everyone lived forever we would run out of room on the planet. He also says that if man could live forever he would still be a fish. There would be no reason to evolve. You could always do it later, and because evolution is hard work, you would blow it off entirely. In a deathless world you would see 200 year old teenagers laying on the couch drooling on themselves. Children would never grow up to inherit the earth because treacherous old people would be hogging all the cool houses and cars. There would be no incentive to grow up anyway. There is barely an incentive to do it now. I have some friends who hang out with their moms all the time and you can't tell who is the mom and who is the kid. You see middle aged people obsessed with their health and appearance. Rinchen says this is all about denial. Everyone, in one way or another, is running from death.

Rinchen says that the ancient Japanese saw aging as an opportunity to become wise. A long life gave you time to think about an inevitable death. This made things urgent. It caused people to make their peace with the world. Wisdom was the natural compensation that you earned as your body began to fail you. It was part of the harmony of the cycle of life. When you are young and stupid like me, you need a strong body that can work hard to learn and be resilient enough to withstand mistakes. As you get older, your mind starts doing all the work. If you are lucky, by the time that it is your moment to die, you understand that life and death are the same thing and with a single breath you merge the two into one. I have been told that this is a very good way to die.

In our world, we have a lot of superstition about death. We have no idea what it really is, but we are scared shitless of it. We live an entire lifetime in denial rather than spending our time engaging the world and savoring it. Rinchen says that, especially in the United States, we are the richest bunch of morons in the world. He says we have so much and understand so little. He says that we are busy trying to get the most and be the most and avoid pain and hardship that we never bother to face our existence. We would much prefer to be distracted. While this is great for the self-help seminar and publishing markets, it is a disaster for our people. Most of us live out our entire lives in a self-scripted drama that was largely stolen from movies and TV. In short, the average American is a mess.

I noticed that by the end of my junior year, I was losing my interest in things at school. I found myself spending more time by myself. The kids in the hall were becoming extremely annoying to me. They were interested in the stupidest things. I was starting to get angry about it. I had already been put on notice by Rinchen that I had to keep a close eye on the anger thing. Here it was once again.

Chapter Eighteen: Born To Be Wild

Tripp and I started hanging out, sometimes with Megan and Matt, but more and more we were slipping off to be by ourselves. It started out as a mostly friendly thing and for a while there I was getting concerned that we were going to get locked into the personal hell of a brother-sister thing. Both Megan and Tripp started coming over to my house on their motorcycles which freaked my parents out of their comfy socks. If they showed up on a Saturday morning, you could see the neighbors stop their yard work to scowl in disdain as they pulled into the driveway. Over time, however, my parents came to like them both very much. At first, my dad hated the motorcycle thing and had told me that I was not allowed to ride on the back of one. He had to know that I had already broken that rule about a million times.

On one particularly sunny afternoon, Tripp came out to our house on his own. He got to talking with my dad, who was cleaning the garage. I heard my dad say that he had driven motorcycles in college and had even thought about buying one of his own once-upon-a-time. Tripp spent the next ten minutes convincing my dad to take his bike for a spin. Eventually, he got him to do it. After a few minutes of reacquainting my dad with the controls of the cherry-red "rocket-of-death" as my mom called it, my dad took the helmet and put it on his head and mounted the bike. He fired it up and revved the engine a few times which brought him to the less-than-favorable attention of the neighbors. He rolled the bike down the driveway to the street and after a click of this and a poke at that, revved the engine again and popped the clutch. It stalled. Tripp said nothing and gestured to my dad to try again. This time, he took it easy and eased out the clutch lever and the bike lurched forward. A few seconds later my dad was riding down the street. You could hear the crotch-rocket making its way around the subdivision. Five minutes passed and he was still not back, but you could hear him. For a second, it sounded like the bike might have stalled again but then engine noise could be heard through the trees a couple of blocks away. After about fifteen minutes we both watched the cherry-red motorcycle round the corner onto my street. There was a sudden roar of the engine and my dad came flying past the house hitting the brakes just in time to make his way around the cul-de-sac leaning into the turn like a pro. One more quick rev and he was back in front of the house with the engine bubbling as he looked for the kickstand.

As my dad sat on the now silent bike and was removing Tripp's helmet, my mom came out of the front door of the house and marched up to my father who looked a little embarrassed -- like he had just been caught taking money from her purse. "Well, Easy Rider, at least you made it back alive," mom said in her boy-are-you-gonna-get-it tone of voice. Although despite her posturing, it seemed to me that she was having a difficult time deciding whether my father was a complete idiot or kind of hot sitting on a bitchin' motorcycle. My dad, sensing her indecision, manned-up. He tossed the helmet to Tripp and said, "Thanks man, that was awesome," trying to sound like he did this sort of thing all the time. He dismounted the bike. The neighbors returned to their yard work and my dad casually walked up the driveway to return to his chores in the garage. My mother followed him with her eyes drilling into the back of his head the entire way to the garage.

"What?", he said turning to her with just a little snap of fake anger.

"Oh, nothing," my mom said as she rolled her eyes and turned toward Tripp and me and told us to come inside to get some lunch.

We all sat down to eat at the kitchen table. My dad came in wiping his hands and joined us. He had a million questions about Tripp's bike. "How fast have you ever taken it?" "How did you learn to ride?" "Did you pay for it yourself?" Tripp handled this interrogation with considerable cool. My parents had already been very impressed with how polite Tripp and Megan were. And now it seemed that my dad was getting into the motorcycles and leather jacket thing. It is like Rinchen says, "good manners always clear the way before you."

Tripp explained that his father had never discouraged the kids from doing potentially dangerous things, but made careful distinctions between managed risk and stupidity. Tripp said, "If you or I were to try to do brain surgery, it would be a disaster – a completely stupid thing to do – and yet brain surgeons do it all the time." My father stopped eating for a second to think about this. Trip paused and then continued, "the point is, the more skill you have, the less risk there is." He went on to explain that his father was all about teaching his kids skills so that they could experience more of life and that recklessness at his house was a serious offense. He told my dad about the time that he had taken his motorcycle up to 145 miles per hour just to see what it would do, but had selected the road for this experiment very carefully. "My father has taught us that only the ignorant play with danger because they are usually into the adrenaline. Adrenaline is useful, but can be turned into just another drug to make you feel some way that you can't feel naturally. My dad says that this use of adrenaline is no better than shooting heroin and is not useful to a mind seeking clarity." Tripp paused again to take a bite of his sandwich. "And occasionally, I like to rip it," he said with the smallest bit of a grin on his face as he flashed his eyes at my dad and stuffed the last piece of his sandwich into his mouth. My mother frowned. I felt my cheeks flush a little.

Apparently, when Tripp, and eventually Megan, had asked their father's permission to buy motorcycles, he did not fight them, but told them that they had his blessing if they developed the skill to ride safely. He made them both take basic riding lessons and then a safety course. They were not allowed to buy their own motorcycles until they had gone through a high-performance racing course. This took ten consecutive weekends to complete and cost a fortune. Rinchen only paid for half. But eventually the twins were trained and were allowed to buy motorcycles. Tripp said that the last thing his father wants to do is prevent his kids from developing mastery in life. I could see my dad was nearly hypnotized by this idea. He had wandered off to some place in his mind and was watching this concept play itself out. When he came back to reality he turned to me unexpectedly and said, "We need to get you a helmet that fits and a leather jacket. Leather is very important on a bike because it can be the only thing that saves you from being skinned alive on the pavement if you fall."

"YOU CAN'T POSSIBLY BE SERIOUS, HENRY!," my mom blurted out spitting little bits of food at my dad. She was completely aghast.

"I am," my dad said looking straight into my mom's bulging eyes.

My mother sat there with her mouth open for what seemed to be minutes. You could see a tornado of anger building within her, suppressed only by the fact that we had company. My dad put his hand on hers and she jerked her hand away.

"Jeanie, listen to me. First of all, if you think that Maddie is going to stay off that bike you are kidding yourself. This young man has done his homework and is not one of those daredevil idiots we see riding wheelies down the freeway. This is just the first of many things that she is going to learn that involves some level of risk, in this case, a fair amount of risk because even the best bikers get hurt by morons. Having said that, Honey, I think Tripp's dad is right – skill is the best way to deal with risk. I do not want my daughter growing up inside a roll of bubble wrap. It is better to coach our kids to be skillful than it is to send them out into the world to do foolish things because no one took the time to show them how to do it right." He stopped trying to hold my mom's hand and returned to eating his lunch. In his mind, this was a done deal.

My mom's attitude softened and she looked at me as if she was holding back tears. "Maddie, this is just so dangerous. People get killed all the time on motorcycles." Then she turned to look at Tripp. "I am sure you are a good driver, but you know that that is not always enough."

Tripp smiled at her and nodded, "you are absolutely right Mrs. Albright, I have been nearly killed twice and neither time was my fault. And if you say that she should not ride with me, I will never let her do it."

"Wait a minute! Don't I have anything to say about this?" Both my mom and Tripp turned to look at me in unison and I could see in both sets of eyes that their initial answer to my question was "no". "Mom, dad's right on this one. I am not a little girl anymore and I have no intention of living my life recklessly, but I also have no intention living my life in the safety of my room either. I have ridden with Tripp many times and, quite frankly, I like it! Mom, I am going to do this with or without your permission."

"Not with me you're not," Tripp said butting into the conversation.

"Whose side are you on?" I snapped back at him.

"Mine."

"What on earth do you mean by that?"

"I am not going to take sides with you against your parents. We either work this out or we don't do it. This is *Aikido*. We either come together with each other for a peaceful outcome, or we walk away, but I will not play the push-me-pull-you game here."

My dad looked up at Tripp and was smiling and nodding his head. He was obviously very impressed. Even my mom was looking at him with admiration and I was clearly the odd-man-out of this conversation.

"It's peace or nothing, Little Bit. That's how we roll." He was dead serious.

A guy's good looks may be the gravity that pulls you into his orbit in the beginning, but it is his character, who he is day-to-day and what he stands for in the long run that determines whether or not you will be his moon. Most of my friends at school, with the exception of a few, like Ack and Julie Roth, did not really stand for anything. The only principles that seemed to guide their lives was amusement. I can't remember anyone ever taking a stand about anything. Life was entertaining, so why interrupt it by being so serious and uptight?

In that moment something ran through my mom's mind. I couldn't tell exactly what it was, but it was something like trust. She looked over at Tripp eyeing him shrewdly and then turned to my father and said, "Get her the helmet and jacket, Henry." She reached out and patted the back of my father's hand and then resumed eating her lunch. Tripp looked up at me with only the slightest trace of a smile on his face as if he was trying to keep a secret or had just cut a fart and got away with it. I sat there in a daze. What the hell just happened here?

It was *Aikido*.

Chapter Nineteen: My Name Is Lhamo

There was only a month of spring semester left and the weather in St. Louis was already heating up. I had gotten ready for school early because Megan was coming to pick me up on the two-wheeled school bus. My dad had taken Tripp and me to a motorcycle dealer near our house to buy a helmet and a jacket right after the Lunch of Holy Transformation.

There are actually quite a number of motorcycle dealers in Westchester. There are the dealers who sell crotch rockets to the children of parents who cannot say "no" to expensive toys . But there are also the dealers who sell to their dads. The garages of Westchester are full of expensive Harley Davidsons with 1500 miles on them. It is a hoot to see the middle age lawyers and accountants don their leather chaps and leather vests and take to the local highways as if they didn't all take Viagra. "Poser" does not even begin to describe it. I guess I can't say much about this given that I don't even have a bike.

Tripp had recommended a dealer several miles away, so we went there. The selection of helmets and jackets was nearly endless. There were all sorts of helmet styles. There were little skull cap-looking things called "beanies" and others that looked more like they were suited for flying fighter jets than riding motorcycles. Tripp said that I needed a fighter jet helmet. When you ride on a bike the wind can whip you all over the place. Aerodynamics become really important. This is particularly true with a helmet. If you buy a cheap helmet that is not well engineered, the wind at high speeds can bat your head around. Tripp also made me get one with full face protection. The one I finally picked out had a button in front that could release the visor and jaw protection so that they could be lifted up when not needed. I chose a black helmet because black goes with everything and I was not about to get a helmet that matched Tripp's bike. I was becoming his girlfriend, but I was not his bitch.

I picked out a black leather jacket that looked a lot like the one Megan had. It was tight fitting through the body and was tailored for a woman's chest, not that I am all that busty or anything. It had laces up the sides that could be adjusted to tighten or loosen the torso so that it fit snuggly whether you were wearing a sweater underneath or only a t-shirt. There were zippers at the end of the sleeves as well as up the front. There were also zippers at the armpits to allow for ventilation. It had a strap around a banded collar so that the entire jacket would not flap in high wind. It looked awesome but it cost a bundle. I thought my dad would have a fit, but he did not say a thing as we walked to the counter. In fact, he stopped and made me try on some riding boots too. Despite the enormous cost, my dad casually flipped his credit card to the guy at the cash register and that was that.

As I was waiting for my road-warrior wear to be rung up, I looked down at the glass-topped counter and saw that there were a whole bunch of small stickers on a shelf in tidy little stacks. They had biker sayings on them like "$15,000 and 1500 miles does not make you a biker" or "does my bike make my butt look fast?" Then I saw the one that I had to have: "ride hard and love your guts out". My dad dropped hundreds of dollars during our little shopping spree, but I paid for the helmet sticker out of my own money. I stuck it to the back of my helmet.

As we headed for the door, my dad kept stopping to look at various bikes parked in a neat row along the shop window. You could see that he was dreaming about one for himself. By the door there was a black Ducati and my dad stopped to take a long look at it. Tripp was checking it out too. "That's a nice bike, Little Bit, that's a really nice bike." My dad suddenly looked at him and then back at the bike. I don't think my dad realized that he was using his outside voice when he quite casually said, "Hmmm, that would go with your jacket, Maddie." He looked up at me nonchalantly and continued his thought, "of course, you would have to take a whole lot of lessons." And with that he opened the door and walked out. Tripp took my hand as we passed through the door and gave it a squeeze.

By the time I heard Megan pull up the driveway, we only had ten minutes to get to school. I zipped up my jacket, pulled on my helmet and grabbed my book bag as I darted out of the house. Riding was getting to be a routine with

Tripp and me, but this was the first time I was going to school on a motorcycle. I fastened my chin strap and slapped the visor shut just as Megan gunned the motor and we flew up the street. Damn, how I love pissing off the civilians. Does that make me a bad person?

We arrived at school with five minutes to spare which was a good thing because there is nothing as uncool as biker chicks running to class. I pulled off my helmet before I reached the school door and gave my hair a shake. The short ride was not long enough to give me helmet-head although the same could not be said about the ride downtown to the *dojo*. Megan and I turned the corner to walk down the hall toward our lockers. The hallway was lined with all of the usual characters all of whom were quite used to Megan strolling down the hall to the clump, clump, clump of her biking boots and her helmet dangling from her hand, but no one was quite prepared for her to have a sidekick. I hadn't paid attention to the heads that were turning as I approached my locker, but Megan was looking at the floor to suppress a smirk.

Megan's locker was around the corner from mine and as I whizzed through my combination she disappeared from view. I stashed my helmet first and then started unloading my book bag when Ack walked up and propped himself against the wall with a frown on his face.

"What's up Ackster?" I said like I always did when we would bump into each other.

"You tell me, what's with the born-to-be-wild thing? It's not Halloween." I turned to look at him in an attempt to determine whether or not he was being a jerk. His jab seemed unusually aggressive. Finally, I decided to give him the benefit of the doubt.

"I have been riding with some friends a lot lately and my dad thought that I could use my own gear." I started searching Ack's face for the first signs that this was a problem for him. I was in no mood to take any crap from anyone because of my new choice of outerwear. Just as Ack was about to say something, Megan popped in between us and said, "I will catch you at lunch, okay, Lhamo?"

"Yeah, I will meet you by the cafeteria. See, ya." Megan headed down the hall.

"Lhamo? Who the heck is Lhamo?" Ack said looking at me like I had suddenly grown a tail and fangs.

"Oh, that's just a nickname that the guys at the *dojo* call me."

"*Dojo*? When did you start going to a *dojo*?" It suddenly dawned on me that I had not seen much of Ack since the night I got into the fight with Nick. He was looking at me with open disapproval which was very unlike the Ack that I knew and loved. He was starting to piss me off. I was searching for a smart-ass thing to say and I found it:

"Since a couple of months after I kicked Nick Thompson's ass," I snarled.

Ack stood there speechless. He was utterly confused and I was late for class. I had planned on taking my jacket off and stowing it in my locker, but at that moment I felt like I really needed to be a biker, so I kept it on. I slammed my locker shut and headed down the hall. As I put some distance between me and Ack I heard him shout down the hall, "who are you and what have you done with Maddie?" I just kept on walking. I could get used to this biker-bitch thing.

It is amazing how people count on you to be your same old self. Change freaks people out. The kids at my school put everyone in a pigeonhole. Sometimes these pigeon holes get assigned to you when you are in third grade. Usually, you have to wear them like the a bright orange jumpsuit until you graduate. It is like no one really wants to know you for real or think about what you are really about. It is much easier to use the Dewey Decimal System of Personality Assignment. He's a jock, she's a stoner and Maddie Albright has just gone from cute to biker chick like her possible lesbian lover, Megan. That last bit would not linger in the halls of Westchester High for long. After school, Tripp picked me up to take me down to the *dojo*. He pulled up to the front door and I ran out, helmet in hand, and put a little extra drama into it for the spectators. I wrapped my arms around him and kissed him while he was sitting on his bike with the motor still running. He is such a smart guy. He figured out what I was up to and played along giving the students pouring out of the doorway quite a show. I climbed on the back of his bike and we broke some eardrums as we made tracks out of the school driveway.

If the nicest guy in school was having a problem with Lhamo, then I was going to get trashed by everyone else. Maybe they would get used to it. Half of them were probably thinking that I was a poser anyway because I wore the biker getup, but had no bike. I could fix that. I knew a certain black Ducati that was just dying to meet me. I was having a hard time giving a damn about social status anyway. My life was becoming less and less about Westchester High and more and more about Byakuren Dojo. I thought to myself as Tripp and I were flying downtown on the freeway, "Maddie, Maddie, Maddie … god, how I hate that name."

Chapter Twenty: Training To Run With Scissors

School was out and I was working at the public pool as a life guard and saving every dime I could. I knew that there was no way I could afford a motorcycle, but I decided that if I took all of the lessons, my motorcycle karma would be much improved. Tripp and Megan took turns teaching me the basics of motorcycle driving in my neighborhood and around the *dojo* downtown. It took days before I could shift without stalling and even longer before I felt comfortable going faster than second gear. They showed me how to do quick stops by using the front hand brake and the rear foot brake at the same time. They showed how to down-shift and use the back pressure of the engine to slow down. Over time, I got more and more comfortable banking turns and jacking the speed. I even popped my first wheelie although it was not on purpose and I almost peed my pants doing it.

I took the basic weekend course required for a motorcycle certification on my driver's license. They gave out a booklet at the beginning of the safety course and my dad found it lying on the kitchen table. I told him that I was training and he said nothing about it. I could tell that it was wigging my mom out, but she also said nothing. By taking the weekend course I was allowed to skip the driving test. I had to take the written test twice, but got enough points the second time to pass. It was official: I was legally a biker.

Being licensed doesn't mean much. Getting driving experience is critical. I was going out to ride with Tripp, Megan and Matt nearly every day. Matt had an electric blue bike that was seriously hopped up. Sometimes Megan would let me drive her bike and she would ride with Matt when the four of us hit the road. The guys would never double up together. They said that "real men don't ride bitch". It struck me as quite a double standard, but you have no right to push a guy to drive his bike.

I was probably not really ready for the performance driving class, but I was on a mission. This class was taught for four hours every Saturday morning for ten weeks. Megan let me use her bike. At first this was a seriously scary experience. There are a host of skills that you learn in performance driving that are way beyond what you see on the street. You do controlled skids at ridiculously high speeds. There is a track racing section where you learn to lean through turns so low that you have to make sure your knee does not scrape on the ground. Some people wipe out. There are acceleration and stopping drills and tight slalom courses. After ten weekends of this training, you barely notice high speeds and your bike feels like an extension of yourself.

Tripp suggested that I ride his bike home from time to time to get my parents acquainted with my biker skills. I took him up on this suggestion and rode his bike home from the *dojo* several times and I have to say, I love, I mean I LOVE ripping it on the freeway. That is the best part of being Lhamo. Be it at the *dojo* or on the road, I have been taught to fly and it never gets old.

By mid-summer I was going down to Forest Park at six in the morning to catch the open outdoor class. Rinchen teaches a lot of weapons classes outside. We do *bokken* (wooden practice sword), *Kendo* (sword training with practice armor) and *jo* (short wooden staff) always training by a stream in the park. It must be quite a sight for the joggers in the morning to come around the bend and see *Budoka* in armor beating each other with *shinai* (bamboo practice swords). I particularly liked *Kendo* training for a variety of reasons. First, it is awesome to hit people with sticks. Second, you get to wear armor. But mostly, when we train in *Kendo* everyone gets to wear a hakama.

I don't know what it is about a hakama, but it just brings the *Budo* right out of me. It is totally silly. No self-respecting martial artist gets hung up on her clothes. I love the way a *hakama* feels with its crisp pleats and its baggy culottes legs. When you bend your knees, a *hakama* just barely touches the ground and conceals your footwork. That's just so cool.

I suck at bokken, but do alright with the lighter shinai. My best weapon is the short staff called a jo. I have quickly taken to doing *kata* (a series of strikes, blocks and stances) even though I do not like the short staff as much as I like the sword. Rinchen does not teach us the sport version of any of these weapons. We are taught to strike through targets. When practicing *Kendo*, legs are a legitimate target, a practice that is not allowed in sport *Kendo*. Rinchen says that striking legs is somewhat dishonorable even in a real sword fight, but that one must know the full potential of the weapon. I had been getting better and better by late summer and was even beating some of the boys who outranked me. Tripp and Megan, of course, could positively shred my butt.

After a while you settle into the rhythm of *dojo* life. You walk into the *dojo* like you always do. You pay respects to the *kamidana* like you always do. Even sweeping the mat becomes part of the practice of breathing and motion that brings life into focus. There is also something special about your *dojo* brothers and sisters. These are people who sweat and bleed for their art. They are courageous and skillful, but most of all thoughtful. You get into the habit of impeccable manners and intentional kindness. After a while you notice that you have an awareness that others do not have. You catch cups falling out of the cupboard before they break on the countertop or you do flying rolls that return you to your feet if you slip on ice.

With strength and awareness comes a love for stillness. I notice that I do not worry about much anymore. I keep my room in order at home and never have to go looking for things because everything in my life is in its proper place. For the most part, I do not listen to music and I never watch TV. I like to read, especially books about old masters, especially women masters. That was a news flash. There are hundreds of stories about women warriors and their battles. You don't find that in our culture. That is the great thing about *Budo* – it is not just a guy thing – it is genderless.

I love training in the park. It takes a while to get used to hitting the ground without a mat. But it makes your *ukemi* very sharp because it simply hurts too much to get sloppy with your rolls and break-falls. I love the way the cold dew feels on my feet when we warm up in the morning. Rinchen found the ideal spot for training. It is a relatively isolated flat area in the park near the bend of a stream. There are a few pines that grow near the water. At six o'clock in the morning, it is not unusual to see mist rising off the grass and the stream as the sun rises. One morning as I was sitting in *seiza* getting ready to meditate with the class, a white egret flew overhead and landed gracefully in the stream. A chill ran up my spine. It was so beautiful. It was so simple. I began to understand the meaning of elegance.

Of course, the workouts were awesome, bodies flying everywhere. We work it hard when we are in the park. Often people stop and watch. It is kind of fun to see their faces as we fly over each other seemingly defying gravity. Everyone seems to embrace our practice with good spirit. Once I remember we were practicing *Kendo*. I was paired with Megan and we were in armor

131

practicing *juwaza*, free fighting technique, by the stream. Megan has a proper *Kendo gi* which is deep navy blue. From a distance her dark *gi* and black *hakama* look like she is wearing a single black robe with an imposing helmet and breast plate. I bought a *hakama* for *Kendo*, but only had a white *gi*. There we were waging war against each other in black and white. Two guys in a garbage truck drove through the park on the other side of the stream and the passenger leaned out of the window and shouted, "use the Force, Luke!" I started cracking up until Megan nearly beat my brains out with a quick series of *shomen* cuts.

At the end of the outdoor classes we all change into our street clothes without bothering to find cover . When you throw people around and grab them in all manner of places, you get to know them pretty intimately. And besides, seeing Tripp stripped down to his boxers is quite a bonus feature. (And maybe it is not so bad seeing Matt and Thor changing clothes either.) Everyone is disciplined and would never stoop so low as to gawk. Besides what is the difference between a sports bra and panties and a bathing suit? But you have got to love a totally ripped warrior in boxers. It puts the fight in the girl.

Every day I would go from the park to work and then back to the *dojo* for evening class. I wouldn't drag home sometimes until 10:00 or 11:00 p.m. Sometimes I would ride home with Megan and sometimes we all would stay at Rinchen's house and crash on the floor. I loved those nights in particular. Megan and I would lie on the floor with our heads in the laps of our boyfriends watching the Samurai Trilogy or a host of other old Japanese movies that Rinchen collected. We would rewind the sword fights and replay them in slow motion and watch the technique in detail. Rinchen had strict rules about the sleeping arrangements. The guys stayed in Tripp's room and the girls in Megan's room. Cheating was out of the question. When your dad is a martial arts master and meditation instructor, you don't get away with anything, so no one even tries. I don't think that Rinchen actually sleeps. He is always awake or meditating when we go to bed and is up cooking breakfast when we get up. The man is a machine. But most of all he is my *sensei*.

Toward the end of the summer, I rode home with Tripp on a Sunday morning after staying at his house. I practically fell asleep with my head on his back as we made our way out to the suburbs. The days of being freaked out by motorcycles were long gone and they seemed second nature to me now. We turned into my subdivision and Tripp made a point to go slow to keep the engine noise down. We rounded the corner onto my street and I could see the familiar Kid Car in the driveway. As Tripp turned to head up the drive, he suddenly slammed on the brakes and brought his bike to an abrupt stop. I was jolted back to awareness. "What the hell, Trippster! Take it easy, dude". He didn't say a word as I crawled off the back of his bike and started taking off my helmet. It took me a second or two to notice that he was looking straight ahead. I followed his gaze up the driveway only a few feet and nearly peed in my pants. There, parked right in front of us concealed from the street by the Kid Car was a shining black Ducati. We had almost hit it coming up the driveway. Holy crap! My dad bought himself a bike!

We headed into the house and found my dad in the kitchen cooking breakfast, a time honored tradition on Sunday mornings in the Albright household. My mom was nowhere to be found and Tyler was in the den playing his video game. "Henry," I said brazenly to my dad, "you got yourself a crotch rocket! Awesome, dude!" My dad looked up at me and smiled and then replied, "no I didn't." As he said this he threw me a set of keys.

"NO WAY!"

My dad said nothing but continued to scramble some eggs. After a second he walked around the island kissing me on the head as he went to the pantry to find some pancake mix.

My mother surfaced from the laundry room looking like she needed a cocktail. She was trying to be happy and chipper but the anxiety was winning the battle for the control of her face. "Hi, sweetie," she said trying to act as casual as a terrified mother can.

"Hey, mom." I stood there looking at her and then I noticed something that surprised me. My mother was being brave. I have seen that look a thousand times in the *dojo*. A guy is called to the front of class to demonstrate an advanced technique. He knows he is going to get thrown through a wall and he is not sure if he can handle it. But he goes up there anyway and takes whatever comes his way. That was what mom was doing in that moment – making herself deal with whatever was coming her way. When you see someone stand for you like that in the *dojo*, it makes you respect them forever. I have always loved my mom, but standing there in the kitchen that morning I felt much more than love. This woman was doing what she thought was right rather than what she wanted to do.

We sat down to breakfast, but the motorcycle keys were burning a hole through the pocket lining of my jeans. I was not going to rush this, though. This was a very special occasion of a kind, in fact, that had never happened in our house before. Henry and Jeanie were not the spontaneous expensive gift giving type. Tripp was almost as anxious as I was to get out to the driveway. We chit-chatted about how the weekend had gone. My dad asked Tripp how his father was doing. My mom didn't eat much but doted on Tripp and made sure he ate his fill. Even Tyler had very little to say. Although Captain Oblivion probably didn't even know what was going on. They may have rehearsed all of this. Finally, the bacon was gone and the syrup mopped up with the last little bit of pancake. My mom and dad got up and started clearing the dishes. Tripp and I started to help them when my dad stopped us and said, "Don't you have somewhere to go?" I kissed him on the cheek and then my mom in turn and both Tripp and I dashed for the door. "Bye mom, bye dad!"

Chapter Twenty-one: Lhamo's Mule

There is a lot to be said for riding on the back of Tripp's bike. It has become practically part of my daily zanshin practice. With my arms wrapped around his waist, I have come to know every muscle in his upper body. As we ride down the road, I can feel his breath in my arms and almost always start breathing in time with him. Sometimes I think I can even feel his heartbeat. But the days of riding bitch were over. I slid onto the seat of my new motorcycle and lowered my body onto the gas tank. This was a work of art. It was jet black, shiny and beautiful. The perfect machine to hurl a young girl's ass down the freeway at speeds that could make a cop crap his pants. It was official: Lhamo had her mule.

By the time I had stopped molesting my new motorcycle, Tripp already had his helmet on and his motor running. He is such a good boy. I turned the key slowly and the bike rumbled to life. I giggled. I grabbed the handle bars and revved the engine. I had never had sex before, but I imagined that it had to be a lot like this. Tripp had rolled his bike backward down the driveway and I soon followed after him. He did not dare take off and go first. Not on this day. He has such good manners, have I mentioned that? I slapped the visor down on my helmet, and wrung the rag. I could feel the front wheel lift off the road and then suddenly realized that my mother was probably lying on the floor inside in need of CPR, so I toned it down as we made our way to the corner.

Tripp followed me as we challenged a few speed limits anxiously finding our way to the freeway. We headed west through the Valley and out to the legendary Highway 94. Highway 94 is a biker's paradise and purgatory all rolled into one narrow ribbon of road. It passes through, but does not stop at the village of Defiance. If you are going to start a road trip, especially on a motorcycle, what better place to begin than in a town called "Defiance". The road curves, rises and dips. It loosely follows the Missouri River through towns like Augusta and Washington. It is treacherous and known for its blind turns that can leave you sucking on the back of a slow moving hay wagon if you do not pay attention.

At Augusta, there are wineries and winery tourists. This only adds to the potential danger. More than one biker has met his doom at the hand of a wine taster in a sensible sedan jacked up on Chardonnay. There is a Buddhist monastery in Augusta as well. Tripp, Megan and I have visited it several times with Rinchen. The abbot there is a *Tai Chi* master and even the nuns work out. On Sundays, the Chinese ladies of the sangha (congregation) put on an awesome vegetarian lunch. It is an incredible place of peace and one of my favorite places on the planet.

Beyond Augusta, is Washington, an old river town that has a modern part at the outskirts, but looks like something out of the 1870s down by the waterfront. Further down the river, is Hermann, Missouri. It was founded by German immigrants and is big with the bed and breakfast crowd. There is good reason for this because the place is absolutely lovely with its old brick buildings rising up through the trees that follow the rolling slope of the landscape down to the bank of the river. I remember from history class that Lewis and Clark passed through all of these towns on their way out west. If they had lived in my time they would have made that trip on motorcycles, I just know it. Missouri may be ranked 47th in the nation in everything, but it is pretty high on the list of scenic highways. The bluffs along the Missouri River are stunning, especially when you are riding over them on your own brand new black beauty. It is as close to heaven as a girl can get.

We rode most of the day. The weather was warm, but motorcycles come equipped with their own breeze. We stopped in Hermann for lunch and sat on the deck of an old inn and watched the river roll by. Tripp produced a small sketch pad out of his jacket and a pencil and started sketching the river. Sometimes he would stop drawing for several minutes at a time and stare at the scene intently. He would cock his head to one side as if to see the river from a completely different point of view and then he would go back to his drawing. He was a quiet guy. Even with me, he did not say a lot, but when he did, it was usually something very profound. He was a lot like his dad that way.

He looked up at me suddenly and caught me checking him out. "What?" he asked as if something were wrong.

"Nothing, just watching a man at work. I like stalking you even when you know I am doing it." I was smiling and I couldn't stop. It was hard not to smile around him. I sometimes felt like I was a first grader with a crush on a rock star when I was with Tripp.

"I thought I would make a little souvenir of the day that you broke in your bike," he said looking back at his pad. Within seconds he was off in the world of the landscape and immersed in his sketch of it.

I stood up and walked to the edge of the deck. I got out my cellphone and turned on the camera function. I held the camera phone up and watched the scenery on the video screen trying to get as much of the landscape in the frame as I could. It wouldn't fit and the video screen made the colors look different. I snapped a picture anyway.

"I am afraid mine is not going to be as good as yours," I said as I walked back to the patio chair next to Tripp.

"Well, you can't expect much from a photograph," Tripp said absentmindedly as he continued to draw. This seemed weird to me. Photographs were exact. They made nearly perfect copies of everything. As good as Tripp was at drawing, and he was outstanding, in his best day he could not get as close to real as a photograph.

"What do you mean by that? What is wrong with photos?"

"Nothing, it's just that they are so limited. Sure they can copy what they see, but they can't tell you how you felt about what you saw. They see things the way a machine sees things, not necessarily the way you see things. Of course, a great photographer with good equipment and a lot of skill can get more from a photograph than you can with the one in your cellphone, but for me it is still not enough." Tripp did not look up as he spoke, but kept looking at the river and its banks and scratching away on his pad.

"What more is there? It's a river. I mean, it's just a river."

"No, it's not. It's an event." By now he had set down his pad and was looking at me with just the faintest smile studying me like I was about to be the subject of his next sketch.

"I am not sure that I am following you." I hated it when I didn't understand him. It seemed to suck all of the equality out of our relationship.

"Well, when I sketch, I am not trying to copy the landscape. There is more going on than just the river flowing by. I am giving the scene meaning when I look at it, so I am trying to capture what it means to me. I am trying to use drawing as a meditation on the real life that I am seeing. It is not really about making a record of where I was. That's just data. When I take the time to draw something, I take the time to be with what I am looking at. I take the time to think about it and absorb it into myself. I guess you could say that my sketch is really just the vapor trail of the collision between me and that river over there. I get to come to know it, but I also come to know me at the same time. It is a great opportunity to sink your teeth into life." He paused to see if I was getting it or not. But I was having a moment of my own and I was falling deeply and hopelessly in love with him.

"I don't even really look at my sketch book that much. It is the act of drawing in the face of beauty that is my meditation. Sometimes I am not really sure if I am drawing the river or if the river is making me draw." He sat back in his chair as if to enjoy the look in my eyes. "So, what do you think about that, Little Bit?" Little Bit. He hadn't called me that in a while, ever since his dad started calling me "Lhamo". He was the only one that called me that, except Megan, but she usually only used that name to tease me.

"It's beautiful," I said as my eyes filled with tears, "absolutely, fucking beautiful." Tripp took my hand and gave it a squeeze, then kissed it. The guy was never too much or too little. He was always paying attention to every little detail around him. It was like he was this light that let you see the world in colors that you never knew existed. I was starting to understand why these Buddhist guys were always talking about illumination.

On a day like that day, when you are breaking in a new bike, you are not in a hurry to get anywhere, but you hurry everywhere just the same. Just before sunset we stopped at a small park on the side of the road on top of a bluff. The air was starting to cool a little, but it was still sticky with humidity. The sun painted golds and reds across the otherwise green landscape. Tripp sat on the bench of an old picnic table leaning back between my legs as I sat on the table top with my arms wrapped around his neck and my chin resting on top of his head. I breathed in and then slowly exhaled; in again and then out. I let go and slipped into mu.

When I came back to the moment, I was filled with the overwhelming sense that all was right in the world. The earth was beautiful, our bikes were fast and I had this wonderful guy to share it all with, a guy who saw even more beauty in the world than I did. My, how times had changed! Less than a year ago, I was Maddie Albright, texting with my friends, shopping for clothes with Beth and perfectly numb from the neck up. Now I spent my time learning how to fight three grown men at a time with my bare hands and could do diving rolls over five of my *dojo* brothers and sisters. I had friends whose idea of a great time was to beat the shit out of each other and then meditate on the sound of doves perched in the trees at Forest Park. I could not begin to absorb just how cool my life was. It seemed like I was in love with everybody and everything although, if I told the truth about it, my school friends were becoming less and less interesting to me. I couldn't handle all the static that seemed to hang like a cloud over them. I hardly saw Beth anymore, or Ack. It dawned on me while I was sitting there on the bluff tickling the palms of my hands on the stubble of Tripp's unshaven face that what I was learning by all of this was that less is more. I was no longer frantic and spread out in thin slices all over my world. I had gone vertical and was drilling down into essence of sunsets and open roads and the sound of my boyfriend's breath.

A few minutes after the sun disappeared under the horizon, Tripp stood up and stretched and then leaned into me and started kissing the side of my face. What a gentle man. He was always relaxed and seemed to want to savor me rather than eat me up. He pushed me back onto the picnic table and slowly crawled up on top of me. He was never in a hurry when we made out. He seemed to like to explore me and stopped to think about what he had discovered and then resumed his kisses. I had come to love the way he smelled, even when he had just worked out. He never once seemed disappointed that we didn't have sex, although I was pretty sure he wouldn't say "no" if I said "yes". That day was coming, but it would have to wait a little while longer. I have to say that I deeply respected that he never once pressured me over anything intimate. He didn't even talk about it. He was in tune with me and did not have to be told what was appropriate in any given moment. That was one of the many truly amazing things about Tripp – he paid attention to everything, even the slightest emotion flashing across someone's eyes. When we would lay on top of each other it was like I could read the thoughts that were crossing his mind, well, maybe not just his mind.

It was getting dark and we were still twenty miles from home. We fired up the bikes and rolled down the bluff weaving and rising over the hills along the river. Highway turned into freeway and freeway turned into business avenue. The roads shrank as we got closer to my house. We pulled into the driveway and I could see my mom peering out from behind the curtains of the living room. I wondered how long she had been waiting by the window for me to come home. I parked my bike in the garage and walked down the driveway to invite Tripp inside. He said he needed to get home and kissed me goodbye. I watched the cherry red motorcycle roll up the street and disappear around the corner. I stood on the driveway until I couldn't hear the sound of his engine anymore.

I had missed dinner, but there was no lecture or even as much as a complaint. My mom looked like she had aged about a decade while I had been out. My dad walked into the kitchen smiling, "how did it go?" "Awesome, dad, just totally awesome! I can't thank you enough for this." My dad grabbed a brownie out of a pan on the counter and simply said, "cool" and left the room munching his dessert. I didn't feel much like talking and wandered off to my room. I took a shower and flopped on my bed. As I looked around my bedroom I noticed that the walls were covered with artifacts of a younger version of me. There were pictures cut out of magazines of cute boys from various television shows. There was a bulletin board with ribbons tacked to it from several science fairs I had entered. The room was pink which was starting to really bug me. The stuffed animals on my bed were probably due to be donated to the next generation of prospective fairy princesses. My room was a record of me growing up and while I drifted in and out of a variety of memories it started to occur to me that it just didn't fit me anymore. It was time to redecorate.

Chapter Twenty-two: The Fine Line Revisited

School starts up in Missouri toward the end of August. It is still hot here and it doesn't start to cool off until autumn is nearly over. Megan came by my house on the first day of school -- my last first day of school at Westchester High. We had planned to ride together. The weather was stifling and the humidity was high. My dad does not like me riding without leather, but it was way too hot for jackets. We rolled into the school parking lot revving our engines as we found a place to park. I had seen Beth a few times over the summer and she knew all about my bike. It was a surprise for everyone else.

We headed down the hallway to our respective lockers taking inventory of what the summer had done to everyone as we passed by. I ran into Beth and she ambushed me with a hug, "hey, girlfriend, we're finally in the home stretch, heh?" It was good to see her. She was the same old Beth and that was a good thing. As I stood there listening to her update, I started to feel sort of sad. Beth had been one of the unintended casualties of my reincarnation into Lhamo. I took a moment just to take her in, to notice the color of her eyes and the way her hair bounced as she talked. I have often put a lot of hard judgment on the kids in my school, maybe it was just so that I could feel better about my choices. But Beth occurred to me, on that last first day of school as truly beautiful. I found myself whispering a little mantra under my breath, "have a wonderful life, have a wonderful life, have a wonderful life."

I toted my helmet and book bag further down the hall and dumped the load into my locker. We did not have our books yet, so the inside of my locker was an unthreatening, optimistic space. That would change soon enough. I looked around to get my bearings. Tommy Davidson must be still together with Annie because they were holding hands as they walked down the hall. Ack was nowhere to be found. I think he was still mad at me anyway. Kwame Johnson was walking down the hall. He was still sporting the educated gangsta look. He stopped to look me up and down and noticed the boots. "Damn girl, you look like you are ready to kick some ass," he said while giving me a hug. He had never done that before. He had always been polite to me, but never openly friendly. I have to say that I liked it. Kwame had his quirks, but I thought he had a great sense of humor and I loved the way he played clarinet. I had heard someone say that they had heard him sing and that he was fantastic. He was also really good at math and wanted to be an engineer. He will someday be the coolest engineer alive.

The best thing about the first day of school is that it is easy. In the confusion that will soon be pulled into a grind, you kind of just float through the day. I had been expecting to see Ack all day. I was wondering if he had gotten over the biker chick thing and was hoping just to check in with him. He was nowhere to be found. When I went out to the parking lot after school I saw his car. He had been in school, I had just not seen him. In fact, I didn't see him for the next several days, not even in the lunch room. This struck me as odd because Ack is a pretty social guy and working the lunch room is one of his favorite things to do. He liked to make the rounds checking in with the various groups of friends he had.

Near the end of the week, I had stayed after school to knock out some homework before heading down to the *dojo*. I was usually pretty beat after training and I knew I would blow off doing homework if I waited until I got home. It is funny that as you become more disciplined in one thing, you become more disciplined in all things.

I was walking out of the library when I saw Ack hurrying down the hall. "ACK!," I shouted. He nearly jumped out of his shoes. He spun around and looked at me. I was the only one in the hall and he immediately began to relax, but only a little. This was not the Ack I knew, not even a little bit.

"What is going on, dude? I have been looking all over for you." Ack seemed surprised to hear this. I couldn't say I blamed him.

"You were?"

"Yeah, it's the beginning of the end Ackster. I know I have been pretty busy, like for the last year, but you are still important to me. We go all the way back to third grade, dude. I haven't seen you in forever and I was hoping to check in."

"You were?" He was starting to soften, but something was weighing him down big-time.

"What's the matter, Ack? You look like you have seen a ghost or something. You are all jumpy."

"Yeah, well I managed to totally piss off Jason Anderson just before school started and I have heard he is looking for me. He is quite ginormous, as you know, and wants to kick my ass."

"What did you do to him?"

"Nothing. You know that he and Amy broke up this summer, right ... maybe you don't know ... you have been MIA for quite a while. Well, he broke up with Amy about a month before school started. She started texting me, telling me her tale of woe. She asked if we could hang out. I thought, 'why not', maybe I might get lucky this time. I didn't. She just wanted a male shoulder to cry on. Last week, we were out getting something to eat and we ran into Jason. He was not very happy to see me and Amy to together. Amy decided to rub it in his face and started crawling all over me, which I thoroughly enjoyed, mind you, but she was just screwing with him."

"Sounds like she was screwing with you too."

"Yeah, I get that a lot. That's what you get when girls think you are harmless."

"So, what's the deal here? He broke up with her, right? She's abandoned property, fair game, back on the market."

"Apparently not. I guess Jason expected a longer grieving period from Amy. He has been going around school telling everyone what a slut she is for taking up with me supposedly the day after he dumped her. What a douche bag. When he started getting bad reviews on Facebook over his macho bullshit, instead of backing down, he ramped up and now he is looking for me. He is a wrestler, Maddie, and I am just a devilishly good looking Hindu boy who is a math genius. What am I supposed to do, smack him with my calculator?" He was pretty darned scared, but he was at least trying to keep up some sense of humor about it.

There was not enough time to get Ack to the *dojo* and man him up. I was starting to get really pissed. Westchester High did not have a lot of fights, but they happened. They were usually not much, one guy would pee a line on the ground and dare another to cross it. Usually the challengee would chicken out and back down. There would be a week or two of humiliation for the vanquished and then the world would go back to normal although if the buzz made you out to be too big a pussy, you could be sent down the social totem pole several notches, if not to the bottom. It would be absolutely unfair for a blockhead like Jason Anderson to do this to Ack. What right does he have anyway? He dumped Amy, that prick! I could feel myself getting mad. I wanted to hunt Jason down and toss his ass around the hallways. I was pretty sure he couldn't take the kind of fall that I had in mind for him.

That night, after practice, Megan, Matt, Tripp and I went to the *sake* house. I told them what was going on with Ack. Megan shook her head and said "you gotta just say 'no' to testosterone". She hadn't really thought out her remark. When she looked up, Matt was staring at her with that *oh, really!* look frozen on his face. Even Tripp and I were looking at her like she had just told a big lie. Megan was only slightly embarrassed. "What?" she said almost brazenly as if to use this one word like a *shinai* to defend herself against all three of us. Tripp and I started to laugh. Matt kept staring her down. "You know what I meant. The guy is a testo-pig. He needs to be bitch slapped back to his ancestors." Matt was holding his ground. "Ohhh Matty, you handsome devil, you know I wasn't talking about your testosterone, don't you?" She picked up his hand off the table and was making doe eyes at Matt and he started to chuckle. Suddenly, she licked the back of his hand destroying her own apology. Matt pulled his hand away and started wiping Megan's slobber off on his jeans.

"Jason needs to get whacked," I said half-seriously.

"He needs to grow up," Megan replied.

"That's not going to help Ack."

Tripp added his two cents: "sometime it is your karma to be attacked out of the blue. It can be a moment of purification." I had expected Megan to make some smart-assed response, but both she and Matt were silent and seemingly in agreement. It occurred to me that it was up to me to state the obvious here.

"What the hell does that mean?" Tripp looked up. He put down his chopsticks. This was going to take a while.

"It is Ack's karma that he is being hunted. If Ack was a badass *kung-fu* nightmare, this Jason guy would not be hunting him. Guys like Jason hunt the weak. There are a lot of things in this life that hunt the weak. Pedophiles, muggers, abusive boyfriends, bitch alpha-chicks … late night fast food commercials."

"What?"

"Why do you think that they put fast food commercials on late at night. You get hungry. You don't want to cook. So you jump in your hoopty and hit the drive through at Burger World. They are targeting you when you are weak. This is the karma of weakness – you are vulnerable. It is everywhere. Cops pull you over for speeding. Some are nice, but some are waving their authority in your face. If you get smart, they get mean. Why? Because they can. Have you ever notice that pro football players almost never get mugged? Why? Because they are not weak, therefore they make unappealing targets. Have you ever noticed that abusive men always wind up with needy women. Why? Because needy women will take their crap. It is the way of the world. Tigers hunt sheep, not other tigers."

"Well, this jack-ass should not be hunting Ack."

"Agreed," Tripp said matter-of-factly. "But he will unless there is an intervening karmic influence that counters the cause and effect that is at play here."

I thought about this long and hard. Megan, Matt and Tripp continued eating without saying anything, allowing me to absorb this lesson. Megan seemed the most interested of the three of them as to how this was going to make its way through the Pachinko machine of my brain. I started to eat too. "No one is going to hunt my friend." Megan looked up at Tripp with a measure of uncertainty in her expression. It was like the three of them were having a telepathic conversation about me and it was undecided how things were going. Matt picked up the conversation and continued the lesson.

"Lhamo, the sense of injustice you have is a good thing, but make sure that you do not become the Jason here."

"What do you mean by that?"

"It means that what makes Jason a bad idea right now is that he is full of hate and he is destructive. What he really needs is different thoughts, not a broken nose. And the truth of it may be that only a broken nose will change his thoughts, but I doubt it. It will most likely cause him to hate more. He needs to see the harm of his way of thinking. He needs to have his own inner turmoil smoothed out. We are all human and prone to surges of uncontrollable emotion. We don't know any better until we get schooled. Usually that schooling comes at great expense. We make flaming asses of ourselves. We fling ourselves against our circumstances like crazy people. After we beat our heads against the wall long enough, hopefully, but certainly not always, we wise up. Both Jason and Ack are human beings. They are goofy and ignorant. But who would we be if we did not stand for the enlightenment of everyone? It would make no sense. Our way is not to judge and destroy. Our way is to transform stupidity into understanding; hate into compassion. Sometimes we have to use some pretty severe methods to accomplish this, but only when there is no other way. We must always come from this intention."

"That may be, but I am not going to let that guy hurt Ack." Megan said nothing but was looking at me with deep concern in her eyes. She looked back at Matt and Tripp and something was communicated and the matter was settled.

I road my motorcycle to school by myself the following Monday. I scanned the parking lot for Ack's car. He was already there. Megan pulled into the parking lot as I was heading for the door. She flipped her visor up and shouted to me as she passed me on the driveway, "wait up!" I waited, but I was edgy and wanted to get inside to find Ack. We walked down the hall together. Megan was chatting casually, but did not head to her locker when we got to the point in the hallway where our paths normally separated. As I rounded the corner, I saw Ack and picked up the pace to catch up to him. I tapped him on the shoulder from behind and he nearly jumped out of his skin. "Maddie! What are you trying to do to me? I have got to get to class."

"Just trying to say 'hey'."

"Well, 'hey'. I gotta go." I followed him down the hall to his class. There was no sign of Jason. I was relieved and with Megan still walking with me, we headed toward our lockers. We were both going to be late.

"You know you can't do this, right?" Megan said as I started to jog for my locker.

"Yes I can."

"No you can't," she snapped and grabbed my arm to get me to stop and talk to her. "What do you think can come of this? You might have enough skill by now to take out Jason, he certainly will not see it coming, but then what? His business with Ack will be far from finished and his business with you will be just beginning. Sooner or later he will get Ack alone. And god knows what he will try to do to you. All you are going to do is unleash more hate because all you are adding is hate. Nothing good will come of this."

"Oh yeah? Well, at least my friend will not stand alone. Isn't that what all this *Budo* bullshit is about? We don't just let our friends go down, Megan, not now, not ever!" Megan softened her grip on my arm.

"I know, Lhamo, I know. But we have to find another way."

"Well as far as I am concerned, Jason is making his own bed here." And with that, I spun around and took off down the hall.

Between every class, I followed Ack and Megan followed me. All three of us knew that lunch would be the most likely opportunity for Jason to find Ack. Ack had been avoiding the lunch room at all cost and had been bringing a sack lunch to school that he ate outside. When he stepped outside the doors, I was there waiting for him. Megan was probably searching the lunch room for us.

We sat on a bench along the sidewalk. Ack looked like he was going to throw up. We had been sitting there for only a minute or two, when the doors of the school burst open and Jason trudged out onto the sidewalk. There were a couple of dozen gawkers following him, and Megan was bringing up the rear. Jason was already pretty stewed in his own juice as he confronted Ack.

"Stand up you fucking sand nigger!" Jason snarled.

"Sand nigger? My family is from India you moron." A wave of calm had come over Ack like he had accepted his doom. He might be about to get his ass kicked, but was not going to let this guy take his dignity. I was suddenly proud of him. He was frowning at his enemy and stood up to face him. I had not noticed Megan moving in from the far side of the circle that was beginning to frame the dueling grounds. Surprisingly, Amy was among the onlookers, apparently quite proud of herself that two guys were going to fight over her.

Jason reached out to grab Ack's shirt and I intercepted his hand. I caught his fingers like a bunch of flowers and squeezed hard and bent them back toward his wrist. *Eubidori*: the finger take-down technique. The pain shot across his face along with the sudden concern that he was only an inch away from having every tendon in his hand torn in one flip of my wrist. He tried to push against me to fight back, but this made the pain suddenly much worse. After one more attempt to break free, he finally came to realize that to fight back was only hurting him more.

"You need to back off my friend, you prick, before I trash your hand so bad you won't even be able to play with yourself." Jason was bent over trying to get out from under the excruciating pain I was shooting through his fingers and wrist. He was seething mad and I suddenly realized that I did not have a very good end-game prepared. All I could think to do was flip his fingers back and bounce him around a bit while I tried to figure out how this was going to end. "Well, bully boy, how is this working out for you? You just got your ass handed to you by a girl. You gonna beat me up too, tough guy?" I was livid, but my anger was wearing off as I searched my mind for a solution to this problem. I may have been controlling the pain in Jason's hand, but I was stuck with him just as much as he was stuck with me.

In a life-or-death situation I have been taught that you might have to injure your attacker to leave him in extreme pain while you make your escape. Given that he was not fighting back at the moment, if I broke all of his fingers I would be in some seriously big trouble. If I let him go, he might come after me. There was no longer an element of surprise. Wrestlers are fighters and if he got me on the ground I would be in big trouble. Megan had now come into the huddle in the middle of the circle and was looking at me with a scowl. She was furious. She quickly turned her attention to Jason and whispered in his ear. Only the four of us could hear what she said: "Lhamo is going to break every one of your fingers if you push this. That is really going to fuck you up. I am going to make her stop in a second and you are going to walk out of here with me and we are going to go and talk this out. Is that alright with you?" Jason looked up at Megan confused. She kissed him on the head and nodded at him reassuringly. This had not gone as he planned and it was pretty embarrassing. Megan was giving him a way out. He faked a smile and nodded. Megan turned to me with a ferocious look. She did not have to say anything. I let go of his fingers. Megan took Jason's hand and walked him through the circle of gawkers like they were going on a date. Amy was clearly disappointed.

Ack turned to look at me and was livid. "What the fuck did you just do?"

"*Eubidori.*"

"You just made me look like a complete asshole. I don't need to be saved by a girl! I was prepared to take my beating like a man, but now you have made me your bitch in front of everybody. What the fuck is wrong with you?"

With that he turned away and left me alone on the sidewalk. I was devastated. I had been warned. Everyone tried to stop me, but NO, I had to be the brave samurai and step in and fight the bad guy. What a clusterfuck! As I flopped down on the bench in shock, I saw Megan out in the parking lot talking to Jason. She was patting his shoulder and it looked like she was trying to get him to laugh. She grabbed his shirt with both hands pretending to shake some sense into him while smiling and shaking him back and forth. Eventually, he cracked a smile. Then I saw her give him a big hug and they headed through the cars toward me. I thought to myself, "oh crap, here it comes."

As the two approached, Jason was looking down at the ground but Megan was staring straight at me. She was not as angry as she had been, but she was by no means happy. Jason sat down and looked at me sheepishly and said, "I am sorry about all that, Maddie. I was being a dick. I am going to find Ack and apologize, but I wanted to tell you that I was sorry." What? I was stunned and I looked up at Megan only to be greeted with a very stern "I-told-you-so" expression that was starting to make me feel sick to my stomach. "By the way, that was a pretty wild finger thing you put on me there. Where did you learn that?" Jason was genuinely interested. I guess it was professional curiosity.

"At my *dojo,*" I said starting to feel like a complete idiot.

"Wow, I knew Megan was into that kind of thing, but I didn't know you got into it too. Maybe I should check it out." With that he patted me on the shoulder and apologized again and headed into the school, presumably to find Ack. Ironically, I was missing his company because now I was alone with Megan and I knew this was not going to be pleasant. She took her time before she spoke.

"Well, Wonder Woman, are you feeling better now?"

"No." I was actually pouting. I am pretty sure there is a rule against pouting somewhere in *Bushido* code.

"You didn't listen. Not one, but three *sempai* warned you and you did not listen. You know this will have to be reported, right?"

"Yes, I know."

"And you know that this may get you kicked out of the *dojo*, right?" That I didn't know. I looked up at Megan in a panic.

"You're kidding me! I was trying to save my friend!"

"Were you? Or were you trying to punish Jason?" Suddenly, I realized that there was no real line for me between the two. Tears started to roll down my cheeks. Megan softened her tone of voice. "Lhamo, this hate thing is not Budo. It is just your ego. A badass is still an ass."

I sat there trying not to cry. Megan's face slowly started to radiate some small measure of compassion. But she was not going to baby me. "I am going to go inside and run damage control. I will see what I can do with Ack." As Megan turned to go back inside, I called out to her.

"What did you say to Jason that got him to turn around like that?"

"It was not so much what I said, it was what he said. I mostly listened."

"That is pretty hard to believe, I mean, one minute he is ready to kill Ack and the next minute he is apologizing like he is ready to go into the art room and make pottery or something. You have to admit that this is a pretty radical change." Megan turned around and came back to the bench and sat next to me. She had decided to run damage control on me first.

"Why do people go nuts like Jason did? We have known him forever and while he is a bit of a muscle-head, he is usually a nice enough guy. What made him flip?"

"The fact that he is a jealous douche bag, maybe?" Megan frowned and I realized that if I wanted her to tell me how she turned this guy around so fast, I had better stop being such a smart-ass.

"No. It was pain."

"But he broke up with Amy. He was the dumpor and she was the dumpee."

"Well, if anyone had bothered to actually talk to Jason, they might have found out that Amy had been distancing herself from him for weeks and was hanging out with Ack to piss him off. I am not exactly sure why. Maybe she didn't have the guts to break up with him straight out and sabotaged things to make him out to be the bad guy. Maybe she thought it would only make him jealous and that he would try harder in their relationship. Who knows? Jason broke up with her because he thought he was being dissed. He was basically trying to save face."

"But why go after Ack?"

"Jason adores Amy and thought he was losing her to Ack. It occurred to him like Ack was breaking the Code of Guys. There is a rule among these knuckle-heads that you do not go after another guy's girl unless she is legitimately back on the market. To Jason, Ack was jumping the gun. The truth is, Amy was probably just using him. She can be that way, you know."

"Yeah, I know. She's a Malibu Barbie and that's how they work it. But what did you say to get him to change like that?"

"First, I listened and got his story and then I gently reinterpreted the facts for him. New interpretation, new emotional vapor trail. I pointed out to him that running around attacking harmless boy-escorts like Ack was beneath him and embarrassing to a guy of his social status. This reminded him of who he knows himself to be which had been threatened. Then I pointed out to him that Ack was, in all likelihood, not really on Amy's radar. This eliminated the threat. Everyone knows that Ack never gets past the brotherly love thing with anyone. This gave him confidence that what I was saying to him was true. Then I pointed out that he was probably being played and that getting him to jump through hoops like a little circus dog attacking Ack and confronting you was all part of the play. By then, he could hear this and it redirected his attention back onto the person that is really pulling his trigger. I told him that he needed to have an adult conversation with Amy. If he still loved her, then he needed to say that. If he did not love her anymore, then he needed to say that. Call it like it is. I then told him that he needed to actually man-up and find out what she wanted even if that hurt his feelings. I basically gave him back his balls."

"You did *Aikido*."

"Yes, I did."

Suddenly, I felt so ashamed of myself. I had used the art of harmonizing energy to beat on Jason, not create anything useful. I had used force on force and in the end the joke was on me, only it wasn't funny. I looked up at Megan with tears in my eyes and said, "Megs I am so sorry. I missed the whole point. I could have really hurt that guy and for what? To prove what?"

"In *Budo*, there is no victory and there is no defeat. This would be an inefficient outcome for humanity. In a conflict, what there is to do is confront ignorance, become one with it and then light it up from inside. There are many idiots who think that violence is actually a solution. People abuse each other in many ways. They try to seize control over others to keep themselves safe or get what they want. They are not sophisticated enough to get what they want by blending with others. They don't even know it is an option. That would actually require that they pay attention to others, to their needs and wants and actually bend themselves into something that accommodates everyone, not just themselves. This is our way. We spend hours and hours learning to pay attention so that we can spot the faintest traces of an opportunity to cause peace even in the middle of a rampage. Sometimes we have to redirect so much hostile energy that the aggressor does get hurt, but this is more proof of our lack of skill, than real necessity. A master is thwarting negativity before she ever encounters those turbulent beings that do so much harm. A master is influencing the space always and always bending the energy around her to illuminate. *Aikidoka* do not train to blacken the sky."

"I am so far away from that. If I get kicked out of the *dojo*, I will never get there."

Megan kissed me on the top of my head. "We'll see, Lhamo. We'll see. But if I were you, I would start creating a tidal wave of positive energy right now. What will happen hours from now started a century ago." She stood up and headed for the door. Just before the building swallowed her up, Megan popped her head back outside. "By the way, the way to clean up a mess starts by owning your mistake and being prepared to take whatever consequence comes out of it."

I missed my next class sitting there thinking about what I had seen and heard. Sometimes the only way to get your fingers out of your ears is to put your foot in your mouth.

Chapter Twenty-three: Face The Music, Then Dance

It was the longest ride to the *dojo,* ever. I think that I must have been practically blocking traffic on the freeway because I was so not in a hurry to see Rinchen, or Tripp for that matter. I remember thinking to myself, "you are such a white belt." That thought was followed by, "you are soon to be a no-belt."

I parked in front of the *dojo* and left my *do-gi* bag tied to my bike. I was not sure I would be staying and I was not going to be presumptuous. I had to wait for fifteen minutes for Rinchen to get there. He greeted me with his usual controlled warmness. "Lhamo, how come you are not dressed? Are you feeling ill?"

"Actually, yes, but I am not sick. I need to talk to you." We stepped into his office and he closed the door. When I sat in *seiza* on the floor, a cloud of concern passed over Rinchen's face. In the *Budo* world, the slightest gesture speaks volumes about a situation. My formality told Rinchen, in language much stronger than mere words, that this was serious, at least as far as I was concerned. Merely talking to him would not have communicated how much I really meant what I was about to say. *Budoka,* that is, practitioners of *Budo,* the art of war in which *Aikido* is one of many methods, never allow themselves to be misunderstood. They use their mental clarity to say precisely what they mean in delicately nuanced ways that ensure that their meaning is fully communicated. They take responsibility for both sides of a conversation, the speaking and the listening. Of course, I was hoping to simply make sure that when I apologized to him, that he knew I meant it. After that, I knew it was pretty much going to be me sitting there trying not to cry.

"What is the matter, Lhamo?" Rinchen asked softly.

"I got into another fight."

"Did you, now? What happened?"

I told him the story about how I had followed Ack and had confronted Jason outside. I told him about the eubidori takedown and how I had threatened to hurt Jason and how I found myself not being able to create an exit from the conflict. I told him about how Megan intervened and how she resolved the situation. I told him about what she had taught me on the bench by the door and that I had considered this very seriously. I told him that I had found both Jason and Ack later in the day and apologized to both of them. Jason was okay with everything, but Ack was still pretty mad. "But mostly, I have come to apologize to you because I knew better than this. I have let you down and let your teachings go to waste. I ignored my *sempai* and I have brought dishonor on this dojo. I am here to offer to quit this place and never come back". As I spoke the last of these words, I bowed and put my face between my hands on the floor. I did not move.

"I see," said Rinchen gravely. He left me frozen in my bow for a few seconds and then said, "Sit up, please. We should talk about this." I sat up and by now my face was burning with sadness and the tears were making it difficult to see. Rinchen reached into his *gi* and pulled out a *hachimaki* , a handkerchief, and handed it to me. "So much sadness in you, Lhamo, so much anger. It is hard to imagine that there is all of this inside such a young lady as yourself. But the truth is that there is all of this and more inside of everyone." He was looking at me with his usual penetrating gaze that always made me feel a bit uncomfortable because it felt like he could see things about me that I couldn't see. After taking a moment to let my flare of emotions recede, he asked, "So why do you offer to quit training when it is obvious, even to you, that what you probably need most is more practice, not less."?"."

"I felt that it was the honorable thing to do and Megan told me that I could get kicked out of the *dojo* for what I have done."

"Ahhh, I see. Sensei Megan has a rather harsh opinion of the situation, I think." His sarcastic reference to Megan as a *sensei* suddenly had me worried that I had just gotten her into trouble. I decided to back-peddle.

"She didn't say it would happen, only that it could. She was actually pretty amazing. She took that wrestler guy out into the parking lot and talked to him. When they came back, he was apologizing to everybody. It was like he was high on happy pills or something. I have no idea how she did that."

Rinchen was smiling. *Sensei* or not, he was still a dad and you could tell that he was both miffed and impressed by the tale he was hearing of Megan's afternoon exploits. "Megan and Tripp have been training with me in the *dojo* since they were four. I used to drag them along mainly to keep an eye on them, but I had always hoped they would get into *Aikido*. They were doing diving rolls by the time they were five. Megan stopped coming to the *dojo* for a while when she was fourteen. That's when her mom and I got divorced. She was gone over a year, but eventually made her way back. She is actually very serious about it, maybe more serious than her brother, and he trains, as you know, pretty much every day. When they were younger, all of the stories about great masters and the teachings about ethics and behavior were, perhaps, a little too high-minded for them. Just the same, I would see them act out some of the stories in the park and I knew some of it was sticking. When Megan was little, we were watching a samurai movie on television and there was a highly dramatic moment in a duel when there was a clash and the famous Japanese actor, Toshiro Mifune, makes this miraculous cut that requires him to change grip over his head in the middle of *shomenuchi*. Megan was about seven at the time and was watching this. I was playing this video in slow motion to see how he moved his hands. After the move was complete, Megan said, 'Wow, daddy, nice cut, wasn't that a nice cut, daddy?' The other character in the movie gets killed and what little Megan notices is the technique. What a thing for a small American child to figure out. In their early teen years, they lost interest, but I made them teach the kids' classes so that they would stay connected. It has only been in the last couple of years that they have really come on strong."

You could tell he was very proud of them. "Why are they still brown belts if they have trained for so long?" I asked.

"What is in the color of a belt? I want them to be more concerned with the content of the character and the refinement of their skill. Belt colors can lead to all sorts of egotistical issues. This is particularly true with black belts. Some people think that they are their belts. More than one fellow has gotten a black belt and gone wandering through dark alleys thinking himself invincible only to get his tail kicked by a street punk. Belts are really only useful to distinguish internal rank and to help build decorum and respect for seniority. In most *dojos*, they would both be at least 2nd degree black belts, Tripp might even be 3rd degree, but I am going to keep them humble for a little while longer."

"Well, your daughter was miraculous today."

"I see, well, I will discuss these matters of *dojo* policy with her later, but I assure you that no one wants you to quit. To the contrary. You have taken to

Aikido very quickly, which is not unusual among women. Women tend to learn this art a bit faster than men, because men tend to have a hard time overcoming their natural tendencies toward aggression and force. Although, given your track record, I think you have some of our male students beat in the aggression department." I laughed a little, but it made me sad at the same time. Rinchen smiled.

"There are a couple of things that I want you to start thinking about. First, mistakes are your friends in that they tell you where to work on your life. We intentionally push ourselves to the point of mistake so that we know where to train. Second, you are getting very skillful, very quickly. We have taught you a hundred ways to potentially hurt people. With this comes a very serious responsibility. For every physical skill you have, you must have equal mental training to be wise enough to control your skill. This mental training is not very well developed in you at the moment and we are going to fix that. You are coming to class at least four times a week, am I right?"

"Yes, sometimes more. I love *Aikido*. And your son and daughter might have something to do with it too."

Rinchen laughed. "Yes, you have become nearly a second daughter in our house in just under a year. And for the record ... we love you too."

It is funny, when you are a weepy confused mess sitting in *seiza* at your master's feet and he tells you that he and his whole family love you, you would think that it would make you cheerful. For me, in that moment, I started blubbering uncontrollably and saying, "I love you too *Sensei*, I love you too. I love your whole family ...." I must have sounded like a slap-happy drunk. By now, Rinchen's *hachimaki* was soaking wet.

"Okay young lady, we need to get to work. First, I only want you to train in *Aikido* class twice a week for the next month, but you can certainly come to the *dojo* anytime you want. Practice your *jo katas* and *bokken* at home several times a week. I want you to come to the *dojo*, however, an hour early as many days as you can. I am going to teach you how to tame that wild horse of yours."

"Wild horse?"

"Your mind, Lhamo, your mind. It is a figure of speech. Everybody's mind, in the beginning is like a wild horse. It wanders after any random thought and sensation that crosses its path. It cannot sit still for even a minute. It is weak and shaky and we need to tame it so that it can sit perfectly still and is fully under your command."

"*Hai, Sensei*". This is the formal way of saying "yes" in a *dojo* using the Japanese word .

"I am going to give you another practice to do as well. We will train here before regular class, but I want you doing this every day. In Tibetan we call it the "Tronglen". It means "taking and sending". It is a form of meditation used all over the Buddhist world, but I have heard that even Jewish and Christian mystics use something similar to it. Basically, it is a breathing meditation, but when you inhale, you visualize yourself sucking in all of the negativity of the world as a cloud of black smoke. You then hold it in your center and transform it in your mind and exhale out a cloud of white smoke that carries blessings of peace and wellbeing to all sentient beings. You repeat this exercise until the entire world in your mind is purified. It is not particularly hard to do, but the effect that it can have on you and the people around you can be profound."

"*Hai, Sensei*," I said obediently.

"Alright then, go get your *gi* and get suited up. I think I will do a little horse taming tonight for the whole class while we are at it." I bowed and smiled and tried to hand him the soggy *hachimaki* . Rinchen nodded to me indicating that I could keep it. I resolved that I would take it home and clean it and return it to him the next time that I saw him. I ran out to my motorcycle to grab my *do-gi* bag. Tripp was already on the corner of the mat. It would be a push not to be late. There is something about nearly losing something, even if it is only in your mind, that makes you appreciate it so deeply when you find out that it will be with you a while longer. I think this is how mothers feel when they are reunited with lost children. When I stepped out into the humid St. Louis air to get my bag off the back of my motorcycle, Byakuren Dojo had never been more mine than in that moment. Rinchen was my *sensei* and the students there were truly my brothers and sisters. Maybe I was being a drama queen about it all, but spending a few hours thinking that I might lose my *dojo* only made it clear to me how much I had come to love the warrior life; how much I had come to love my version of *Budo*. I was going to get to keep my license to fly and I was already a mile off the ground.

Chapter Twenty-four: The Wild Horse

You don't realize how much crap runs through your mind until you try to have no thought at all. There is so much mental noise between our ears that we eventually don't even notice it. But when you tune in, you do notice, and for me it was disturbing.

Rinchen had us all sitting in our customary line with our hands folded in front of us and our breathing regulated in long, even doses of in and out. When you breathe properly, your body has plenty of oxygen and your body becomes relaxed while your mind rises to a heightened state of alertness. Though my mind was alert, my thoughts scampered around my brain like a herd of hyper chipmunks … thoughts of this, pictures of that, a song I couldn't get out of my head. It is amazing how random and ultimately useless it all is.

Rinchen took the class on a tour of our own minds. As I sat there, I wonder what it is like inside his head. Then I wonder what it was like inside Tripp's head. I imagined that Tripp could empty his mind completely and made a note to ask him. But wait! This was a thought. I was supposed to be letting thoughts go. Then another thought. I was going to forget to ask him. Crap! Another thought – I am not getting this right. Now there was music. I fought to push it out of my mind, but it not only got louder, it morphed into a really annoying tune nothing like what was on my iPod. The beat, that damned beat. Then I started thinking about how mad I was getting. This was impossible.

Rinchen took a deep breath and exhaled. Then he said, "Notice for some of you that your thoughts are almost like static. Notice how nervously your mind darts from object to object. Notice how your mind, without your permission, jumps at the slightest sound. The worst thing that you can do is fight it. Your mind is rebellious by nature and will resist your efforts to suppress it. Instead, let your thoughts simply pass out of your mind like floating clouds. Notice and then let them float away."

I tried this, and it worked a little bit, but some of my thoughts only floated an inch or two and then sat there taunting me. I had the thought that I need to purify my mind and instead of having my thoughts file out of my mind single file, I envisioned a pile of dog poop. Then I thought of Tripp with his shirt off. A little embarrassed by this thought forcing itself into my mind while I was in class trying to purify my mind, I fought against this mental picture and he was suddenly down to his boxers. Then he was kissing an old naked fat lady. Oh my god! How does this crap come into my mind? I panicked. "I am such a pervert", I thought. It got worse. I had to open my eyes. The sight of the *kamidana* and the students sitting in *seiza* was an immediate relief.

Rinchen was sitting in *seiza* with his eyes open but whatever he was looking at was only about two feet from his face and only in his mind. "Try to imagine a round sphere of light just off the end of your nose. It is simply a ball of white light floating there." I closed my eyes and tried to visualize a ball of light, but the mish mash of mind sludge was splattered everywhere. I would start to see a circle, but it was not light. I could get flutters of light, but no sphere. This was not working out at all.

"You cannot force the ball to appear, you must relax it into existence. You must invite it."

I relaxed a little and a fuzzy circular shape appeared and then faded away. I tried again, and this time I got a sphere for about a second and it then went away fading faster as I chased after it.

"Try an experiment, imagine an apple in front of you," Rinchen said without changing the focus of his eyes. I giggled. I could actually see a foggy version of an apple! Why was this easy and a ball of light so hard?

"Now visualize a baseball. See its shape and the threads on the ball." Without much effort, my apple morphed into a baseball with red threads. It was even clearer than the apple and I could get it to radiate a little bit of white. This was not so hard.

"Now turn you baseball into a ping pong ball, a pure white ping pong ball and keep it floating in front of your face." The baseball morphed into a smaller white ping pong ball, but this immediately began to fade and flicker in my mind. It was dim and wobbly. "Now light that ping pong ball up like a light bulb" commanded Rinchen. I got a slight bit of light to radiate out of my fuzzy ping pong ball and then it disappeared nearly entirely. After a second, Rinchen asked all of his students to come back and pay attention to him.

"Why is the ball of light so hard to get and the baseball relatively easy?" he asked. No one answered him.

"It is because you were trying to create the ball of light out of pure imagination. The apple and the baseball, and even the ping pong ball are familiar and can be sourced by your memory. Even though you are not remembering a specific baseball, per se, you are reaching into your experience to concoct the image. When you get good at this practice, you can visualize objects at will in front of you as if they were really there. That, however, takes a really strong and well trained mind." I started to wonder about that. I could see immediately how far away my own mind was from that ability. But a thought struck me: this was not impossible, it just took practice. You can build your mind just like you can build your body. Who knew?

In the last exercise, Rinchen had us focus on our imaginary baseballs. Then he said, "I am going to show you how fragile the human mind really is. Take a minute to get your mind settled and focused on your imaginary baseball." There was a minute of silence. "Now, no matter what happens, do not think about pink elephants." In a flash a blob of pink appeared in my mind, but as I returned my attention back to my baseball it disappeared. That was interesting. I had forced it out of my mind by focusing on something else. And then Rinchen said, "Do not see a plump pink elephant with a little pink tutu, doing the shimmy-shake in your mind. A plump pink elephant with a long pink trunk dancing in circles around your mind. Now there are two pink elephants and they are dancing in a line." There they were, two pink elephants and every time he added more description, they got clearer and clearer and I could not get them out of my mind to save my life. I could hear some of the students giggling. They were infected with pink elephants too.

"Come back into the room," Rinchen commanded. When I opened my eyes he was looking at me smiling. "Do you see how little it takes to take over your mind? I can put any message or picture I want into your thoughts and you can do little about it. Now imagine what television is doing to you. Imagine what the internet is doing to you. Imagine what the radio is doing to you. Why do you allow such unworthy things to take over your precious mind? Do you really need to carry a fast food jingle in your head all day? Can you see how polluted your mind really is?" I had never thought about it that way. I have watched hours and hours of TV and, even now I am going through withdraw from the Disney Channel. Only a few friends like Beth and Ack even know this about me and they both give me crap about it. They think that I should have graduated to more mature reality-based television like Project Supermodel or The House on cable. Up until the pink elephant exercise, I had not realized how pounded my brain was. No wonder I could not visualize a simple ball of light. Where, in all that clutter, would I put it?

Chapter Twenty-five: Eddie Manta

Eddie Manta was a pretty cool guy. He graduated from Metro as I was I finishing my junior year and was working as a designer in a tattoo shop downtown. He was one of the few friends that Tripp had that was not a member of the *dojo*. Eddie was a walking piece of art. He had tattoos everywhere. He was also into piercings. He had a ring in his eyebrow and tubes that stretched holes into his earlobes. He would have scared the crap out of most people in Westchester, but when you got to know him, you realized that not only were his looks deceiving, sometimes they were just plain wrong.

Tripp sometimes helped Eddie come up with new designs for tattoos. They both got into abstract designs and motifs rather than actual pictures of things, although Tripp sometimes drew pictures of wrathful Buddhist deities that Eddie turned into tattoo designs that his boss etched onto the skin of urban hipsters who had no idea what they were. The point was that they looked ferocious and apparently ferocious is a pretty big deal in tattoos. These unsuspecting customers had no idea that they were actually wearing pictures of the Buddha, symbols of universal compassion and the commitment to ultimate consciousness. I am pretty sure that getting a tattoo will not move you closer to enlightenment, although Rinchen says that if they connect to the image in their minds, it might influence them in a future life. I have to say, I have not bought into the reincarnation thing as of yet, but I am open to hearing what Rinchen and others have to say about it.

Unlike Tripp, Eddie was anything but laid back. In fact, he was totally hyper. He drove a black crotch rocket that had the back of the tailpipe worn off from riding wheelies. On a bike, Eddie was a menace. He always drove 20 miles per hour faster than was sane on the freeway and was known to ride "the suicide line", the line between his lane and oncoming traffic. Tripp said he had been riding for years and had never had an accident which was pretty hard to believe.

Tripp and I would run into him on Washington Avenue and he would come by Tripp's house from time to time. He hated samurai movies, but loved Japanese Anime, so at least when he made us take out the videos we were watching, there was something else to watch. I remember one Saturday night, Tripp and I were flopped on the couch waiting for Megan and Matt who were busy in the kitchen making pot stickers and fried rice when there was a banging at the door. Matt peeked through the peep hole and said half under his breath, "oh shit, here we go …." He opened the door and Eddie strode in. He was slightly heavier than Matt or Tripp largely because the only work-out that Eddie did was lifting a beer bottle. He always had a trucker wallet hanging half out of the back pocket of his jeans with a long steel chain draped across his hip that attached to his belt by way of a leather strap. His biking boots were beat to hell and the heels were worn at the back from dragging them across the pavement when he slowed down or took off on his bike. It was summer and already too hot for leather jackets. Eddie had a jacket that was truly badass with a skull wearing a crown of roses painted on the back. He had painted it himself. On this occasion, however, he was sporting only a wife-beater that showed off the beginning of a paunch.

As he made his entrance, he knuckle bumped Matt and gave a shout out to Megan in the kitchen. "Hello Edward," said Megan. She seemed genuinely happy to see him.

"Miss Laskowitz, you look ravishing as ever." Eddie then turned quickly to look at Matt and holding up his hands in mock submissiveness said, "I didn't mean nothing by that, big guy, just being friendly." Matt grinned and shook his head.

Eddie marched across the room and practically leaped onto the couch next to me immediately putting his arm around my shoulders over the top of Tripp's arm that had already claimed the territory. Eddie then started playing with the back of Tripp's hair as if he had only put his arm around me as a cover for a more elicit maneuver. "What are we watching, kids? Oh hell no, don't tell me it's another 101 Ninjas of Death movie. You guys have got to get out more." There was no use resisting. He was just going to keep making fun of the movie until we turned it off or put something else on, so Tripp found the remote and clicked over to cable. We both pretended that we were suddenly really interested in a do-it-yourself home make-over program hoping that Eddie would get the message that we were punishing him. Eddie put his head on my shoulder but kept twirling Tripp's hair. "Ah, drywall, much better," he said. What a goof.

Megan set out the feast on the coffee table in front of the couch. Matt brought plates and chop sticks. Eddie took a single chop stick and skewered a pot sticker making as big a show as he could out of neglecting the proper use of the foreign utensils. Megan brought a pot of green tea and poured a cup for me. I had developed quite a fondness for green tea. Rinchen says it has many health benefits. I like it because it seems to calm me down and does not have a particularly strong taste.

I reached across the coffee table with my chop sticks to snatch a pot sticker and Eddie gently ran his fingers over my forearm. "Look at all that empty space," he said, "the things we could draw on that." Tripp smirked although I don't know why; he did not have any tattoos, that I knew of anyway. "I don't do tatts," I said as if this was a deeply committed moral decision. The truth was that I had never really thought about it. There were a few girls at school who had them. They were usually very small, on an ankle or just above the bikini line. I had heard that Rita Montrose had a tramp-stamp on the top of her ass crack, but this was an unconfirmed report from Ack and, therefore, highly unreliable. Even if Ack had the opportunity to see the top of Rita Montrose's butt, he would be too polite to look at it.

"You ought to let me draw something for you. Now that you are an ass-kicking-*dojo*-biker-chick, you cannot let all that virgin skin go to waste."

"I don't think so," I replied.

"Aw, why not? It is just a drawing. We can even put it on you in henna so that you can try it out . In about a month, it will wear off." This actually sounded fun, but then I thought about my parents. My mom would crap herself if she even thought that I was thinking about getting a tattoo.

I remember once stopping by a coffee shop with my mom and the barista, a girl a bit older than me, but not by much, handed us our drinks over the counter. When she stretched out her arms, I noticed that she was covered in tattoos from her elbows up. I then noticed that she must have had them on her chest too because you could see little patches of blue and red shapes just around the neckline of her shirt. As we turned away to find seats, my mom whispered to me "she is going to deeply regret that."

"What?"

"Those tattoos. They may seem like a fun thing to do now, but if she ever hopes to get a job anywhere other than a coffee shop, those things are going to really get in her way."

"A lot of people these days get tattoos, what's the big deal?'

"Everybody goes through a rebellious phase of some sort. There is nothing wrong with that. I know that I did. Of course, in my day it was mostly just teased-up hair and multiple piercings in your ears. Those are things you can take off. But a tattoo is forever."

"I have heard you can get them removed."

"Not when they are that big."

"Well, there are so many people with them these days that I think that most employers will understand."

"No they won't. No large company that I know of will hire someone who looks like a comic book. It is too hard to take a person like that seriously. If you have a choice between a marked or unmarked employee, you are going to pick the unmarked one." This suddenly bothered me. Why should something like tattoos automatically exclude you from being hired for a job if you are otherwise qualified? What right does an employer have to judge your appearance like that?

"It doesn't seem fair," I said after taking a second to mull over the injustice of it.

"Who says life is fair," my mom said sipping her coffee. "You are being judged by your appearance all the time."

This revelation landed, for some reason, with a particular crash. She was right. That was the reason for the whole shopping exercise at the mall. There was a difference, although sometimes quite subtle, between styles and brand names. If your parents could afford it, you wore clothing from the top designers. If they couldn't, you wore copies. But at school, "poser-wear" could drop the value of your personal brand. Wow. I remember thinking in that moment how incredibly shallow and stupid that was. Then it dawned on me. This was everywhere. At school, appearances helped to determine how popular you were and who your friends were likely to be. If you were black, you had to play into the gangsta role because that was one of the only cool roles available for black kids in lily-white Westchester – even if you were a musical genius like Kwame Johnson. You had to play the game or stay outside the loop. I thought to myself, as I sat there with my mom, that this truly sucked.

I nearly got a tattoo after my moment of awakening at the coffee shop. The problem was that I was pretty sure that I would get in deep trouble if I got one. Furthermore, what I felt like saying at that moment was "stop fucking judging me" and having that permanently etched into my skin was never going to happen. But it was tantalizing. To put that one thing on your body that is your own personal symbol, your brand, you shouting what you have to say to a world that is busy processing you was suddenly quite appealing. It would be worth it just to see the looks on their faces at school when I came walking down the hall with a tattoo on my shoulder of a hand flipping everyone the bird. Wouldn't that be something?

My real problem with tattoos is that I could never think of anything so definitive and timeless to say that I would want it permanently attached to my body. Thinking back to just a year or two ago, what would I have had tattooed on me then? A butterfly, a unicorn, a picture of my favorite boy-band singer? Yikes! To have to live with a reminder of my immaturity forever would be deeply annoying. Could you see reading your grandchildren a bedtime story and them asking who the droopy guy tattooed to your shoulder was?

I don't think that people using their bodies as art is foolish, it is just that if you think that what you come up with today will not utterly bother the crap out of you later, then it seems to me that you are asking for trouble. That is the part that is so shortsighted about tattoos. Eddie Manta is nineteen years old and while I sometimes doubt that he will ever be mature, he is certainly going to change. And yet he will be stuck with the graffiti of his youth to remind him always of what an idiot he was back in the day.

Maybe if I was devoutly religious I would have a crucifix or a Star of David tattooed over my heart. Kwame Johnson has his parents' names tattooed on the sides of his neck. I kind of like the gesture of respect that that is, but "Henry" and "Jeanie" on my neck? I don't think so.

Tattoos are like epitaphs for the living. They are those ultimate statements of identification that need to be well thought out. Epitaphs are written for you by people who knew you and maybe saw you more objectively then you saw yourself. They are sometimes complete bullshit. Like the girl who kills herself because she hates her parents but winds up buried under a rock that says "Loving Daughter". An epitaph can be an apology, a denial or a complete fantasy depending on what suits the needs of whomever gets that final say. What would my parents put on my stone? "Here lies Madison Albright, a girl once filled with promise and possibility but threw it all away on motorcycles and martial arts." That is the rip-off of epitaphs: somebody else gets the last word about you.

But a tattoo cannot be blamed on your surviving family. It is all about you and you are solely responsible for its content. But when you are seventeen what is there to say about who you are that is worthy of being forever carved into your skin? I have no idea who I am going to be or how I am going to turn out. I am, for sure, a work in progress. What? Am I going to get Tripp's name tattooed on my butt inside a picture of a heart with an arrow stuck in it? I really love Tripp, but a year from now I am going off to college and then what? As Eddie sat there contemplating all of the cool stuff he could draw on my skin, I realized that I needed to be a blank slate for a while longer.

But it was an intriguing thought: if you had to make an eternal statement about yourself, what would it be?

Chapter Twenty-six: Dojo Moan

By early October, I had been in the *dojo* for a year. I had trained like a maniac during the summer and was getting pretty good at most of it, especially ukemi. I was break-falling which meant that no one in the *dojo* had to go easy on me anymore. A break-fall is a pretty creepy thing when you are first learning how to do it. Normally, most of *Aikido* is about re-routing an attacker's energy so that you can control his movement with mechanics, pain or both. This usually leaves him on the ground with you pinning him by bending his arm in directions that are not natural. To avoid getting hurt when you are being tossed around like a rag doll on the mat, you are first taught to roll out of a throw. The *nage* (pronounced "na-gay"), the person throwing, will bend a wrist or an elbow to redirect the energy and this forces the *uke* (pronounced "oo-kay"), the person being thrown, to try to get out from under the pain or escape injury in some other way. Flipping over your own arm is one of many ways to do this. Initially, this looks like the rolls you are taught on the first day, but requires the *nage* to let go of you once you start rolling. If the *nage* intends to pin you, however, you do not get to roll out. Instead, you are flipped up into the air and you land flat on your back. In a real fight, this would knock the wind out of most anyone, if they did not know how to fall. In the case of a trained *Aikidoka*, however, you are taught how to manipulate your landing while in mid-air and to distribute the shock of crashing onto the ground by slapping the ground just before you land. The slap transfers as much excess kinetic energy as possible into the ground reducing the force of the landing when the rest of you catches up to your hand. It looks much more dramatic than it actually is.

167

On a training mat, the slap-out combined with your body hitting the mat makes a large banging sound. The "slap-thunk-slap-thunk" sound of students practicing this controlled method of slamming onto the floor is what the heartbeat of the *dojo* sounds like.

Sensei Rinchen never tells you when it is your day to learn break-falling. Usually, he has his students practice the slap-out while rolling, a way of simulating the mechanics of a break-fall, for a month or two before you he launches them into one. The difference between the two techniques is that when you are thrown into a roll, the *nage* lets go of your hand or arm once you are airborne. In a breakfall, however, the *nage* does not let go and maintains her connection to you as she slams you into the ground. You train and train on rolling out of a hold until one day he calls you up to the front of the class to demonstrate a technique and lets you have it. It is probably a good thing that he doesn't tell you it's coming. The last thing you want to do when someone is pile-driving you into the mat is think. He lets you think that you know what you are doing, which you do, and then "WHAM"!

His teaching technique on this is flawless. He knows that the student will be perfectly safe as long as they are not afraid and starts over-thinking the situation. And that's how it happened to me. One day he called me up to the front of class to demonstrate a technique. I attacked him; he threw me, which by the way, is an experience similar to being shot out of a cannon, and as I started into my roll I realized that I was being kept on the leash. BANG! There it was -- a perfect break-fall. I just so happened that my first break-fall didn't happen on the mat in the *dojo*. My introduction to the violent use of gravity was on the grass out in the park. It had been dry for weeks and that St. Louis clay was as hard as concrete. When I hit the ground, I laughed.

"What is so funny?" Rinchen asked.

"It doesn't hurt," I said still amazed at what I had just done.

"Good then, you can do it again." For the next several minutes, Sensei Rinchen slammed me onto the ground over and over. Joggers passing by stopped to watch. Each time I slapped out with a "whack". After about the fifth or sixth break-fall, my earlier statement about it not hurting was starting to turn into a lie. Rinchen did not stop. Again and again, he flipped me onto the ground. When he could see that I was starting to really feel it, he bowed and instructed the class to practice what he had just shown. And that was it. After that, I was certified to take a full beating. I was allowed to start staying over for the advanced class and while most of the advanced students took it easy on me at first, there were no holds barred.

They say that "practice makes perfect". Rinchen says that "practice makes permanent". What I began to notice was that the more I practiced, the better I got at something that most people cannot do. This opened a huge door for me. I could see from that point on that I could do anything if I was willing to invest the time to develop the skill. This is how concert pianists are made. This is how pro-athletes are made. This is how doctors and lawyers are made. Technique, practice, sweat. It is a very simple formula. Rinchen says that it is the key to enlightenment and the secret to a happy life. It is all about skill.

Skill comes at a cost. I have never had so many bruises in my life as I had gotten that first summer in the park. By the time we moved back inside in the fall, the mat felt like diving into a pile of marshmallows by comparison. After a couple of weeks, however, we were all missing the park. One of the best things about rock-hard ground is that it teaches you how to fall softly. It teaches you to be precise. It teaches you to eke out perfection.. Precision is the difference between landing from a throw without injury and losing a ligament in your elbow. The ground is a great teacher. It shows you exactly what a good landing is by putting pain everywhere that it is not. The seniors in the *dojo* had always said that the park would toughen me up. I now knew what they meant.

My relationship to pain has completely changed. When I was a little girl, I would cry when my mom tried to comb the tangles out of my hair. Now I had grown men throwing me onto the ground and this was my new idea of a good time. My mother had been particularly concerned about me when the summer had gotten underway. I was coming home from training sore and bruised. Sometimes I had cuts and scratches. When you think of the thousands of skin care products that you see in commercials, not one of them is designed to help grow skin back onto your hip after you have gotten a raspberry from being slid across the ground in a break-fall gone wrong. In fact, you see the occasional sports remedy, like heat packs and what not, being marketed for women, but they are always runners or tennis players. What is up with that? You always see the chick with the nice legs, perfect running shoes and a sports bra as the image of a woman athlete. And yet, I saw on the internet that there are women hockey and rugby teams. Why don't they make commercials for those us who actually get slammed? It is as if our culture is afraid to see women in a fight.

I remember in history class that we studied the Israeli Army in the 1960s. They put women in combat. I remember being told about the debate over it. Some were afraid that women combat troops would weaken the fighting ability of the men because they would always be worried about the women or would freak out at the sight of a woman killed in battle. As it turned out, the women in the Israeli military were ferocious. Young women my age in Israel are expected to be soldiers and they are expected to kick-ass. There is something attractive about a culture that sees women in this way.

In the *dojo,* I am not coddled. It is the only place that I have been in my life where I have known myself as a true equal to boys and men. I get my ass kicked just like everyone else. I like being known as powerful. I like being known as potentially dangerous. And I really like being taken seriously. On the mat, my *dojo* brothers and sisters know that I can take them out and they respect that. They respect me. Not just because I can hurt people but because I have walked the hard mile. I have taken the beating. I just cannot put into words what it means to be a member of this kind of tribe.

I like the fact that I am no longer a second class citizen in a world that, while admittedly much improved from my grandmother's day, still expects girls to take a seat behind boys in all things but menstruating. I am beginning to resent the expectation that I be soft while boys get to be hard. My dad says, however, that boys these days are becoming softer. What he really means is that they are less assertive and confrontational. I fail to see what that has to do with gender. A wimp is a wimp, penis or none. I used to think that being assertive or confrontational was a sign of power. It is actually kind of ignorant when you think about it. Rinchen says that aggression is what people do when they run out of wisdom. It is not the toughness that I admire, now that I think about it. It is the courage. That's it. It is all about conquering fear.

I have a friend at school, his name is Jeffery Willis. He is the only openly gay guy at Westchester High School where that is anything but a safe thing to be. Some people would say he is a wimp in that he is effeminate and hardly a fighter. But the truth is that it takes more guts to be him than it does to be anyone else in school. His strength is in his persistence to be himself regardless of what people say about him or do to him. He has been the victim of more than one senseless act of hostility. He has had his locker painted pink. He has been jumped in the hallway and dragged into the bathroom and given a swirly in the toilet. He has endured every attempt to humiliate him and yet there he is – unshakably himself. He is a warrior – a real warrior.

Megan says that there is one rule that her father always held her to: "thou shalt not take crap from a boy". She says that he never let Tripp try to assert male dominance between them. Tripp benefitted, too, from this lesson. He had a twin sister, the very copy of himself, but in the other gender flavor. Tripp says that when he looks at Megan he sees the female version of himself. They are by no means gender-bending twins. Tripp is what I call a "real man".

He is smart, strong and thoughtful. He is artistic and patient. One thing he is not is macho. Megan is confident and strong too. She is loving and yet she would fight to the death for her family and her friends. They are not even close to the same and yet, they are clearly made from the same mold.

That is the cool thing about the *dojo*. Every personality is valued and the only roles that are expected are those of the *Aikido* tradition. Senior students are expected to take responsibility for the junior students. Everyone is expected to be flawless in their manners and their courtesy to others. Everyone is expected to train hard and evolve. If someone is going through a tough time, it is not seen as a sign of personal weakness or fault, but as a training opportunity for everyone. It is a never-ending exploration of what can be learned from everyday occurrences.

By the time October had brought cooler weather to St. Louis, all thoughts were on the upcoming test for rank. At Byakuren Dojo everyone starts out as a Gokyu, or fifth rank. I was a Yonkyu, fourth rank, by the time I started my senior year at Westchester High. I was told by Megan that I needed to prepare for the *Sankyu* test. This was the test that separated the beginners from the advanced students. To pass this test you have to know all of the five basic technique groups, be able to do all of the rolls and falls, be able to perform the long and short *jo katas* (exercise forms), and work your way through what is called the *Seven Suburi* , or cutting exercises with a wooden *bokken* (practice sword). The last part of the test is an exercise that all younger students dread. It is called Ping-Pong in our *dojo*. The student being tested stands in the middle of a ring of senior students. Seniors take turns, in no particular order, pushing their *kohai* in any direction they want. The *kohai* must use the appropriate roll, front, back or sideways to escape the force of the push. During this test, the seniors can unexpectedly throw the *kohai* into a break-fall. The object for the *kohai* is to stay loose and take whatever comes. For most students, it is not the rolls and falls that are the problem, it is the conservation of energy and loss of oxygen. You are not allowed to quit, even if you think you are going to throw up or pass out. That is actually the point. Ping-Pong is not testing your falling technique – it is a test of your mind to see how far the *kohai* can push herself without giving up.

The weeks that precede a test are intense. Tests only happen twice a year and you do not want to miss your chance to advance. It is not the rank that matters, but testing determines what you get to learn. The higher you are, the closer to the good stuff you get. I really, really wanted to train in the advanced class. I had been watching these classes for months and I wanted to be part of them in the worst way. The classes before a test are hard. Everyone stays after class to train even harder. It is tradition that your *sempai*, the senior student responsible for bringing you into the *dojo*, will work with you to help you get ready. It is considered a deep embarrassment for a *sempai* if they tell the *sensei* that a student is ready to test and the student fails. It is the *sempai* that has to shoulder the blame for the *kohai*'s failure. In the *dojo*, students do not fail, only teachers do.

Megan and Tripp were training their *kohai* to death. Every night I would come home completely exhausted. Every morning I was taking six ibuprofen tablets before class and six more before I got to the *dojo*. One of the many useful little tidbits of knowledge that you learn in the *dojo* is that ibuprofen becomes an anti-inflammatory when you take 800 milligrams or more. Every serious student at our *dojo* keeps an economy-sized bottle in their *do-gi* bags along with an awesome camphor liniment that you can buy at most Chinese variety stores called "Tiger Cream". This stuff smells like the stuff my mom used to rub on my chest when I had a cold and it really helps relieve muscle aches. During test season, everyone in the *dojo* pays frequent visits to the Chinese variety stores. Some buy ginseng tonics, others buy herbal teas that supposedly help your concentration. Everyone has their own system.

My routine was Megan's routine. I got up in the morning and stretched for fifteen minutes. I showered and then had a breakfast of oatmeal and fruit. During test season, I gave up most of my bad eating habits. No breakfast bars and certainly no fast food. I had pretty much given up soda anyway by the fall of my senior year opting for water or tea when it was available. I trained so much that I could technically eat anything, but I was starting to get sensitive to the effects of sugar and had cut most of it out of my diet. I still ate starches like rice and potatoes and probably needed to because I was burning hundreds of calories a night during training. Some *dojo* people were vegetarians, but not me. Tripp said that meat helped with muscle development, but was bad karma and that I should eventually try to get off of it, if I could. I was eating less meat, except during test season.

I went to school, studied on my lunch hour because study time was getting harder and harder to come by. I had even arranged my schedule at school to give myself a study hall that helped me stay current with my school work. Parties and socializing were out. I was not even hanging out with Megan and Tripp after class. Megan made me go home and rest. When I could pull it off, I took long hot baths and let my muscles try to recover.

My parents took my schedule in stride although my mom was getting worried. She noticed the bruises on my arms and would sometimes give me back rubs when I had had a particularly hard class. She was mostly concerned about my hands. It is a rule in the *dojo* that you must keep your fingernails cut short. This is to prevent your fellow students from being cut or scratched by them. Your hands get sore after practice and mine were no longer the soft, well-hydrated girlie hands that I had once worked so hard to maintain. My mom even remarked one evening while she was rubbing down my arms that I had "man hands." I laughed. Alrighty then.

I have to say that by the time that test week came around, I was fully obsessed. There was nothing in my life except the test. School was just something that I had to wade through on my way to the *dojo*. Meals became fuel for the test. Every waking thought become a visualization of technique. I was standing in the lunch line in the middle of the week working through *jo* kata in my mind, or so I thought, but apparently I was working through the motions physically. I heard a voice from behind me, "it must be test week". It was Beth. The semester was nearly half over and I had hardly seen her at all. I was startled out of my concentration and a little bit embarrassed that my practice had leaked out of my mind and into my hands in front of everyone. "Yeah, how do you know about test week?"

"Megan told me."

"Really, you hang out with Megan?"

"I have Calculus with her and we sit together. She is my news source for all things LMAO," Beth said with a grin and perhaps just a little bit of hurt in her eyes.

"I am sorry about that Beth, really I am. I have gotten into this whole *dojo* thing up to my ears. I really, really like it and can't seem to help myself."

"I know. We all find our thing and move on. We were all destined to scatter after this year anyway." I could see that her subtle indication of hurt was blossoming in to sadness. It made me sad too. Beth used to be the center of my world. We grew up together. We explored what we thought life was together. We shared notes on boys and music, clothing and food. We used to text each other constantly. Now half the time, I didn't even know where my cellphone was.

"You know I love you B, really I do." Beth smiled, "I know and I love you too." Now I was really sad and I was pretty sure that if she said one more thing, I was going to burst into tears and wreck my whole warrior-chick mystique in front of the whole school. She hugged me and whispered into my ear as she did, "I can see how happy this makes you and I have only ever wanted you to be happy." That was it. I was mush. I held her tight as the tears poured out of my eyes. I was trying desperately not to make any audible sounds of crying, but I began to shake and I could feel the ratings and evaluations go out over the Gossipedia in a flurry of texts. One idiot even took my picture on her cellphone camera. Great.

I composed myself and resolved that I needed to put the test aside and have lunch with my old friend. That is the great thing about Beth, she can disappear off my radar for months, but when we finally get back together, our friendship picks up right where we left off. Well, almost.

Things had been changing for Beth too. She was applying to colleges. She had crushed the SAT test and was looking at the Ivy League schools. She said her mom wanted her to go to Wellesley, but that she really wanted to go to a school that had men. Beth had always liked math and art and was thinking about being an architectural engineer. She said she was thinking about Cornell, but had heard that they had the highest suicide rate of any college. She was thinking about Vassar if she could get in, or maybe Duke. She really wanted to live in Atlanta, which made Emory a possibility. So many schools, so little time. This was all pretty impressive as far as I was concerned. My parents had started to bug me about getting my college applications in too. I was really conflicted about this. I kind of wanted to stay in Missouri so I could continue to train at the *dojo*. My parents really wanted me to go to school out of state to learn a thing or two about independence. A year ago, I was all for heading east or west to school, but now it seemed like I would have to give up my whole life. Tripp had not decided where he wanted to go and Megan had already applied at University of California, Irvine, but was considering Washington University in St. Louis so that she could stay near her mom. Rinchen was against this idea, but there was no telling Megan how to manage her relationship to her mother.

Thinking of Beth moving hundreds of miles away seemed incredibly unnatural. Since the day I started riding my bike over to her house, she had always been near. Even with my new center of gravity at the *dojo*, there was something reassuring about knowing that Beth was always near. I had often felt guilty about drifting away from her, but had the consolation that she was never more than a few blocks away. I guess it was unfair to console myself with her nearness when I was putting so much distance between us. But that was the thing about Beth for me. What she meant to me was always there even when she wasn't. Would that always be true? When she had become some famous building designer in New York City, would she still mean anything to me? Would I still be comforted to know that the world did not completely suck as long as she was on the planet? I was missing her already and she was sitting right in front of me.

"B, you are awesome. A lot of girls would be trashing me up and down for ignoring you like I have."

"I am not a lot of girls and while I might do that to someone I don't really care about, I could never do that to you. You are my best friend and that is how it is going to be."

Best friend. Who was my best friend these days? I spent most of my time with Tripp and Megan. They certainly knew Lhamo the best. They were helping build Lhamo, if the truth was told. I decided that having a best friend was no longer useful to me. There were people I really, really loved and others that I liked. There were a few that I disliked and one or two I despised. Beth would always be in the "really, really loved" category.

I walked with Beth to her locker after lunch. She wished me luck on my test. "Text me when you know how it came out," she said with a smile. I promised that I would and then I got a better idea.

"I want you to be there."

"I will be, you know I will be thinking about you.," she said almost like she were my mom.

"No, I mean, I want you to be there to watch. You were there when I started this whole thing. I really, really want you to come to the *dojo* and be there while I get my ass kicked. You might even find it amusing." I was getting excited about this idea. Beth had never been interested in doing *Aikido*, but I had never asked her if she wanted to watch. I really wanted to share this with her and it did not feel right to do this without her.

"When?"

"Saturday night, six o'clock and if I am still alive, we can got out of sushi afterwards, my treat." This was not as enticing an offer for her as I thought it was, although sushi was tipping the scale in my favor. Then Beth broke into a big smile. "I will be there." I hugged her and then, realizing that I was going to be late for class, skipped down the hall to get my books.

Rinchen says that when you are faced with difficulty, it is helpful to surround yourself with things that give you power. When I used to get stressed out, I used to surround myself with ice cream and that made me feel better although I am pretty sure that I never got much power out of it. But as I was walking to my class, I realized that my life was like a constellation of stars.

There was an alignment to them. I had always had a vague intuition about this. Before the fight with Nick, life broke down into several important key ingredients: school, home, girlfriends, boys, clothes, hair. If these things were all working at the same time, life was good. Anyone of them, however, could throw my universe out of whack. If several of these things were screwed up at once, my life would suck.

My constellation was different now. There was mind, body, technique, motorcycles, Tripp and Megan, Rinchen and, at the moment, Beth. These were the sources of my being. These were the batteries to my flashlight. And they were all going to be at the *dojo* on Saturday night.

Chapter Twenty-seven: When There Is Nothing Left To Give

On test day, everyone shows up on time. Everybody has a clean gi. Everybody is quiet. The manners in the *dojo* are formal and impeccable. You can feel the nervous anxiety of the junior students as they get dressed and then go out to sweep the mat. The seniors are much more focused. They have learned to take all of their energy and focus it so that it could dance on the head of a pin.

Tripp, Matt, Megan, Thor and Tracy were already on the mat sweeping. Normally, seniors don't sweep the mat because it is tradition that *kohai* never let a senior do such menial work. It is considered dishonorable to allow a senior to clean. But there are times when you cannot take the broom from them and test night was one of those nights.

I had ridden my bike down to the *dojo*. It was getting cooler in St. Louis; certainly leather weather. I did not see Beth when I got there and sent her a quick text to see if she was still planning to come. I got a rapid reply: "OMW." I have no idea why this was reassuring, but it was.

Old Bob stepped onto the mat in his very worn, nearly ratty looking *gi* and hakama. The dressing rooms were crowded. Attendance at tests was obligatory. I got changed into my *gi* as quickly as possible, bowed to the *kamidana* and stepped on to the mat. The *dojo* had been cleaned thoroughly and everyone was quietly stretching or practicing their rolls in a distant corner. Tripp was off on the *joseki* end of the mat standing perfectly straight with his hands clasped. He was shaking his hands up and down. This is an exercise called "soul shaking" that helps build internal energy and free the mind. Megan was stretching in a hurdler's stride.

As I went through my own routine, I heard the front door open and my dad walked in. Holy crap! What was *he* doing here? He smiled and took a seat in the foyer area. I tried to focus past this unexpected turn of events. I had told my parents about the test, but had not specifically invited them. I did not think that it was that big of a deal and figured that it would freak my mom out. I guess she thought so too because she apparently had not come with my dad to watch. A few minutes later, the door opened again. It was Rinchen. He always shows up late on test days. I am not sure why, but it is as if he deliberately wants to keep his students in a state of anxiety. That is the white-belt's view of it, at least. Within just a few minutes, Rinchen was dressed and had stepped out into the foyer area to introduce himself to his guests. There were several civilians who had come to watch. Out of the corner of my eye, I saw him bow and shake my father's hand. I heard my dad say his own name and Rinchen suddenly became quite animated glancing out on the mat at me only briefly. A minute later, the front door opened again and Beth walked in. She was as surprised to see my dad as I was and gave him a big hug. Rinchen bowed to her too and shook her hand and asked her to take a seat. The stars were aligned.

Unlike a regular class, Rinchen lead the warm-up himself. He sat in *seiza* in front of the *kamidana* and clapped in. He turned briskly to his students and bowed and spoke the traditional word of thanks in unison with the class - *onegaishimasu*! Within seconds the class was on its feet and working its way through the traditional stretching exercises. Rinchen took his time letting the class stretch thoroughly. He was going to make sure everyone was completely ready. There was a sudden clap of hands and everyone raced to the end of the mat to start *ukemi* practice. One after another we rolled across the mat, first forward, then backwards. Another clap of hands and the class formed a line and the newest student went out to the center of the mat curled up on his knees to be the first human hurdle. One by one, the class flew over the obstacle and returned to the back of the line. With each round another white belt was added as the class flew through the air over them, rolling and then popping to their feet. I stayed focused on the exercise and tried to ignore my dad and Beth. Why had I invited them? Oh yeah, I wanted to show off. That was a mistake. The distraction was going to get me killed or at least embarrassed if I did not watch it.

There were five human hurdles when it was once again my turn to fly, I dashed from my starting point and ran toward them as fast as I could. I was airborne, then ducked my head, rolled and popped into the air. In my exuberance, however, I had pushed it too hard and when I hit the mat I was off balance and nearly did a face-plant. In my panic, I ducked into a second roll and popped to my feet like it was all part of the plan. My goof, however, was not lost on Rinchen and he called out to me, "are you alright , Lhamo?"

"*Hai, Sensei*" I responded pretending that I had not just made an ass of myself by trying to show off.

As I got back in line I saw both Tripp and Megan suppressing their amusement. I have since found that if you find yourself trying to do something difficult in front of people important to you, that it is best to release your inner idiot early so that you can get down to business. With all hope of looking good shot to hell, I was now free to focus.

Until the night of the test, I had done diving rolls over five people, but never more than that. When it came around to my turn at six, I decided that tonight was the night. I took off, dove and tucked into my roll feeling myself graze over the last person hunched in the now tightly packed row of human obstacles. The landing, was perfect and I popped to my feet without as much as wobble. There were only a handful of students still in the line. The others did not attempt to jump over this many people and were sitting in *seiza* on the mat waiting for the end of the exercise. I got back in line for seven. Tripp took off and flew over the seven crouched students like a raven. Then Megan took off and her *hakama* fluttered as she cleared the obstacle. Thor was next, then Matt and then Tracy each sailing into their rolls with what looked like considerable ease. They were all brown belts, except Tracy. She should have been a brown belt, but had missed the last test. The rumor was that she was not that interested in testing.

Next in line was Ty Lauer. Ty was testing for *sankyu* with me that night and was also pushing the envelope in this exercise. He took off, but his foot slipped on the mat. He tried to recover, but as he approached the seven crouching students, he did not have enough speed to make it and had too much speed to stop. At the last second, he dove into the air, but had deliberately aimed to the side. He flew over the first few students until he found some clear mat at their feet and crashed into a heap having spared the hurdles from having to absorb his crash landing. This was the honorable thing to do, but it came at a cost. As he got to his feet he was holding his shoulder. Shoulders are always at risk during rolls. One little miscalculation and you can crunch your shoulder and even tear your rotator cuff or worse. Every *Aikidoka* had crunched a shoulder at least once. It usually happens early in your training and for some people, it can put an end to their *Aikido* training altogether.

Rinchen called out to Ty, "are you okay, Mr. Lauer?"

"*Hai, Sensei,*" replied Ty, but he was unconvincing. Rinchen looked at Tripp and with a slight nod instructed him to check Ty's shoulder. Rinchen then looked at me as I was getting ready to take off. I could see that he was trying to decide whether I was ready to attempt seven. Too late. I took off. As I dashed across the mat, I let go of all of my thoughts. I let go of Rinchen's hesitation at letting me take the leap. I forgot about my dad and Beth in the foyer. I forgot about the students crouched in a row. I don't remember running, but I remember sucking in as much air as I could and heaving it out of my lungs in forceful bursts. I did not have to adjust my steps as I placed my foot nearly in the ribs of the first student in the row . I could feel the firmness of the mat under my feet. It felt like it was shooting power up my legs as I dove into the air. And then, I was flying. I saw the last white belt pass underneath me, but I still had plenty of air. I lowered my head and my arm and ducked into tight roll and sucked in a deep inhale of breath. As I rolled I felt my feet come underneath me and, once again, the mat under my feet seemed to shoot me into the air. Oh, how I love to fly! I heard the thump of my feet hit the mat as I nailed the landing. A lightness passed through my whole body. I did not want the feeling to end. I just stood there for a moment taking it all in. I was at peace. I was in love. I just was.

When I turned around I could see all the faces staring at me, some with their mouths open. Tripp's eyes were bulging out of his head and Megan was nodding and smiling. I was standing only a foot or two from the far wall. I had cleared the hurdle with several feet to spare – the distance of nine, maybe ten crouching students. I had nearly shot myself through the wall. At first, I did not realize what I had done. Rinchen was staring at me intently as if to take in what he had just seen. Beth's mouth was wide open and my dad looked like he was trying to decide whether to laugh or cry. I shook it off. I didn't want to know what it meant. I simply wanted to burn the feeling of it into my mind.

The students took their places in order of rank at the back edge of the mat to leave plenty of room for those who were being tested. Those testing for *yonkyu* went first. Most of their test consisted of rolling and a few basic throws. They did most of this together. Then came my test. There were supposed to be five of us testing that night, but Ty's shoulder was too messed up for him to continue. With only four of us remaining, the test went quicker because we could work in even pairs. *Sensei* put us through the rolling test quickly and then had us throw each other in break-falls. You could hear the bang, bang, bang of the break-falls as we each took turns slamming each other onto the mat. Then we were each assigned a senior student and instructed us to show three variations of each major category of throws that we knew. Megan had prepared me well for this part of the test and had insisted that I know five variations instead of just three. The extra training over the summer paid off in that my techniques were natural and well-practiced as I went through the routine.

The *sankyu* test was considerably longer than the *yonkyu* test. I was getting tired, but Rinchen was relentless. After what seemed like an hour, but was probably only fifteen or twenty minutes we came to the part that I was dreading: Ping-Pong. I had seen this exercise done many times before and had even practiced it in class a couple of times. The last time I had seen it was at my *yonkyu* test and two people passed out doing it and a third ran off the mat to throw up. I did not care about passing out so much, but I most definitely did not want to hurl. Getting sick to your stomach on the mat happens rarely, but it does happen. There is an unspoken rule that if you feel like you have to barf and cannot get off the mat in time, you are supposed to open your *gi* and vomit on yourself without getting any on the mat. If you hurl on the mat, class has to be stopped and the mat has to be thoroughly cleaned and disinfected. No one wants to be responsible for such junior varsity move as that.

I was third of four to do the exercise. The first guy, Raj Gupta, went for several minutes before finally being thrown into a wicked break-fall and passing out. The second, Becky Danwick, was sucking air so hard that it looked like she might hurt herself. Rinchen made her stop and then start again. She nearly started crying when he made her do the exercise a second time. Then it was my turn. It is funny that when you have to stand up and get tossed around the *dojo* like a rag doll in front of your friends and your father that the pain or the difficulty is not the first thing you worry about; it is not looking like a fool that creates the most panic.

I stood up and took my place in the center of a circle of *hakamas*. Tripp, Megan, Matt, Thor, Tracy, Old Bob and a couple of others were looking at me with just a little too much glee and it was making me really uncomfortable. Rinchen shouted *hajime* (pronounced "ha-ji-may"), or "begin." From behind me, I felt a violent shove into my shoulder blades and I fell forward into a roll. No sooner had I gotten to my feet, then Megan gave me a shove backward by slamming the butts of her hands into my shoulders. I started to fall backwards but rotated mid-fall into a forward roll. This was a trick she had taught me. Forward rolls take less energy than backward rolls and you can turn nearly any fall, so long as a person is not holding onto part of you, into the easier forward roll. Megan had also shown me how to stay limp, literally like the rag doll, so as to not expend a single speck of energy more on standing up than was absolutely necessary. Over and over, I was shoved first one way and then the other, each time rolling and rising to my feet. Then, suddenly I felt someone grab my wrist from behind and twirl me around. It was Rinchen. As I spun around to face him, he hit me in the throat with the web of his hand just under the chin. This is called *irimi nage* and if you know what you are doing, you flip your head back with the strike and throw your feet up in the air as quickly as you can. Breaking your connection with the ground makes you momentarily weightless. A strike to your neck will only hurt you if you stay connected to the ground. Instead of taking your head off, the strike merely flips you backwards and you land on your upper back. Most of the seniors are really good at taking this fall. I had tried it before and survived, but I was not expecting this at all. I got my chin up and arched my back which is the most important part of this *ukemi*.

The force of the strike flipped my feet over my head. For a split second, I was hanging in mid-air upside down. Rinchen gave my arm a quick tug and I fell on the back of my shoulders slapping the mat with a loud bang. I rocked back up to my feet. The adrenaline was now burning up all my oxygen and I was having trouble breathing. Someone shoved me from behind. I rolled out. Out of nowhere, Tripp appeared. He had my hand in wrist lock; this was *nikyo*, second technique. Pain shot up my arm. Out of sheer reaction I gave up my feet to break my connection to the earth and its gravity. We pivoted together, Tripp forcing my hand back against my own wrist and me escaping the wrist lock by arching backward and floating in the air. Bang! Another break-fall.

It was getting hard to get off the mat. I could feel myself staggering to get to my feet. Then Old Bob swooped in on all fours striking my shins with his ribs and forcing me to flip forward over the top of him. I had almost nothing left. It was all I could do to get my arm out in front of me and tuck my head into a forward roll. I was breathing hard; sucking air with all my might. I was getting dizzy. Suddenly, my shoulders were jammed forward from behind and I flew forward. In mid-air, I curled in to a ball. This was the only position that I could muster as I thumped onto the mat and rolled. Only this time, there was no getting up. I couldn't breathe. I let go. I had always been told that we all chose the moment of our death because we always have just one more breath if we really want it. I didn't care anymore. I tried to stand up. Everyone was yelling at me to stand. I strained with all my might to get to my feet and just as I was almost there, I felt the back of my calves being swept out from under me while a man's bicep slammed across my throat. My head snapped back; my feet flew up. It seemed like I was suspended in the air for a whole minute. I slapped. There was a bang. My hand stung from slapping so much. And then everything went completely black.

Rinchen says that most people never know failure because they quit way before they fail. Quitting is choosing to surrender. It is the choice to stop before you are at the end of yourself. Failure is letting go of a need to reach the end, giving it your all and accepting whatever happens. It is a beautiful place, failure. Almost nobody ever really knows it. It is the ability to push yourself to the point that you physically cannot continue because your body has nothing left. It is death. This is a point of consciousness that very few people know. To this day, it was the most important thing I have learned from my practice of *Aikido*. There is no quit. This is just do until you die. Words cannot describe how much freedom I felt in that split second before the lights went out. Now I know why *Budoka* do not fear death. It is just another moment. It is just the end of time.

I was told that it only took about ten seconds for me to open my eyes. I was breathing hard but not sucking air like I had been. I was amazed at how fast my energy came back. Within another ten seconds or so, I was able to pull myself up to sit in *seiza*. Then I realized that everyone was clapping. The whole *dojo* was clapping and smiling. I looked up and saw Tripp clapping and smiling at me. I couldn't tell if Megan was crying or if the water on her cheeks was just sweat. Even Rinchen was clapping – an expression of emotion that he does not normally allow himself to make. After a few more breaths I stood up and bowed to Rinchen and he bowed back. He motioned for me to take my place at the back of the mat and called the last candidate for *sankyu* to the center of the mat.

As I watched the last round of Ping-Pong, I found myself sitting in *seiza* with my hands forming a circle as is the tradition when meditating. My breath had returned completely and I was now enjoying fresh air by the lung-full. By habit, my inhalation took the same length of time as my exhalation. I was aware of every little sound in the room; every breath of every student; every rustle of a *gi*, every thump of my brother break-falling in front of me. I did not try to focus on any of it, but remained one with all of it. It was over. All there was to do was sit there in peace and bear witness to life unfolding around me.

Chapter Twenty-eight: Daddy's Little Girl Is Gone

After the test was over and we had meditated for about a quarter of an hour, we concluded the way we always did. Two thunderous claps from our teacher in unison with his students. There were deep bows of respect. Megan bowed off the mat and ran into the dressing room bringing the hakama that I had stashed in my *do-gi* bag. Up until now, I only wore it when we practiced *Kendo*. She handed it to me and bowed. "Your clothes, Lhamo. You do not have to train in your underwear anymore!"

From across the room I heard Rinchen's voice boom, "Miss Megan, have you promoted yourself to *sensei* again? Are you now doing the promoting here?" Megan was suddenly very embarrassed. This was a significant breach of protocol. Only the *sensei* announces promotions and that would not usually happen until the next class and only for those whom he thought had earned it. Megan bowed to her father and apologized. Rinchen started to laugh as he untied his hakama. "Well, you might as well make sure that she remembers how to tie that thing. There is nothing worse than a *sankyu* that doesn't know how to dress herself." Megan spun on her knees and handed me the hakama. I stood up and slipped my legs into the baggy trousers and wove the *himo*, the black straps, through my belt and tied the three-pronged knot in the front. I heard my dad call my name from the foyer. He had his cellphone out and was motioning for us all to bunch together for a picture. He was smiling ear to ear. I still have that picture. I printed it out and framed it.

Tripp took his father's *hakama* and folded it for him as was the custom. This was the job of the senior-most student and was rarely delegated. Megan and I, along with the rest of the advanced students, folded our own. We bowed off the mat and disappeared into the dressing room. By the time I got my street clothes on, I was starting to get sore. This was going to take days to get over, but I did not care.

The whole class gathered in the foyer. It was a long-standing tradition to go out for sushi after a test and this was not going to be an exception. Rinchen personally invited my dad, who was quickly becoming a *dojo* groupie. Beth on the other hand, gave me a hug and said that she had to get going. She did not say where and I knew her well enough to know that she did not really have to be anywhere. She looked into my eyes and there were tears in hers. "I love you Lhamo – you are amazing!" She hugged me again and then headed for her car. I was confused and a little bit concerned. What was that all about?

The fact of the matter is that I did not see much of Beth after that. She would stop and say "hello" in the hallways at school and occasionally we would have lunch together. I would suggest that we hang out and she would always have something else to do. What was so weird about it was that I felt as close to her as I always had and I could feel genuine warmth from her during what little time we spent together after the test. Something had changed for her. I had changed. I was someone different and it seemed to amaze her like she had said, but at the same time she did not completely understand it. For years, we had had so much in common, but not this. I had now gone down a path in my life and she simply could not follow me as she had done so many times before. We had always been the Frick and Frack of Westchester High, but now I might as well have been part of an entirely different species. She had always said that she wanted me to be happy and I guess she felt that she had to let me go. Maybe it was her way of encouraging me to follow my new path knowing that it was good for me. From time to time, I would hear other people recount Beth's story of my test and how it was like magic; that I flew through air and got beat up by eight seniors at once and survived. This did nothing but improve my reputation at school, but despite that, we had never been further apart.

As the *dojo* gang walked down Washington Avenue to take over Terried Sake House, my dad put his arm around me, but said next to nothing. The others got ahead of us and before we went into the restaurant, he took me by the shoulders with a look on his face that could have been pain as much as it could have been overwhelming joy. All he could say was, "I had no idea." Then he hugged me.

I know that warriors, especially those who have recently been promoted to the advanced class at Byakuren Dojo, are not supposed to cry on their daddy's shoulders, but I indulged myself in that moment anyway. Becoming an advanced-class *Budoka* would have to wait one more day. I put my face on his chest and held him tight and just cried. My tears started to soak through his shirt. We just stood there; my dad and his little girl, just like when I was five years old and had jumped into bed with him because I was scared of a thunderstorm. I would always be his daughter. Forever and ever, I would be his daughter. But we both knew that the moment we walked into the *sake* house, his little girl would be gone for good. He might remember me as a girl in his mind's eye, but he would never again see it in my face in this lifetime - not after he had seen me take a beating like the one I had just taken. For the first time in our lives, I could do things that he could not do. I had a power that was unique to me. He held me tight and I could feel how proud he was. I could feel how happy he was, but there was sadness. He was at a loss for words. What does a father say when he meets his daughter as a woman for the first time?

I could feel my dad take a deep breath and with a squeeze, he let go of me. "Let's check this place out. You have to be starving." As a matter of fact I was. As we walked into the *sake* house, I noticed that the students had already taken over most of the tables. It was late and the crowd had thinned out. The gang was already filling out their sushi orders. Rinchen was sitting at his usual place, a smaller table next to the wall, but adjacent to the three of four other tables that had been lined up for his students. He waved at my father to join him. My dad held a chair for me; one conveniently located next to Tripp and yet closest to where he would be sitting. Rinchen had already ordered a flask of *sake* and offered my dad a cup as he sat down. This was a whole new world for Henry, but he seemed excited to be a part of it. The student table was already roaring with jokes and commentary as they recalled the events of the test. Tripp put his arm around me and gave me a kiss on my forehead. "That was one hell of a test, Little Bit, one hell of a test."

"That's 'Lhamo' to you, you big lug," I said whispering into his ear.

"Alrighty, then," he said with a single nod

"Alrighty, then" I replied kissing him on the ear.

I took a look around the table as if to take inventory of who was there and how they were doing. Two parallel rows of happiness. Thor was sitting back in his chair with his arm around Tracy. They kept their relationship on the down-low, for the most part, but tonight they seemed to have decided to come

186

out of the closet. Old Bob had taken a seat next to Megan. Normally, he would sit with Rinchen, but on this night he was accommodating my father. Ty had ice wrapped with an elastic bandage on his shoulder. This was not a good sign. Becky seemed a bit down in the dumps but the white belts next to her were making every effort to reassure her that she had most likely passed the test. Megan was retelling the play-by-play of my ping-pong round. It was much more exciting to hear her version of it. As for me, I did not have a lot to say. I really just wanted to take it all in and then go home and pass out – only this time in my bed. It is a truly beautiful thing when there is nothing to say. Sometimes life just speaks for itself and if you open your mouth, even just to order food, you will mess it up. The sushi lady brought hot green tea. I sipped it slowly as I listened to the conversations all around me. She brought three or four pitchers of ice water and that shut everyone up as they scrambled to fill their glasses.

I could hear Rinchen ask my dad what he did for a living. My dad asked how he had become an *Aikido* master. I tuned into this part of the conversation with particular interest, but without looking at them. Rinchen said that he had been a student of several very prominent *Aikido* masters over the years and had even trained in Osaka for a while with one of the greatest living masters in all of Japan. He was young when he started, not much older than Tripp. He spent seven years in Japan learning all that he could about *Aikido*, *Kendo* and even studied the tea ceremony with a *Chado* master who was also a Zen monk. While in Japan he learned to do mostly Zen-style meditation which is a meditation form that largely focuses on emptiness. He said this is a particularly difficult form of meditation for a beginner and takes years and years to learn. He became frustrated with his practice and eventually crossed paths with a monk that practiced Vajrayanna Buddhism. Vajrayanna is practiced, for the most part, in only two parts of the world, Japan and Tibet. The Tibetans have a much broader network of practitioners and a very large variety of individual practices. Eventually, Rinchen went to northern India and took up studies in one of the four great Tibetan lineages, the Shangpa Kagyu.

My dad was absolutely spellbound by Rinchen's life story. So was I. Rinchen explained that he studied under a master that had tried to flee Tibet when the Chinese invaded in 1959. That happened to be the year that Rinchen was born. His master had been caught, imprisoned and tortured, but had managed to survive and eventually escaped to India. According to Rinchen, his master believed that Rinchen was the reincarnation of a lama that had been killed by the Chinese Army during the invasion.

Rinchen said that his master believed that it was highly unlikely that an American would find himself attracted to Tibetan Buddhism, let alone train with the intensity that Rinchen had. Only someone with a predisposition to this kind of practice would do that. He said that his teacher had said that it would be easier to find someone who had survived being struck by lightning twice in the same day.

He said that he did not believe in reincarnation, but did not disbelieve in it either. He said that the Buddha taught that one should never believe anything, especially about religion, unless it could be proven in one's own experience. My dad particularly liked that idea and so did I.

Rinchen went on to tell my father that he came back to the United States after having been gone for fourteen years. Seven had been spent in Japan and seven had been spent in Northern India. When he got home he had considerable difficulty adjusting to the American lifestyle. "There was so much commotion," he said. "People talked just to hear their own voices and there was an advertisement stuck on everything." He took a job translating business documents from Japanese into English and met Tripp and Megan's mother. They got married had two kids, but he still struggled with what he called "the noise". His wife developed depression and their relationship deteriorated. She was yelling at him a lot and yelling at the kids. He felt that the situation was unhealthy, especially for the children. When the twins were about thirteen, he filed for divorce. The legal proceedings had been particularly vicious because his wife wanted exclusive custody of the children and planned to move with them out of state. Rinchen thought that this would be disastrous for them and wasn't even sure that she was mentally healthy enough to have joint custody of the twins let alone exclusive custody. Eventually, the court asked the kids what they wanted. Tripp chose to live with his dad and Megan chose to live with her mom. "Time may not heal old wounds, but it does take away the ache," said Rinchen to my father. "Now that the storm is passed, things have calmed down. The kids have figured out how to be part of both households."

"My wife and I have really enjoyed getting to know Tripp and Megan. They are very fine, fine young people," my dad said to Rinchen.

"Thank you. You have done a pretty good job as a father yourself, I think."

My dad turned to look at me and said, "Yeah, I got really lucky."

"I beg to differ. Luck had nothing to do with it. Your daughter is the karmic consequence of how you and your wife treated her, taught her and while you were not her only influences, the apple never falls far from the tree, if you know what I mean."

"Thank you for saying so." And with that, my dad lifted his *sake* cup as if to toast my master and said "to our children". Rinchen was more than happy to oblige in this gesture and tapped his cup to my father's and they downed their *sake*.

There was food and tea and more than a gallon or two of ice water. Rinchen and my dad chatted on and on, but eventually people started to leave. Old Bob was first. He stood up and walked over to offer a handshake to my father. "You have one hell of a daughter Mr. Albright, one hell of a daughter. She is one tough cookie." My dad looked up at him not entirely sure what to say to such a compliment. It was a bit new to him to have *Budoka* complimenting him on how tough his daughter was. "Thanks" was enough. Bob bowed to Rinchen, patted me on the shoulder and waved good-bye to everyone as he left. Thor and Tracy were next. Thor reached into his pocket and pulled out a wad of bills and slid them over to Tripp. "This should cover our share". Tripp stood up and took his hand as if he was going to shake it but pulled it sharply to his chest and hugged his *dojo* brother instead. He gave Tracy a peck on the cheek as he hugged her over the table.

One by one and in pairs, the members of my clan stood up, hugged each other, paid their respects to Rinchen and my father and departed. Each one added more and more money to the pile to cover the bill. Never once did Tripp bother to count it or check to make sure that his brothers and sisters were paying their fair share. When the group had shrunk to just Tripp, Megan, Rinchen, my dad and me, I turned to Tripp and said jokingly, "well, we will see how honest our *dojo* is; you had better count the money."

"I don't have to," Tripp said abruptly as he arranged the mess of bills into a tidy pile and handed it to the sushi lady with the check. This surprised me and surprised my dad even more. Rinchen smiled. "No one in the *dojo* would ever dishonor themselves by not paying their share of a bill. Sometimes the tip is as high as fifty percent. A devious man could make good money being the last person here with the responsibility for paying the check. There is always way more than enough, but none of us would dishonor ourselves by profiting from the generosity of our students, so it all goes to the house. That is why the sushi lady is always so happy to see us." My dad pulled out his wallet, but was quickly informed that he would not be allowed to pay. Rinchen had already added a handful of bills to the stack. "Tonight, you are our guest."

My dad did not want to leave, but he also did not want to be a bore and keep his new friend captive in a sushi restaurant. We all stood up and exchanged hugs, though I bowed to Rinchen. It is considered totally rude to be so presumptuous as to hug your master. I kissed Tripp good-bye. We stepped out into the cool autumn air in the middle of the night. There were still people bar hopping along Washington Avenue at that hour, in fact it was quite a lively scene. My dad walked me back to my motorcycle. "Are you going to be alright to ride, you have had one hell of a night?" I thought about riding home with him and how much easier that would be, but I did not want to leave my bike downtown on a Saturday night.

"I will be fine. You can follow me and honk if I look like I am falling asleep," I said. My dad was not amused by my tired attempt at humor, but did not resist my decision to ride home. I zipped up my leather jacket and put on my helmet. The bike felt heavy as my sore arms pulled it upright. The motor rumbled to life. My dad walked down the street to his car and waited for me to pass him before pulling out behind me. It takes a half an hour to get to Westchester from downtown. I was not looking forward to the cold ride home. The air is twenty degrees colder at 65 mile per hour, but the traffic would be thin so there would be few obstacles between me and my bed.

As I turned off of Washington Avenue and onto 14th Street, there was nothing but green lights all the way to the freeway. Ordinarily, I would have gunned it, but thought better of it given that my dad was right behind me. He had had enough excitement for one night. I was still feeling a little warm from the tea and the food and lifted my visor to get some cold air on my face. In the corner of my eye I saw a car pulling up to the intersection to my right. It was moving too fast to stop at the red light. I turned to look just as I was reaching the point-of-no-return at the intersection and realized that the car was not going to stop at the light at all. I hit the brakes hard. The tail of my bike started to slide out from under me and I was now skidding almost sideways into the intersection. The driver, a young guy a little older than me, was laughing as he shot through the light. Half way across the street, there was an eruption of car horns as he turned left cutting off a string of cars. As I was skidding toward his door I could see every detail of his face and the sudden "oh shit" that formed in his mouth as his smile was suddenly erased by sheer panic. I skidded past his rear bumper with only inches to spare and pulled hard to keep the bike from lying down. I wobbled for half a block, but ultimately found myself rolling in a very welcome straight line. My heart was racing. I was gasping for breath. This was the second time tonight that I had come to the end of myself only this time I was far from being at peace with it.

I pulled over to the curb figuring that my dad had to be completely freaking out. He was. He pulled up behind me and jumped out of the car nearly getting hit by a bus as it passed. "Holy shit, Maddie, are you alright?" I pulled off my helmet and tried to catch my breath.

"Yeah, but that was close."

"That prick could have killed you."

"Yeah, I noticed that." I was still trying to get my mind to calm down. I turned to look down the street. A police car had pulled out behind Party Boy with sirens blazing and was chasing him down the street.

"We should call the police" my dad said.

"No, we should go home. It looks like the cops saw what they needed to see." My dad was not convinced. I wanted to change the subject and get back on the road.

"Good thing mom wasn't here, heh?" This did not have the effect on my dad that I had hoped for. He was going to have to tell her what happened and she was going to absolutely lose it.

"Jesus, Maddie, you were almost killed. Maybe this motorcycle thing was a very bad idea." I was wondering the same thing myself. I took a deep breath and then looked my dad in the eye.

"No, Dad, the motorcycle is not the bad idea here. An idiot like that can kill me in a car or walking down the sidewalk. He could fly up over a curb and crash through a restaurant window. He was not dangerous just to me, but to everyone out here tonight. To be honest with you, had I been in a car, I would have plowed right into him." My dad was still very upset. He was pacing back and forth and looking down the street as if he was trying to see the police catch the guy.

"Let's go home," I said putting my helmet back on. My dad reluctantly walked back to his car. He followed me to the freeway with his emergency flashers on. Halfway home, I looked back through my rear-view mirrors and saw that he still had his flashers on even though we were doing 65 miles per hour in the middle lane. He flipped them off when we pulled into our neighborhood. We both rolled up the driveway and he pulled his car into the garage. I left the bike outside. I caught up to him before he went inside.

"Maybe we don't need to tell mom about the near-miss, what do you think?" I could tell my dad did not like this idea at all. He had a pretty open and honest relationship with my mom, good news or bad. "It is just going to freak her out."

"It's freaking me out, Maddie, really, it is freaking me right the hell out." He was getting loud and I was afraid that my mom might still be up and would, at any minute, come out to the driveway to find out what all the fuss was about.

"I know dad, but I didn't get hurt and I do not want to get into a fight with either of you about me riding a motorcycle. We have covered that ground already."

"I am not sure that we have. This was a very close call. I thought for a second there, that I was going to be scraping you off of the side of that asshole's car."

"But you didn't have to do that and do you know why?"

"Luck, that's why, sheer, dumb luck."

"No Dad -- *skill*. I saw him before he entered the intersection. I saw him. I knew that he wasn't going to stop and I hit the brakes before he ever blew the light. They teach you that kind of stop in the riding classes that I took. He missed me because *I made him miss me*." This seemed to bring my dad's heart rate down substantially.

"Holy shit, Maddie, it has been quite a night. First, I watch you dive over half your class at your *Aikido* school."

"'*Dojo*'. It's called a '*dojo*'."

"Okay, '*dojo*'. And then I watch these samurai kids beat the crap out of you until you passed out."

"They were *Aikidoka*, Dad, not samurai; let's not exaggerate."

"Okay, *Aikidoka*, whatever, but then I watched you cheat death by skidding sideways around some drunk running a red light! I thought one of the best nights of my life was going turn into a disaster. It has been one hell of a night, Maddie, one hell of a night!" I could see that my dad was in quite a turmoil – bouncing back and forth somewhere between rational thought and terror.

"And yet, here we are, safe and sound at home. It has all worked out. Rinchen says if a punch misses you by an inch or misses you by a mile, either way it still misses you."

"But it could have been different."

"No, Dad, it couldn't. Things work out the only way that they *can* work out. This is the only way that it could have worked out because it is the way that it *did* work out. Do you get that? Why be upset about hypothetical things that didn't happen?"

"When did you become such an Eastern mystic?"

"A little over a year ago," I said with a smile. Things were starting to lighten up. "Your girl's got skills Dad, some serious skills." He finally let go of a smile and hugged me.

"Yes, you do," he said resting his chin on the top of my head, "yes, you do."

Chapter Twenty-nine: The Usefulness of Muck

I was sore for days after the test. My shoulders hurt. My legs hurt. My butt hurt. Tripp, Megan and Eddie Banta rode out the next morning to see if I wanted to take a ride out to the temple at Augusta. My mom had big hugs for Tripp and Megan as they walked in through the laundry room from the garage. Eddie was last in line and hugged my mom just like he had seen Megan and Tripp do pretending that he had known her for years. My mom was not at all sure what to make of Eddie, but he was with Tripp and Megan so he had to be okay on some plane of existence.

As we were standing in the kitchen, my mom started to inspect Eddie's tattoos. "I hope those wash off" she said with an overfamiliarity directed at Eddie that was clearly meant as pay-back for his overfamiliarity with her when he first walked in.

"Nope, permanent ink," he replied spying a pan of brownies on the counter.

"Your mother must be proud."

"No, my mother's dead," said Eddie nonchalantly.

My mom was suddenly mortified. She had only meant to play with Eddie to see what kind of guy he really was, but she suddenly found herself in the middle of her own kitchen with her foot in her mouth. "I am so, so sorry. Please forgive me for being so rude."

"I will forgive you for one of those brownies."

"Of course, help yourself" said my mom quickly snatching the pan off the counter to make a peace offering to her unexpected guest.

"Oh no you don't!" snapped Megan as she snatched the pan from my mom just as Eddie was zeroing in on a brownie. My mom was now quite confused. Megan was scowling at Eddie, "you can have a brownie when your mother actually dies, you jerk."

Eddie did not miss a beat and turned to my mother and said, "gotcha". My mom was at first annoyed at such a tasteless joke, but as she thought about it, she must have decided that she had it coming to her for being so judgmental about his tattoos. She lifted the pan of brownies from Megan's hands and offered one to Eddie. Just as he was once again about to take one, my mom jerked the pan away and said, "gotcha!" Eddie was impressed. He wasn't expecting so much sass in the suburbs. My mom finally handed him the whole pan of brownies and told him to knock himself out. Megan continued to glare at Eddie until an urgent thought crossed her mind.

"Oh yeah, Lhamo, you might be needing this," she said reaching into the pocket of her leather jacket. She pulled out a PEZ dispenser with the head of a goofy looking dog on it.

"Candy? Gee thanks, Megs." I accepted her gift wondering what the heck this was all about. This was uncharacteristically cute for Megan. As I was inspecting the candy dispenser, Megan pulled the dog's head back and a little orange tablet ejected from the device.

"*Dojo* candy -- it's ibuprofen, baby".

"That's more like it!" I said as I unloaded three tablets and popped them into my mouth. Only a warrior would fully appreciate the humor in this. My mom wasn't getting it and decided to leave us to our conversation. "Okay, well, I think I will go find your father and tell him that we have company."

When my dad finally made his way into the kitchen to say "hello" he was not in his usual happy-to-see-you mood that had become his normal reaction to seeing Megan and Tripp. For starters, there was an unknown biker covered in tattoos in his kitchen gnawing on the last of the brownies and my dad really loves brownies. But despite Eddie's unexpected appearance in our house, something else was clearly bothering him even though he was trying not to show it. My mom came back holding her purse and saying something about going to the grocery store and wanting to know if the gang would be staying for lunch. Tripp explained that he was hoping that I would go with them to the temple although I really needed to think that one over for a minute. My mom said that she hoped that everyone would still be there when she got back and walked out to her car. My dad claimed to have some important leaf raking to do and ducked out through the garage. Eddie looked up with brownie crumbs still caked on his lips and said, "Was it something I said?"

As soon as my dad was out of ear-shot, Megan turned to me and asked what was wrong.

"I nearly bought the farm last night on my way home and my dad saw the whole thing." This revelation got even Eddie's attention and he put down the brownie pan to hear what I had to say. I told them about turning off Washington Avenue and having the green light and how the party car had ran the red light and shot into the intersection. I told them about the skid and the near miss. I also told them that my dad was still really upset and while he was not making me lay off the bike just yet, he was clearly having motorcycle issues. Frankly, I was having issues too.

Tripp and Megan decided that a ride out to the temple was probably not such a good idea given the events of the previous night. They asked Eddie if he would mind if they hung out at my house instead of going to the temple and invited him to hang out with us. "As long as we do not have to watch any those damned Ninja movies, I'm cool." We made our way to the den. Tyler was playing X-box and Eddie immediately became his best friend. Ten minutes later, Tyler and Eddie were going at it beating the virtual crap out of each other. This made it possible for Tripp, Megan and I to have an undistracted conversation in the living room.

I sat on the couch next to Tripp and put my head on his chest. It was so good to feel him next to me. Megan was deep in thought about what I had just told her. Finally, she looked over at me and said, "You know, it was a matter of time. Every biker has close calls."

"Yeah, I know. I was just hoping not to have them in front of my parents. My dad is really, really shook up. He is trying hard to be brave about it, but this has knocked the wind right out of him."

"He's a parent, what would you expect? He has been keeping you alive for years and he came close to watching you die. That's a mind-fuck for anybody," Tripp said though his mind seemed to be somewhere else as he spoke.

"It was a mind-fuck for me. I am still freaking out about it." There was a moment of silence. The twins seemed to be remembering, each in their own experiences, the close calls that they had had and the times that they too had cheated death.

Most kids at my school, and I suspect at most schools, do not give much thought to death. They say when you are young, you think that you will live forever. That's not really true; you mostly just think that death, like most bad things that happen to people, happens only to *other* people. We live in such a comfortable little bubble that it does not occur to us that life is a 100% fatal experience for everyone. Ever so often, you see in the news that a kid gets killed on his bike or a teenager is killed in a drunk driving accident. The truth is, that there is so much news of really bad crap happening to people who you have never met that you don't give it much thought until death is in your face.

I remember a classmate of mine from the sixth grade, her name was Jenny Rose. She died of leukemia just before school got out for the summer that year. I had known her pretty well. I had played with her on the playground many times. She had disappeared from class about half-way through the year and I had thought that she had moved. Then one day our teacher told us that Jenny had died. I didn't know what to make of it. This was the first time that someone my age, someone I knew, had died. I remember how it took me hours to become sad about it because I had to piece together what the consequences of death were. As I thought about how I would never see her again or wondered if it hurt to die, I began to feel sad for her. But once that door was open, once I had become aware of her being permanently gone, once I had let the hurt grow, I almost immediately wanted it to stop. I tried to forget about it, but she kept popping up in my mind and every time she did, I started feeling worse and worse. For days, I would have sudden shocks of recognition and memory as I thought about her. Eventually, it passed and I forgot about her almost entirely. She died years ago.

Rinchen says that in these times we are jammed with information, but never have enough time to contemplate the meaning of any of it. We jump from new event to new event as texts and emails, web pages and videos sail in and out of our brains. We live in a world of a million little shocks, but none ever really sink in because some other thing is right behind it pushing it out of the way of our attention. Rinchen says that it is the lack of contemplation and reflection that makes our species so incredibly ignorant and shallow. It is why we cannot work out our problems and why we really don't ever get to know people all that well. We are a generation of over-stimulated children sizzling in the fizz of a constant bombardment of information that is mostly useless and irrelevant to our lives.

I had been noticing that when you lay off the internet, turn off the TV, stop texting and talking on the phone about nothing important that you start to actually think about the meaning of things. You start connecting the dots between the various things that you know and you start to understand how everything in the world fits together as a whole. You notice your father's fear and your girlfriend's kindness. You not only feel your boyfriend in your arms, but you smell him and taste him like you can know him in his molecules. We have a lot of bandwidth, but do not drill down into our experience. Apparently, they used to do that in the olden days. Rinchen says we are all blinded by the dazzle and never really see what anything is made of. We do not have any knowledge of the essence of true existence because we let it get covered in glitter. We have mistaken our amusements for the mind of god.

As I sat there on the couch next to Tripp, I could hear his heartbeat. I could smell him; his scent of boy and leather. The three of us sat quietly for nearly a half an hour, just thinking and being together. I used to be too jumpy to enjoy the quiet. If my phone did not go off with a text notification every ten minutes, I would get anxious. I remember constantly having to be stimulated. It was my dope.

This was one of the thousands of times over the past couple of years that I realized that I was becoming different from most of the people I knew. The more I changed, the more I sought peace and quiet while the joy of my own breathing caused me to feel increasingly isolated from the world I used to know. I started rooting myself deeper and deeper in the *dojo* and into the lives of my brothers and sisters there because they knew – they knew what I knew. They loved what I loved. Sometimes it felt like my whole existence was shrinking down to a handful of people. But at least I had them.

It is funny, as I look back on my last years in high school, I see now that I had spent way too much time decorating my life. Now I was chewing on it - chewing on it to the bone. Pain and joy were becoming equally welcome in my experience. It was the proof that I was alive. I remember hearing kids use the expression "keep it real" in the hallways at school. Kwame Johnson said that a lot. For him, he may have had some idea of what that meant because his life was not always a bed of roses. He lived in the city and he spent half of his life on a bus. I did not know what his home life was like, but there had to be some reason why his family put him through the ordeal of long bus rides to go to school miles and miles from home. But everyone else at school, with a few notable exceptions, I suppose, really were the walking-almost-dead. A generation of lost children floating on an endless sea of chatter without meaning or any real understanding of what was happening to them.

I was starting to get sleepy and slid my head down to use Tripp's thigh as a pillow. He pulled out his sketch pad started drawing on it. He was lost in thought. Megan was paging through a coffee table book that my mom used more as a décor item than as a source of information. It was a book on Paris and had pictures of old buildings and simple people selling exotic foods in markets and stuff. Every now and then Megan would cock her head as if one of the pictures was really making her think. I loved watching her, but soon I was asleep.

When I woke up, the twins and Eddie were in the kitchen talking to my mom. I had drool running down the side of my mouth and was suddenly grateful that I was not slobbering on my boyfriend. There was a page from Tripp's sketchbook on the coffee table. It was a design, the flower of a lily pad with what looked like fire floating over the top of it. It was beautiful. You can always see more than the image in what Tripp draws. It is like he leaves a little piece of himself behind on the paper. What a Buddha-boy. He loved the imagery of the Buddhist world and used drawing as a meditation on his subject, as if the act of drawing exposed the deep mystery of the thing. I recognized this image and remembered the story that Rinchen had told me about it. This was the lotus blossom, the symbol of enlightenment seen everywhere in the Buddhist world.

Rinchen says that the lotus seed is planted in the mud of a swamp but grows up out of the murky water to blossom in the fresh air and sunlight in much the same way as the human mind rises out of the mud of its own confusion and ignorance to expand into what Rinchen calls "the great luminosity". I don't think he means the ball of light from the Taming the Wild Horse exercise. Rinchen's luminosity seems to be a much bigger deal. The lotus cannot grow in a tidy garden, but needs the chaotic muck just as enlightenment can only come from a mind that starts out as a mess. Rinchen says that you can use the mess, contemplate the facets of it and come to know it and chisel away at all the static until you reach a clear, empty space that lies within the true core of everyone's mind. If we didn't have the mess, we would never have the flower. What a lovely thing to put on paper. What a lovely thing to have on your mind.

Chapter Thirty: Randori

It was raining on my next training day, so I drove into the city in the Kid Car. I spent half the trip wondering if I was too scared to ride my motorcycle again after my near-death experience. This, of course, was ridiculous. It was a moot point, at least for the time being, irrelevant given that it was pouring down sheets of icy rain. It was mid-November, after all, and the hot weather here doesn't last forever. St. Louis sits on the eastern edge of the Great Plains and gets the screwiest weather ever, especially in the late fall and winter. I remember one year, in the middle of February, it was so warm in the morning that I wore shorts to school, but by the time school was out, it was snowing. We get flash blizzards from the Rocky Mountains and nearly tropical days from the Gulf of Mexico. The most common weather in November, however, is rainy, snowy sleet. It sucks and St. Louis drivers are nothing to brag about. I once heard my dad, who is originally from Wisconsin, say that "when the first flake hits the street in St. Louis, the first flake hits a light pole."

The weather had turned quickly and I had decided to stow my bike away in the garage for the winter, but still I wondered … was I losing my nerve?

It was a pretty good turnout at Byakuren Dojo. There were a few newbies struggling with their belt knots that I hadn't seen before. Megan was already on the mat focused on the *kamidana* and *soul shaking*. Soul shaking is an interesting meditative exercise that is done by clasping your hands together and shaking them in such a way as to send vibrations through your entire body while standing in meditation. The idea is to use the vibration shake your mind loose from your body so that both can flow uninhibited. Seeing her in front of the *kamidana* meditating seemed a bit odd. Where was Tripp, I wondered? He hadn't mentioned that he was going to miss class. On the rare occasion that he did, Megan was next in rank and lead the warm-up. There were several skirts on the mat. Thor and Tracy were there, Old Bob and, of course, me. I was disappointed that Tripp was going to miss my debut in a *hakama*. After the test, I had moved up the line and was now the first skirt after the white belts.

Megan led a much more rigorous warm-up than Tripp did. She doesn't really like warming up so she pushes through it pretty quickly. Personally, I like to take my time. Stretching is one of the most important safety precautions that a martial artist can take. It is amazing the number of injuries that happen because someone was not flexible enough. I was getting Gumby-flexible. I could sit on my shins and lay all the way backward with my back flat on the floor. I could put the palms of my hands on the bottoms of my feet without bending my knees. It was something you had to keep working at. I noticed that even though several days had passed since the test, I was still feeling mighty sore. The backs of my legs were burning as I stretched.

The beginner's class sailed by. I was getting a kick out of hearing my *hakama* flutter as I rolled and flipped through the air. I even tripped on it a few times. When you run in a *hakama* you have to curl your toes upward so that they do not get caught in the blousy pant legs. Despite a few initial clothing related issues, I was getting the hang of it. Only an idiot thinks that her uniform means anything, but the *hakama* made me aware that I was heading for my first advanced class as a bona fide advanced student and it had me playing my A-game. It was all in my head, but I felt different – somehow more mature.

We took a water break between the beginner's class and the advanced class. I stayed on the mat. Tripp and Matt showed up just in time to catch round two. I gave Tripp a look like "where the hell have you been, you light-weight". They both headed for the men's dressing room smiling at me. As Matt passed by, he caught me looking the other way and gave me a shove. I went flying and had to duck into a roll to save myself from total embarrassment. "Awesome, fresh meat," he said as he ducked into the dressing room behind Tripp.

It is absolutely forbidden to pick on anyone in the *dojo*. Respect is always mandatory. But that does not mean that there isn't a certain amount of hazing and dues-paying that goes on. You are expected to earn your place and when you step into a new rank you are immediately being put to the test for the next one. You come to like this kind of thing. It's a kind of an overly male, ass-slapping sort of mentality, but it gives you a certain strength of mind. It is that little edge of aggression that makes sure that your inner victim stays away. It rouses your ego to rise to the challenge. Eventually your ego will be beat out of you which usually means you are ready for promotion. Over all, there is a bravado in the *dojo* that I have come to find very motivating. True, it is your inner badass, but it can be a good thing as long as you keep it tamed with proper manners.

Rinchen says that in the beginning it is our egos that give us the thrust that helps us break the gravitational pull of ordinary consciousness and propels us into the emptiness of space. Enlightenment is weightless and vast, but you have to get there somehow and in the beginning, ego is all that you have to work with.

Tripp and Matt quickly stretched and Rinchen doddled a bit to let them get loose. After a few minutes the line formed by rank. Tripp had taken his place in *joseki* and I was at the other end in *shimoseki*. It was a short line. There were only seven of us.

The advanced class does not start with a warm up or rolls. Rinchen gets straight to the point and the pace of class is much faster. Seniors are expected to know their shit and very little time is spent with explanations. Rinchen can take the class through a dozen variations of a technique in twenty minutes. Even the experienced *Aikidoka* break into a hard sweat. Rinchen calls a student up, an *uke*, to help him demonstrate. The joke in our *dojo* is that the word "*uke*" is Japanese for "guy-who-falls-down-and-goes-boom". He pounds the crap out of you when you are his *uke*. *Flip, bang, flip, bang, flip, bang.* After a minute or less of demonstration the class breaks up into pairs changing partners after every technique. When there is an odd number in class, Rinchen trains right along with everyone else. If you draw him as your partner during an exercise, you need to be prepared to get your ass kicked. At the same time, it is an honor to train with your teacher. From the first day you enter the *dojo* you are told to always seek the hard path, to always train with the strongest students when you can get their attention. They call this *shugyo* – or "conducting oneself in a way that inspires mastery". In short, we say that it is the suffering that you do to gain wisdom. The harder the better.

What I have come to know about *dojo* life is that it runs in the exact opposite direction of normal life. At home or at school, I was always seeking comfort and the easy way out. I took easy classes and dodged strict teachers. Comfort is practically a religion with most people. It is worshipped. That's why Rinchen says that we live in a "comfort culture". But what kind of evolution can you expect from that? Some of my friends blow their minds on drugs to take comfort to a whole new level, but all that it seems to do is make it that much harder for them to deal with the bad times that find everybody eventually. Mrs. Chavez, my psychology teacher, says that people need coping skills. Learning to deal with pain and disappointment is, and this has been very big news to me over the past year or so, a very necessary thing. My friends at school are marshmallows both physically and mentally. Kids scream at their parents on their cellphones because they are being ordered home when they don't want to go. And discipline, what the hell is that to the average teenager?

I have come to love the hard life, or at least what I consider to be my harder life in comparison to what it used to be. I cannot believe how much stronger I feel; how much more love is in my heart – how much better my food tastes! I get off completely on learning to do things that I once thought impossible. I am not sure that I think anything is impossible anymore. Damn, I am starting to sound like my guidance counselor at school. It's funny. I used to think that the phrase "no pain, no gain" referred to bikini waxing.

There was only about fifteen minutes left of class when Rinchen motioned for us to form a line at the back edge of the mat. This could mean only one thing: *randori*. *Randori* is one of those Japanese words that does not translate well into English, so I am told, but it's rough meaning is to "create order out of chaos". At our *dojo*, there is usually more chaos than order when we do this exercise. I have seen *randori* done many times. In the beginner's class it consists of one student sitting in *seiza* at one end of the mat and two other students sitting in *seiza* at the opposite side of the mat. The instructor calls out *hajime*! and the players snap into action. Everyone jumps to their feet and the two attack the one. At the beginner's level the two attacking students approach at a jogging speed in order to give the *nage*, the person performing the technique, the opportunity to work things out.

At the advanced level, *randori* is a completely different deal. First of all, there are three attackers instead of two. Second of all, they don't walk, they run at you and are allowed to take you down in any way they can. They can punch you, tackle you, grab you by the hair – whatever it takes to put you down. No one survives *randori* except for perhaps Rinchen and a few other masters. You are considered to be pretty good at it if you can stay on your feet for fifteen seconds. I have seen big-kid *randori* and the pounding that people take as they are learning. If you didn't know that everyone in the exercise was controlling the action, you would think it was absolute mayhem. I have to say that during my first advanced class I was pretty scared. Tradition has it, by the way, that if you are new, you get to go first.

Rinchen had no intention of going easy on me. He called for three *ukes*, Thor, Matt and Old Bob. They took their places on the mat without a shred of acknowledgment, friendliness or emotion of any kind. Okay, so that freaked me out. These guys were being just a little too frosty for my liking. I was hoping for some sympathy for the new girl, but apparently that was not in the plan.

I took my place at the opposite end of the mat. Rinchen gave me only one instruction: "do not try to throw anybody, just try to stay on your feet and parry their hands as they try to grab you." This seemed simple enough. Hand parries are taught from day-one. You basically turn your arms into swords and deflect anything that enters your personal bubble of space. "I can do that," I said to myself. We all bowed to each other as is the custom before any exercise. My heart was racing. I was even starting to panic a little. "*Hajime!*" shouted Rinchen.

I have never seen three men move faster in all my life. It was a blur of white and black. They were nearly on top of me before I was even on my feet. I had just dropped into a stance when I was jammed in both shoulders with such force that it was like being hit by a truck. I flew up in the air backwards landing flat on my butt and sliding the rest of the way off the mat. I could feel myself freaking out and I wanted to cry. That wasn't going to happen. I immediately turned fear into anger and got up and took my place again.

"*Hajime!*" Once again, there was a blur and the flutter of *hakamas* as the three men charged at me. I tried to step out of the way and let them run past me, but they didn't fall for it. Thor grabbed the collar of my *gi* with both hands. I tried to strike his throat with *irimi nage*, but I was so clumsy at it that I hit him in the face with the palm of my hand. This did not even slow him down, but he got a little pissed off and hurled me across the mat. I landed with a thump and rolled sideways like I had just fallen out of speeding car.

There is a rule in the *dojo* that you never allow yourself to get angry, but in the heat of *randori* this rule gets broken frequently. Thor was standing over me frowning and daring me to get up. His nose was pink from where I had mistakenly hit him. Accidents happen, but if you are clumsy and hurt someone, especially a senior, they will not necessarily complain, but they will teach you a lesson. "Take a seat!" Rinchen commanded. Thor bowed to his teacher and stepped away from me as I dragged myself to my feet.

"I told you not to throw anyone, Lhamo. You are not ready to do that yet. The point of this exercise today is to avoid, not confront. Do you understand?"

"*Hai, Sensei,*" I barked putting the palms of my hands together as I bowed to make my apology.

"Do it again. This time, half speed."

By now I was no longer afraid. I had my eye on Thor, not being sure if he had calmed down yet, but I was not going to give him the satisfaction of seeing as much as a fleck of weakness in me. These guys were so fast. There was very little I could do with them other than swat at their hands as they tried to grab me. This time, however, they came at me in a light trot. I had time to get to my feet. *Ukes* are trained to simulate the momentum of an attack when they are moving artificially slow. If you step out of their way, they will continue on in their original direction for at least one step before correcting themselves and adjusting to your new position. This imitates the natural momentum of higher speeds and lets the *nage* think through the situation so that she can try to work out the very complicated art of managing chaos.

As they came upon me, Old Bob had his hands outstretched to grab me and I slashed at his outside wrist using my hand like a knife blade pivoting down his arm as he passed by me. The three missed me on the first pass and stopped and turned around. This is a big advantage when you are fighting multiple people. The first rush is focused and furious, but if you can get by them, not unlike a bull fighter might try to do to a charging bull, they have to stop despite their momentum, turn around, and start from zero energy. This is an opportunity to take advantage of the situation and enter toward them before they can completely regroup. As I turned to face the three of them, they were turning almost in unison Matt was now on the outside and Thor was in the middle of the three. Matt's arm swung around to try to snag my *gi*, but I intercepted his wrist, pivoted under his arm and now had his arm locked straight out behind his back. I stepped into him and he fell into Thor who collided into Old Bob. Old Bob was taken by surprise and lost his balance and fell into a forward roll. "*Yame!*" (stop) shouted Rinchen in his familiar deep, commanding tone. Everyone came to a complete halt.

"I thought I said no throws tonight, Lhamo."

"Sorry, *Sensei*. It just kind of showed up." Rinchen chuckled, so did Thor.

"Yes, that happens and when opportunity knocks in the chaos, it is best to open the door and take advantage of it. Nicely done."

He waved us off the mat and waved Tracy out to take my place. He then nodded at Tripp and Megan to come out to join Matt in the attack. "Full speed. *Hajime!*"

None of the four had even had a chance to get completely seated when they leapt to their feet.

Tracy had been in the advanced class for over a year and had been through *randori* practice many times before. She was a pretty amazing *Aikidoka*. In fact, Tracy was pretty amazing in general. She was in nursing school. She looked like a swimsuit model. She ran marathons. She had perfect teeth. She and Thor were older than the rest of us with the exception of Old Bob. They both worked out together at the *dojo* and at a private gym nearby. They lived in a loft just a couple of blocks from the *dojo*. Thor was a natural body builder meaning that he did not take steroids to put on muscle. The guy was ripped; I mean, drop-your-panties gorgeous. (Did I just say that in my outside voice?) When they worked out on the mat together they were so graceful. Both of them had fluid, nearly flawless technique.

When you are watching *randori* as a spectator, it seems like the attackers move slower. Maybe not in this case. Tripp, Megan and Matt were on her in a flash, but she swiped Tripp's hands away from her just as he was about to grab her *gi* and pivoted down his arm. She circled around behind the three of them as they were trying to turn around to attack again. She didn't wait. She attacked them. She collided with Megan first striking her under the chin with the web of her hand. This was the *irimi nage* that I had attempted, but the difference was that Tracy did it right. Megan flew backward into the air arching her back and then rotating into a forward roll in mid-air. By the time she was back on her feet, she was ten feet away from the fight. Matt had sidestepped Megan as she was falling and got a hand on Tracy's collar. She quickly ducked her head under his arm entangling his hand in her *gi* and locking his arm out so that he had to stand on his toes to avoid having his elbow bent the wrong way. She pivoted increasing the pressure on his arm by merely twisting her torso without ever grabbing him. By continuing to try to hold on, he was hurting himself. Matt dove into the air and transforming his motion into a roll to save his arm. Her pivot had slowed her down, however, and Tripp dove at her in an attempt to tackle her around the waist, but she placed her hand on the top of his head as he ducked to drive his shoulder into her. She forced herself into a wide sword stance sliding backwards with both feet on the floor and jamming Tripp's head downward. He wound up face-down on the mat unable to hold on to her as she looked around to find the next attacker.

Randori is more myth than truth. In real life, it would be very difficult to manage multiple attackers without hurting one or two of them. This is the street reality of *randori*. In the *dojo* you might throw an attacker over and over, but on the street you would deal with each one once and only once. They say if you are attacked by only one person, you can let him live. If you are attacked by two, you will have to hurt one and pin the other. If you are attacked by three, the first one slips by, the second one gets thrown and the third one gets killed or incapacitated so that on the next pass you are down to only two. The more skill you have the less damage gets done, but in the end, you have to do what you have to do.

As in all *randori* exercises in the *dojo*, eventually you go down. Megan was charging straight at Tracy so she did not see Matt coming from behind. Matt tackled her around the waist pinning one arm to her side as he did. Tracy started to fall forward just as Megan leapt into the air to tackle her around the neck. Megan's forearm struck Tracy across the bridge of her nose as the two collided in mid-air. Tracy's head snapped back with such violence that you could see the on-lookers cringe in unison. All four *Aikidoka* wound up in a heap in the middle of the mat. Megan was the first to realize that there was no way that her collision did not do damage. She rolled to her knees and immediately crawled over to where Tracy was lying perfectly still, face-down on the mat. Within seconds, Rinchen and all of the skirts were in circle around her. She was not moving and Megan started to cry.

No one trains in the martial arts without getting hurt. It is an occupational hazard. Teachers try to contain those risks as best they can by allowing students to take on only what they can handle. At the same time, everyone is constantly trying to push themselves to new levels. In the process, accidents happened to all of us. Seniors are particularly safety conscious and get very angry at reckless newbies that have watched too many action movies.

I remember once, a guy came to class who said that he was a black belt in *Tai Kwando* and claimed that he was looking to learn a new style. What he was really up to was to prove that his art was better than ours. During the exercises he kept thwarting his training partners' attempts to perform the exercises and was making fun of them. One white belt who had trained with this guy had to leave the mat with an injured wrist. Rinchen said nothing, but shot a glance at Tripp who made a point of choosing this clown to be his next training partner. They did an exercise at a safe practice speed and the visitor cheated the technique by speeding up and said, "See, this crap doesn't work." Tripp bowed and said, "Let's try again". This time, the visitor simulated the attack and, once again, tried to cheat the technique by speeding up only he picked the wrong guy to do that to. Like lighting, Tripp had the visitor on his knees in a wrist lock. The visitor was howling in pain. Tripp quickly reversed the wrist lock and flipped the visitor on his back. When he tried to get up, Tripp spun around him and dropped him from behind. Every time the visitor tried to get up or tried to attack, Tripp put him down. The guy started getting really mad and decided that enough was enough. He jumped to his feet and started punching and kicking as Tripp deflected and parried every strike. It was clear that Tripp was just playing with this guy. Finally, the visitor made an angry and committed attack and Tripp entered into the center of the violent energy between them wrapping his arm around a very surprised attacker's neck. As Tripp bent forward the visitor was pulled off his feet backward stretched over Tripp's hip. Tripp held him suspended for seconds and with a quick flick of his hips, threw the guy on his butt. He then stood over the once-arrogant attacker and said, "Come in peace or leave". The guy stormed off the mat never to return.

But this class was different. This had been a normal practice. No one had lost their temper and yet, Tracy was face-down and not moving. Rinchen made everyone stand back and put his hand on Tracy's back to check her breathing. She started to come around and tried to push herself off the mat. Her hair had been knocked out of its pony tail and was hanging over her face on all sides as she tried to get up. She took a minute to catch her breath and then rose to sit in *seiza*. As she pulled her hair back away from her face, Megan suddenly gasped and said, "Oh shit!" under her breath.

Tracy's nose was bent to one side and was obviously broken. She had blood trickling out of both nostrils. The skin around her eyes was pink and already starting to get puffy. Worse, the white part of her left eye was deep red with blood. This could not be good. There were tears in her eyes as she reached up to touch her nose. She winced.

"Get some ice," said Rinchen to Thor. Thor dashed off the mat disappearing into Rinchen's office where there was a refrigerator. He soon bounded back onto the mat with a couple of small blue ice packs that were kept in the refrigerator for just such an occasion. "I'm okay," Tracy said, "Just give me a minute". Rinchen told her to do her breathing exercise. This was a warrior's first cure for everything, intentional breathing, and it does help. In fact, it is amazing how important your breath and breathing are – I mean, beyond the obvious. When you have a sudden injury, like stubbing your toe, your initial panic reaction dumps adrenaline into your blood and you start to burn up oxygen much faster than normal. This helps you have a little burst of strength, but it also can make you have to breathe harder to replace the lost air. After a few seconds, the loss of oxygen actually makes you start getting weaker.

Getting your breath under control gives the body what it needs, when it needs it most.

In the *dojo* we are taught to manage our breathing constantly. Actually, it eventually becomes a subconscious habit. When you are about to get hit or tackled you never want to have the impact occur while you are inhaling. This can result in getting the wind knocked out of you and developing a muscle spasm in your diaphragm that makes it impossible to inhale. You can pass out from having the wind knocked out of you and you certainly cannot defend yourself in that condition. As a consequence, we are taught from our first moments to synchronize our breathing with our body movements so that we are exhaling and compressing our breath on exertion. This tightens all of the muscles in your torso at once and makes your body one solid mass with no hollow bag of air inside to soften it. It is the difference between exerting yourself as a rock rather than as a balloon. This makes you a single, solid object directly connected to the ground and allows you to translate that strength from the earth, through your body, so that you can actually shoot it out of your hands. Planned breathing is a part of every *Aikido* technique.

Rinchen teaches us to do what is called a *kiai* (pronounced "key-eye"). A *kiai* is the "hi-ya" sound that the *Karate* guys make when they are breaking a board. It actually serves a very important purpose. When you make a *kiai*, you are actually exhaling and compressing your entire body, if only for a split second, into an extremely hard object. The sound helps you control your exhale while you are compressing your breath and clears your mind so that you can focus every thought, every emotion and all your energy into a single pulse of power and shoot it out of your muscles in a single direction. It is amazing how strong you can be if you are organized and focused, if only for a split second. You may only be able to summon this power for an instant, but that is all it takes to make the difference between life and death.

Rinchen has many ways to prove this point. To show the strength of breath, he has his students, even the new ones, lie down on their backs on the mat. He tells them to take a breath and hold it. He then starts to step on their stomach which usually forces the air out of their lungs making them sound like a tire with a leak. He then tells them to take a breath and actually compress their breath into a controlled exhale while shouting a single syllable. Vowel sounds work best . He tells them to shoot the strength of the *kiai* from their stomachs up his leg as he steps on them. He then walks across the *dojo* on the stomachs of his students, each shouting a *kiai* at the precise moment that he is putting his full weight on them. It is a lesson you do not forget. The day he first taught me this he also had a stack of boards. We do not kick or punch in *Aikido*, but after about ten minutes of instruction about how to compress the muscles in our hands and how to focus our power from the earth through the board, we were all snapping boards in half. It was amazing to me then. I thought that this took years of training to do. I would not go out and crack bricks or anything like that. I will leave that to the *Karate* guys, but I could not believe that I could be taught to do such a thing that fast.

The day that Rinchen walked on my stomach and I broke a board with my hand, a whole new world started to open for me. I started to notice that every movement I made could be coordinated with my breath to make that movement more powerful, graceful and even easier. The night of my test, when I dove over seven students but could have probably dove over more, I pulled my whole being into one single expression of power. I inhaled deeply as I took my last step. I compressed my breath and made my *kiai* expelling every ounce of everything into the split second pulse of power that I shot through my legs. These are not mysterious things – they are skills. Very simple, logical skills. The more you know about what is possible for the mind and body, the easier life gets. It is incredible how blind we are to this.

Aikido, like all martial arts, was born of necessity in a time when you did not have a machine to do everything for you. Rinchen says that it took centuries for people to figure it out. Each generation passed on what it had learned to the next generation. Over the centuries, this created a culture of people with nearly super-human abilities. It makes you wonder. What are we passing on to future generations now? It is as if all of this knowledge that people struggled so hard to gather and combine into arts that were not just good for staying alive, but for making life itself intense and beautiful, are disappearing in a cloud of digital fog. I don't want to be a virtual Maddie. *I want to be Lhamo for real.*

It reminds me of the story of Pinocchio. This guy makes a puppet out of wood and it is very life-like, but it is not real. But the puppet wants to be a real boy. That comes at a cost. If you want to be more than a puppet, a thing that does not really know what it is doing or why, a thing that chatters and makes noise but does not create anything of any importance with its words, a thing that is devoted to its own shallow emotions only seeking to be amused or comfortable, then you have to be prepared to get messy. Puppets don't die, but they don't truly live either. Rinchen says that this is the trade-off consciousness. If you choose to wake yourself up, you wake yourself up to all of life, to pain and joy, to life and death. He says that they are actually all one thing, but I am really having a hard time figuring that one out. Otherwise, you can continue to tickle your mind with amusement and distraction and you will never ever know who or what you really are.

Tracy brought her breathing under control. This, I am sure, made the pain much less. Rinchen called for the line and we moved quickly to our proper places. He lead us in a few minutes of meditation and then ended class. Thor took Tracy to the hospital to have her nose and eye checked out. Megan was very upset. She felt responsible for hurting Tracy. Matt wasn't feeling much better. There was no need to lecture anybody about being careful next time. Megan was already drilling into her own brain about it. She had apologized to Tracy over and over. Tracy wasn't angry, but she was not happy about getting her face all messed up either.

She did not come back to the *dojo* for a week and when she did finally show up, she did not train. She had two really black eyes. The guys called it being "raccooned". She said that her nose was broken and that the doctor at the emergency room had had to set it back in place. Thor bragged about her, "you should have seen her, she was like a rock. The doctor offered to give her some pain killers, but she just said, 'set it'. What a beast! He put his hand on both sides of her nose and "pop", just like new. Well, it was a bit black and blue, but at least it was straight." Tracy was watching him tell the story like he was talking about someone else other than her. She shook her head and turned to me and said, "Boys will be boys. They wear their injuries like badges of honor; like getting hurt is the whole idea. They are idiots, you know that, right?" I started to smile. I was impressed by how calm she was even about being irritated with Thor. I smiled and nodded. I felt in that moment like I was getting woman lessons from a professional.

Tracy said that the doctors told her that she was lucky and that her eye would eventually heal and that she would not lose any of her eyesight. You could tell that her injury had hurt her in ways more than just physical. Megan practically offered to be her slave to make it up to her, but Tracy just laughed. "You did not do this to me; I did this to me." Tracy really liked Megan and kind of treated her like a kid sister even though Megan technically out ranked her.

After a couple of weeks, Tracy started to train again occasionally. She was not allowed to do *randori* practice. Rinchen only lets us practice *randori* twice a month or so because it can be so hard on your body. After a month, we were seeing less and less of Tracy although Thor still came to the *dojo* regularly. I finally asked him what was going on.

"She is giving up *Aikido*," he said.

"What?"

"Yeah, she said that she doesn't want to go through life torn to shreds and looking like a prize fighter." Tracy did not look anything like a prize fighter. At first, I thought that Thor was implying that she valued her looks and did not want to risk another injury that might disfigure her. I thought that that sounded awfully prissy for Tracy and then I kind of got mad at her because it seemed like she was taking the bus to Vanityville. Of course, the news that Tracy was dropping out of the *dojo* tortured Megan.

Around Christmas, Tracy showed up at the *dojo* to meet Thor after training. She looked like her old, totally hot self. Rinchen stepped off the mat to greet her and inquire how she was doing. He never made any mention of her leaving and treated her just like he always had, maybe even better now that she was a *civilian*. A gang of us went out for sushi after training and she came along. I walked with her down the street. I told her that I missed her and that I really wanted her to come back and train again. "That ship has sailed," she said smiling at me. She wrapped her arm around mine and we walked the rest of the way down the street like we were BFFs.

I sat next to her at the plank table that was now pretty much always reserved for us after training. Some nights we did not go to the *sake* house, but we were there often enough that the sushi lady made sure that we always had places to sit. Thor sat at the other end of the table with Tripp and Matt. Tracy sat next to me and asked me how my training was going. I told her that I was starting to like *randori*. I told her that I had scraped most of the skin off of my elbow a week or so ago and showed her the massive scab. "Another *dojo* memory," I said. She looked at me with concern and said, "It is easy to get sucked into the pseudo-samurai thing, you know, but you don't have to do it that way." I wasn't sure what she meant.

She told me that in ancient Japan, martial artists trained with extreme severity. This was because in their world you did not survive mistakes. Their training had to suit their real needs. "Most modern people could not handle the way they trained. In the old *dojos*, people did not just get hurt, they got killed." I was glad that times had changed. She continued, "some of these guys take great pride in getting hurt and get all manly about it. They brag about injuries and do the whole macho thing. It can be like being on a professional football team sometimes."

"You ought to know, Thor would be the quarterback of that team," I said. Tracy looked into her tea cup and nodded. "I really don't like that part of him," she said as if she was talking to herself. She looked into my eyes and said, "you know this is not about being tough, right; you know that that's not *Aikido*. That macho bullshit is way off the mark. Yes, you get hurt from time to time. Yes, you should control your mind not to make more of it than it is. But you should not throw a party in your pants celebrating damage like you want to be hurt or you think it's okay for someone else to get hurt. That is some really evil stuff. Those boxers who beat their chests over the unconscious bodies of their victims, those so called 'champions' who can barely see through their own swollen eyelids, that stand there and beat their chest like they are some kind of god -- those guys are barbarians, not warriors." I could suddenly see that I had done that. There was a running joke in the *dojo* that was saved for the rare moments when you pulled off a particularly slick move and felt like gloating about it. After you really nailed somebody, you would stand over them and say, "whose your daddy?" It was particularly funny when it was a woman saying it to a man. But I could see the problem now – this was taking pleasure in suffering even if the suffering was *shugyo*. It might toughen you up, but I was getting the idea from Tracy that this kind of "tough" might be a bad thing.

Tracy told me this saying; she said it was Chinese, but it made her point: "beware of the brave man for he shall commit murder by the end of the day." When she said this to me, I had no idea what it meant.

"It addresses a particular type of bravery, that charge-across-the-field-in-a-hail-of-bullets kind of bravery that you see in war movies. Do you know what I am talking about?"

I nodded.

"That kind of macho bravado stuff is really ignorance. A guy who leaps into danger without giving it a second thought does not care about himself. If he does not care about himself, he does not care about others. Therefore, a brave man who does not care about getting killed, does not care about killing – he is capable of murder by the end of the day. Empathy is caring about others as much as you would care about yourself. This is the key to compassion. It might actually cause you to stand up and take a bullet for someone, but out of your love for them not pride of self or arrogance and certainly not out of ignorance. The point is that if you don't care about yourself, you are not going to care about others. That's why those big macho athletes not only wreck themselves, but trash each other. It is nothing to admire."

I thought of how I had popped Thor in the face by accident at my first advanced class and how he had hurled me across the *dojo*. I could see Tracy's point. Thor was a really nice guy most of the time, but he had this mean streak in him when he got mad. I was starting to figure out that Tracy may have seen this mean streak up close. I was thinking about what she said. Something was bugging me about it.

"Yeah, but you don't want to go through life a complete sissy, do you?" I said. Tracy laughed, "no you don't, but it is one thing to be courageous and at the same time aware of your own suffering and the suffering of others and quite another thing to be a beast." A thought shot into my mind: "beast", that was the word Thor had used to describe Tracy when the doctor had set her broken nose. I hadn't realized it at the time, but his comment had really pissed her off. She had found it insulting.

"Thor called you that when he told us about you being at the hospital after you got hurt. He said you had been a 'beast'." I was starting to feel the insult myself. My statement took the shine out of Tracy's eyes for a second, but she regrouped.

"Yeah, he did, and he didn't realize what he was saying and that is exactly my point. That sort of thing is all pump, all ego. It isn't useful. It is a type of blindness. He wasn't even aware of what I was going through. He is not always like that, but he can really get stoned on his own testosterone sometimes. To tell you the truth, I told the doctor to fix my nose without drugs out of medical curiosity. I wanted to know what patients with broken noses went through. It sucks. It hurt like hell." She started laughing as if she was confessing to an act of incredible stupidity rather than exposing a part of her that was going to help her be a fantastic nurse someday. I laughed with her. Before, I had a kind of reverence for Tracy, but now I just loved her to death.

She had it all, I thought; she was smart and good looking and she really seemed to know what she was about. It made me kind of wonder why she was with Thor. I looked down the table and saw Thor listening to Matt tell a joke. He burst into laughter and slapped the table. You could see the veins in his bicep bulge. His long blond hair swirled across his face as he shook his head laughing his ass off. It must have been a funny joke. But I could see what Tracy saw in him. He was more than just a very well arranged bundle of muscles. He had a heart and it did beat for his friends. It beat for Tracy probably most of all. This man-thing was going to take some more study. The guys at my school were mostly boys. Even Ack was something less than the guys at the end of that table. Tripp was laughing too and Matt was slapping him on his back. It was like watching the Three Musketeers. There was something awesome about them and it was not just that they were handsome and could get your hormones racing. There is something inspiring about real

213

men. I could not quite figure out what it was, but it had something to do with how they just live full out. They laugh hard, they play hard and they hurt hard. What is that?

Tracy saw me staring at the guys at the end of the table and said, "They're beautiful aren't they?" I turned to look at her and a tear was rolling down her cheek. "They can smell really bad and they will forget your birthday, but god damn it they are gorgeous." I knew that she was talking about something much more than their looks. They were beautiful, like egrets are beautiful when they swoop down over the stream in Forest Park flapping their large outstretched wings to descend slowly into the cool water.

We sipped some more tea and picked over the sushi with chop sticks. Then Tracy stopped and looked at me. "I have heard that you really hate your given name, but what do you think about being called 'Lhamo'?" This was out of blue. I couldn't imagine where her question was coming from.

"I like it a hell of a lot better than 'Madison'", I said stuffing a piece of tuna roll in my mouth.

"Do you know what it means?"

"Yeah, it's short for 'Palden Lhamo'. She's a wrathful deity. I looked it up on Wikipedia. She's a badass. Killed her own son because he was going to destroy Buddhism. That's seemed a bit harsh to me, but it is a name that reminds me to be strong. 'Madison' used to remind me to be cute."

Tracy had to spit her tea back into her cup. It was good to see her laughing. She is even prettier when she laughs. "Yeah, well I know all about *cute*," she said. "I joined the *dojo* thinking that it would help me be taken more seriously by men."

"You're kidding."

"Oh yeah. Most men think that the sound that I make when I am talking comes out of my tits. At least that's what they look at when I talk. And being blond, well, I might as well get at tattoo on my forehead that says 'idiot'. It is a real problem for me in school. Some of my teachers, I swear to god, give me lower grades because I am blond. Unless, of course, they want to sleep with me, and then you have to worry about flunking a class because you told some idiot professor to keep it in his pants."

"So why the *dojo*?"

"I thought that if I became a 'badass', as you say -- that I would get more respect. It worked inside the *dojo*, but it is not like you can wear a *gi* and *hakama* around campus. I mean you could, but the respect thing wouldn't happen, now would it?" We both laughed.

"So now what?"

"So, now nothing. I have learned a lot in the *dojo* and from Rinchen. I have learned that being a badass still makes you an ass."

"You got that from Megan!"

"No, she got that from me."

"Very cool."

"Thanks. So, I have also learned that you cannot save people from themselves and the world will always be full of shallow assholes regardless of what you do. Actually, that is not entirely true. The world if full of people, whether they are assholes or not is a matter of how you choose to see them and is not so much about who they choose to be. I get to decide what I see in people and who someone is to me. If I think that someone is being a jerk, I need to look into myself first to see why I need to see them as a jerk. It usually boils down to some egotistical thing that makes me right and them wrong. I have an endless ability to justify myself. But ... I don't let people tell blond jokes around me anymore, or black jokes, or Jewish jokes or any other kind of joke that demeans people based on a stereotype. I confront them about it. It makes me a pain in the ass at parties, but why should anyone have to live with stereotypes? '*Slap 'em up against the side of their heads and make them think about who you really are*' – that's my motto."

"What if you are not completely sure who you are?"

"Then you are in the right place. The *dojo* is the perfect place to figure that out. Just remember that you do not have to be any particular way. You should be what makes sense to you after drilling into it for a while. You get to draw the picture. Although, it doesn't hurt to get some education in 'Lhamo design' first."

"How would I do that?" I was getting what she was saying, but how do you even know what the possibilities are let alone figure out where you can learn about such things?

"Do what you are doing. Learn. Explore. Dig in. Get your hands dirty. Try new things. Read cool books. Seek out teachers – all the stuff that people have been doing for centuries to expand their minds."

"Oh yeah, that" I said sarcastically.

"Do you have anything better to do with your life?" she asked. I had to think about that. It seems like I used to be so busy. Now it seemed that all there was to do was learn cool shit.

"You will be dead soon enough. So, light your own fuse and explode while you can. Don't waste a single minute." If I had liked her before, I was now completely drinking the Kool-Aid of her awesomeness. This chick rocked!

Tracy took my hand and said, "Life is a journey through a matrix of very fine lines. Step to one side or the other of any one of these lines and the world looks completely different. If you can make out the tiny distinctions that separate useful things from wastes of time, your life will just get better and better. Crawl, walk, run, fly. It is all about evolution. There is no end to it. You will know some of the greatest things you will ever know in your last breath. But be patient with yourself. Try to learn a thing or two about grace. Grace is the art of forgiveness and patience. And then go out and grant grace to yourself so that you will also grant it to everybody else." This was getting over my head. Grace? Evolution? I am still thinking through it all.

I would see Tracy from time to time after that night. For a while longer, she would stop by the *dojo* to meet up with Thor and she occasionally came to the gatherings of the clan. She said that she had taken up Tai Chi with a Chinese master that Rinchen had recommended to her and she was really getting into it. She ran in the Boston Marathon that spring. I did not see her again until late May. I had heard that she broke up with Thor. He didn't talk about it. I think about her all the time, especially when I am just about to do *randori*. In that moment when I start to make the mistake of using ferocity to become brave, I think of her and find real courage instead.

Chapter Thirty-one: Learning How To Walk

Dojo life is a continuous conversation. *Aikido* and *Budo* becomes the thing that everybody talks about almost all the time. Before and after class, students are constantly working out techniques alone, or with each other, in their street clothes, in the foyer of the *dojo* or on the sidewalk or even while standing in line to see a movie. It is common to see one of your *dojo* brothers or sisters suddenly close her eyes and start moving her body through a technique, visualizing the precise way the back of the hand intercepts a punch and slides along the attacker's arm in a parry. Over time, *Aikido* becomes a dance with all the intimacy of a waltz. You start to notice how people move and you subconsciously start to adjust your movement to those around you. This awareness of other people becomes a big part of how you think. Even when I am walking down the hall at school or through the mall with my mom, I am noticing what people are carrying in their hands or how they carry their body weight. Are they walking up on their toes or down on their heels? Rinchen told me when I first started in the *dojo* that a trained *Budoka* always knows another trained *Budoka* simply by the way she moves.

Before I joined the *dojo*, I just walked down a hall. Occasionally, especially when it was icy outside, I would slip or trip on something and wipe out. In my worst day, I was never anywhere near as clumsy as Beth. Holy crap, that girl couldn't have more accidents if she spent her whole life on stilts. She should never even step outside in the winter. She has scars on her knees from the many dives she has taken, sometimes down stairs. Solid movement is one of the many odd little quirks that you develop when you train in *Aikido* or *Kendo*.

Both of these arts have essentially the same footwork. This means that you learn how to move forward, backward and sideways while keeping your center, or your *hara*, as it is called in Japanese, in a stable relationship to the ground. Instead of lifting your feet when you walk or run, you kind of slide them over the ground so that you are never very far from being able to suddenly plant your feet and shoot the strength of the earth through your body. It becomes, in time, a very efficient way to move. In fact, because this type of movement is so efficient, creating the greatest strength with the least effort, it feels like you could walk for miles and miles without getting tired. Most people pay no mind to how they move or breathe and because they never think it through, they never get very good at it.

Managing your breath, I have learned, is actually a way to enhance your health and extend your life. In the *dojo*, Rinchen says that no self-respecting *Budoka* would ever do anything for the sole purpose of extending his life or even give it a second thought. Living a healthy, well organized existence, however, is not about living longer. As Rinchen says, "an entire lifetime happens in the flash of a blade." This is not just some spooky saying. What he means is that life is not about *quantity*, it is about *quality*. Eating a thousand delicious apples is actually less valuable to our experience than having only one and taking in each bite with complete awareness. He once told us a story about this:

> There was a samurai who had a beautiful home that had a wall that was covered with flowers. Another samurai, a good friend of the first, always admired the wall of flowers and complimented the owner on their beauty every time he visited. One day, this friend wrote to the samurai who owned the wall of flowers telling him that he wanted to pay a visit so that he could see the flowers that should be in bloom by the time he arrived. He was whole-heartedly invited.
>
> As the visitor passed through the wall surrounding the house, he noticed, much to his great sadness, that the flowers had all been cut down. He entered the house and was greeted by his friend and invited to sit and have tea. As they sat in the tea room, the visitor expressed his deep sadness at the loss of the flowers. His host smiled and presented him with ancient tea cup filled with water. Floating in the center of the cup was a single perfect blossom. The visitor's heart burst with joy and he was overwhelmed with satisfaction.

When I first heard this story, I thought that it was the stupidest thing that I had ever heard. I had no idea why someone would think that a single blossom that would be dead in a day or two was more beautiful than a whole wall of living flowers. But then again, that is how we all live our lives. We are only vaguely aware of beauty when we wallow in excess. Our minds are so overwhelmed by the pile of sand that we cannot notice the crystalline beauty of a single grain.

When I think about Rinchen's story, I think about the pile of shoes in my closet. I have at least twenty pairs. Most of them I don't even wear anymore. Sometimes I give them away or trade them with my friends, but most of the time they just sit there. In fact, when I used to go into shoe stores, I would walk down the aisles and my heart would jump at every cute pair. By the hundredth pair the thrill was gone. In fact, more than once have I gotten burned out on shoe shopping.

There is actually an even deeper cut to this teaching. Rinchen says that we humans are devoted to the superstition of "more". We think that living to be one hundred years old is somehow better than living to be fifty even if the last fifty years are lived in a coma. But this turns out to be purely a delusion. Rinchen says that life is only one second long and it is the second that you are living right now. You may have memories of other moments and dreams for the future, but those are all fantasies and do not exist. Only "now" exists. And when you die, there is no conscious mind left to worry about "more".

He says that you can never really know your own death because this requires a fully functional brain. Your last waking moment is not of death, but of the last moment of life. Since you will never know death, why worry about it? Even if you are dying of some disease, you never have any more or less life than anyone else. You can look back at the shadow of the past with longing and your mind might start craving more. You might think about the future and regret that it will not be around for much longer and crave longevity, but in reality these thoughts are just as fanciful as wishing for the moon to be made out of cheese. He says that it is like wishing for more food when your mouth is already full. You can only chew one bite at time. Any thought of more life than you have already can only reside in a world of concepts and dreams.

What I am starting to figure out is that more is not better. You can like a million things a little or you can come to know a single thing so well that it becomes the center of your existence because you can see through this one thing, all things. This is really only a passing thought for me. I have to sit quietly and really focus to be able to understand this, but I want it to be the way I always think. I don't want a world made of a million pieces of junk. I am starting to wonder if I want anything at all except for a clean *gi*. I want each moment of my life to knock me down with beauty. I want the taste of my food to saturate my mind entirely and without distraction. When I kiss someone, I want to become completely one with them, even if it is my grandma. I know that sounds gross, but a kiss does not always have to be sexual. Get your mind out of the gutter. Rinchen says that the key to a happy life is intimacy. I had no idea what that was at first. I have only ever heard that word used in the same sentence with sex. Yet another lie told to me in the hallways of Westchester High and on TV.

Rinchen is always trying to get us to be intimate with everything. Our feet should be intimate with the floor. When someone grabs us, we should be intimate with the hands of our attackers. We should be intimate with the air we breathe. Here's a kicker. He caught me on this one. Do you actually smell the air when you breathe? Rinchen's sense of smell is like a dog's. When you walk into the *dojo,* he knows what you had for lunch. Rinchen once asked us, "how can you know all about your world if you don't even use all of your senses?" When I breathe now, I breathe on purpose. I use all of my lung capacity, not just part of it. I breathe deeply and have to expand my stomach to take it all in. What I notice is that I don't get tired hardly ever. That is because my body has enough oxygen – always. Megan showed me a really cool trick. When you are sitting in class and it is boring as hell and you start getting sleepy, start breathing in slow deep breaths. Basically, breathing meditation wakes you up. Who needs energy drinks when you have your own breath? Who knew?

I came to love the smell of Tripp. I would have not noticed this part of him if I had not been taught to open my eyes, or my nose, I should say. Don't get me wrong, there were days when Tripp smelled like a gym sock that has been sitting at the bottom of a locker for a month. I actually started to notice that how he smelled changed all the time. It would change with the food he ate and sometimes from the places he had been. If someone hadn't told me about this, I would have missed it.

I have come to really notice this when I am riding my motorcycle. When you drive down a road in a car you do not feel all of the bumps. You don't notice that the temperature changes as you move from place to place. In a car you don't realize that every foot of road has a different smell. On a motorcycle, you do not need to be a Buddha to learn this. It is obvious. I noticed it the first night that Tripp drove me around downtown St. Louis. You can smell the sewers and the exhaust from busses, but you can also smell the kitchens of the restaurants and, of course, there was the smell of Tripp's leather jacket. Waking up is a really good thing.

And food – wow! I have always been a big eater. I have a sweet tooth and can devour a bag of candy in a hurry. What I have started to notice is that most candy is flavored for the walking almost dead. It is always super sweet and has usually a single overpowering flavor. I guess they have to do that to make an impression on people who are eating candy while watching TV and listening to music while doing homework all at one time. How can any sensation make it through all that distraction? A candy maker has to use flavors that are strong and simple just to crack through the crust that smothers the brains of most of their customers. I have actually started to like fruit more and more because the flavors are actually more complex and interesting.

I did try an experiment, however, on a bag of Skittles. Instead of eating the whole bag in a minute or two like I have been doing for years, I bought a bag and picked out a single Skittle in my favorite color -- I like the purple ones. I threw the rest of the bag away, though it pained me to do it. I spent a minute studying the Chosen One. I noticed its shape and its color. Then I popped it into my mouth and sucked on it for a minute. What I noticed was that there was a burst of flavor, but pretty soon it was hard to taste. I bit into it and felt the crunch on my teeth and then the soft, chewy center. There was another burst of flavor, but by the time it had dissolved in my mouth I couldn't really taste it anymore. It was like the flavor would wear off or I would become numb to it. Of course, I was dying for another one. I wanted that burst. I think these big corporations know this. I think they make these things to pop and fade just so you will eat more of them. But, I have to say, for the second or two that I could taste the burst of purple flavor (I would like to say that it was grape, but I have never tasted a grape that tastes like a purple Skittle), it was rather pleasant – even memorable. Since my experiment, whenever someone has a bag of candy and is sharing, I always have just one and go through my ritual of knowing my Chosen One – intimately. I guess that is what was happening with the samurai who was given the single blossom in a tea cup. He was given the opportunity to be intimate and one with a thing that he loved without the distraction of too much of a good thing.

Aikido and *Kendo* taught me that we are always dancing with everything around us, all the time. Sometimes we are better at it than others. As you learn more about *zanshin*, the sense of lingering awareness of all that is around you, you start to tune in to everything. In the *dojo*, you are taught about *zanshin* so that you can be constantly aware of attackers, but it has a wonderful side benefit. You begin to connect with everything, not just the things that can kill you. It is amazing. For example, I have known Ack for a decade and only recently noticed that one of his nostrils is larger than the other. Or Beth, she always walks favoring her left leg. Mrs. Chavez has eyes that are not exactly the same color. Kwame Johnson has a very extensive vocabulary, but hides it behind gangsta jargon. My dad always, without fail, kisses my mom on her forehead when he sees her after work. Never on the lips, never on her cheek, always on her forehead. He might kiss her on the lips as a second kiss, but never on the first kiss. I am not sure why, but there is something really, really sweet about that.

The more you notice, the more you want to notice. There is this entire intense world that is happening right in front of your eyes and if you are too busy texting, you will miss it. You will miss it completely.

Zanshin has another side effect. The world starts to make you want to cry almost all the time. Sometimes because it is just so fucking beautiful and sometimes because it is just so fucking sad. I was out having pizza with Tripp once and a lady came into the pizza place with a young girl in a wheelchair. This child had very serious deformities. Her arms were curled up and her head was cocked to one side permanently. She was drooling on herself and trying to talk which sounded more like wailing than words. The lady ordered and sat at a table next to us. The mother had carefully checked out the people at the different tables as if she was trying to figure out who would be most accepting of her and her daughter. She chose us. I could see why. Tripp was smiling at her and looking at her daughter with appreciation. He later told me that this was a conscious practice for him; that he did this on purpose. He said that when he walked down the street, he intentionally let people know that he liked them. He said that, first of all, it made the streets safer, but also that it took a burden off of people. When we meet people, the first thing that we are all concerned about is whether or not they are a threat. Tripp advertised that he was a safe space – to everyone.

As the lady tried to get her daughter ready to eat, people were complaining quietly about the groaning. I wanted to get up and smack them. How rude. "I am sorry that this poor child is ruining your dining experience, you assholes," I thought to myself. And then I watched the mother. She was so courageous. She would not back down. She was taking her child out for pizza regardless of what other people thought about it. She loved her girl. You could see it in her devotion to her; the way she tended to her without getting upset or embarrassed. This woman was a saint and it was obvious within seconds of watching her. I felt my chin start to quiver and tears were forming in my eyes. I was not sad. I was in love with this mother and her child in the wheelchair;

deeply and forever in love with them. The mother saw my tears and was immediately concerned, "are we bothering you?', she asked.

"No," I said, "not at all." I realized that I owed her some explanation. "You are both just so beautiful, that's all; just really awesome." By now the tears were rolling down my cheeks. Tripp was looking at me and his eyes were getting watery too. When the cashier called out the lady's name she started to get up to get her pizza and Tripp stood up quickly and told her that he would get it for her. He came back to her table and placed the pizza in front of the girl. She got very excited and her groaning turned into what some would say was nearly a screech. Some of the other customers shot the girl a dirty look. I stood up to help the lady tuck a bib around the girl's neck while staring down the other customers with a don't-you-fucking-dare-say-a-word kind of look. Eventually, the lady got everything in order and started feeding her daughter pizza. Some people might have found this scene to be disgusting. The girl chewed with her mouth open and half of the chewed pizza wound up on her bib or on the floor. But to me, and I don't know why, I just got it. I can't even say what it is that I got, but I just got it. I got why compassion is the preferred tool of Buddhist to train their minds to wake up. I got the bravery of mothers and beauty of all children. When I am old and gray, if someone asks me how I reached enlightenment, that is, if I ever get there, I will say to them "pizza".

Chapter Thirty-two: War, What Is It Good For?

At Byakuren Dojo, it is not all about learning how to manage your body as a lean, mean fighting machine. Rinchen says that the bulk of real *Aikido*, *Kendo* and pretty much all of *Budo* never gets taught in the West. He says that there are hundreds of teachers who are really fine athletes, but have never had the mental training that is the greater part of all *Budo* arts. According to him, in the ancient times, the mind training was as important, if not more important, than the physical training. A samurai with a quick blade but a dull mind was a dead man.

There are very few instructors in the West who have "put callouses on their asses with a meditation cushion" as Rinchen puts it. This is actually as close to being vulgar as Rinchen gets, but he explained this remark by noting that he was actually paraphrasing a great Tibetan Buddhist teacher -- a guy named Milarepa.

Rinchen told the story this way:

> In Tibet, centuries ago, there was a man named Milarepa who was not a particularly nice guy. When Milarepa's father died, his uncle took all the money and left Milarepa and his mother penniless. His mother told her son to study sorcery, which he did, and one day while his uncle was throwing a wedding feast for his own son with the money that he had stolen, Milarepa summoned an enormous hailstorm and smashed his uncle's house killing 35 people. When the clan organized to go and look for Milarepa, he summoned another large hailstorm and wiped out all of their crops.

Eventually, Milarepa crossed paths with a Buddhist teacher named Marpa. Marpa told Milarepa about teachings far more powerful than sorcery. Milarepa wanted to learn. Marpa told him that he needed to do a few things to become worthy of the teachings and instructed him to build a house for Marpa's son. Milarepa did this by himself. He gathered the rocks and cut trees for timber and built a fine house. Marpa, upon inspecting the house, told Milarepa that he had built it in the wrong place and made him tear it down and rebuild it on another site, not too far from the first. Milarepa, did what his teacher told him, but again, Marpa found fault with the house.

Over and over Marpa made Milarepa build and tear down the house. Many times Milarepa would get frustrated that he was not getting any teachings about Buddha-dharma and several times he tried to quit. Marpa's wife, however, would intervene and encourage Milarepa to keep going. At one point, Milarepa wore a hole through the skin of his back that was so deep that you could see the muscle and bone underneath. Eventually, Milarepa stopped worrying about getting it right and just built and tore down the house. It was when he got to this point that Marpa finally agreed to teach him Buddha-dharma. Because his mind had been so well prepared and all the ego had been worked out of it, he learned everything in a matter of months, instead of years.

Milarepa went on to be a great vajra master. Eventually, he took on a student named Gampopa. Milarepa was as hard on Gampopa as Marpa had been on him. It is said that eventually Milarepa sent Gampopa out into the world to teach in a distant region near Nepal. He walked with his student part of the way until they reached a stream. He turned to Gampopa and said, 'Now you go on my son' and then paused to say, "I haven't given you my most important secret teaching, but maybe it is best that I don't." Gampopa fell on his face prostrating to his teacher and begged for the teaching. Milarepa said, "No, I don't think I will" and turned to walk away. Gampopa crossed the stream and as he was climbing the bank on the other side, he heard his master shouting to him. "You are my best disciple after all and if I do not give this teaching to you, who would I give it to?" And with that Milarepa turned away and lifted his clothes and showed Gampopa his butt. It was covered with scars and callouses from sitting in meditation for years and years. "Look my son, this is my final instruction to you."

There is no awakening without instruction, practice and effort. Some things cannot be downloaded from the internet. Some things take longer than what can be worked into a commercial break on TV. And by the way, you gotta love a guy who teaches his student by mooning him.

At the *dojo*, nearly everyone has a book in their *do-gi* bag. Among the favorites are Miyamoto Musashi's *The Book of Five Rings*, Takuan Soho's *The Unfettered Mind* and Mumon's *Gateless Gate*. And of course, it would not be a *dojo* if at least half the students were not reading Sun Tzu's *The Art Of War*. These books get quoted all the time, especially by white belts that think they understand them. I ought to know because I am a white belt and I have read them all and, yes, quoted them from time to time. I read them because Megan read them. At first I quoted them because I thought it made me sound smart. Sometimes, Rinchen would look at me as if he was impressed when I would whip a Takuan Soho quote on him. Here's a good one:

> *When facing a single tree, if you look at a single one of its red leaves, you will not see all the others. When the eye is not set on any one leaf, and you face the tree with nothing at all in mind, any number of leaves are visible to the eye without limit. But if a single leaf holds the eye, it will be as if the remaining leaves were not there.*

But you can get busted. If you quote something that you pretended to understand, but really didn't, Rinchen will put you on the grill and eat you for lunch. Take for instance, the first *koan* of *The Gateless Gate*. *Koans* are stories that seem to make no sense whatsoever; they are kind of like riddles. Zen teachers tell them to their students, give them some time to think about it, and then ask them what they mean. It tests the student's level of insight and gives the student something to work on while she is trying to understand how something and nothing have the same nature. Confused? You are supposed to be. Even the name *The Gateless Gate* is a koan. It is a pretty bad idea to tell Rinchen that you have figured out a *koan* unless you have and the odds are that you haven't. I tried this once.

The first *koan* is called *Joshu's Dog*. It goes like this:

> *A monk asked Joshu, a Chinese Zen master: "Has a dog Buddha-nature or not?"*
>
> *Joshu answered: "Mu."*

Now, Mumon does not leave you completely in the dark. He has provided handy commentaries that are sometimes more confusing than the *koan*:

> *Has a dog Buddha-nature?*
> *This is the most serious question of all.*

If you say yes or no,
You lose your own Buddha-nature.

The real problem here is understanding what *mu* (pronounced "moo") means and why that is the answer to the original question. I was told that *mu* meant "nothing" or "emptiness". But how can you answer the monk's question with "emptiness"? The monk is not asking if the dog has to pee and the response emptiness means that he doesn't. I mean, Joshu might as well have said hamburger or push-up bra or something.

I thought I was starting to figure this out so I went up to Rinchen and said, "In the story about Joshu's dog the monk asks if a dog has Buddha-nature, right?"

"Yes," said Rinchen, suddenly interested to know where I was going with this.

"Joshu says, 'mu', right? So what he is saying is that the question is unanswerable. That's why he says 'mu'. I mean, Mumon even says so in the commentary when he says that if you answer "yes" or "no" you will lose your own Buddha nature, right? So it is a trick. There is no answer." I was looking at Rinchen hoping to see some indication that I was correct. But it didn't happen. He simply smiled and said, "No, there is an answer to the question and it is 'mu'". With that he turned around and walked away and I am pretty sure that he was laughing at me under his breath.

But Rinchen did not always keep you guessing. Sometimes he would go to great pains to try to explain certain ideas that were particularly hard to understand. One time, I remember that someone had asked him if he could explain what the *bu* in *Budo* meant. As he started to answer the question, people all around the *dojo* started to tune in. Class was over and some people were still in their *gis* while others were already in their street clothes. As his explanation started to pour out into the quiet of the *dojo*, he eventually wound up in the middle of the mat sitting down with nearly all of his students gathered around him in a very intense discussion about the meaning of war.

He started his comments with "well, *bu* means 'war', but perhaps the better question is what is war?'" I remember this conversation because, well, it blew my mind. It was cold outside. The evaporated sweat from training had condensed and was frozen on the glass of the front door in a white sheet of frost. I had been in the *dojo* for a year and half, maybe a little more. As the conversation took off, even Tripp and Megan took a seat and joined in. Tripp was almost always genuinely interested in Rinchen's teachings. He really, really admired his dad and tried to be like him in many ways. Megan's relationship to

Rinchen was different. She loved her father in a cuddle-up-on-the-couch kind of way more than she admired his brilliance. She would never admit this, but she actually settled for getting tossed around the *dojo* because it was Rinchen's way of giving her a hug. She was interested in *Budo*, but liked to study it on her own. But there were some occasions when Rinchen would start talking about a subject that she had not figured out yet and it would catch her attention.

Thor was there and he asked the obvious opening question: "Okay, so I'll take the bait, what is war then?"

Rinchen pointed out that war was really just conflict - one force pitted against another force. He said that, in nature, this happens all the time and that, in fact, all of existence depends on it. "Look at the moon when it is clear and full. With the naked eye you can sometimes see the craters. This is the result of conflict. An asteroid, minding its own business, travels through space and crosses paths with the moon that is also minding its own business and traveling in its customary orbit. The asteroid hasn't the ability to change its course, nor does the moon, so they collide. The outcome is the destruction of the asteroid as it explodes and the creation of the crater. The asteroid and the moon, after their war, become one. After their war, the physical universe has a different shape. This is the way of all things."

"How is it the way of all things?" Tripp asked.

"Well, to begin with, everything in existence is the product of one kind of collision or another. Scientists like to talk about The Big Bang. They say there was an explosion and all of the solid matter in the universe scattered from the blast. Personally, I think this is only one step beyond the theory that the universe is held up by four enormous sea turtles, but the point is that every particle in the universe is in motion. Or at least that is how we see it. Everything is moving. Atoms move, subatomic particles move, people move. This creates a huge matrix of collisions that is ever-ongoing. The molecules in your own bodies are the products of these collisions; conflicts resolved by the formation of bigger and bigger molecules right up to your own DNA. The point is that we are trained in our comfort culture to see conflict between forces as a bad thing. I have no idea why. It is utterly superstitious. We would not exist without it. In fact, our whole reality is shaped and unfolds as things move through space, collide, and change into other things. This is true even with ideas. You say tomāto, I say tomăto, but eventually we call it a spaghetti sauce and it all works out. Think of it as a cosmic lava lamp."

"But what does that have to do with *Budo*?" I asked.

"You have to let go of your natural prejudice against the word "war". Normally, when we think of war, we think of anger and ferocity, death and destruction. War evokes in us a very negative visceral response. It is hard to see anything useful in it. This may, indeed, be what is going on in the minds of ordinary people trapped in war, but what is actually happening is something more akin to white blood cells attacking a bacterium. It is just an interaction. To a practitioner of *Budo*, that is *exactly* the experience. *Budoka* understand that an event is just an event. The feelings or horror or fear that we might have in a conflict do not arise from the conflict, but from the emotional attachments that we have created in our own minds. War is just another event without all of the drama that the normal hysterical mind associates with it. Try to look at it as simply the synthesis of energy bumping up against energy as it moves in different directions. On a personal level, it might be one sword striking another; on a broader level, it is two armies charging at each other. They are no different than the asteroid and the moon. One army believes that it needs to take one course of action and the other objects and opposes it. In other words, for whatever reason, the two forces collide. Why they do this is usually unimportant. The moon and the stars and the earth under your feet don't care about your reasons and justifications. The real world is the direct consequence of what actually happens and not the interpretive fairy tale we make up about it. Take language out of human activity and simply observe it as action and you see the same swirling forces colliding, merging and emerging over and over just like you might see in the confluence of two rivers. It is like watching a galaxy being formed. This is the nature of things and how existence in the world of things really works."

I tried to image all human activity like a big silent movie. In my mind there were people scurrying around, building things, destroying things, killing, dying and giving birth. It was just as he said. It began to look like shapes melting together and separating into something new.

Rinchen continued his thought: "Human beings add an extra dimension to all of this karmic activity. We think, we imagine and we dream. We whip everything that happens to us into our version of *Macbeth*. Sometimes I think that we have all seen so many movies and televisions shows that we process our own lives into a perpetual and hysterical narrative out of sheer habit. It is a form of insanity. We build huge mental structures, thoughts stacked upon other thoughts, like a giant house of cards and call it "reality". But it's not. It is just a house of concept, a virtual reality that is mostly fiction.

"If you have a religion, you might experience a sunrise as a gift from the divine rewarding you for donating to your church or temple. You might see a Western business man as a living devil trying to thwart the emergence of the Caliphate. Human beings live in a perpetual state of amusement and distraction that is disconnecting them from their own bodies let alone the rest of the world. Like drug addicts, we wander the darkness slashing at phantoms. But while we wander through our nightmares attacking each other, falling in love with shadows and fantasies, we are leaving real foot prints on the ground and cannot, for the life of us, understand why we are killing off our planet and beginning to resent much of the human race. We hate the people on the streets who get in our way because they are at odds with our internal fantasy. They are *other*.

"Like a race of spoiled children, we want to be left alone sucking on candy that is killing us as we wallow in the fantasy of our virtual lives imagined for us on televisions, computer screens and even on our cell phones. We cling, like starving beasts, to these figments of our imagination in a self-absorbed euphoria that arises in our minds as we are being tickled and stimulated by machines. We don't even bother to know our real world anymore. We thought we were becoming gods, but we really have become hungry ghosts."

"Wow, that's a buzz kill," I said absentmindedly as I was considering what Rinchen had just said.

"Maybe your buzz needs to be killed. Kill the buzz and get a life", Rinchen said with a startling look of ferocity in his eyes. He drew in a long breath and exhaled slowly as he was watching me closely awaiting a response that did not come.

"*Budoka* do not live in their heads. They live on the earth and because they do this, they develop an intimate relationship to everything around them, even death. They care about real trees and hear the sounds of cicadas. They love real people for what they are instead of performing surgery on them to please some arbitrary standard that has been sold to the masses as beauty. They possess the ultimate coping skills because they accept everything as it is and find perfection in common things. This power cannot be underestimated. Real warriors assume perfection and try to clear their minds to see it rather than entertain their whims and petty emotions with concocted stimulation. They know that life unaltered is magnificent and that it is only the obscurations of their own thinking that diminish the awe that they experience in contemplation of a single grain of sand. *Budoka* clear their minds to find heaven where they stand, in every moment and in every breath. They wage war on ignorance and delusion and resist the force of greedy people to impose addiction and obsession upon the human race. You will not find us staring off into an imaginary distance utterly distracted by mind-cartoons or catchy lyrics from a song about co-dependent love gone predictably wrong. You will find us smelling the air that we breath and opening our minds and our hearts to the chaos of the world around us. There is no higher calling than this."

"Wait a minute," said Megan. "You make it sound like people are complete idiots. I think we all probably agree that much of what you say is true. But people do *some* thinking and they make choices. They have some power over how they look at things and they can choose whether or not to take a stand."

"Yes, this is true, and the war of thoughts is just as karmically potent as a war in action. The difference is that a war of thoughts while colliding and changing like physical things do, has no substance. You can murder a thousand people in your mind while stuck in a traffic jam and have no fear of causing real harm because imaginary murder has no effect on the physical world, at least not directly. Likewise, you can cut a man down with your blade because he killed your brother or because he sneezed on your wife, but either way, you have killed him just the same. He is just as gone. The fantasy in your mind that inspired you to take such drastic action may be interesting in that it informed your blade to take a life, but in the end, all there is to say about it is a prayer for the dead. We spend an enormous amount of our time waging a war of thoughts trying to find motivation. Perhaps this is backwards. Perhaps we should simply look at the world and choose what we want to put in the space and do that. We need no reasons. Knee-jerk reactions are for dogs. Ultimately, this kind of war is an act of creation. We can simply form an intention and cause something to come into the world – so long as we have the skill to make it so."

"So what you are saying is that we should just go out into the world and do whatever we feel like doing because, in the end, it does not make a difference? Jesus, dad, if that is the case then why the hell do we have all of these rules in the *dojo*? Why should we choose compassion instead of hate, if it doesn't really make a difference?" This was rare for Megan. Rinchen was not her *sensei* in this moment, but rather, her dad and she was not buying what he was saying, not even a little bit.

Rinchen looked at his daughter with a calm smile. He wanted her to challenge him. He had nothing to defend. "You still have to be concerned about the consequences of your actions because you are filling up the future with them as you are stepping into it. If you go through life abusing everyone you meet, eventually you will step into a moment where everyone hates you and someone puts an end to you. Sure, you can do whatever you want, as long as you can live with your own vapor trail. Many people do just that. They drink and drug, rob and injure, fling themselves through their lives without the slightest concern for what they are causing in the world. We see teenagers making porn videos, drinking themselves into oblivion, gossiping about their friends and slandering their enemies. Then one day, they are grown up and on their second divorce. Their own children hate them and they find themselves alone. They take a new kind of drug, antidepressants, and no amount of therapy seems to make them happy. They have come to sit in the cesspool of their own crap and they have no idea how their lives came to be so unrewarding. And that's the point: just because you *can* doesn't mean you *should.*

"What if we made it our religion to take responsibility for the consequences of our actions instead? What if we did not blame the future on God or the way our parents raised us. What if we built a relationship with the consequences of our thoughts and actions before we made a mess of things. What if we used this new found power to clean up the messes that we made by careless living. If you do something rude to me, I could choose to get angry. I could easily justify retaliation or revenge with a list of good reasons. Everyone around me might even agree that I had a right to respond to you with hostility. I can even add this public approval to my endless list of reasons why. But if what I stand for is clarity, peace and happiness, then I cannot follow the path of reasons. I have to simply choose to cause peace for no reason at all; simply because that is what I have chosen to stand for. I can choose to interrupt the normal chain of cause and effect. I can choose to answer your rudeness with my kindness, because it is a chance to transform a hateful act into a loving consequence. It is like magic. If I respond with hostility and the animosity escalates, then I have only created a purgatory in my own backyard. Beating the hell out of each other is what reasonable people do. I want none of that. I want to cause awareness and harmony even if you don't deserve it. I want to be a big black hole that absorbs the fire of negativity and allows it to have no further consequence. With a committed mind, I can take this kind of a stand. I can say there shall be love in the face of hell fire and confusion."

I was breathless. Rinchen had built up his comments with a preacher's passion and lit my mind on fire. Megan, on the other hand, looked like a wolf moving in for the kill. "So, why not just let me kill you and there will be peace enough?" She smirked in anticipation of triumph.

Her father was unmoved. "There are occasions when that type of sacrifice might serve a compassionate intention. There have certainly been many great beings who have chosen to perish for the benefit of others. Most notably Jesus, for example. The benefit to sentient beings that comes from choosing to forfeit your life or fight for it depends on the depth of your insight and the skill you possess when you make your choice in the moment. If a monk sets himself on fire to show the world that enlightened consciousness can defeat suffering, he had better deliver the goods. If he runs through the streets ablaze screaming as he dies, he is no saint, but a fool. He will have thwarted his own intention with his own lack of skill. And yet, when Thich Quang Duc lit himself on fire in the streets of Saigon in 1963, this single gesture made an enormous impact on the entire world. Twelve thousand miles away, it turned a Midwestern farm boy into a Buddhist."

Rinchen did not elaborate on this last comment, but we all assumed that he was referring to himself. I had seen the photograph of the monk on fire and, at first, it scared the hell out of me. But as I learned more and more about *Budo*, I came to see the awesome power of that monk's serenity and sheer beauty in that photograph. It is funny how my training has so completely changed my mind about such things.

Rinchen could talk for hours and hours on a variety of subjects. Some of his teachings were like taking an elevator to the bottom of a mine shaft. He would meticulously take you down through each level of understanding so that you could appreciate the next layer as he drilled deeper and deeper into his subject. If you did not understand what he was doing, it would be quite easy to mistake him for a talkative bore. But if you thought that of him, then you were clearly not listening. Nothing that came out of his mouth was idle chatter. With every word that he spoke, he was trying to illuminate the darkest corner of every dull mind, one inch at a time, if need be.

Thor brought the subject back to fighting. "I can see how sacrifice can benefit people, but how is an adversary's mind improved by kicking his ass." Everyone wanted to know the answer to this question.

Rinchen paused for a minute to think about it. "A person can benefit from almost anything if it causes his mind to open and understand. You can get great teachings from a crack in the sidewalk, if you are open to learning. Simply stopping something from happening does not illuminate consciousness. The mind has to see something that it did not notice before. Sometimes the best we can do is to prevent someone from digging their hole deeper. If you stop a robbery, you may have also prevented a murder. If you calm a friend who is upset, you may have prevented her from being mean to someone else. But you have not necessarily changed how they think. What I do know is that compassion is very good medicine. Understanding the condition of others and trying to enable realization does no harm and often does a great deal of good. When we fight, we do not set our minds to 'kicking ass' as Thor-san has suggested. We are never trying to destroy someone. And yet, we may have to. We might, however, try to destroy the ignorance and mental obscurations that were motivating their harmful behavior. This is true enough. We do this with great prejudice, in fact. But what we are really trying to do is transform consciousness – ours and theirs. This is the high art of *Budo*. If you truly have skill, you will never have to lift a finger against anyone. The conflict will disappear before it become a fight. Fighting only happens when one or both sides just doesn't get it. There is no merit in learning how to crush other beings. This is the business of ignorant simpletons. This being said, we do make ourselves capable of withstanding and prevailing in attacks launched upon us. Our real fight, however, is with hate and malice, ignorance and greed. When those things provoke destructive behavior, we aspire to have the skill to engage this maelstrom and turn the hurricane into a gentle breeze. We *Budoka*, in fact, prefer to live in the eye of the storm – *taifu no me*, as the Japanese say."

The senior students all began to smile. They knew the *eye of the storm* all too well. The eye of a storm, especially a hurricane or typhoon, is the tranquil center around which rages violent winds. When you are attacked, sometimes the safest place to be is right in the center of flailing fists and blades. There are certain positions around an attacker's body that are referred to as "dead angles" or *shikaku*, in Japanese. They are like blind spots where an attacker has no real power. Many *Aikido* techniques involve stepping into the center of the storm or these blind spots and using them as safe havens to subdue the attacker's violence by influencing her own energy to work against her own hostile intention. Rinchen smiled as he observed the spark of recognition light up in the eyes of his students.

"The harm that beings do is almost always caused by ignorance or some delusional thinking that finds its way into our behavior. This is the real enemy, not the body that is merely following orders. We all do foul things. We all have moments of incredible ignorance. We must always remember that only the confused can rise up to enlightenment and, therefore, we should respect this inner chaos as the beginning of luminosity. At the same time, it is the intention of all true *Budoka* to deprive hate and ignorance of a place to live. Who's responsibility is it to make this so? Who's responsibility is it to engage these harmful acts that are born of confusion or malice? Because most people do not step up to this task, because they are afraid of the danger or too lazy to take on such a noble effort for the benefit of others, we are all forced to live in a world of mayhem. The suffering of humanity is only as great as we are willing to tolerate or unable to distinguish as suffering."

"Are you trying to suggest that we should go around wiping out bad guys like we are some kind of superheroes or something?" I asked.

Rinchen chuckled. "No, that would make us all quite annoying. And besides, domination is a fool's victory. Forcing people to behave a certain way does not relieve suffering because it does not change their minds, the source of the suffering, in fact, domination usually adds to it. Skillful *Budoka* seek to *blend* with the turmoil and bring it to order safely with as little harm done as possible. It is not oppressive. It is transformative. This is the *Aiki* way. We fill the natural spaces of our lives with compassion in an attempt to influence karma. We engage violence and transform it into harmony. But most of all, we take on the responsibility for the wellbeing of everything. This is our purpose. This is our commitment. If we are going to draw breath and walk this earth, we might as well make ourselves useful."

Megan was silent. She was thinking intently on what her father had just said. We all were. Rinchen gave us time to think this over and then he continued his lesson.

"My grandmother used to say that it does not matter whether or not you are sorry for the milk you spilled; you have still made a mess. Cleaning it up is the only real way to apologize. In other words, the road to hell is paved with good intentions, so get busy and make things right. How you feel about it is a useless fantasy. I have heard of a young woman who was driving down the freeway talking on her cellphone and putting on lipstick in her rearview mirror while trying to steer the car with her elbows. We have all seen something like this. In this case, the young woman struck a man changing his tire on the side of the freeway and killed him. The news report said that when the police interviewed her to get her version of what happened, her first word to the police officer was "ooops". This is a person who lives in darkness. This is a tornado that lashes out of its own mental oblivion and takes fathers away from innocent children forever. This is the danger of confusion. This is the danger of a shallow mind. In the history of the world, no one has ever caused an accident while paying attention. My point is that the only way to take suffering out of the world is to wake up, tune in and take responsibility for what happens. It means, as *Budoka*, we live a life by design rather than by accident. We strive to be clear headed by focusing our minds on what is going on around us and engaging the chaos when we think we can make a difference. This is our way, but it takes skill and clarity and so this is why we train."

Ho-lee-shit. Everything that I thought I knew disintegrated as I considered what Rinchen was saying. I had been living my life backward, like riding in the back of a pick-up truck and seeing only what I had already passed. By the time I had an opportunity to take in the scenery, it was already a mile behind me. I had rarely seen anything in real time and almost never noticed what I was creating in the future. But now, a new possibility was emerging. Now, I could look ahead into the empty space of a future that had yet to be born and plant a seed in it. I could cause love. I could cause awareness. I could cause almost anything. This is why the great masters say that they can see the end of the fight before it begins. Whoa.

This was getting way over my head, but it was still so fascinating to me. While my *dojo* brothers and sisters may have been thinking about samurai out on the battlefield or an encounter in a dark alley, I was thinking about the sources of conflict that were most familiar to me. My parents came to mind immediately, of course, but so did every argument I had ever had with anybody. It was all the same process. One person saw things one way, the other saw them another and both sides were clinging to their perceptions as if they were divine truths. When you think that truth is on your side, you are willing to make a big-ass stink about things. Isn't that pretty much how all conflicts go? Does it matter if it is a war in Iraq or a fight over the television remote? It is all the same thing, though the consequences can be drastically different, or not. I am sure someone has been killed over a television remote.

Tripp looked at his father and said thoughtfully, "If I understand you correctly then, all of existence is a product of war. Is that right?"

"Yes."

"So, war is not really destruction so much as it is the reorganization of energies, intentions, ideas and actions that will ultimately create whatever is next."

"Yes."

"How far does the power of human creation go?"

"As far as we have the skill to make it go."

"Are you saying that when we come to the end of our skill, existence is pretty much a random deal?'"

"What lies at the end of our skill is the natural chaos of the universe but it is not random. It only seems random to us because we cannot always comprehend the complexity of the interrelationships that are at play. There is no such thing as "random". There are limits to everyone's abilities merely by the fact that we have mortal bodies. The human being as thing, is as impermanent and finite as all other things inevitably are. The quality of your consciousness cannot help you with impermanence. You can take a fully enlightened being and chain him to a tree and shoot him and despite his enlightenment, he is still going to die. Even Buddha died. In the physical world, sometimes that is what there is to do – just die. Every one of us will face that moment eventually. No matter what diet you keep, no matter how much exercise you get, sooner or later you are done for. There comes a time when the only thing to do is to simply cease. Events are not infinitely alterable because they depend on what came before them and the conditions in the moment. The karma of everything, however, eventually exhausts itself as a practical matter. "Random" is just the term that we use when we are ignorant of how the chain of cause and effect has unfolded. We might as well exchange that word with the phrase "blind to how it really works". In the Buddhist world, we call this interconnection of all things *dependent origination*. In other words, everything that happens depends on a very precise set of circumstances and interconnections, a web if you will, that causes them to happen in the only way that they can happen. While some connections between phenomenon may seem to be stronger and more obvious than others, if a grasshopper sneezes in China, it is still felt on the moon."

Holy crap! You don't learn about that in Vogue (although you might learn about it in Vanity Fair). As Rinchen was talking, an idea rose in my mind. Suddenly the whole universe was just this big swirl of energies and forces pushing on each other. The actual shape of the world was being molded like clay by all of these forces pushing and tugging on it in every direction. Even my own body was the product of this kind of war.

Elvis had officially left the building. I was getting a headache trying to follow this conversation even though I kind of, sort of, got the gist of it. But I was getting one thing out of it for sure: I was starting to understand why all this talk about emptiness was important. Even though it was very hard to keep it all straight in my mind, I could see that this was why *Budoka*, Buddhists, Hindus and others were always saying things like "existence is a delusion," "life is empty and meaningless" and stuff like that. They weren't kidding, it really is like that.

"So that's how all this emptiness stuff works," I said. Rinchen smiled and replied, "sorry, but no. You see, the minute you create an idea that there is a way that it works, you have created a distinction, a concept, and you are no longer experiencing what is in front of you, but rather, you are now relating to your idea of it. You are chewing on your own thoughts. It is like trying to know a rose by its shadow. The thought of a rose is not a flower. It's a thought. It is like we cannot simply look directly at something and see it for what it is. We have to draw a picture of it in our mind and then admire our interpretation of it. You have cut at the uncarved block. This is the shadow world; sorry, no cookie for you!"

"Ohhhhh, so that's what Joshu was talking about. The minute you create the concept of Buddha nature and try to stick it onto your dog like a post-it note, you have actually destroyed Buddha nature by creating the concept. What a crafty dude that guy was! Ooops, I just destroyed my own Buddha nature by saying that!" I was really just rambling and trying to chase this stuff around in my mind, but when I brought my attention back into the room and looked at Rinchen, he was staring at me with the sweetest, most loving expression on his face.

"That's exactly so, Lhamo, exactly so. Good for you!" he said softly.

When I was born, my mom started a scrap book that has all sorts of things in it that she thought were important. She called it my "Baby Book". There was my hospital bracelet from when I was born; a lock of hair from my first hair cut; a picture that I had scribbled on the back of an envelope. Everything that she felt was a souvenir of my life was in that book. Around our house, it came to represent the record of my life; sometimes as a joke. I remember coming home with my first speeding ticket. My mom was pissed. She said sarcastically, "great, we can put this in your Baby Book". I think that if I was the keeper of my own Baby Book, I would need to put the *koan* about Joshu's dog in it. After that night when I learned about the art of war for real, I would never see anything the same again. It was a moment that changed my past, present and future all at the same time. From that moment on, and as I would come to understand *mu* better and better, my point of view began to shift and my choices began to change at a dizzying speed. My mind had collided with Rinchen's and it had left a crater on the surface of the moon.

Chapter Thirty-three: All I Want For Christmas Is A Very Sharp Katana

Swords and guns are considered boys' toys although I saw on the internet that they now make real guns in pink. I am not sure how pink became the banner color of women. In my mind, it is a color of weakness. It lacks the passion of red and the purity of white. It seems to have settled on being cute. It is a hard color to take seriously. But I just made that up. I am pretty sure that you would take the color pink seriously enough if a pink gun just shot you in the face.

Swords have pretty much gone extinct. They are not very effective against an Uzi. Swords and knives are the last vestiges of a race that once had to train its children how to kill using manual labor. Now we have machines to do it for us. Rinchen says that facing an enemy created the opportunity for peace in the middle of war. If you had to look someone in the eye, it was much harder to kill them. You had to face death, know who did the killing and watch someone die, that is, if you won the fight. You could not escape your responsibility in the matter. You were up close and personal to a life and death struggle and that made you have to think about it. It was a very hard thing to take lightly. Shooting a missile off a ship, however, makes killing a piece of cake.

At the *dojo* they drum it into your brain that *Aikido* is *Budo* – part of the art of war. As a girl growing up, I didn't give much thought to war. It was not part of my process, at least, not like it was for the boys at school. While women are joining the Army by the thousands, modern war is still mostly a guy thing. It is still about dominance and control. Modern war still has a penis.

But it hasn't always been that way. In the Japanese tradition, there are many stories about famous women who won battles and saved clans. Rinchen told me once about a woman named Tomoe Gozen. She was an expert at sword and bow and played a pivotal role in capturing the city of Kyoto during the Genpei War in the Twelfth Century. Japanese history does not diminish the role of women in history quite as much as Western History does. Have you ever noticed that if you open up an art history book it is mostly filled with the work of men? I suppose that men had more access to education and training in the arts, but there were many, many educated women throughout Western history that were really good artists. Many of their pieces hang in fancy museums all over the world with the names of men painted on them.

I remember having to do a report on Auguste Rodin, the dude who supposedly made *The Thinker* sculpture. I say "supposedly" because when I started Googling this guy, I found several articles about a woman named Camille Claudel. She supposedly did a lot of Rodin's work for him although, in the end, it all had his signature on it. If a guy tried to pull that crap in my school, he would get suspended for plagiarism. How this Rodin guy got away with it, I don't know, but someone should have straightened his ass out.

Sometimes the woman got the props. Take Joan of Arc, for instance. At first, the men would not let a chick fight against the English in the Hundred Years War even though the French all-guy army had been getting its ass kicked for decades and were getting kind of desperate. She claimed to have been told by angels that the French could win and this inspired the soldiers who really wanted to go home and forget about the English altogether. Eventually, she got so pushy about it, that they gave her a chance. The soldiers believed that God was on her side, so they got their act together and beat up on the English. She is a fluke of Western history in that no one seems to have been interested in trying to diminish what she did, except for the English, of course, who were thoroughly pissed that they got beat up by a girl. They captured her and burnt her at the stake because they could not wrap their minds around the fact that a chick with a bunch of her guy-friends could kick their butts like that. It had to be devils' work. What assholes.

In American history there were women warriors, most of whom no one bothered to remember. There was Deborah Sampson who dressed up like a man and fought in the American Revolution. That cross-dressing-to-serve-your-country theme is actually a fairly common one. There were lots of women who disguised themselves as men to fight in the Civil War and were not discovered until they were shot and someone took off their clothing.

One of my favorites is a woman that Tripp actually told me about, Mary Edwards Walker. She was a hoot. She actually went to medical school, became a doctor and married a guy who was also a doctor. She and her husband started up a medical practice together even though most people would ask for her husband instead of her because she was a woman. When the Civil War broke out, she volunteered as a surgeon with the Union Army, but was only allowed to be a nurse. At the Battle of Bull Run, however, they apparently ran short of doctors so they allowed her to perform surgery. She saved a lot of lives. She was eventually promoted to be an actual field surgeon and was known for treating soldiers of either army and civilians too. She was eventually captured wandering behind enemy lines looking for injured people to help and was imprisoned by the Confederates as a spy. I guess that the Confederate army guys must have been descended of the same English guys who burnt Joan of Arc at the stake just because she kicked their asses. It seems that the Confederate brass had a hard time wrapping their minds around the idea that a woman could be a doctor and that a Northern woman doctor could care about wounded Southern soldiers. Why is it that when a woman does something exceptional in history she is either a witch, a spy, or a lesbian?

She was so well thought of by the Union Army, that they negotiated to get her back during a prisoner exchange while the war was still going on. She went right back to the front lines and marched with the Union Army all the way to Atlanta. She is the only woman to be awarded the Congressional Medal of Honor for combat service.

The cool thing about Mary Edwards Walker is that she hated wearing dresses. She was actually arrested for wearing men's clothing several times. Supposedly, she was not gay or anything, but just thought men's clothing was more practical. She went on to be a big deal in the fight for women's rights. She died in 1919, one year before they amended the Constitution to allow women to vote. According to an article that I read on the internet, she was buried in a man's suit with the American flag draped on her coffin as a military honor. Now that's a power chick.

So it came as a complete surprise to my parents, probably as much as Mary Edward's Walker's suits came as a complete surprise to her parents, if they ever lived to see her wear them, when I put at the top of my Christmas list my senior year, a real, very sharp sword called a *katana*. I am pretty sure, I was the only girl in Westchester to ask for one of those in the history of that place and it threw my mom and dad for a loop, because you cannot get them at Macy's. "Why on earth, do you want a real *katana?*" asked my mom.

"So that I can start taking *tame shigiri* lessons," I replied matter-of-factly.

"Tommy who?"

"*Tame shigiri* -- the art of making real cuts with a sword. It is not as easy as it looks and you cannot practice with the wooden *bokkens* that I already have. I really want to learn how to do this and I have to have the equipment to do it." My mom had come to be a good sport about the motorcycle, but asking for a real sword was just a hair's width away from asking for a gun. The truth of it is that she never minded the practice weapons like the bamboo practice sword called a *shinai* (pronounced "shin-eye") that we use for *Kendo* practice or the wooden practice sword called a *bokken* that we use to practice sword forms. She figured that those couldn't actually hurt anyone. Actually, they are both as lethal as a real sword in the hands of someone who knows how to be lethal. In fact, Rinchen once told us that Miyamoto Mushashi once fought his most famous duel with a *bokken* that he carved out of a boat oar on his way to the fight. A *bokken*, in particular, can screw you up, but I could think of no reason to mention this to my mom.

I got on the internet with my mom and showed her the web site of the company that made the sword that Rinchen had recommended that I get. They were not made like real historical blades. Real *katanas* made by real Japanese sword smiths cost thousands of dollars. For centuries, Japanese sword smiths experimented and tested new techniques to come up with a sword blade that was sharp, would stay sharp and would not shatter when used to block another sword. Back in the day, this was the most important military technology in Japan. Secrets were stolen and smiths were even kidnapped to find out how they made their blades. This was a matter of extremely high priority for the samurai.

Cutting anything with a sword eventually dulls the blade. Cutting through a guy's neck really dulls a blade. Swords were tested on dead bodies and sometimes on living ones. They would take a number of dead bodies and stack them on a sand pile and would then do the classic downward cut called *shomenuchi.* The number of bodies that the blade could cut through in a single stroke would become the rating of the sword. The smith would engrave the rating on the tang of the blade and it would read something like "two in one stroke" or "four in one cut". Rinchen said that the best swords ever made were rated at "five in one cut". Sword making awesomeness was not always determined by dead guys. Rinchen said that the most legendary sword smith ever, a guy named Masamune, made blades so sharp that they could be dipped into a stream and cut leaves being pushed along by the current.

Fun fact: Rinchen says that occasionally they tested blades on live slaves. A lot of slaves took issue with this practice. Occasionally, a slave knew that he was going to be used for live blade testing would get even by swallowing rocks before the sword test. They would still get killed, but the rocks in their stomachs would destroy the blade by chipping it. It is pretty grim stuff, but if I was going to get cut in half to test a blade, I would want to make sure they remembered me too.

The *tame shigiri* sword that I wanted, however, was not that exotic. Modern practice blades are made of spring steel and have hardened cutting edges that can hold up to hundreds of practice cuts. To the untrained eye, they look like historical blades, but they are not that sophisticated. Traditionally, swords were fitted to the precise body size, strength and fighting style of its owner. On the internet, however, you have to choose from four or five basic styles in small, medium and large. Richen said that I needed a medium.

If you had told me a year and a half ago that Japanese swords were amazing, I would have changed the subject. But they are real works of art if you know how to appreciate them. Rinchen has been collecting real swords for years and has an incredible collection of them that Tripp says is extremely valuable. He keeps some of them in a safe in his bedroom at his loft. There are many parts to a *katana*, but the ones to really look at are the blade, the hand guard called a *tsuba*, the handle called a *tsuka* and the sheath called a *saya*. *Sayas* are usually, but not always, coated in shiny black lacquer. You can see yourself in the shine of these things. The *tsukas* have a core of wood that is wrapped in the skin of a manta ray and then there is a kind of braided wrapping around them to form a grip. Under the braided wrapping are two metal charms called *menuki*. These help improve the grip, but are also used to bring some kind of blessing or good luck. I wanted *menuki* in the shape of *vajras* for my sword. A *vajra* is supposed to represent a lightning bolt of awareness. It is the kind of spark of light that jolts you into enlightenment. In Tibetan, it is called a *dorje*. The symbol looks like two small bird cages on either side of a handle. (This is supposed to be the lightning.) I wanted these *menuki* on my sword, because that is the symbol of Rinchen's dharma name. Rinchen Dorje means "precious *vajra*" and he most certainly has been a precious bolt of lightning that has shocked my ass awake.

Since Jeanie and Henry had never ordered a weapon before, let alone a live *katana*, I made it easy for them and wrote down the website and product codes to make their buying experience more pleasurable. I told my mom that if she really loved me that she could also buy me the matching *wakasashi*, that is the shorter second sword that samurai carried in their belts, but I knew that I would be really pushing my luck to get the *katana*.

My family has no real religion anymore. Neither of my parents were ever big on going to church even though both of them come from sort of Christian families and went to church when they were young. There are all types of religions in Westchester; we even have a mosque. There are Catholics, Jews, Evangelicals and a whole lot of Mormons in my suburb. I have never met a Buddhist there, but I am sure if you looked for them that there are probably some closet Buddhists around somewhere because there are a fair number of Chinese people that live near me. Most of the Chinese parents are scientists or college professors and I hear their kids complain at school about having to go to the temple in Augusta from time to time.

Religion or not, Christmas is part of our tradition. In fact, it is one of our *only* traditions. Like most families, we totally overdo it at our house. It is an orgy of conspicuous consumption. Every year, I get clothes and make-up, a book or two and the Grand Prize, whatever that might be. The Grand Prize is that one big thing that, if you have done your calculations carefully, will stretch, but not break, your parents' Christmas budget. It is the offering that you know that they will make to you to show you that they really do love you because why else would they max out their credit cards. You usually have to lobby for a Grand Prize over a period of months. This starts by dropping hints and can end up with begging if you have no self-esteem. Sometimes you don't always get what you want. I remember the year that my brother asked for a motorized go-kart and got a new bicycle instead. One year, I wanted tickets to see a rap group called Boy Toyz and didn't even get the CD. My mom said it had something to do with the lyrics of the songs that talked about "beating bitches" or something like that. I had to settle for a new digital music player. Of course, I copied someone else's CD and put every Boy Toyz song on it anyway.

In this year, it was going to be tough because my parents had already popped for a motorcycle and that pretty much blew up their discretionary income and was way beyond the normal gift. The *katana* I wanted was $300. This was within the normal range of Grand Prize spending, but the motorcycle was threatening to undo the whole thing. It didn't really matter that much. My parents had racked up a decade of bonus points with the motorcycle purchase and I was not about to complain.

As it turned out, I got my *katana*. I was so excited! My brother wanted to play with it and had to be told that it was a lethal weapon. I found a place to hide it in my room so that he could not find it and cut his fingers off when nobody was looking and, more importantly, not wreck it.

Shortly after Christmas we had a couple of inches of snow that, in typical St. Louis fashion, stayed on the ground for all of three days. Tripp and I had once watched an old Japanese samurai movie where the hero trains in his bare feet in the snow. I wanted to try that out. I was ready to join the ranks of real samurai now that I had a real sword. So, I put on my *gi* and *hakama* and took my *katana* out into the backyard. The snow had just fallen and barely reached the top of my feet, but it was enough to live the dream. I got through about three or four sword forms before my feet turned beet-red and then started to go numb. The Slavin kids next door were watching me through the sliding glass door of their kitchen. When Mrs. Slavin came to see what they were looking at, she was quite startled and whisked them away. I used to babysit for the Slavins until I got my motorcycle. The sword was just another bit of proof that I was a deeply troubled girl in Mrs. Slavin's eyes. As it turned out, I guess I am no samurai. After five minutes I had to come in and soak my feet in hot water.

Tame shigiri practice only happened twice a month. There were only about five people in any one class. Only three students, Tripp, Megan and now me, had swords. Rinchen makes us take thin sheets of plywood that have been painted to prevent splinters and place them on the mat. During *tame shigiri* practice, occasionally a sword slips from someone's hands and while he does not care if you punch a hole in your foot, he will not allow holes in his mat. In the summer, *tame shigiri* practice is always done outside.

Cutting an object with a sword looks easy, but it is not. Rinchen has these bamboo mats that are soaked in water before they are used and they take on the consistency of a bunch of carrots. The mats are rolled to a size that approximates a man's neck and are mounted on a wooden rack at various heights to represent various limbs. The idea is to cut through the rolled mat with a single stroke. To watch an expert, like Rinchen, this looks easy. To watch a beginner, like me, it is hilarious. Most people, despite hours of sword form training (Rinchen will only allow you to do *tame shigiri* when you are part of the advanced class) will swing the sword like an axe. The blade hits the target and bounces off barely making a nick. This is because a Japanese sword is really a slicing weapon. The blade has to actually be pulled across the surface of the target in order for it to cut. This means that you have to manage the stroke in such a way so as to be able to pull the blade across the surface of the target while moving the sword toward the target at the same time. This is a very hard movement to learn. I did not get through my first target until my third class.

Rinchen says that in the olden days, in order to become a Shinto priest, you had to demonstrate that you had mastered control over your mind and body to the extent that you could defeat the cutting properties of *katanas* in an ultimate test of courage and skill. They would make a ladder out of *katana* blades with the sharp edges facing up and then make the candidate climb up the ladder of blades in bare feet. If you pressed your foot exactly straight down on a blade, it would not cut you. Slip just one millimeter to the side and this would start the slicing action of the sword and it would cut your foot in half. This test proved that you were in complete control of mind and body and, of course, had guts. As far into this *Aiki-Budo* thing as I have gotten, there is no fucking way I am ever going to try something like that. Of course, I would have said the same thing about diving rolls two years ago.

Before I joined the *dojo*, New Year's Eve meant going to a sleep-over at someone's house or watching TV with my parents. At the *dojo*, New Year's Eve is celebrated the same way we celebrate everything else – with training. Rinchen holds a special class that starts at 11:30 pm and ends at 12:30 am. The point of this class is to end the year and begin the next one doing the one thing that we are supposed to be the most committed to – developing ourselves. This workout is slower paced than a regular class, more meditative, and is taught in absolute silence. The only acknowledgement of midnight is that the senior student strikes a gong once at 12:00 a.m. The class ends with a longer period of meditation than normal and I have to say that I really, really love the whole idea of this. It is a completely different deal than the drunken bashes that my friends go to. It is just another way in which *dojo* life is on purpose.

After training, small tables are set up on the mat and food is brought in and there is *sake* for those old enough to drink and soda for those who don't drink alcohol. Megan worked it out so that we had *sake* with the adults. At her father's house, when his kids turned fifteen, they were always offered alcohol if it was being served. Rinchen's rule was that the twins could drink at home but never, ever anywhere else unless he gave his permission and he never did. Rinchen, however, only applies this rule to his own children and the children of other parents are never offered alcohol at all unless they are twenty-one years old. Megan says that her dad thinks that the reason kids are so interested in intoxication is because Americans have made such a big deal out of it and because of that, everyone associates drinking with being an adult. He says that kids drink because they think it makes them grown up, when it really just proves that they are not. Rinchen, personally, rarely drinks any kind of alcohol preferring tea or water. I have seen Tripp occasionally drink a beer at home, but generally speaking neither Tripp nor Megan really like to drink although they will hit the *sake* at the *dojo* on New Year's Eve. Rinchen pretended that he did not notice me drinking *sake* which was unusual for him. His ethics are usually non-negotiable. We were going to crash at his house that night and no one would be driving. He was watching the other young people, however, like a hawk. I guess I was really becoming his "other daughter" as he often called me when we were not around the *dojo*.

Drinking toasts with *sake* is an ancient *Budo* tradition. It happens at parties and even memorials for the dead. I have heard that the samurai could be incredible drunks. I asked Rinchen about this once. He said that personally he did not like to drink because he worked too hard to get his mind clear and that he could feel the effects of even a single glass of wine for days after he drank it. He said that he hated it when his mind was foggy and that he didn't take some medicines for the same reason. He said that drinking for a *Budoka* is like washing your car and then throwing mud on it. It was something that simply did not make sense. He also said that many people drink to feel better and that if you maintained your mind in a clear state, no amount of drinking could make you feel better than that. He said a clear mind has real courage. It has a natural ability to face difficulty despite being afraid, and does not need anything to hold it up. He said that drugs and alcohol are the medicines of hungry ghosts and unsettled minds that have never learned how to engage reality as it is. And yet, on New Year's Eve, even Rinchen was drinking *sake*. There are a few things like that in the *dojo*; things that don't make perfect sense or are inconsistent as if on purpose. It is as if, on rare occasions, that discipline and tradition must be tarnished for a brief moment so that there is something to polish and renew when we resume our training.

I have never been a big drinker mainly because I never wanted to look like a fool. My dad likes to have scotch every once in a while. I have sipped a little out of my dad's glass and it nearly made me gag. Beer is not so bad, but it makes you feel bloated and who needs all those carbs? Some girls that I know like to drink things like flavored vodka and I have even tried some drinks that taste like soda pop. I did get drunk once and it wasn't so bad. It was kind of fun. And I didn't even get a hangover. At the New Year's Eve party, I had more than a few cups of *sake* and I was getting a little happy. I noticed that I was pretty much ready to jump Tripp's bones. But then again, I was almost always ready to jump Tripp's bones. I noticed that the *sake* made it a little bit harder to want to restrain myself. I had to think about that for a while. Why would someone want to take something that gave them the opportunity to step outside themselves like that? I mean, I get the whole freedom thing, but shouldn't you be free naturally? I don't get that getting drunk makes you free so much as it turns you into a moron. I am not interested in being out of control. I am just starting to figure out how to bring myself under control and it is hard work. And yet, I do like to drive over the speed limit on my motorcycle. I love the rush of leaning into a curve at high speed. That can kill me deader than a few beers or a joint. I guess what I like about riding my motorcycle is that I know where my limits are and I push them outward through practice and skill. When you are getting fucked up, you are going past your limits, but there is no skill there to help you. In fact, it is the opposite of skill. It is pretty stupid when you think about it. And yet, that *sake*, while it tasted kind of crappy, or at least to me it did, was warm in my tummy and was making me feel mighty fine.

Rinchen says that you cannot use training to try to tie yourself to a tree so that you are safe from making mistakes. He says that the greatest wisdom sometimes come from making a perfect ass of yourself. It is one thing to make an ass of yourself and learn from it and quite another thing to make being an ass a lifestyle. He says that his Buddhist teacher once sat down with one of his own teachers and they killed a fifth of tequila because they wanted to know what getting drunk was like. They saw all these people wrecking their lives on booze and had no idea what it was about, so they decided to find out first hand. Rinchen said that his teacher told him that he did not like it, that all that happened was that he got a headache. "Why you Americans give yourselves big headache?" Rinchen said, imitating his teacher's accent. It was funny to watch Rinchen imitate his teacher. He says that neither his teacher's teacher, nor his teacher ever bothered to drink again. While I am pretty sure that this will not be my experience, I have come to love the clarity of my own mind. Joy is a much sweeter experience when you know that it arises from the facts of your life rather than from a bottle, pill or pipe. There is strength in always facing what is as it is.

Chapter Thirty-four: You Can't Bring A Llama Into The Dojo, They Spit

Rinchen knows a lot of teachers from all over the world. Occasionally, some of these teachers come to visit and do weekend seminars. Some stay even longer. In January, word was passed through the *dojo* that a special guest was coming to visit. His name was Lama Yeshe Jinpa, but the only part of the memo that landed in my mind was that he was Rinchen's Buddhist teacher. I was getting dressed for class in the dressing room when Megan came in with Becky Danwick. "We are going to have a lama here next week," Megan said as she dumped her *do-gi* bag on a chair and started pulling off her T-shirt.

"Who is being assigned to take care of him?" asked Becky.

"Probably Tripp, although my dad does most of the work by himself because he considers it to be his obligation."

"How long is he in for?"

"A week, I think," said Megan.

"Okay, well we better get the place tidied up, then."

"Yeah, I will get a schedule together tonight; there is a lot of cleaning that needs to be done." I had no idea what they were talking about.

"Whose coming?" I asked.

"We are bringing in a lama next Monday. He will be in the *dojo* for a week. My dad expects this place to be spotless. This is not just *any* lama, this is *his* lama and next week is very important to him." I thought to myself, why on earth would anyone bring a llama into a *dojo*. This was alarming to me.

"You can't bring a llama in here, they spit. My god, the place will be a mess." I was just a little put out by the mere idea of it. Normally, Megan was the one correcting me. I couldn't believe that she did not know this.

Becky and Megan burst into laughter, Becky was nearly crying because she was laughing so hard. Megan started to hold her crotch and was jumping up and down saying, "oh shit, oh shit, I'm going to pee," but she couldn't stop laughing.

"What's so funny?" I asked just a little pissed off. I may have still been in high school, but I took biology and we studied llamas and everyone knows that llamas spit.

Finally, Megan got a hold of herself, and said, "He's not a *llama* like the animal, he is a Tibetan Buddhist teacher, they call them *lamas*. It literally means *high mother*, but most of them are men. But, oh, my dad and Tripp are going to *love* this!"

Suddenly, I was embarrassed. For once, I thought that I had the 411 on something, but instead I had made a perfect idiot of myself. Great. Rinchen always referred to his teachers using the term *master*. Megan and Tripp had always used the term *teacher*. They had mentioned numerous times *our dharma teacher*, *my dad's master* and one time they had even referred to him as *rinpoche* (pronounced *rin-po-shay*), but who knew that his actual title was *lama*?

The joke spread through the *dojo* like wildfire. You could hear someone mumble a little bit and then there was a burst of laughter. The one thing about *dojo* life is that you will eventually make a complete ass of yourself and how you handle your humiliation is very important. If you get defensive you will be coached by your *sempai* or your *sensei* about taming your ego. If you laugh at yourself too much, you will have given up your self-respect. The best thing to do is just take your beating and say as little about it as possible.

When Rinchen came out to start class, he looked as blank and empty as always. He clapped us in and then turned to face the class. We bowed, but when he came out of his bow he had the slightest trace of a smile on his face. "We are going to have a special guest here next week. Lama Yeshe Jinpa will be here. Tripp, Megan and I will largely be responsible for his care and feeding …"

Tripp started to snicker but was desperately trying to suppress it. He would spit out a giggle or two and then contain himself. Then Megan would start to giggle and he would start losing it all over again.

Rinchen looked at the two of them with mock sternness and cleared his throat loudly as if to warn them to be quiet.

"As I was saying, we will be having a lama here, and not just any lama, but *my lama* ... "

This time it was Becky Danwick trying mightily not to laugh. Rinchen looked over at her and raised his eyebrows, but was still smiling just ever so slightly. Becky quieted down.

"AS I WAS SAYING," said Rinchen, raising his voice, "we are bringing a lama here and you each will have a job to do to keep the *dojo* in order. Becky, I would like you to make sure that the mats are clean. Thor please tidy up the office. Lhamo, I want you to make sure that the lama gets a haircut, because I want to make a sweater...."

That was it. The entire *dojo* lost it at once. Tripp was lying on his side in convulsions. Megan was bent over with her forehead on the mat and holding her stomach and heaving up and down. Matt, was slapping the mat in hysterics. But Rinchen kept a mostly straight face and was looking around pretending that he didn't know what all the fuss was about.

The *dojo* is usually a very formal place, but every formal place needs to be desecrated for its own good every now and then. While Rinchen rarely broke form, when he did, the sheer rarity of it made a huge impression on everyone. A good teacher knows to be rigid when it is time to be rigid and funny when it is time to be funny. Rinchen was a master of keeping balance in the *dojo*. He never let it get too slack and he never let it get too serious. He always seemed to know how to set the right tone. And on that particular day, it was entirely at my expense.

To this day when the subject of lamas comes up in *dojo* in my presence, someone always says, "oh shit, not a lama, watch out they spit!" or something equally stupid. I could train at Byakuren Dojo for a hundred years and they will still be beating me over the head with a bag of llama spit at every opportunity. So be it. They even told Lama Jinpa about it when he got there and he laughed his ass off.

I had never met a human lama before. I had seen pictures of the Dalai Lama and could have saved myself a whole lot of embarrassment had I made the connection between his title and his name. I knew that he was highly respected around the world. Everyone who had met Lama Jinpa spoke well of him and said that he was a really cool guy, but I was not that familiar with Tibetan Buddhism despite my Tibetan nickname. I had Googled Tibetan Buddhism a little, but everything I read made it seem like a wild and crazy religion with gobs of deities that looked like demons chewing on people's heads and stuff. But the fact that Rinchen, Tripp and Megan practiced this type of

Buddhism gave it a lot of credibility as far as I was concerned. It was what my boyfriend thought about when he sketched flaming lotus blossoms.

After class was over and everyone had gotten their jabs in about llama spit, Tripp and I walked down Washington Avenue to his loft. He was merciful and had let the joke pass. It was already pretty worn out. I had a lot of questions about his religious ideas. He did not usually talk about it much, but with Lama Jinpa coming, I wanted to know more about it.

"Have you always been Buddhist?" I asked.

"Sort of," he said. "My dad has practiced for as long as I can remember and I kind of just grew up in it. My mom is Christian and there was always this subtle holy war thing going on in our house when my parents were together. My dad did not push it on us, but we were up to our ears in it. Sometimes my mom would start banging the bible pretty hard and my dad felt that some of it was harmful to us so we would always get a Buddhist counter argument regarding one thing or another. My dad particularly dislikes the idea that religion should make you feel guilty and my mom is all about guilt so that was pretty much an ongoing dispute. I was always more interested in it than Megan. It is what my dad did and so I figured that it is what boys are supposed to do."

"Wow. As if it isn't hard enough to deal with parents as it is."

"I suppose it could have been worse."

"But you seem to really get into this stuff. It doesn't seem to me that it is all about your dad." Tripp looked down the street as if the thought he was having was standing on the corner. After a second he said, "it isn't about my dad at all. It's about me. Both the *Budo* and Buddhist worlds make sense to me. They are logical. Karma is logical. Shit in, shit out. Love in, love out. I was raised to live a thoughtful life and I guess I can't see how I would do it any other way."

"I am glad that you can't. Your way is pretty damn cool."

"I don't know about cool, but I like getting up in the morning knowing what I am about. I like knowing that I can walk into the *dojo* and make myself a better man every day without fail. A lot of my friends are lost and wandering around throwing themselves at useless and even desperate things. They don't have a path. I watch them struggle to figure out why they even draw breath let alone what they should be when they grow up. There is something really valuable in having a method to your madness. You don't know where it is always going to take you, but you always know where to look for answers when you need them."

I had to stop and just take him in for a second. What teenage guy says stuff like that? The sexiest, coolest most loveable thing in all of guydom is a man who knows who he is and what he is about and isn't selling any of it to anyone -- especially, when what he is about is strength, love and compassion. Holy crap! All I could do was just stand there and look at him.

"What?" he said suddenly wondering what he had said that had left me thunderstruck like that.

"I want to be like you," I said. "I want to care like you care. I want to push my limits like you do. I might want to be a little smarter than you and I definitely want to be better looking than you, but god fucking damn it, I want to be like you." As I said this, I realized that I had taken two handfuls of his leather coat and was shaking him back and forth, much to his amusement.

"Well, you are already doing *Aikido*. I suppose, you could take refuge and do the Chenrezig empowerment. I know I got a lot out of it."

"What did you get out of it, exactly?" I asked. Tripp looked deep into my eyes as if he was considering whether or not I would understand what he was about to say.

"A purpose." That is all he said. That is all he had to say. I knew exactly what he meant and it was awesome.

When we got to the loft, Tripp made some tea and we sat on the couch with our feet on the coffee table sipping away and discussing big things like the origin of the mind, whether physical stuff was really there and what was up with all of those funny looking Tibetan deities. Tripp told me that before Lama Jinpa gave the Chenrezig empowerment, he would provide students with the opportunity to take *refuge*.

"What is refuge?" I asked.

"I guess you could say it is like Buddhist baptism. It is the thing that we do to become an official Buddhists, not that being *official* makes a real difference. It is a pretty simple ceremony, really. You start out by renouncing your attachment to the material world and to your own ego and promise to cut through mental delusions to reach enlightenment. There is one catch. You have to promise that you will reach enlightenment for the benefit of all sentient beings. Of course, there is no way to reach enlightenment through selfishness, so it is really no big deal. Basically you are saying that you want to come in from the storm of craziness and seek shelter in sanity."

"That's it?" It seemed so simple.

"Well, that and you then have to prove that you mean it by cutting off all of your hair. But that's no big deal. It grows back." He was serious. I couldn't believe it. I was hoping to become a Buddhist and slip it by my parents, but getting a cue-ball cut was going to be a give-away. Henry and Jeannie would crap their pants and the wrath of shit that I would take at school would be overwhelming. I really wanted something a little less committed. This was a game changer for me. "Holy shit, Trippster, there is no way. Even the Girls Scouts start you out as a Brownie. Don't you guys have something like that?"

"See how you are clinging to your looks? It means that you are not ready to renounce the things that you have to give up to really start working on this. If you can't get past the hair cut, how are you ever going to give up eating meat and donating all of your free time to the poor. And three hours of meditation a day, well forget it. Maybe you should try one of those internet religions. I hear that for thirty-five bucks you can call yourself 'reverend'".

"What? Nobody said anything about any of this stuff? There has to be a baby-step way into this where you give up eating meat two days a week and try to be nice to people for a probation period or something. Wait a minute! We just had hamburgers after training last night. You're a lying little shit!" Tripp could no longer keep a straight face. He had played me bad. There was only one thing to do – kick his ass.

As I jumped on top of him and was beating him with one of the couch cushions, Rinchen and Megan walked in. Megan turned nonchalantly to her father as he closed the door behind them and said, "See, I told you he would screw this relationship up." She was joking, of course. Tripp was laughing too hard to make anyone believe that there was any kind of real trouble. When I heard the door close, I looked up through the hair that had fallen over my face during the smack-down and suddenly realized that I was trashing my *sensei's* loft. Not good.

The truth finally came out. While it is true that in some parts of the world people do shave their heads when they take refuge, the dumbed-down American custom was to simply snip off a symbolic lock of your hair. According to Rinchen, a far more reliable source than Tripp, you do promise, however, to work toward mental clarity and enlightenment for the benefit of all beings. There is no save-your-own-butt thing going on here. The Buddhist idea is to reach complete enlightenment for yourself only after all other sentient beings get there first. Oh yeah, and you get a new name. I was not that crazy about that part because I was getting into being called *Lhamo*.

In the Tibetan Buddhist tradition, you receive an empowerment from your teacher before you start certain kinds of practices. Megan had told me earlier that these were ceremonies where the teacher actually transfers the practice to you by giving you a piece of his mind, like, literally. They say that when this happens you are actually getting the mind of the Buddha himself because he transferred part of his mind to his students and they transferred it to their students. Tripp said that Lama Jinpa could trace his lineage, generation by generation all the way back to the Buddha 2,500 years ago. This was amazing to me. I was not sure what I thought about the Tibetan mind-meld thing, but it was incredible to me that the teachings had been handed down with such care.

So this is where they get it from, I thought to myself musing over how unusual Rinchen, Tripp and Megan were compared to the rest of the world.

Lama Jinpa was scheduled to teach classes for the public in the evenings. Rinchen had cancelled advance classes to make room for these teachings right after the beginner's class was finished. Lama Jinpa taught late into the evening and then would go home with Rinchen and Tripp. Every day during his visit, he showed up at the *dojo* before the beginner's class. He liked to watch *Aikido*. Everyone was on their best behavior around him. Unlike the other students that bowed to Lama Jinpa, I noticed that Tripp would lie face-down on the mat completely outstretched with the palms of his hands pressed together over his head like he was diving into a swimming pool. He told me later that this was called a "prostration" and that disciples do this for their teachers, provided that they are in an appropriate place to do so. Otherwise, they bow and keep their heads lower than their teacher's head out of respect. Even Rinchen prostrated to Lama Jinpa. Only a few students practiced Buddhism, but everyone paid respects just the same.

Lama Jinpa was an older man though it was not all that easy to determine his age. What little stubble of hair he had was gray, and he wore big wire rimmed glasses. He had a set of prayer beads like the ones that I had seen Rinchen, Tripp and Megan wear on their wrists. Their beads were brown, but Lama Jinpa' s beads were yellowish-white and looked like they might have been made out of bone. He spoke English well enough, but with an accent. He always wore a red skirt-like bottom robe and a yellow shirt with very short sleeves. He had a red shawl that was very long and looked like it could wrap around his shoulders several times. One striking feature about Lama Jinpa was that despite his appearance as a genuine holy man, he never walked outside without wearing a baseball cap.

I went to his first talk which was about the *Tronglen* practice that Rinchen had shown me months before. I had done this practice many times, but Lama Jinpa talked about it in great detail and I started to realize that I had already experienced many of the things that he said that develops from this practice.

"*Tronglen* is practice about compassion. In order to do practice, you must be able to see suffering. In order to see suffering, you have to know what it is." While you could understand everything he said, his English was sometimes broken and he left out words or made words up to fit his purpose. "All of human experience is suffering even when feels good. There are people who do drug. They feel good when they do drug. But without drug, they unhappy. We always chasing and craving things we do not have. We may have plenty to eat, but because it not ice cream we are sad. You understand this?" The people in the crowd nodded. He continued, "ice cream no better than rice. It is sweet so we crave taste, but food is food. Food is supposed to be fuel only, not drug to make us intoxicated. In our world, we do not know our own real mind because we make drunk with our addictions, delusions and conflicting emotions like putting mud in clear water. It makes us very unstable."

Lama Jinpa told us a story about when he was younger and was captured by Chinese soldiers in Tibet. They put him in prison when he was just a young monk. They told him that they would kill him if he did not renounce the Dalai Lama as the head of the Tibetan government. He could not understand why anyone would go so far as to make another person say words they did not mean. They were just words. He said that he refused because, at that time, he was young and defiant. During his imprisonment, the soldiers tied him up by his wrists and hung him over an oil barrel and then lit a fire in the barrel to roast his feet. Another time they stripped away his clothes and pushed him down on a concrete floor covered in broken glass. He said that many of his friends were killed in prison. He said that there were nuns that had been taken from his monastery and who were raped in order to force them to break their vow of celibacy. Monks were used as human plow horses to turn over the soil in fields and if they got too tired to pull the plow, they were buried alive where they fell.

These things were shocking to me. It is one thing to see them on TV or read about them in a book, but to sit there with a man who has seen all of these terrible things with his own eyes, who had been tortured for real – it gets way past your not-my-problem filter. I was stunned that Lama Jinpa could talk about his imprisonment and torture with very little emotion in his voice and with a calm, even loving, expression on his face like he was remembering a trip to summer camp. Someone asked him, "you say that we should love every being on the planet, but how can you love a person who does something like that to you?"

Lama Jinpa smiled. "Who better to love? I wish I could say that I had perfect compassion for those soldiers. There were times when I could feel my hate, but had to ask myself, where hate come from? I realized that my anger was caused by my love of self, by my ego and the more I clung to my identity and my life, the more I get angry. It was not so much about the pain, but was insulting to my ego. When I realize this, I could see that soldiers did not know what they were doing. That they hate me like I hate them. We were the same. We hate each other for reasons that we make up in mind. They had no awareness of what they were causing. To them, I was animal. This is ignorance. I started to feel sorry for them because they were so lost. In the world there is no real blame. Blame is just your ego pointing finger at what you not like. We do not blame tiger for killing goat. The only way to stop this ignorance and hate is to teach people to see what they really doing; to see the harm that comes from their ignorance and give them skill to see better way. Without skill, they will keep killing and ultimately will get killed. This is the true sadness of my imprisonment. For me, had I died, I would have died with a clear mind. This would be no bad thing."

"How can you say that being killed as a young man is not a bad thing?" I asked, "It would have been horrible."

"Not for me. I would be dead."

"But the world would lose a very good person. The soldiers would have gotten away with murder. That's just wrong!" I blurted out.

"The world loses all good men and all good young women like you eventually. Death is death and it takes us all in time. All things are impermanent. If you have only five minutes to live, why waste it on hate. It is the condition of your mind in any given moment that matters. Your hate does not hurt your enemy. Your enemy ignores it. Your hate only hurts you. If I let soldiers fill me with hate, I would go through world doing what they did. I would kill and rape. Hate is disease. So why set yourself on fire to burn down your enemy's house. You will burn to death before you get to his door. I choose to have my being filled with love always. Why cloud your mind with anything less than compassion and clarity? Why live one minute of your life without compassion and clarity? No one, not even soldiers with broken glass can take away your pure mind, if you have the skill to keep it. No one can force such delusion on you – only you say when you hate or hurt. Only you say when you become lost to delusion."

"I am sorry Lama, but I do not understand this. If someone cuts you and burns you it will hurt, will it not?" I asked.

"For most people, yes. There are those who have transcended pain, but yes it will hurt."

"If you are in such pain and someone is giving you that pain, anyone would be mad and want them to stop."

"Not necessarily. You might want them to stop hurting you, but I assure you, the hate is, how you say? It is optional." Lama Jinpa smiled and watched me closely to see if I was understanding him. When he saw me struggling, he continued, "do you eat meat?"

"Yes, although I am starting to wonder if I should."

"What makes you wonder?"

"The thought of killing animals, taking life to eat, it bothers me."

"Has it always bothered you?"

"No, I didn't used to think about it at all. I am not even sure that I really stopped to think that meat was from living animals."

"Yes, this is like the soldiers I just tell you about . They did not stop to think. They do not see that I am just like them. They see me and see something other. You now see the animals and are starting to think about the real cost of hamburger. Why does killing animal bother you?"

"I think it is cruel. We hurt them and do not let them live their normal lives."

"Yes, but why you see this now and not before?"

"I don't know. I am thinking about a lot of things that I was not thinking about before. Sensei Rinchen used to tease me that I was one of the walking almost dead".

Lama Jinpa laughed. "Yes, yes, we all start that way. But what has made you start to wake up?"

I had to think about this for a minute or two. Lama seemed in no hurry for me to answer and sat there in front of the *kamidana* with a smile on his face as if waiting for my answer was just as interesting as hearing it. Finally, I said, "I have learned to pay attention. I used to notice hardly anything, but now I see bees on flowers, birds in trees and the facial expression on everyone I meet. I notice the cracks in the sidewalk, the smell of the air and the sounds all around me. The more I notice the details of my life, the more I seem to care about everything."

Lama Jinpa slapped his hands together in one, loud SMACK! "Ha! Well done! This is good news for me, such good news!"

"Why is that?" I asked.

"First, you are really waking up and this is wonderful thing! Every teacher wants to know that his students are learning. In this case, my student Rinchen Dorje has taught you well and this pleases me much and I am sure it pleases him much."

I broke into a smile. Lama Jinpa was kind of like an Asian version of Santa Claus. He was jolly and cared so deeply about everything. I looked over at Rinchen and he was smiling too. It was strange to hear Lama Jinpa talk about Rinchen as a student and not the great teacher that I knew him to be. For a second, and only for a second, it was like we were the same. I have heard Rinchen comment on this many times that he was a teacher to us, but a student in his own mind. This is the *dojo* way.

Each person stands in a line with her teachers and her teachers' teachers each in a cascade of ever-flowing contribution. To everyone on the *joseki* side, we listen with respect and try to learn as much as we can from those with more experience. On the *shimoseki* side, we owe the same duty of patience and compassion that was shown to us by those who are wiser. Rank is not given out as a privilege. Rank is merely your place in the chain of responsibility. As we all progress, we are included in a greater and greater circle of responsibility. Even my master has a master. It is a beautiful thing when you think about it. It is the organization of wisdom and, more importantly, the organized transfer of this wisdom down the line, through the centuries from the Buddha, O-Sensei and the great samurai to me. I can feel the compassion of all of the people who died centuries before me and yet who have contributed to me because they took the time to teach their students how to love and, these students went on to teach their own students in turn. You can't teach what you don't know.

I realized in that moment, why Rinchen had taught me the *Tronglen* practice. Breath by breath, it made me think about where all that black smoke was coming from. It made me look at suffering and pay attention to it. Every day, I was seeing deeper and deeper into the condition of the world and by this simple practice I was taking on the responsibility of caring for all of it. You do not grow this kind of awareness by thinking about these kinds of things only once. You cannot change the channel and suddenly get a whole new world. It is the repetition, the discipline of drilling into things over and over that not only trains your mind to make compassion a natural habit, but lets you see subtle things that you may have missed after the first twenty times you looked at them.

Rinchen called this the art of contemplation and said that it is nearly extinct because these days we spend our time chasing tidbits of useless information like snowflakes in a blizzard. We do not think through anything. It takes too long. But through the *Tronglen* practice, I was making the pain of the world my business and it was filling my mind with compassion. After doing this for months, it had changed me in ways that I was just then beginning to notice.

It was actually getting intense, to the point that I was noticing even the slightest little things about people. Beth said that I was becoming kind of a badass on one hand and a flowerchild on the other. She went as far as to say that I might be going schizo. I noticed, though, that I was taking the time to really talk to my friends and listen to them. I was becoming sensitive to the things that upset them. I started to worry more about the people that I knew. Most of all, I was losing my interest in chit-chat. It seemed that every time I talked to somebody, I would dig into the conversation to get to something that really mattered. Some kids at school would look at me and say, "whoa that's too deep for me, LMAO."

As Lama Jinpa continued his talk about *Tronglen* he pointed out that the whole point of the practice was to get good at compassion. Like any other skill, you can start to build it up only after you know what it is. Lama Jinpa said that it was one thing to watch a person suffer, but quite another thing to know the suffering person's experience. He said it was like in Roman times when they would throw people to the lions. The Romans would watch and be entertained. It would not be nearly as amusing to them if they had taken the time to imagine what it felt like to face a hungry lion and then be torn to shreds by it. Their society did not always value compassion and, therefore, they did not practice it. He said taking on real compassion is a critical leap of awareness. When you are a spectator, you are merely watching an experience without being in the experience. Compassion is something completely different. It is the art of seeing through someone else's eyes, even if you can only imagine it. This can be hard to do. You have to set aside your judgments and really get yourself out of the way to do this. It is much harder than it looks and that is probably why these Buddhist guys practice it so much.

Lama Jinpa said that our judgments about people are not helpful. People are the only way that they can be. I was having a particularly difficult time understanding this. Lama Jinpa took us back to the Chinese prison camp to help us figure it out.

"When I was in prison, Chinese soldier cannot help what he do for many reasons He was told by his government that Buddhists were enslaving the population of Tibet by making them believe in religion that tells everybody to be happy being poor. They tell soldier that Dalai Lama lives in palace and steals money from poor people. These soldiers very angry and think that we are bad guys. Most did not have much education. They think they serve their country. They think we are traitors to China even though Tibet had not been part of China for eight hundred years. You see this in America all the time. The newspaper say this guy, bad guy. They tell you story about bad things. You never meet this guy, but you hate him just the same. The newspaper does not tell you how he is same as you. Instead, they tell you how is different. If human being knew what it was like to be like enemy, there would be no enemy. All human beings think they have good reasons. All people believe themselves to be reasonable. It is the reasons that we make up that cause so much trouble. Buddha says give up your reasons and care about people for no reason. This act destroys the Great Liar."

I raised my hand. "Who is the Great Liar?"

"You are." Lama Jinpa replied looking at me like he was hoping that this was going to lead to another debate. He got his wish.

"Say what? How am I the Great Liar?"

"Not you the young woman sitting in *jodo*." (Lama Jinpa always got the pronunciation of *dojo* backwards calling it *jodo*. He still does it to this day even though the proper pronunciation has been explained to him a million times.) "I am referring to corruptor of all things -- your ego."

"How is my ego a liar?"

"Do you have enemy?" I had to think about this. There was Nick who had not exactly been my friend, but he was dead and did not fit into the present tense of the question. Almost as quickly as Nick had come and gone out of my mind, Rita Montrose popped into my head.

"I don't know that I would call her an "enemy", but I know a person that I do not get along with very well."

"Why you not get along?" Lama asked.

"She is mean to me and other people and tells lies about me."

"This make you mad?"

"Sometimes 'livid' would be a better word." I said. Megan laughed. She knew exactly who I was talking about.

"Why you get so mad, does your enemy torture you?" I had to think about it. Some of the rumors that Rita had spread about me did feel like torture, but I was pretty sure that compared to being roasted alive over a fire in Chinese prison camp, this did not meet Lama Jinpa's definition.

261

"No."

"Does she take your money or burn your house?" I was starting to get a little embarrassed. My problem with Rita was starting to seem to me and everyone in the room as pretty lame.

"No."

"Then what she do that makes you hate her so much?"

"Like I said, she tells lies about me and tries to make me look stupid in front of other people?"

"And what you do about it?" Lama Jinpa asked as if he genuinely wanted to know the answer to his question.

"I don't know. Sometimes I confront her, but usually, I just let it go." I said not entirely convinced that this was the whole truth.

"Really, you let go? To me looks like you are carrying it even now." Ouch. He was right. I was busted.

"Yeah, maybe a little."

"You are suffering not because of what she says, but because you carry anger with you like monkey on your back. Why you do that?" I was surprised by this remark and the more I thought about it, the more I realized that it was true. And why was I still carrying this crap around anyway?

"You know, Lama, I have absolutely no idea." As these words passed my lips I could feel the weight of Rita Montrose being lifted off of my mind. But Lama Jinpa was not finished with me yet.

"When she say bad things, why this hurt you? It is just breath. Just hot air."

"I am afraid people might believe her and think that I am a bad person."

"So your pride that gets hurt?"

"I guess so."

"This your ego. Is just image of self, but we go crazy to protect it. In Buddhism we call ego by name of devil, 'Mara'. Mara is liar. Mara turn everything into jealous and hate. The real battle for sanity in the human race is with Mara and our principle weapon is compassion. Compassion is opposite of ego. It only come from awareness of other person, not self. The more we pay attention to what is outside of us, the less power we give to Mara." Lama Jinpa was searching my eyes for some sliver of understanding but he was not finding it. So he continued his thought.

"All suffering come from concern for self. We do not suffer for others. When we see family killed by soldier, we may have some compassion for them, but mostly we think about what has been taken from us. When we are angry it is selfish. When we are sad, we pity ourselves. True happiness exist only when we abandon ourselves. When we care about others we do not feel jealous or angry. Negative emotions only come when we looking in, not out. When we notice what is outside and care about it, all negative disappear. When this person say mean things about you, it only causes suffering when you look at yourself and your own condition. But if you stop and wonder why she harming other people and have concern for the negative karma she build up for herself, suddenly anger is gone and perhaps sadness comes. But sadness for her is love, not negative. Suddenly you are whole and empty with no negative emotions at all. This is power of compassion."

It seems like such a simple thing, not particularly earthshattering, but when I really thought about it, it nearly knocked me down. You can actually practice compassion until you get it right. Ack does that. Practicing compassion forces you to deal with your crap. It forces you to notice your sniveling hateful little inner demon. It occasionally requires you to spank your inner child. But the effect is awesome. Compassion knocks the crust off of your life. Love gives us the motive to come when called and to go where needed. It is the force that used to bring neighbors together to rebuild a burnt barn. It is what compels a Coast Guard diver to drop from a perfectly comfortable helicopter into the Bering Sea to save a fisherman. It is the thing that makes real heroes and causes one to live a truly useful life. All of the best people who have ever lived have had huge hearts and an inexhaustible ability to love others. Some have died for us. While they might make a statue of some greedy bastard and set it in front of an office building or a bank for the pigeons to shit on, our highest admiration is reserved for those who have loved their guts out.

To be a true warrior you have to have compassion and loving kindness. You have to appreciate where everyone's personal journey has taken them and the story that they have made up about it along the way. Everyone is trapped in their story every bit as much as they are trapped in the facts of their life. It is disgusting what I have based my story on up until now. Do I really want to let MTV tell me who I am? Am I really going to let a bunch of high school kids, who do not know their asses from speed bumps, tell me what my life is about? Am I going to jump into some religion and trust that it is telling me the truth just because someone said so?

There are a whole lot of dead Arab kids out there who didn't get their seventy virgins, but were tricked into using their deaths to build hate when they could have used their lives to build love. Those old guys that strapped bombs on to those kids are not going to make me hate anybody – not even them. I know why they did what they did. They bought into a lie just like my friends and I are buying into a different kind of lie. We have all been misled. Mara is kicking our asses and she has created an entire digital culture of fantasy and marketing persuasion to pump us full of our own bullshit. Our culture has let us down and we are to blame. We let it happen.

Where was Lama Jinpa's message all this time? Why was I not told to hold Jenny Rose's hand while she died of leukemia? Why did I not follow Ack's example sooner and speak only kindness about my classmates despite the temptation to trash them? I could have eased their nervousness, but instead I fanned it like a fire. Why was I not told that love and compassion are, like for real, the strongest powers in the universe -- the power of life itself. Why was I told that wealth was the strongest power? Why the hell isn't this on TV? Instead, we are bombarded with a thousand advertisements telling us to smell good so that people will like us. We are sculpted by a million little messages that say to us that we are fucked up, but that if we just go out and buy something we will be better. Who is running this planet anyway? Are they complete idiots?

Oh yeah. I am running this planet - me and my friends and our families and the families of those dead kids in Israel and Palestine. What the hell have we been thinking?

Chapter Thirty-five: Give Me Shelter

The high points of my life used to be thrills, but lately they have become moments of insight that make me want to cry for joy. You can see something as simple as a firefly on a warm summer night and, if you get it, if you can wrap your mind all the way around it, there is this sense of wholeness that takes your breath away. Of course, it took a lot of teachers to show me what wholeness was. I don't know what it was about Lama Jinpa's talk, but it brought together a whole bunch of things that I had been thinking about into a single sense of WOW. My mind was blown wide open by a new understanding that seemed so obvious that I could not figure out why it was new to me or why everyone else didn't know about it.

The day after Lama Jinpa's teaching on compassion was like a dream. I floated down the halls of Westchester High School watching the commotion of students. They no longer seemed like part of a single herd. Each person stood out as I looked at them. I noticed their clothes and the color of their shoes. I could see the emotions that were twitching through their minds. There were kids who I had never noticed before. One or two of them walked through the hallways looking quite sad. I saw Julie Roth walking down the hall holding her books in front of her and she caught me smiling at her. It is amazing how a smile can be contagious. She veered through the traffic toward my locker.

"Aren't you just a beaming ray of sunshine today. What happened? You look like you just got laid," she said returning the smile I had just sent her.

"No, something much better than that."

"There's something better than that?" she replied in mock disbelief.

"Yeah, last night I pulled my head out of my ass. It was fantastic."

Julie cracked up. "What the hell are you talking about?"

"I would like to say that I have had some sort of religious experience, but I haven't. It's just that, suddenly, I realize that there are all these people and they are going through some kind of shit and yet they are really, really beautiful if you stop and think about it -- magnificent even. Their hearts beat with fear and confusion and love and hunger, but they are, each one them, little miracles."

"Whoa, what have you been smoking this morning?"

"Not a damn thing," I said still smiling at her. I could hear myself fumbling for a way to put this all into words and realized that my dork factor was running pretty high. "It is just that when you cut through your own bullshit, things are pretty damned cool. You find yourself with these very lovely lesbian friends who are really smart and actually give a shit about stuff and suddenly life just doesn't seem to suck. You know what I mean?" I grabbed the hair that was tucked behind her ears and hanging down along both sides of her neck and pulled her face toward mine and kissed her on the lips. "You are awesome!"

"Damn, girl! I want whatever you've been taking," Julie said still not sure what to make of the mood I was in.

"Black smoke, white smoke, baby. Black smoke, white smoke." I smiled and slammed my locker shut. "It's a warrior thing." We walked together down the hall watching the creatures of that jungle forage and do their thing.

At lunch I saw Ack standing in line for food and cut in front of several freshmen to talk to him.

"Hey, I used to know a girl who looked a lot like you," he said as I stepped up beside him.

"Okay, okay, so I have been missing in action lately."

"Lately? I think I have only seen you three or four times this year so far. I get the boyfriend thing and all, but damn, I knew you first."

"True, my handsome Hindu prince, so true. But unfortunately you cannot blame it all on Tripp. Actually, I only get to see him when we train and maybe once over the weekend. But you're right, I have been a bit of shit and have been ducking the scene here."

"You haven't missed much."

"I have missed you."

"I'll bet," he said sarcastically.

"Dude, did you just pout? Seriously? You totally pouted! What? Are you running for homecoming queen here or something?" I was jabbing him in the ribs with my finger trying to make him defend himself and he nearly backed over one of the freshmen who was standing quietly in line trying very hard not to draw any unnecessary attention to himself. I finally got Ack to laugh. It was so good to see him laugh. I really did miss him.

"Okay, alright already. I'm busted. I pouted. I confess."

"I love you too."

"What? You think that just because I got a little miffed because I haven't hardly seen you in, what has it been, a year now, that I love you. No, no. Bitch, you still owe me money."

"I do not," I said indignantly.

"Yes, you do. Remember that time in sixth grade when your mom forgot to send you to school with lunch money and I bought you lunch? That will be three bucks … and you can cough it up right now." He was standing in front of me holding his hand out, so I spit in it.

"That's gross!" he said wiping his hand on the sleeve of my shirt.

"You know, I think I really do owe you money. Uh, wait a minute, uh, no, I don't. As I recall you told the entire sixth grade that it was our first date … and I didn't rat your sorry ass out. So, dude, sorry, no cookie for you."

We got our lunch. I slipped in front of Ack and paid for his just to rub it in. We found a table where we could talk.

"Ack, I know that I haven't been around much, but I think about you all the time. I just want you to know that you are one of the finest people that I have ever met. I really, really mean that. When I grow up, I want to be just like you."

"Okay, now you are just getting weird," Ack said stuffing half of a sandwich in his mouth.

"Actually, I mean it. You have always paid attention to people and done what you could to make things easier for them. I got kind of sucked into the whole social tornado thing and played the game. I should have followed your example. You had it right all along."

"You're serious, aren't you?" he said studying my eyes and trying to figure out where this was going. "You're not sick are you? The doctors haven't given you one week to live or something like that, have they?"

"No dumbass, I am being serious here. I am trying to tell you that after all these years, I have noticed. I have noticed what a great guy you are. I have noticed that you are careful about how you treat people. It is amazing. Really, it is a miracle, actually. I am sorry that it took so long for me to figure it out."

"Yeah, it would have been great if you could have had this epiphany before you met that Tripp guy."

"What the hell is an 'epiphany'? You are like the only guy at Westchester that could even use a word like that in a sentence." I was trying to divert the course of the conversation away from boyfriend issues. And, I really didn't know what 'epiphany' meant either.

Ack smiled. "It's cool. That was a cheap shot. Tripp is a great guy from what I hear. And, believe it or not, I am very happy for you. At least you didn't wind up with some macho dipshit in a polo shirt that is a size too small. Megan says that Tripp is actually really smart and I hear that he is an artist too. Is that true?"

"You know, this is the first time that you have ever asked me about him, for real. Does this mean that the subject is no longer taboo?" I think my facial expression was failing to conceal my hopefulness that Ack would finally be cool with me seeing Tripp.

"Yeah. That's what it means. But you call me if he ever does you wrong. I want to be your rebound relationship."

"Oooh. Nice one!" I said in full appreciation of a truly creative diss. "Did I just say that I should follow your example because you are so good to people? What the fuck was I thinking?" We both laughed. It was good to have him back in my world again.

After lunch I ran into Megan on my way to class. She noticed my unusually happy mood immediately. "What's up with you? You look like you just got laid."

"What is up with that? Why does everybody think that just because I am happy that sex was involved? Damn. You're yucking my yum here, chica."

"Easy, Lhamo, no need to get testy. So what *is* going on?"

"I think I had an epiphany, but I am not really sure what that is yet, so let's just say that the whole compassion and loving kindness thing clicked for me and I am enjoying being in love and shit. I was even in love with you a minute ago until you, like, dissed my ass." I was trying not to smile, but my inner badass was nowhere to be found. Megan started to chuckle.

"Ahh, I see. You're surfing the bliss."

"What? What's that mean?"

"You clicked into the teachings last night and you are jacked up on a wave of compassion. You're surfing the bliss."

"Yeah, I guess I am. Is that bad?" I asked.

"Not necessarily. But be careful. You can get just as hooked on bliss as you can smoking dope or eating chocolate cake. It is one thing to be moved by all of this stuff, but it's another thing to crave it or use it as an emotional crutch. You know, Little Bit, there is no charismatic version of Buddhism, right? If you find yourself floating in yah-yah land, it is pretty safe to say that that's not it."

It's funny, usually Megan calls me "Lhamo", but when she really wants to get my attention, when she wants to have a private chat on Girl-Net, she calls me "Little Bit" like Tripp had done the night I met him. It kind of makes me feel like a little kid, but in a good way. I got what she meant. You could spend your whole life going around doing good deeds and gushing over people just to cop a buzz. Even compassion is corruptible. Our minds have an infinite capacity to turn everything into all-about-us. You have to be careful not to drag you higher nature into the suck.

"Are you coming into town tonight?" Megan asked after giving me time to digest what she had said.

"Yeah, I think so. Lama is going to do the Refuge Ceremony tonight. I have been thinking that it is time to step up to that."

"There's no rush. Think it through. You don't need to take refuge in the Buddha to be a good person or even to practice Buddhism for that matter. But if you are going to say that you will, then you need to be for real about it. You don't do something like this on a whim. It sucks the meaning out of it for everyone." She was staring at me intently as if to see whether I was sincere about taking refuge or not. I was sincerely thinking about it, but I was new to this religious stuff. I wasn't sure how it was supposed to feel.

Finally I asked, "Are you going to be there?"

"Oh yeah. This is a holy day of obligation with my dad. I already have this empowerment, but I kind of like them anyway. You can never be too blessed, you know." It was funny to hear Megan talk about attending *vajra* empowerments like she was being coerced to go to church on Easter. Her experience of this was always going to be quite different than mine. For her, this was part of her family tradition, or, at least, half of her family tradition. For me, I was breaking all sorts of habits by choosing this for myself.

The bell was ringing and I was late. "I will see you tonight, " I said as I dashed off to class.

"Try to walk on the ground until then," Megan replied as she headed off in the opposite direction.

When I arrived at the *dojo*, I walked in with my *do-gi* bag and headed for the dressing room to get ready for the beginner's class. The day before, Lama Jinpa had watched the class while sitting in the foyer. This evening, he was sitting in front of the *tokonoma* chanting in Tibetan. Some people had already suited up, but it did not look to me like we were going to have class. I decided that it was better to be safe than late. So I slipped into the dressing room and put on my *gi* and *hakama*.

The word passed through the *dojo* that class was going to be cancelled because Lama Jinpa needed to consecrate the space in preparation for the empowerment later that evening. Some of us had gone out onto a remote section of the mat and were already stretching when we heard about the change of plan. *So that was what he was doing.* He was meditating and purifying the space. He chanted in deep, low tones that sounded like they were coming from halfway down his throat. The sounds croaked into the *dojo* with a pulsating rhythm that, while completely foreign to me, sounded oddly soothing. In a way, it was kind of hypnotic and drew my mind into its profound, but simple pattern. Occasionally, the chanting would be suddenly interrupted by the sound of a bell and a funny little drum that made sound when Lama Jinpa twirled it back and forth so that two little balls attached to strings would swing and strike one side then the other. Even if you heard these sounds in an alley you would know that they were sacred.

I sat through most of the consecration doing my own newbie meditation, listening to the sounds, breathing in black smoke and exhaling white. Eventually, the *dojo* filled with people who had come to take refuge and receive the Chenrezig empowerment. It was odd to me to see so many civilians sitting on the mat. There were several of us from the *dojo*. Even though class had been canceled, we all were wearing our uniforms. We were our own kind of monks and nuns. Rinchen had been off somewhere running errands and preparing for the empowerment. Tripp came in and, there being no reason for him to change his clothing, sat beside me in his street clothes. He kissed me on the cheek as he sat down. Normally, the *dojo* was an affection-free zone, but apparently these Buddhist gatherings were different.

Lama Jinpa's consecration of the *dojo* ended in a flurry of bell ringing and drum beating. He had set up what appeared to be his version of a shrine on the *tokonoma*. He sat for a moment or two continuing to meditate in front of the shrine and then slid to the side and turned around to face the guests. He looked like he was stoned, but even with my small amount of Buddhist training I knew that the opposite was true. His entire body was relaxed and he looked out at the audience with no emotion in his face. He just sat there for some minutes noticing and waiting for people to get settled. When his attention turned toward Tripp and me sitting in the back, he smiled slightly and a twinkle came to his eyes.

Empowerments are usually only given to ordained Buddhists, though there are some exceptions I am told. To become an ordained Buddhist you go through a process called "taking refuge". Before letting anyone take refuge, Lama Jinpa gave us an explanation as to what refuge was and why someone would want to do it. Like *Aikido*, Buddhism has been refined to a very precise method of training. Even the explanation of why someone might want to become a Buddhist is an exact lesson with numbered parts. In this case, it was called "The Four Thoughts That Turn The Mind To Buddha-dharma." While I am sure that there are many other thoughts that do this, Lama Jinpa talked about only these four.

Tripp had told me once that Tibetan Buddhism, while certainly a wild thing to look at with all of its colorful peaceful deities and demonic looking wrathful ones, is a very highly organized system of mental training. Apparently, these Tibetan guys have been working on it for a while. He said that nearly everything is reduced to numbered lists to make it easier to remember. There are four noble truths, an eight-fold path, a seven branches prayer, two turtle doves and a partridge in a pear tree. Books were rare in Tibet and had to be printed by hand, so usually only the monasteries had them. Students were trained to remember the complexities of the system by memorizing images that had critical graphical elements representing different qualities that could be recited in an itemized list. The teaching that Lama Jinpa was giving to the audience had been given for centuries in precisely the same way. I have to say, there is something kind of exciting about being given an ancient teaching that people thought was so important that they preserved it in detail and made sure that it got handed down correctly.

The first thing that Lama Jinpa discussed was the history of his lineage. He was a teacher in the Kagyu tradition, one of four great lineages of Tibetan Buddhism and the second oldest. It has been around for nearly thirteen hundred years although the teachings of the Buddha are nearly twice as old as that. After discussing a bunch of ancient guys and describing in detail how one taught the other all the way up to Lama Jinpa teaching me, he started in on a discussion of the Four Thoughts that Turn the Mind to Buddha-dharma. If I were texting this I would call this teaching 4TTTTMTBD because it is a title that is just way too long. See, texting is not a complete waste of time.

Lama Jinpa talked about 4TTTTMTBD for nearly an hour, but the short form looks like this: the first thought is that human existence is rare and extremely fortunate. He calls it "precious human existence". The second thought is that all things are impermanent, even the solar system and the universe itself. Everything has a shelf life and will cease to exist eventually. The third thought is the law of karma. This word gets beat up and misused in our culture. Karma actually means "cause and effect". In other words, things happen only because certain other things caused them to happen. Think of it as the universe being like a massive network of dominoes, one falling into the next. The fourth thought is that life as it is dished out is full of suffering, ignorance and foolishness. Lama Jinpa called this "*samsara*" or "the ocean of suffering". Some suffering, does not necessarily involve pain. Being stoned on drugs, for example, can feel good, but turns you into an idiot incapable of knowing what is really going on around you. Therefore, the fourth thought is that this state of constant suffering basically sucks and everyone should look for a way out of it.

When he first presented this list, it seemed like these four thoughts were not really connected with one another. While I could see a certain logic behind them, I didn't get how this added up to shaving your head and renouncing the world. This is why, of course, that it took Lama Jinpa an hour to explain this stuff. It gets pretty deep.

It all starts with the first thought: that human existence is precious. These Tibetan guys see the world as divided up into not one realm of existence, but six. These range from hell realms where all of the beings there experience nothing but pain and have no ability to have any thought other than "OMFG this hurts." Only slightly better is the karma of the beings in the hungry ghost realm. They are trapped in a world of extreme craving and addiction. They get so overwhelmed with their cravings that they can die of thirst in the sight of clear water because their delusional minds make water look like blood and pus. Tibetans have very vivid imaginations. And yet, you hear about beings like this in the news. These are the guys who get strung out on drugs and then kill their own children mistaking them for demons.

The next realm of consciousness is the animal realm. Lama Jinpa pointed out that animals have a lot of mental characteristics in common with people. They have cravings, but can satisfy them. They feel pain, but only when they are hurt. They care for their young, so they have a sense of compassion. As Lama Jinpa put it: "even mother tiger take care of puppies." This misuse of the word "puppies" became an inside joke with Tripp, Megan and me. "Puppies" became the word of choice for all offspring. Pigeons had nests full of puppies and the ducks in Forest Park waddled across the bike paths with a line of little puppies following behind them. Having fun at the expense of Lama Jinpa's word choice was probably not the best way to show devotion to him as a teacher, but to this day, every time I misuse the word "puppy", I get a warm, fond feeling and think of Lama Jinpa.

According to the good lama's six realms of existence theory, the biggest problem with the animal realm is that they are hopelessly ignorant. You can sit with them for days on end trying to teach them calculus and they will never get it. The ability for abstract reasoning and the nuances of real language are just not part of the intellectual scope of a dog. While animals might have a sense of self, they do not have any ability to consider the complex meanings of things. The upside is that they do not need therapists.

The whole six realms thing started getting a bit weird when Lama Jinpa started explaining the god realms. According to him, there are two. The jealous god realm is a state of consciousness where the beings are very powerful, but also very egotistical and competitive. Because of this, they do not play nice with the other jealous gods. He says that these guys fight all the time and are constantly trying to dominate each other with their powers. It sounded like a bunch of corporate CEOs only these guys can shoot lightning bolts at each other. The last realm, the god realm, was different in that gods could create anything they wanted, even whole universes and living things. Some gods assumed a form and other did not, but they all lived for eons of time and had absolute control over their physical environments. This started to sound like a fairy tale and I have to say I was not really buying into it. But then Lama Jinpa said something that really made me stop and wonder about it all. He said, "scientists now know that universe is billions and billions of years old and that there are other planets like ours that very likely have life on them. It would be hard to believe that other beings somewhere are not more evolved than us. Even similar species only few centuries older would have more power. We are making life with our science now and scientists tell us that they are close to making whole universes with atom cutters and big machines. Do you really believe that human beings, who have only not been monkey for a few million years is most evolved being in universe? This not likely."

Several people in the audience raised their hands to get a piece of this conversation.

"So what you are saying is that the Christian god may very well have created human beings just to have someone worship him?" asked a middle aged woman in the front of the audience.

"Is possible," Lama Jinpa replied. "God is god. A god can create beings for any purpose just like we use animal for our purpose. Better to be human supposed to worship god than mouse killed for experiment, no?" The woman was frowning. It seemed like she had been counting on Buddhism as a way to prove Christians wrong. I have learned since this day that no Buddhist has any interest in proving any such thing. The woman was not satisfied with his answer.

"So you are saying that we might very well be offending God by not worshiping him and that he may actually have created us just to stroke his ego?"

"Is possible."

"What kind of god is that? That sounds pretty arrogant to me."

"We say that beings in god realm are very proud. Arrogant even. This is kind of thing god might actually do, just like we make people slave. This not new to universe."

"Well, what do you think about the Christian god?" asked the woman as if she was trying to get Lama Jinpa to denounce Christianity and its god in public.

"I not know. I not meet him. I would like to meet some god sometime. Be very interesting conversation, no?"

"But what if he damns you and sends you to hell?"

"I apologize to him, but if he that mad at me, I go to hell. It would be my karma. Might be my karma to be eaten by tiger or killed by crazy man. Karma is karma. If you meet some god and he get mad, he powerful, you just human, you go to hell realm. But you only go to hell realm if god can make you suffer. If you are enlightened, he cannot make you suffer."

The woman was now confused. Megan had told me that lamas are trained in debate. Apparently, Buddhists love to debate and always try to put their ideas to the test. Lama sat patiently waiting for her to say something.

"But gods are all powerful, so they say," she said after some deliberation.

"Nothing more powerful than enlightened mind. For clear mind, god can put you on red hot copper plate and you no suffer. You ever see picture of Buddhist abbot in Vietnam? Light himself on fire and die without even blink eye. This is enlightenment. This is power beyond power. If god cannot stab you, burn you, drown you or trick you into delusion of pain, then how he make you suffer? How anything make you suffer, if your mind clear and sitting in emptiness of all delusion?"

"Good point" said the woman as her facial expression softened.

"Why god want to hurt in first place? Why human want to hurt other beings? Only confused mind do such thing. We say gods confused by their own power. They can be arrogant or not, just like us. They can reach enlightenment or not, just like us. Just like gods, humans often confused by own power. So arrogant. Start war, kill, torture other beings. Kill animal for fun. Only mind that not see clearly do these things. Only mind that not know true nature cause suffering to other beings. We not do that. We say this madness must stop. We train ourselves and tame our minds to make delusion stop. We stand in face of all other beings and say 'no more'. Even if they kill us or torture us, we not allow our mind to take on craziness."

Wow. Now that was an idea a girl could get behind. I had never heard anything that made more sense than that.

Lama Jinpa went on to say that human beings actually had the best opportunity to reach enlightenment. He said that they had the ability to reason and could understand infinite possibility just like gods, but because death was always on their doorstep, there was a greater urgency to finding an answer to suffering. There was no time to be lazy about it. Death also makes us humble. Gods could always look for an answer to suffering later, if it occurred to them to look for one at all, which was unlikely because they had no reason to change their status quo. Apparently, they just sit around their celestial cribs and spend their time blinking groovy things into existence by having groovy thoughts until one day the magic does not work anymore. According to Lama Jinpa, gods may live a really long time, but the party comes to an end eventually, and when it does, it freaks them out. They are completely unprepared for death or an existence without absolute power. Lama Jinpa said that this comes as such a shock to them that they often wind up being reborn in hell realms.

The jury is still out for me on the whole reincarnation thing, but what I was beginning to see was that Lama Jinpa was describing the mechanics of consciousness. I remember seeing a TV show once where a camera crew was following around a woman who at one time had been fabulously rich, but had lost everything. Her life was a mess. She did not even know how to get a job, let alone know how to work. She eventually killed herself. I could totally see how that could happen to a fallen god.

Humans have the potential to be more humble beings, yet one with a fully developed mind, is a precious thing. We humans can be brilliant and yet death and suffering is always nearby to keep us from getting cocky. There is a path somewhere down the middle, a path between genius and road-kill that might just have something to offer a curious girl. It looked like just my kind of rabbit hole and I was ready to jump in.

I spent weeks thinking about the 4TTTTMTBD formula. Human life was an opportunity to get to the bottom of this mind stuff. Everything was impermanent and that meant I had to get busy. The world was interconnected and things only happened because other things happened. And while this was all perfectly understandable, you could get crushed by a meteor at any moment and lose your chance to step out of the endless cycle of delusion and ignorance. He was right. Being trapped in the chaos of cause and effect sucks in the big picture. After giving it some thought, I figured that he had just given me four really good reasons to get busy breaking through.

So, this is why people take refuge. I thought about how much my own thinking had changed since I had joined the *dojo*. I still wasn't sure what enlightenment was, but my mind was changing really fast so there had to be something to it. I had seen too many things in completely new ways to know that my first impression of things, or even my third or fourth impressions, were not always true. One thing I knew for sure – there was way more to my mind than I had ever thought possible just a couple of years ago and I really wanted to know more about it.

One other thing caught my attention during Lama Jinpa's talk on refuge. He said that we should not accept anything he had said, anything that anyone says, on faith alone. He said that the Buddha had told his own students not to believe a word of his teachings until they could verify it in their own experience. This sounded like the sanest thing I had ever heard come out of any religion. Lama Jinpa said that there might be times when a teacher tells you that something is possible before you can experience it and that it is generally a good idea to have confidence that your teacher knows what he or she is talking about. Having confidence in your teacher is something quite different, however, from following someone blindly without question. Following blindly is, by definition, ignorance.

Lama Jinpa asked if there was anyone who wanted to take refuge before he gave the Chenrezig empowerment. Matt, who had been sitting next to Megan on the other side of the *dojo*, raised his hand. The woman who had debated about god with Lama Jinpa raised her hand along with two young people who appeared to be her children. I took a deep breath and raised my hand too. Tripp did not turn his head, but a smile spread across his face as my hand rose in the air.

Lama Jinpa nodded and smiled at me. Apparently, my choice to take refuge was already bringing joy to the world around me. Of course, that could change when I got home. Lama Jinpa put his hands together as if in prayer and began to chant in Tibetan. Rinchen, Tripp and Megan were chanting along with him. In fact, all of the Buddhists in the room seemed to know this prayer even though it was in a foreign language.

After several prayers and some more bell ringing and drum beating, Lama Jinpa came out of his meditation and looked around the room. He was smiling and there was a twinkle in his eyes. He looked like the living manifestation of peace itself. He looked over at Matt and nodded. Megan whispered something in Matt's ear and he rose to his knees. In the *dojo* we have a way of walking on our knees called *shikko* (pronounced *"shee-ko"*). When you are asked to approach your teacher, walking in *shikko* is a sign of respect. This is a Japanese custom, not a Tibetan one. You could tell that Matt had been in the *dojo* for quite a while because he crossed the mat in seconds never once rising to his feet. Lama smiled and while chanting something in Tibetan, took a tiny pair of scissors and clipped a strand of Matt's hair.

He then pulled out a red silk string and tied it around Matt's neck. This, I learned later, was called a "protection cord". It was a piece of silk cord with a knot in it. Lamas prepare protection cords by whispering a prayer into a loop of cord that is then pulled into a knot to trap the blessing of the prayer in the cord. They give protection cords to students on auspicious occasions. You are supposed to wear it for at least three days and it is said that it will prevent you from being reborn in a lower realm.

Lama Jinpa then reached down into a silk bag sitting next to him and pulled out a little booklet. He opened it up and read from it. "Karma Dorje", he said. This was apparently, Matt's new dharma name. Matt took the booklet from Lama Jinpa, bowed and walked on his knees back to his place on the mat next to Megan. The others made their way to where Lama Jinpa was sitting and he repeated the hair snipping and cord tying each time concluding with the pronouncement of a new dharma name for each of them.

"Is there anyone else?" asked Lama Jinpa looking at me with an almost mischievous smile. The cat was already out of the bag so I rose to my knees. I had deliberately not said anything before the ceremony to Tripp or Megan because if I was going to do this, I needed to do it for me and not because it was the thing to do. A second or two slipped by, I found myself walking in *shikko* toward Lama Jinpa. If he could teach people like Rinchen, there had to be things he could teach me. As I drew close to Lama Jinpa, he was smiling ear to ear. "I was hoping you would join us," he said warmly. I did not look back to see the others. This was between me and him. I bowed with my palms pressed together. I heard him begin a brief chant. Then I heard the snip of the scissors. I watched Lama reach into his silk bag and pull out a booklet. I was intensely curious to learn what they would be calling me next. He looked at the booklet and returned it to the bag and then pulled out another. He looked at that one and, again, returned it to the bag. When he opened up the third booklet, he smiled and read it out loud. "Jigme Lhamo", he said handing me the booklet and then tying a red protection cord around my neck. He seemed to be quite pleased. I guess they were going to keep calling me "Lhamo" after all that. Cool.

And that's how I found my religion.

As I made my way back to my place next to Tripp, Rinchen was smiling at me. Megan was clapping her hands excitedly, yet silently to show me her happiness. Tripp just smiled and as I sat down next to him he reached over and pulled me close. I could hear him just barely sound out my new name under his breath – "Jigme Lhamo."

I had known since the beginning of my time at Byakuren Dojo that "Lhamo" meant "protectress" and that it was the name of a wrathful deity that protected all of Buddhism. "Jigme" means "fearless". When Tripp told me after the teaching what my name meant, it went straight to my head. I said, "Awesome, strong name, good deal". Tripp chuckled. "I am pretty sure that it is a mistake to use your dharma name to stroke your own ego." I looked up at him at first a bit miffed and then embarrassed. "I'm just saying ...", he said trying to take the sting out of his comment. Of course, he was right and I was glad that he straightened me out from the beginning.

"Why didn't lama give me the first name out of the bag?"

"Your dharma name is supposed to be a matter of karma, but I have seen him do this before. I am told that he did the same thing when my dad took refuge. If he pulls out a name that does not seem to him to fit you, he will pass it up. He will only do this for people that he has taken an interest in." It warmed me a little that this meant that he had taken an interest in me. I like it when my teachers like me. Tripp continued his thought, "sometimes I think he passes over names because he wants you to have one that guides you where he hopes you will go. My guess is that he wanted you to keep the name 'Lhamo'. He knows that my dad gave you that name and I think he was showing his agreement with it. So, when he got to one that had 'Lhamo' in it, he knew it was right for you."

Lama Jinpa had written my new name inside the cover the small refuge booklet that had two prayers written in it. One was called *The Refuge Prayer* which is a vow that says you will take your place with your teacher, the Buddha and the congregation of other Buddhists of your lineage, past and present, called a *sangha*. There was also another prayer in the booklet called *The Seven Branches Prayer* that walks you through seven gestures and offerings that you promise to undertake as part of your practice. The first branch is to show reverence to the Buddha and your teachers through the act of prostration. The second is to make offerings to the Buddha and your teachers to develop generosity. The third branch is to confess misdeeds and to call attention to your own faults so that they cannot grow and can be corrected. The fourth is my favorite: to rejoice in the merit of others and celebrate their contributions and achievements. This is an antidote to jealousy. The fifth branch is to ask those who reach enlightenment to remain in the world to help others. The sixth is to pray for the continued benefit all sentient beings. The last branch is one that is part of every Tibetan Buddhist practice. It is believed that Buddhist practice accumulates merit in the practitioner. The last branch dedicates all of this merit to others.

I used to really hate rules. The fun of growing up and getting to drive a car and to stay out late was all about being free from rules. And yet, here I was nearly two years in the *dojo* adding new rules to my life nearly every day. When I was younger I thought that freedom meant doing whatever you wanted to whenever you wanted to do it. I now realize that this kind of freedom is really a trap. It is not really freedom. It is an undirected accidental existence that turns you into the "walking almost dead." It is very ironic to me, that after all those fights with my mom about what I could or could not wear to school, that real freedom would be found in taking responsibility for my life and choosing to live it a certain way. That's a revelation that should be noted in my Baby Book It is the moment when I started living like a fully empowered human being.

Some of the non-Buddhists in the *dojo* follow a set of rules for their lives that comes from a part of the ancient samurai code that written by a famous swordsman named Miyamoto Musashi. Musashi, oddly enough, was a Buddhist though of a Japanese school. He set down twenty-one rules for life in what is called the *Dokkōdō*. These rules, called "precepts", actually hang in both dressing rooms of the *dojo*. Some are easier to follow than others:

1. Accept everything just the way it is.
2. Do not seek pleasure for its own sake.
3. Do not, under any circumstances, depend on a partial feeling.
4. Think lightly of yourself and deeply of the world.
5. Be detached from desire your whole life long.
6. Do not regret what you have done.
7. Never be jealous.
8. Never let yourself be saddened by a separation.

9. Resentment and complaint are appropriate neither for oneself nor others.
10. Do not let yourself be guided by the feeling of lust or love.
11. In all things have no preferences.
12. Be indifferent to where you live.
13. Do not pursue the taste of good food.
14. Do not hold on to possessions you no longer need.
15. Do not act following customary beliefs.
16. Do not collect weapons or practice with weapons beyond what is useful.
17. Do not fear death.
18. Do not seek to possess either goods or fiefs for your old age.
19. Respect Buddha and the gods without counting on their help.
20. You may abandon your own body but you must preserve your honor.
21. Never stray from the Way.

Regardless of your religion or culture, I think it is important to have a code. These are not just a bunch of rules that some guy forced on somebody else. You have to choose to live by a code for it to be a real part of your heart and mind. But what I have noticed in nearly everything I have read about warriors and lamas is that they think deeply about life and then figure out rules for themselves so that they know how to act even in moments when they are not thinking things through. Rules form habits. This is how they tame their inner drunken monkey.

Warriors and priests do not throw themselves into chaos without a plan. They do not just do "whatever". They sharpen themselves to cut through the crap with thoughtfulness and dedication. Even if they get killed doing this thing or that, they do not allow themselves to run through life like they have a squirrel in their pants. They are not accidental people. They are watchers and doers that create a protective ring around humanity so that it can evolve. What better purpose can a young woman have for life than this? When you open your eyes to life and really start to take it seriously, it is hard to spend a lot of time mulling over fashion accessories. The best thing about my new life is that it is devoted to things that I believe are important and worth standing for. I get to say who I shall be in this life and this is where I am taking my stand. I have thought it over. I am going to be this until I am skillful enough to give up the need to be anything.

Chapter Thirty-six: The Yidam Who Does Not Blink

I wasn't sure what to expect after I took refuge. In the back of my mind, I may have thought that I was supposed to feel different somehow. After all, I was no longer Maddie Albright of no real religion. I was Jigme Lhamo, official member of the Kagyu lineage. I was now a part of a thirteen hundred year old tradition in a twenty-five hundred year old religion. It can make a girl feel kind of special, but Lama Jinpa says that if being Buddhist is making you feel special, then you are getting it wrong.

The way that this whole empowerment thing works is that you go through a ritual where the teacher supposedly transfers a piece of his consciousness into yours. It doesn't hurt or anything. Lama Jinpa compared it to planting a seed. While I did not have a real expectation around it, I thought that there would be at least a Buddhisty tingle or something to mark the change. But I guess that is the point. There was no change, at least, not from taking refuge. When you plant a seed in the dirt and cover it up, you do not even notice that it is there. It has to be nurtured and grown before that seed amounts to anything. You can call yourself anything you want, but until you actually wrap your mind around the teachings and shake it and bake it for a while, you are still the same old you. After all, buying a concert T-shirt does not make you a member of the band. There is no magic Buddhist fairy dust that is going to instantly change my eighteen year habit of being me.

The empowerment ritual itself was mostly spoken in Tibetan. It was mysterious and made me feel like I was about to be struck by lightning. My mind was paying very close attention to itself, looking for any sign of magic. I thought I felt a tingle at a couple of different points in the ceremony like when we were given a handful of saffron water to wash away karmic impurities. The group formed a line and one by one we went up to Lama Jinpa holding out our hands. He poured some of the yellow water into the cup of our hands from a thing that looked like a teapot with peacock feathers sticking out of it. You were supposed to put the water in your mouth and then go outside and spit it out. The bad karma is supposed to leave with the spit, but I saw at least two or three people walk outside who were obviously confused because they had swallowed the saffron water before they figured out that they were supposed to spit it out. The experienced students like Rinchen, Tripp and Megan spit out the water and then dried their hands on their hair as they walked back inside. Rinchen does not really have hair enough to dry his hands on, but he made this gesture just the same. I figured that this was an advanced class thing, so I did it too. I am still not sure what that was all about.

It would take another class for Lama Jinpa to teach us newbies how to do the actual practice. It seemed, at first, to be incredibly complicated. There are prayers with melodies and prayers with visualizations. There is one part where you are supposed to empty your mind of all thought. There are songs for your teachers. Lama Jinpa said that if you do this practice you accumulate merit. This is kind of like brownie points or gold stars. At the end of the practice you dedicate all of this merit to other sentient beings. I like that part. He had to explain what a "sentient being" which was a good thing because I did not know. It is a being that thinks. Rinchen says that I am becoming more *sentient* every day.

After the empowerment, he explained how the practice works and gave us a few tips on how to get the most out of it. Rinchen says that the Tibetan system is very advanced. He pointed out to me that visualization tends to make things come to life so that you relate to it like it is real. This lets the training method slip by your doubting mind more easily than if you were just sitting there trying to have happy thoughts waiting for something good to happen. If you can visualize something, it can become a part of your thinking very quickly. He said that it is very useful, even for martial arts training.

I received this empowerment half a year ago and it has grown on me like crazy. It really is like a plant growing out of a seed in your mind. It branches out and touches every part of your life. And once it gets going, it seems to have a power of its own. It is kind of cool, but it can also be kind of scary. I have found myself thinking in ways that were exactly the opposite of how I used to think. Some of my friends think that I have gotten really weird. I suppose that sanity in a nuthouse does look weird depending on which side of the straightjacket you are on.

Lama Jinpa calls *Vajrayanna* visualization a "strong method". I thought that this was a pretty interesting choice of words. There was very little discussion of whether *yidams* were real or not. Buddhists, I have since learned, have a problem calling anything "real". It has something to do with this whole idea that everything is ultimately empty making the word "real" a bit squishy. But whether something is real or not is kind of irrelevant. You imagine stuff all the time that turns into real things. Rinchen says that this is the ordinary creative process. Architects imagine buildings, clothing designers imagine fashion; it is the way things come into existence.

Just because a being is in your mind, does not mean that it cannot create real consequences in the world of things. If you believe that the Hunga-Bunga god told you to paint yourself purple and you followed this advice, the god might not be real, but you are still going to have trouble getting a date. But what if you focused your attention on a handsome green guy who sits in meditation being one with the suffering of the world? What if you always noticed that his eyes were open and that he never even blinked? What inspiration could you draw from a being that cared so much about the world that he did that? What if this guy had four arms each holding really noble and thoughtful things like a gem that grants wishes for the benefit to all sentient beings. In one of his other hands he holds a string of practice beads called a *mala* to remind you to practice kindness and to work at this all the time. In yet another hand, he holds a lotus blossom to remind you that your mind is like a flower that rises out of the muck of suffering and can become peaceful and beautiful regardless of where it comes from. Being able to actually see these qualities, rather than just have some abstract thought about them, is the first step toward bringing them into the living world. It is one thing to go around thinking "I should be nice to people," whatever that means to you. It is quite another thing to look into the clear eyes of the deity of compassion and see that you have been indifferent to nearly everything. Even dreaming about getting smacked up the side of your head can wake you up.

Over the past six months of doing the Chenrezig practice, I have noticed that he has become more and more real to me, whatever that word even means anymore. We have a relationship and just like any other friend, Chenrezig is beginning to have a pretty big influence on my life. He is becoming tangible. When I find myself acting like an asshole and I suddenly see his face in my thoughts, I realize that he has come to change my mind so that I can change my behavior.

Rinchen has even suggested that visualization can help you do things that you have to do, but don't want to do. I have even tried visualizing cleaning my room. Having walked through it in my mind makes it considerably less painful when I actually do it. A lot of the students at the *dojo* use visualization with *Aikido* and sword techniques. You will see them close their eyes and work through the movements. It is a way of getting mentally and emotionally organized. One interesting side effect of the visualization process is that when you go to actually do the thing that you have visualized, usually you can do it more accurately and much quicker. Rinchen says that this is because after you have visualized something, you have experience with it. You are not fumbling through something new. This is a very fast way to develop skill even if you are just training yourself to be polite.

Lama Jinpa warned us that when you first start doing *puja* that there are all sorts of nasty little thoughts and feelings that rise up out of your mind. When the lotus starts growing out of its seed and rises through the muck, it stirs things up a bit. This is kind of like what happened when I first started practicing Wild Horse meditation. My mind would buck like a bronco because it did not want to sit down. In a *puja*, this can get even weirder. You can sit there visualizing Chenrezig and suddenly have the thought that you are bored and the next thing you know, Chenrezig is wearing a tie-dyed shirt and is smoking a joint. Lama Jinpa said that you have to stay calm and just make note of the rebellious nature of your mind and let it go. In the first few months that I did this practice, I had to be really patient with myself, but the chanting and counting mantras on my *mala* gave my mind something to chew on while I was working through it.

I have since become a big fan of *yidams* . A lot of religions believe in gods or some kind of spirit. Wars have been fought over whether or not these gods are real or not. For the Tibetan Buddhist, to question the reality of a *yidam* is a waste of time.

I am getting better at seeing the details of Chenrezig when I bring him into my meditation. Chenrezig is visualized wearing silks and jewelry along with a crown. In the Buddhist world they do not feel guilty about wealth. It is a sign of good karma and, in this case, shows that Chenrezig wants for nothing. Wealth, in this sense, is a tool that can be used to alleviate suffering. Lama Jinpa mentioned that Buddha had been born a prince and came from a very wealthy family. He eventually gave up all of his wealth because he did not need it and saw that it was just one more thing to be addicted to. His privileged upbringing, however, actually gave him the ability to study and learn. It is said in the Buddhist world that those of us that are born with wealth enough to have spare time are in the best position to reach enlightenment because we can step outside the struggle to survive and study and meditate. This is very good fortune if you don't waste it partying or buying stuff you don't need. It almost made me nauseous when Lama Jinpa made this point. I suddenly thought of all the ridiculous things that my friends and I do with all of the free time we have. Watching television shows about spoiled teenagers wasting small fortunes on birthday parties for themselves when you could be evolving the human race is pretty hard to justify. Of course, when I was doing it, it never occurred to me that there was a more useful alternative. Looking back on it now, I cannot for the life of me tell you what the fuck I was thinking. Maybe that's not true. Maybe the point is that I was not thinking at all.

So this guy, Chenrezig, sees all of existence at once and does not blink. He sees people being hacked to pieces in the Congo and getting married in the Bahamas. He sees children being sold into prostitution in Mumbai and Atlanta while doctors are saving a mother's life in Pakistan. He does not miss a second of it, not even to blink. He stares it down. He confronts life as it is. This takes a very big heart and a very big mind. If you sit in meditation and really sit with the suffering of the world, at first it seems like it will blow you away. We all start pulling the window shade down at the sight of the first mangled child, but that child does not go away. We simply make ourselves ignorant of her so that we do not have to think about her or do anything about her sorry condition. Chenrezig does not do that and when you are holding this *yidam* in your heart and mind he doesn't let you close your eyes. If the suffering of the world breaks your heart, then this guy is telling you to go and grow a bigger one.

Lama Jinpa warned me that waking up would not be a bed of roses. It is a dumpster with a body in it. It is a freshly made donut with chocolate milk. It is the whole enchilada. To look at the world and not back down takes practice. We are not born with muscles, a mind or a heart big enough to handle this massive ocean of suffering, but we can hit the gym and rise to the challenge. We can practice facing pain and suffering. We can build ourselves up to be able to lift the weight of the human experience, but first we have to look at it – and not blink.

The idea behind the empowerment ritual is to have Chenrezig on your mind. You synchronize yourself to his being so that it will become not just an influence on your behavior, but part of your intuition as well. Chenrezig is a cool green dude who, unlike your real friends, doesn't talk you into one more beer before you drive home. The guy neither judges nor requires that you be any certain way. Only your best of friends are like that. But when you conjure this being in your heart center, it is like shining the light of the sun through the glass of your mind. You may have thought that the glass was clear, but up against this kind of illumination you can see the smudges of selfishness, streaks of anger and your own fingerprints left over from where you were clinging to stuff that was hurting you. It is kind of like when you pull a shirt out of a pile of dirty laundry and after a quick sniff test, you tell yourself that it is not that dirty. But when you get to school and step under the bright fluorescent lights of the hallway, you suddenly realize why the shirt was in the dirty laundry pile.

So this is what I had gotten myself into. The Chenrezig empowerment was not just a lecture or a ritual. It was a form of mind surgery. Lama Jinpa planted a seed that had been planted in him by a line of teachers that went all the way back to Buddha himself. At the time, this kind of freaked me out a bit. First of all, I wasn't all that sure that I wanted even a part of Tibetan-old-guy-mind in my mind. That could get seriously creepy. But then Lama Jinpa explained that we actually do this to each other all the time. Rinchen says that if you are nice to the people around you, they will receive a real, measurable piece of happiness that changes the way that they will treat others while the experience of your gift of kindness lingers. This, in turn, causes them to be gentle and do kind things and returns to them a loving echo from the consequences of their own positive action. This can sweep through the whole human race, but it does not have to be an accident. It does not have to wait for you to be in a good mood. You can intentionally empower the people around you, even people that you do not even know, by infecting everyone around you with the virus of kindness simply because you have trained yourself to do so.

Likewise, when you are mean to someone, that hatefulness passes itself on to others whom you have never met. A single moment of road rage can trip the trigger of disaster. Every day, we hear about people who suddenly snap after one too many psychic nastygrams have piled up in their in-box. We are bombing people constantly with our crap as if they are our own personal whipping posts. If I had to work in India as a customer service person, I would just shoot myself and get it over with. You wonder how many of these people go home and beat their children, or at least their dogs, because of the hate that got dumped on them from around the world by angry consumers of defective widgets. What a price to pay just to provide customer service for a home appliance. It is just a fucking toaster, for crying out loud.

All that the Tibetans are saying is that maybe we might want to be more careful about dumping our bullshit into shared human spaces.

It will take me a long time to figure out Chenrezig. For right now he is a being that lives in my mind. He changes my thoughts from my natural random mish-mash into a focused intention to give a damn. Until I ran into Chenrezig, I had no idea how much of my personal bandwidth was being consumed by mind-spam. The minute Chenrezig pops into my mind, all that crap freaks out and runs away like scared rats. His mantra, *om mani pema hung*, snaps my mind into his rhythm and we become one. You can say that you stand for something, but until you make it the deity you pray to, the jewel that you bury in the deepest core of who you are, you are really just talking smack. I really like the idea that they found a way to take the mind of the Buddha and put it in this handy, easy to remember package and then went out and planted it into the minds of human beings over the course of centuries. It is so much better than having the image of a cheeseburger or fancy new dust mop stuck in your head from watching TV commercials. There is so much crap floating in our brain waves. It was hurting me and I did not even notice it. It was causing me to hurt others and that was worse.

Chenrezig is my *yidam* and my teacher and he teaches me that what you let run through your thinking is really important. It is really hard for me to be a jerk when he is on my mind.

Chapter Thirty-seven: Puja In The Suburbs

I did not tell my parents about taking refuge for a couple of weeks. I figured that after joining a *dojo*, getting a motorcycle and training with a real sword, this was going to be pretty much a no-brainer for them, but I wasn't completely sure about that. Eventually, my mom noticed the protection cord around my neck and asked me what it was. I told her that Lama Jinpa had given it to me and that it contained a blessing that was supposed to keep me safe from lower rebirth. This was not exactly what she had expected to hear. She thought it was the high school version of the friendship bracelets my friends and I used to braid for each other in elementary school.

"I think you are getting into this stuff a little bit too far, don't you Maddie?" she said.

"No, not really. I am very interested in this way of life. I know that it is pretty different to the way things work around here, but it is all about thoughtfulness and compassion. How bad can that be?"

"Sometimes, I think that you have joined a cult or something. I am not sure that it is a good thing for people to change so much so quickly. You are always talking about what Rinchen says and I am concerned that what Maddie says is no longer important to you. They are not going to make you start handing out pamphlets at the airport, are they?" She was serious.

"Mom, first those guys at the airport are Hare Krishna, not Buddhists. Second, you have always said that I was heading into a man's world. That I was going to have to learn to be strong. Well ... I can kick the shit out of most guys I know. Not that I would, exactly, but the girlie-girl thing doesn't work

288

for me anymore and besides, I really, really like my life." It was this last thing that really calmed my mom down.

"Well, you have been much happier. Your father and I can see that. We just thought it was because you had a boyfriend."

"That is part of it. I love Tripp, but I love my *dojo* and my friends. I am doing things that people only dream about. I do not have an imaginary life – mine is for real."

Just as I was making my passionate claim to an extraordinary life, my dad walked in from the garage.

"What's going on? Am I interrupting a mother-daughter bonding moment?" he said casually.

"Your daughter has become a Buddhist and I have a few concerns about that," my mom said, not entirely sure that the matter was resolved.

"Really? I always thought Buddhism was pretty cool. I took a class in it in college," he said opening the refrigerator to forage for a snack.

"Henry, this is serious. Don't you think that she is getting sucked into this *dojo* thing a bit too far?" My dad closed the refrigerator door and turned to look at my mom.

"No, Jeanie, I don't. Not at all. In fact, I wish more kids would dig into life like Maddie, I mean, Lhamo, does. If I was younger, I might even go downtown and dig into it myself." My dad was not angry, but he was very serious about what he said. It was not winning my mom over, but I could see that she was taking his opinion into account.

"But Henry, what's going to be next? The next thing you know she will be walking around with her head shaved wearing funny robes and sandals. This isn't ancient Japan or Tibet. This is Missouri for crying out loud!"

"Jeanie listen to yourself. What happened to the college girl who locked herself in the dean's office to protest apartheid in South Africa? Where is the young woman who was president of the campus women's interest group and pestered everyone she knew to support the Equal Rights Amendment? When I met you, you didn't shave your legs and you wore a T-shirt with a picture of Ché Guevera on it. What happened to that woman, huh?" Wow! Dad was on the soapbox here and who knew that Jeanie had ever had a cool phase? My mom suddenly smiled and said, "I loved that T-shirt."

My dad lowered his voice and said, "Jeanie, you should be proud of your daughter. She is living a thoughtful life based on really, really great principles and hanging out with kids who think that exercise and compassion are the coolest things in town. Other people's kids are killing themselves in drunk driving accidents or being dragged to the hospital after having passed out at a party. What exactly is the problem here?"

"It doesn't include me and it is stuff that I don't understand. That's what it is. And I am kind of jealous. I would like to be the woman in the meeting that can kick butt and then go meditate in my cubicle." My mom's eyes were beginning to get soggy. "I am sorry, Maddie, I guess that what is really bothering me is that I used to have all these ideals and principles and they have all kind of fallen by the wayside. Sometimes when I see you doing your *dojo* thing, I feel like I really sold out. I get a little bit ashamed of myself."

I gave my mom a hug. "How can you say that? You have provided us with everything. You have taken care of us when we were sick. You do honest work. How can you say that you abandoned your principles? And by the way, who is Ché Guevara?"

My mom laughed. "He was a Marxist revolutionary who fought to free his people from oppression. He was eventually killed by the CIA, but has become a symbol of freedom and revolt on college campuses everywhere."

"A warrior. Cool."

"Yeah, cool," said my mom kissing me on the forehead.

Once I came out of the closet about me being an official Buddhist, my mom was still worried that I was going to undergo even more radical life changes than I already had. She was constantly asking me, sometimes in a mocking tone, whether it was okay for Buddhists to have ketchup on French fries or whether or not she should get rid of my bikini. Eventually, she realized that my lifestyle was pretty much what she was already used to.

I had mentioned to my dad, that I wanted to set up a personal shrine in my bedroom and he nearly hurt himself trying to build one for me in the garage. He looked up pictures of shrines on the internet and opted for a small table with a sword rack and a small cabinet with a pair of doors that opened in the middle. The cabinet had a shelf in it for a statue and another little shelf that could be pulled out of the base of the cabinet and used to hold an incense burner. He actually bought the table at a store, but the cabinet was all Henry. It took him a week to build it. In my former life, I would have thought that his little cabinet thingy was kind of stupid, but when he showed it to me, I could see how hard he had worked on it and that it was not just a box, but a shrine built with his love for me. I would have missed that completely in my old days. We had to come up with a pedestal for the shrine box so that when it was open you could see into it over top of the sword rack. When it was all finished, however, it looked kind of cool and it certainly did its job.

At first, I used a pillow off of the couch to sit on when I practiced meditation. Before, I had done most of my Wild Horse and *Tronglen* practice sitting in *seiza*, but I wanted to do things like Lama Jinpa did them, so the pillow disappeared into my bedroom. Eventually, Tripp took me to a store downtown that sold Buddhist artifacts and supplies and I got a proper prayer cushion. Lama Jinpa does not actually sit on a cushion, but he recommends them to his American students because they do not have "Asian knees." While we were at the Buddhist shop, I picked out a *mala*.

The Chenrezig practice requires the use of these prayer beads when you recite mantra. A mantra is a phrase that you repeat over and over while you visualize the deity in your mind. In the case of Chenrezig practice, the mantra is *"om mani pema hung"*. During the explanation of the Chenrezig practice, it took Lama Jinpa over an hour to explain what it means. Half of that time was spent on the *"om"*..". Chenrezig *puja* is a series of prayers and practices that are written down in a text. *"Puja"* actually refers to the idea of devotional acts and during the practice of *puja* you do different things like repeat a prayer or chant a mantra. There is even a part where you do absolutely nothing while you try to empty your mind. When you chant mantra, the idea is to completely occupy yourself in body, speech and mind. To do this, you count the mantras using your *mala* which occupies our body. You speak the mantra occupying your speech while simultaneously visualizing Chenrezig in your heart center which takes a lot of concentration. This occupies your mind. The cool thing about *puja* is that there is no room in your brain for anything else. The practice is designed to occupy your body, speech and mind completely. Even a beginner can sit through *puja* without hardly twitching. This is one of the reasons why they say that *Vajrayanna* is the "lightning vehicle". It works pretty fast. When I was trying to learn the Wild Horse meditation, it was really frustrating because my mind would wander all over the place. Visualization meditation is much more effective on my attention deficit disordered brain.

I bought a practice compact disc from Lama Jinpa's dharma center in California that features Lama Jinpa and some of his students who know what they are doing, reciting the practice. This is very useful, but the practice is chanted in Tibetan. Lama Jinpa told us to start doing the practice in English so that we knew what we were saying. The *puja* text has the practice written out three ways: in Tibetan script, in an English phonetic description of the Tibetan script and in English. Most of the practice has a melody making it sound all mysterious and Buddha-like. I have to say, I much prefer the Tibetan version because it sounds really cool. So what I do is go through the practice in

English first kind of fast and then do it in Tibetan trying to chant along with Lama Jinpa and his students on the CD. It makes me feel ancient and serious like I am part of twenty-five hundred years of tradition - which, actually, I am. Tripp said that you don't have to do the Tibetan part to be a part of the tradition, but it's cool; I am doing it that way and I am not changing my mind.

After doing this practice for a couple of weeks, I started to have dreams about Chenrezig. In the first one, I was sitting on a hill overlooking a very beautiful valley. I could see this guy sitting slightly further down the hill from me looking at the same thing that I was looking at. He then turned around and looked at me and said without moving his lips, "it is beautiful, isn't it?" When I saw his face, I was suddenly scared in my dream because it was not the cartoon character that I had been visualizing. His face looked so real, but not the face of a human being exactly. There was something different in his facial features like they were not proportioned exactly the same as a human being. It scared me so much that I woke up.

A month into the practice, I had another dream where I saw Lama Jinpa lit up like he was a holiday lawn ornament. He just sat there smiling at me. After a minute, I saw the Dalai Lama lit up just like Lama Jinpa and he was also just sitting there smiling at me. There were a few other old guys in robes who showed up, but I did not know who they were. A week or so later, I was in a book shop with Megan and I picked up a book about Tibetan Buddhism. As I paged through it, I came to an old photograph of this guy, a famous lama, who had been in my dream. That just creeped me out. I asked Rinchen about it and he said that meditation unlocks subtleties in your mind and that I should not make too much of it. Dude, I am dreaming of dead guys that I have never met and it turns out that they were real people. How could I know that?

Rinchen said that sometimes meditation unlocks certain psychic processes that seem like magic or ESP. He says that it is really important to ignore this stuff because if you start meditating to have creepy powers you will lose your way and can go down a very dark path. He said that Buddha had a cousin who was also his brother-in-law who started doing this kind of stuff and then tried to take over Buddha's followers by suggesting that his powers were something more important than enlightenment. At first, Buddha ignored him, but eventually the cousin tried to kill the Buddha and he had to be banished. According to Rinchen, this guy, his name was Devadatta, didn't figure out what a jerk he had been until he got really sick and tried to see the Buddha before he died. Too bad for him because he kicked the bucket at the outer gates of the monastery where Buddha was staying. Rinchen says that Devadatta is a warning to anyone who tries to turn Buddhism into party tricks. He also says that it is written that someday Devadatta will be reborn to be a Buddha, so go figure.

Chapter Thirty-eight: The Mystery of Tuesday Nights

After the new year, my life settled into an easy rhythm of school, training and date nights on Saturdays. Before I knew it, January was already gone. During these first several weeks of the year, I hadn't noticed that neither Tripp nor Megan were training on Tuesday nights. In fact, I would have probably not noticed it for quite a while longer if it hadn't been for the fact that Valentine's Day just happened to fall on Tuesday.

It is pretty cool to be in a relationship on Valentine's Day and I expected it to be a celebration of us. It is supposed to be one of the automatic perks of having a boyfriend. I mean, it is a holy day of obligation -- especially for guys. Tripp and I had had a pretty good time on our first Valentine's Day together. He had made arrangements with my parents to cook dinner for me at my house while my parents went out on a date of their own. He brought flowers and made lasagna with real garlic bread and everything. Of course, it was a little bit weird to have Tyler there for dinner, but it was the thought that counted. I was thinking that it was my turn to do something for him and I had been saving my money to take him someplace special. I figured that going out that Tuesday night was a no-brainer and did not say much about it until the weekend before.

We were at his dad's loft sitting at the kitchen table having tea when I decided to make my move on him. "Trippster ... watcha doing on Tuesday night?" I was expecting him to say something like, "whatever you want to do" or "I will be spending Valentine's Day with my best girl" or .... It didn't happen. Captain Oblivion said "I am going to Victoria's house like I always do."

"Who the hell is Victoria and why the fuck are you spending Valentine's Day with her?" Tripp was in shock. He had not realized that Tuesday was Valentine's Day and that he had just managed to trip the trigger of an emotional landmine. Unlike many guys, Tripp had no skill in the manly art of improvised bullshit. All he could say was, "oh crap, I forgot." Wrong answer.

"What a dick! You're blowing me off on Valentine's Day for some chick named Victoria – and she had better be your aunt! What is wrong with you?" Rinchen came through the front door just as I was lighting into his son. He could see the look of shock and awe on Tripp's face and froze in the doorway as if he was trying to assess how dangerous the situation was. Tripp was clearly unprepared for the tongue-lashing he was getting and seemed not to be entirely sure why he was getting it. I was just about to go in for round two when I heard the door close behind Rinchen and realized that we were not alone. I turned around to see who was there and Rinchen was holding his keys and looking at me not sure of whether it was safe to even say "hello". He looked at Tripp and asked, "What's the matter? Did I interrupt something?"

Tripp shrugged his shoulders and said, "I was just in the middle of getting my butt kicked, I guess. I am not sure what is going on."

"Well, I can go back outside if you two need to finish your conversation," said Rinchen. He didn't even finish his sentence before Tripp was saying, "oh no, please don't." It sounded like he was begging his father to stay so that there would be a witness to his murder.

Rinchen looked at me and asked, "Miss Lhamo, what has you so riled up?" This was not fair. It was bad enough that Tripp's dad had just interrupted a perfectly justified ass chewing, but he was my *sensei* and he was never not my *sensei*. I was required to calm myself. I took a deep breath and started to make my case.

"Your son, instead of letting me take him out for dinner on Valentine's Day this Tuesday night, is blowing me off to go hang out with someone named 'Victoria' at her house … and I AM REALLY NOT AMUSED!" Rinchen burst out laughing.

"Excuse me *Sensei*, but I am not getting the joke here. I have been dating your son for over a year and a half now and I don't think that this is a very nice thing to do." Rinchen composed himself and looked at Tripp with an expression that said, "It's okay son, I got this." He crossed the kitchen and put his hands on both of my shoulders and looked me straight in the eye and speaking softly he said, "He's not going to Victoria's house, he is going to *Victoria House*. It's a battered women's shelter and he and Megan go there every

Tuesday night to tutor the children of the women who live there. I am friends with one of the nuns there and thought that it would be a good idea for these guys to help out. They have been going there for the last month or so. So, you see, this is really my fault."

"Oh." That was all I could think of to say. I was suddenly so embarrassed. I couldn't even turn around to face Tripp. How could I think that he was a cheating bastard when he was really the patron saint of battered women. I felt like a complete jerk. I started to cry and Rinchen pulled me toward him and hugged me laughing not at me, but to express his relief that all was actually well. As I cried into his shoulder, he motioned for Tripp to come over to where we were standing and gently handed me over to his son. "This is your job," he said to Tripp and disappeared into his room. Tripp held me close. "I am so sorry Tripp. I am such an asshole."

"No you're not. I should have told you what we've been up to. It's just that I didn't really want to make a big deal out of it. Megs and I have been going there occasionally for a couple of years, but not on a regular schedule like we are doing now. We used to just help out when we could, but now we are kind of part of the program." He kissed me on my forehead and held my head to his shoulder. "Are we good?"

"Yeah, we're great, Trippster, we're great."

We decided that instead of going out on Valentine's Day, I would go with him and Megan to Victoria House. He said that they actually needed more volunteers, but that it had to be cleared with the staff of the shelter. The night before, Megan came over to my house and we put together a whole bunch of little bags of cookies and candies as a treat for the residents. Tripp said that there were usually at least fifteen kids there and about ten women. So we made up about thirty-five goodie bags to be on the safe side. On Tuesday night, Megan picked me up and we headed downtown. While we were driving down the freeway, she just couldn't help but pop me with a cheap shot: "wow, I can't believe that Tripp is letting you go over to Victoria's house; it's gonna be awkward having both of you there at the same time. You better watch yourself, she's pretty hot."

"Bitch," I said smiling, but slightly annoyed that this was not the last Victoria joke I was likely to face.

Megan chuckled.

We picked up Tripp and made our way through north St. Louis. Some parts were nicer than others, but where we were going looked like left-overs from a war movie. There were two entire city blocks covered with nothing but foundations of houses that used to be there. When we turned to head up the street toward an old church, I realized that the church was abandoned. Apparently, not even God wanted to live here.

Victoria House looked like an ordinary St. Louis-style brownstone duplex. There were no signs or any indication that the building housed thirty people. Megan explained the anonymous appearance: "this place is kept secret and you can't talk about where it is. You'd be amazed at how many of these woman have very violent men looking for them. It is really screwed up. First, they beat the shit of them and when they try to leave, these guys hunt them down so that they can beat the shit out of them again. Just having volunteers coming and going is a risk. So when we pull up, we get out of the car and head to the side door, not the front door – you got it?" Megan parked, and the three of us got out of the car walked directly to a door on the side of the three story brick building. Tripp rang the bell and within just a few seconds a nun with a beautiful face and dark brown skin appeared at the door to let us in.

"Hello Sister Constance, we brought a friend," Megan said cheerfully as we stepped into what looked like an ordinary apartment. Sister Constance shook my hand and said with a slight accent that I did not recognize, "it's a pleasure to meet you; you must be Madison."

"Yes, but most people call me 'Lhamo'."

"Lhamo, that's an unusual name. Well, Lhamo, welcome to Victoria House." No sooner had Sister Constance taken our coats, than what sounded like a large herd of small ponies came running down the hallway. As the first little kid rounded the corner, I heard "HI-YA!" as a little boy jumped in front of Tripp landing in what looked like a *Karate* stance. "Hey, DeShaun," said Tripp leaning over to pat the boy on the head. DeShaun swept away Tripp's hand and tried to get off a snap kick. "No fighting in the house!" scolded Sister Constance. Two little girls in pigtails ran up to Megan and hugged her leg. They started jumping up and down with their arms up trying to get Megan to pick them up yelling, "Megan! Megan! Megan!" Sister Constance let the kids have their moment of excitement and then told them to head into the living room and get their books out. As fast as they had stormed into the hall, the stampede now took off in the opposite direction.

I handed Sister Constance the box of Valentine treats. "We won't tell them about these until after they have done their homework, otherwise we won't get anything done this evening," the nun said turning to take the box back into the kitchen. As I walked down the hallway, the heads of some older kids, all girls, peeked around the corner from the living room. Some were younger than me and at first I assumed that they were the daughters of some of the women that were living there. When I went into the living room, I saw several of them pick up smaller children and hold them on their hips. It was then that I realized that anyone over twelve years old in this place was a battered woman and not a battered woman's child.

There were four kids that sat with Tripp at one of two card tables set up in the living room. They were only about six or seven years old. Megan sat at another table on the other side of the room with several other kids, all of whom were older. One of them seemed to be a mom and sat at the table with a tiny baby propped up on her knee. Tripp started by picking out a book and reading it to the kids at his table. He held up the book from time to time so that everyone could see the pictures. He would read a page and then pass the book to a child and ask him if he could try to read the same page. Two of the children could read most of the words. The other two could not read at all. Tripp was patient and showed each child how to sound out the words and match the words to the picture.

Megan was working on math with the older kids. They were doing long division. She had paper and pencils on the table and made each kid work out a problem in front of everyone else at the table. One of the girls, who looked to be about fourteen, was working on a problem while balancing a baby on her knee. "Tamika, why don't you let Lhamo hold Jasmine so you can work?" asked Megan as she motioned for me to come over to the table and take the baby. As I started to take Jasmine from Tamika, she started to cry. "Don't you start that cryin' shit baby girl, I'm right here," said Tamika. It took several minutes of bouncing the baby and walking around the living room to get her to calm down, but eventually she found the red protection cord tied around my neck and started pulling on it. To keep Jasmine quiet, we started wandering around the house and pointing at objects and people saying, "what's that? What's in here? Who's that?"

As I walked toward the back of the house, I met Sister Constance. "Ah, I see you have found one of our pretty little bundles," offering her finger to Jasmine who grabbed it and tried to stick it into her mouth.

"How many people live here?" I asked.

"There is only supposed to be eight women and a total of twelve kids, plus the four of us who run the place, but we are cheating at the moment. We don't usually get too much trouble from the city, but we are subject to the housing codes just like everybody else."

"Some of the mothers seem really young," I said.

"Well, some of them start having kids at eleven or twelve years old when they are still children themselves. We see the whole spectrum here. Some have drug problems; some get pregnant through incest or rape. Most of them, get sweet talked by an older guy and when their families find out that they are pregnant, they get beaten up, thrown out or both. We take the ones who have the highest risk of being victims of violence. There are other shelters in the city that take the ones that are simply homeless."

"It's amazing that someone would beat a girl up because she is pregnant."

"Hah! It happens every day; sometimes by fathers, but you would be amazed at how many mothers beat up their daughters because they got pregnant. And it is not just poor people. We see girls coming in here from middle class neighborhoods sometimes. They have nowhere to go at first. Abuse is an equal opportunity sin."

"How many women are there like these in St. Louis?" I asked.

"Hundreds. We only see the ones that are lucky enough to get help. Most of our residents come to us through social workers working with the police. The police usually get to them first because there has been an altercation. They are then assigned a case worker who assesses their situation and tries to figure out a solution. Some of these women have been in the hospital before they were well enough to come here."

It is one thing to hear about homeless shelters on the news or read about them. It was quite another to stand in one and look into the faces of women and children who have lives so horrible that they must be hidden away to keep them safe. This was not Africa. This was not Afghanistan. This was in the very heart of the United States. This was twenty-five miles from my home and two miles from my *dojo*.

Sister Constance told me that they do not allow cellphones in the house and try to control the communication that the women have with the outside world. She said that it is not unusual for a woman to call the person who beat her up and ask them to come and get her. Sometimes they leave the house without taking their children with them, which Sister Constance says can sometimes be a blessing for the children. They figure that the nuns will take care of the kids. Some of these women try to come back after a day or two of partying and some try to come back after being beaten up again. If they leave without permission, however, they cannot come back. They are considered a risk to the rest of the house and even if they have to live in a dumpster they are out for good. The kids are put in foster care. Sister Constance says that the chances for a woman who gets kicked out of Victoria House are not very good although some have amazing survival skills.

"It sounds kind of cruel to kick them out like that, " I said.

"We cannot let this place turn into a flop house. Many of these women would disappear for a few days and go out and have a good time while we looked after their children and then come back when they had nowhere else to go bringing drugs and God knows what else with them. The first rule of Victoria House is that it is an absolute drug-free zone. Drugs can spread through a place like this like the flu. The rule here is that you can stay until another situation can be figured out, but you must be a mom and you must help out. A lot of our guests are not very well trained in taking responsibility. The point is that there is a nearly endless list of women who need our help, so we have to focus on the ones who play by the rules and will help themselves. We have had to bury quite a few of the women who we have tried to help and put their children in foster care."

As I got the tour of Victoria House, I realized that Sister Constance was a warrior of the highest order. She had seen more human damage than I could imagine and yet chose to devote her life to confronting it. She was not a person who had been swept away by a religious whim. She said that she had been born in Haiti and had been very poor. Her parents died when she was in her early teens and she was taken in by an orphanage run by an order of Catholic nuns. They made sure that she was educated and when she was old enough, she applied to go to college in the United States. She said that she was a graduate of Georgetown University and while she had been taught about Christianity in the orphanage, she had only really come to accept it as her true religion in college. She was so impressed with the help that she had gotten, that she decided to take the vows to become a nun and was assigned to live in St. Louis. Like all warriors, her eyes were wide open. She could see the suffering in the world that was all around her and because of the clarity of her mind and the quality of her experience, there was no way that she could ignore it. Sister Constance woke up and then she stood up.

My new favorite nun took me upstairs to see the living quarters. As we walked down the hall, I would peek into the rooms as I passed. There were cribs in some and makeshift children's beds in others. Some were neat and some were quite messy. The nuns had a rule that everyone who was old enough to help out had to help keep the house clean. She said that some of the women would refuse to clean up even their own rooms and on rare occasions the nuns made them leave the house for it.

"Some of these women do not have even the slightest discipline and many cannot write their own names. They grow up pretty much like animals in some cases. Their parents, if they know them, are frequently substance abusers and very poor. Some of these women have no immediate family at all and have been living with extended family until an uncle or an uncle's friend attacked them. It is amazing how many "uncles" these women have. They grow up with nearly none of the emotional and educational support that you or I had. They are thrown to the dogs from birth and then society wonders why they are the way they are."

"I had no idea that it could get this bad. I mean, you hear about this in places like where you came from, but it is hard to believe that it happens here," I said.

"My dear Lhamo, suffering happens everywhere. I did not have to go back to Haiti to find it. Every major city on earth has places like this. They sent me here because it is just as good a place as any to try to help. Although it is true that it gets much worse than this, but not just in poor countries -- even here. There are worse places than this in this metropolitan area." As she spoke, she looked at me with great kindness as if my lack of understanding was no different than the lack of understanding that brought women to live in this house.

"I can't believe with all of the wealth and technology in this country that we allow this to happen," I said indignantly.

"There have always been poor people, my dear. There has always been a bottom of the pile and there always will be. Money would help, and people getting involved would help even more, but the truth is that even if we had big budgets and an army of highly educated volunteers, there would still be suffering. Some of these women have lived in government housing that was as nice as any apartment in town. Some have had access to food and medical care most of their lives. Physical assets are not enough for anyone. What made you who you are is *a family* that actually cared about you. They were there for you. They fed you and clothed you and they set an example for your behavior. Surely you know a few messed up kids in Westchester, no?"

"Yes, several," I said immediately thinking of Nick Thompson.

"They had all the material things that they needed, did they not?"

"Yes, some are quite wealthy in fact."

"So what happened to them?"

"Usually, it is their parents not caring, but not always. Sometimes you can't tell why things go wrong for them. A couple of my friends are bi-polar. I don't know, I am not sure that there is always a convenient pattern."

"That's right, there's not. Suffering comes in all shapes and sizes and finds everyone at some point. It is how we are taught to relate to suffering that, in my opinion, makes the biggest difference. I have a friend in Washington Park across the river in Illinois. He runs a church over there that has buried more than a hundred gang bangers and young people since he has been there. He tells the youth of his congregation that it does not matter whether life is fair or not. That it does not matter how high your mountain is. He tells them that however tough their life might be, they must confront it and never feel sorry for themselves because to do so will just give their minds a reason to give up. Most of them don't listen. They fall into drugs and things like that because no matter how bad your life feels, drugs are an easy way to feel better. Doing drugs is much easier than getting an education or fighting your way out of a bad situation. The good reverend tries to get them to climb their mountains. He tries to show them how to do it, just like your parents and friends have shown you. The more resolved you are to face difficulty, the better off you will be regardless of whether you live in a housing project or a mansion. Those kids you know that have troubles, I will bet that they are just as angry and feel just as sorry for themselves as anyone in this house."

I thought about what Sister Constance was telling me. I could see that in many cases that she was right. I could remember times when I was unhappy because I didn't get what I wanted or felt that I was being treated unfairly. Oh the tantrums I have thrown. Those were the darkest times of my life, but compared to the people living in Victoria House they seemed ridiculous by comparison. As I stood in the hallway on the second floor of the women's shelter, I was suddenly embarrassed by the hundreds of things that I had been upset about in my life. Some of them were the stupidest things, like not getting the shoes I wanted or not being allowed to go out on a school night. Here I was talking to a woman who had grown up in one of the poorest countries in the world, lost both her parents when she was young but still found a way to go to one of the best universities in the world. And rather than go out into the world to make all the money she never had and live in comfort, she voluntarily returned to the pit of hell, to a world of poverty and trouble, a world of lost souls and people hurting each other in ignorance and anger. It takes a whole lot of love to do that. Only a true warrior has the character to even consider such a thing.

"Why did you become a nun?" I asked. Sister Constance smiled and patted my shoulder.

"I have known poverty and despair all my life. But the one thing I know, from my own experience, is that it can be beaten. I know what these women know. I have seen what they have seen, but with a big difference. I have seen a way out. They can't see that. It is right in front of them sometimes but they just can't see it. If you were in a burning building and you could see the door what would you do? Would you run through it and save yourself? Would you try to show everyone else in the house where the door was? If you saved yourself and everyone else perished in the fire, could you live with that? Could you live with yourself knowing that you could have done something?"

Her answer gave me chills. As she spoke I could see all the things that I could have done in my life, but that I had not done. At first, I started to feel guilty, but then I realized that my life was far from over. I couldn't imagine doing what Sister Constance had done. I did not want to immerse myself in a constant world of suffering. Surely a girl is entitled to have some joy in her life? But on the other hand, how do you go out and have fun knowing what is happening to people like these poor young women. It felt like a trap. I felt guilty for not helping those in need and sad for myself if my whole world were to become a donation to others. "Do you ever get a chance to get out of here and do things for yourself?" I asked Sister Constance.

She smiled and said, "Of course! I take a Yoga class at the YMCA and Rinchen is teaching me mindfulness meditation. I belong to the St. Louis Inter-Faith Council and occasionally, when I am feeling run-down or sad, I go to the zoo. I love the zoo."

St. Louis has one of the best zoos in the country and the best thing about it is that admission is free. You can go there every day if you want. But what really surprised me about what Sister Constance had just said was that Rinchen was teaching her mindfulness meditation.

"You train with Rinchen?"

"Yes, I love it. It is really relaxing and I find that mindfulness practice does wonders for my own spiritual practice."

"But you're a Christian, right? And not just a little bit Christian, you're a Catholic nun. Won't you get in trouble for taking meditation lessons from a Buddhist?"

Sister Constance started to laugh. "Maybe if this were the fifteenth century. I am pretty sure that they are not going to excommunicate me for learning how to meditate, besides Bishop Monahan takes the same class. In fact, he's the one who introduced me to Rinchen."

"You're kidding me!"

"No, my child, I am a nun. We don't kid around. I don't even have a sense of humor," she said holding her hands together as if she were praying and rolling her eyes upward trying to look as innocent as possible. I cracked up. She was the coolest nun ever.

When we came back into the living room, Tripp was laying faced-down on the floor with a pile of kids on top of him. Megan was still sitting at the card table, but was shouting "get him; nail him to the floor!"

Sister Constance stood in the doorway watching the wrestling match. "These kids get so few opportunities to just be kids. That Tripp, he is a character. He loves to get them all riled up. They need physical contact like this. They need to see men showing them kindness. He is quite a young man." She kept her eyes on the wiggling pile of Tripp and the children on the floor and then looked at me and said, "But I'd bet that you already knew that, didn't you?" She took Jasmine from my arms and handed her over to her mother and then she said, "I think it is time for those goodie bags, don't you?"

We stuck around to clean up the living room. It was amazing to see how fast a dozen little kids could tear into candy wrappers. I had bags for the mothers too and plenty left over for the nuns.

We got ready to leave and as we stepped out onto the landing by the side door and into cold night air, DeShaun would not let go of Tripp's pant leg. "Don't go, don't go," he cried working himself up into quite a tantrum. Tripp sat down in *seiza* in front of the boy and said, "How do samurai say good-bye?" DeShaun dropped to his knees and bowed. Tripp returned his bow, but when he sat up they did a ritual I had not seen before. They punched knuckles cross-handed, Tripp's large fist bumping DeShaun's tiny one, and then repeating the move with the other hand. Then they both threw their fists downward and screamed "hi-yaaaa" while touching foreheads. DeShaun grabbed Tripp around the neck. "Until we meet again, samurai," said Tripp in a fake deep voice. DeShaun crunched up his face to look tough and bowed. Quickly, we made our escape down the stairs.

Megan had already crossed the street to the car and was climbing into the driver's seat when she heard Sister Constance yell out, "DeShaun come back here!"

Tripp was on the far side of the car and turned to look. I was barely to the curb behind the car when I saw the little boy jump off the bottom step and run straight for the street. I only saw the headlights sliding down the pavement, but I could hear the loud base tones of music rumbling out of a car. Without a conscious thought, I dashed for the boy. I only had to take a few steps until DeShaun was nearly at my feet, I bent down and snatched him up off the street grabbing him under his arms. I could hear the car. It was close. It was in my ear. I pulled DeShaun close to my chest covering him with both of my arms and dove forward into the air. As I felt our bodies descending to the ground I tucked my head downward and began the roll that was pure habit for me. I could feel the curb strike my upper shoulders, but was immediately relieved to feel my feet rise up and over in the air. It was not my prettiest forward roll and the landing was one nasty break-fall on the cold concrete of the sidewalk, but when I started thinking consciously again, I was on my back looking up with DeShaun held tightly to my chest. I heard the screech of brakes as the car stopped. "Get out of the fucking road you crazy-ass bitch". The driver gunned the motor and took off around the corner. It all happened in a flash. I was never once afraid. It was like I flew in slow motion never doubting what needed to be done and without giving it a second thought. Within seconds, I was looking up at a circle of faces. Sister Constance leaned over to take DeShaun off of my chest while Tripp and Megan were helping me to my feet.

"Are you okay?" Tripp asked looking like he had just seen a ghost.

"Yeah, but my ass is going to hurt tomorrow," I said straightening my clothes.

"Damn, Lhamo, that was awesome. It was like watching a momma panther. You got skills, girl", Megan said brushing off my back. Sister Constance was holding DeShaun and tears were forming in her eyes. "You're an angel," she said looking at me. She turned to walk back into Victoria House with several of the mothers in front of her. I could hear the mothers talking about what they had just seen.

"Damn, did you see that? That girl flew through the air and snatched little DeShaun right off that street like she was some kind of an eagle or something."

"Those motherfuckers in that car weren't even going to try to stop, damn motherfuckers." The side door closed and the street became silent except for the sound of a bus taking off from a stop somewhere in the distance. As I opened the car door, Tripp came up to me and held me tight.

"You're amazing," he said softly in my ear.

"No, you're amazing coming down here and helping these kids."

"No you're amazing," he said teasing me.

"No, you're amazing."

"Alright, alright, you're both fucking amazing. Can we go now?" Megan was looking at us with a smile, but it was dark and we were in a pretty bad part of town and her instincts were telling her that it was time to move.

As we made our way back to the loft to drop off Tripp, I thought about Sister Constance and her devotion and how I didn't think twice before running out in front of that car to snatch DeShaun from the street. It was a pretty good warrior moment for me. I realized that that's what we are about. When we see the need we must do what we must do. It doesn't make you a superhero. But there is something deeply satisfying about living your life on purpose in a fight for the benefit of others. I want to be like Sister Constance, at least as much as I can. I want to be one of those people who comes when called, who rises up, who takes a stand. Maybe I don't have to be a nun or a *sensei*. Maybe I can just be me, but I realized right then and there, that you have to make some decisions ahead of time so that there is no decision to make when people really need you.

Chapter Thirty-nine: A Different Kind Of Spring Break

Senior year in high school is marked by more rituals than other years. The biggest, of course, is graduation, but there are others like spring break and senior prom. Spring break for many college kids has turned into an orgy somewhere in Florida or Cancun where you are supposed to do all the stuff that you will regret when you are older, but will make interesting Facebook content. If you really go whacko on spring break, you might even find yourself in a porn video.

When I was a sophomore, Beth and I had promised each other that we would go to the beach for spring break our senior year. I don't think we ever thought that we would get particularly wild, but we both were going to turn eighteen before spring break was scheduled and in our minds that meant we could do whatever we wanted. It never occurred to us that we might have the right to vote for the president of the United States, but we did not have the right to take off for a week without our parents' permission. It didn't matter much. Without financial assistance, a spring break trip was not going to happen anyway.

Spring break at Westchester High was scheduled for the third week in March and by February, Beth had not checked in with me to see if I was going to go anywhere. She had not made plans and had figured that I would probably do something with Megan and Tripp now that they were the center of my orbit. Tripp and I had talked about riding down to the Gulf shore on our motorcycles if we could get the parents to agree. That wasn't going to happen.

It was still too rainy in Missouri for motorcycles in March. So, the dream of our first open road trip together would have to be put on hold.

As March was drawing nearer, Rinchen pulled me aside in the *dojo* one evening to tell me that we had all been invited by Lama Jinpa to go to a Buddhist retreat in up-state New York over spring break. Tripp wanted to go and Megan said that she would go if I went. Matt was also invited, but he had a job and could not get off work for the whole week. Rinchen was planning to drive and would act as chaperone which meant that Henry and Jeanie would probably let me go. Why wouldn't they? If you were a parent and had a choice between having your eighteen year old daughter dancing on the beach with a bunch of drunks or tucked away safely in a Buddhist monastery, which would you choose? Even if you were Catholic, you might consider this a pretty good deal.

I can't say that the retreat was that much of a draw for me, but the chance to take a road trip with Tripp and Megan was certainly cool and a week in a farmhouse practicing Buddhism with Lama Jinpa was not exactly Fort Lauderdale, but it could work out. Besides, Tripp said that Lama Jinpa was going to be leading the *Nyung Ne* (pronounced "nyoong-nay") practice which is supposed to wipeout all of your bad karma from previous lives. I was still not sold on the reincarnation thing, but I liked the idea of a practice, a thing that you could physically do, that would put things in the past and leave them there. I had just turned eighteen and had not built up a lot of regrets yet, but I knew as time passed that I would go out and get some. So I figured that this practice would be useful when I was old, like thirty or something, and needed to clean up my college karma. I had no idea what *Nyung Ne* was or how you did it, but at that point in my life, I was so far down the rabbit hole anyway, that it did not even sound all that unusual to me. A bunch of my friends from school are Catholic and they go to confession, so I pretty much figured that *Nyung Ne* was kind of like that.

We left on Friday after school. Tripp said that we should travel light, but told me to bring a *do-gi* bag and weapons. This struck me as kind of strange -- that we would go to a Tibetan Buddhist retreat and take weapons. I was turning into as big a cultural mutt as Rinchen and his kids. The retreat center is on an old farm converted into a monastery and Tripp said that there would be time to train nearly every day in a barn or out on the lawn.

Rinchen walks almost everywhere he goes, but he does own a car. Unfortunately it is too small for long trips with four people, so he rented a minivan. My experience of minivans had been that they were privately owned school busses with kiddie debris all over the back seat – evidence that your mother did not have a life. When my mom got her convertible, I didn't mind so much waiting in line to be dropped off at the front door of my school. But her old minivan was kind of embarrassing. You would open the side door and the first thing that would happen is a pile of crumpled up fast food bags and paper cups would fall out onto the sidewalk. The minivan that Rinchen rented, however, was brand new. There were no dried up French fries wedged in the seats or empty water bottles on the floor. If you did not know that you were in a minivan, you would have thought that you were in a really nice, spacious car. We stowed all of our gear in the back and there was plenty of room for us to stretch our legs. This was a truly useful vehicle.

I used to think that cars needed to make you look cool. Some of my friends drove awesome cars. Ack drove a Mercedes. It was ten years old, but it was black and looked like new. Rachel Miller, a girl in my psychology class, drove a Lexus with a stereo that could be heard for miles when she rolled down the windows. The coolest kid-car ever was the car Rita Montrose drove to school – a lipstick red Jaguar convertible. As much as I hated that bitch, I wanted her car. But as we started rolling down the freeway toward New York, I started thinking about the difference between looking good and being actually useful. I started thinking about all of the money I had spent on shoes that I had only worn once, the drawer full of slightly used nail polish bottles and eye shadow cases that would never see the light of day again. I thought about the closet full of clothes that were no longer cool enough to wear. There were hundreds of dollars tied up in that stuff and it was all going to get thrown away eventually. I remember Rinchen once saying to us in class that when you walk into a large retail store and you look around, you notice the thousands of things on the shelves. He said "now think that those thousands of things, every scrap of it, will be in a landfill in five years." He said, they might as well drive the delivery trucks straight to the dump and save us the trouble of having to throw it all away.

It is amazing what we waste on looking good or our amusement. We buy new stuff to replace our old new stuff nearly every day. We download songs instead of actually learning how to play music. I have had at least five cellphones that I can think of and I didn't get my first one until I was eleven. When you think about it, we are actually choking on our own toys which would not be so bad, but after all of that consumption we are still bored shitless.

Without really realizing it, I had stopped dressing up for school. I wore mostly the same two pairs of cheap jeans that were baggy and comfortable.

When you wear a *gi* and realize that you can twist yourself into a pretzel without feeling pinched by your clothes, you get to like baggy. I have seen girls show up at school dances with skirts so tight that they could not take full steps and heels so high that if they did take full steps, they would fall on their faces. You see these girls doing the mommy-shoes-shuffle across the polished floors at school and wonder why they torture themselves to please a bunch of moron boys who are working really hard to imagine them wearing nothing. I used to think that this was really cool and even went to the homecoming dance my sophomore year dressed like a fashion mummy. I think the designers in Paris and Los Angeles should make the *hakama* part of their collections. Now that's a skirt I would love to wear to school.

I got into wearing baggy sweaters too when it got cold and T-shirts when it was warm. It was funny, I ran into Ack in the hall and he almost didn't recognize me. No one really paid attention to me anymore because I didn't make an effort to be on anybody's radar. It is amazing how much extra time you have to think about really cool stuff when you are not thinking about whether people like you or not. In fact, I kind of started not thinking about myself at all because I was too busy thinking about why my locker smelled like fake strawberries or how they got the little flecks of color into the stone-hard floors of the hallways or what kind of bird was chirping outside of the window of my classroom. I had found a new freedom in my clothes and in my mind and it was making my life simple and light.

When you travel with Rinchen, I think that it would help if you were already enlightened. It is not like the guy sings show tunes rolling down the freeway. In fact, Rinchen does not listen to music. He doesn't like to have the radio on and he doesn't talk much when he drives. He actually spends his time noticing the scenery which is incredible because to get to New York from Missouri, you have to cut across whole states of flat farmland. Tripp and Megan are used to this. Tripp actually likes the quiet too and Megan came prepared with headphones and listened to music on her cellphone. We changed seats when we stopped for gas. Tripp started out up front with his dad and Megan and I sat in back and chatted about school and people we found annoying. You had to be careful what you said around Rinchen. He would let a lot of things slide, but if you dissed someone or said something particularly ditzy, you could find yourself in the middle of an educational opportunity.

In Indiana, Rinchen asked Tripp to drive for a while. He crawled into the passenger seat and within ten minutes, he was fast asleep. In twenty minutes he was snoring so loudly that it was interrupting our conversation. Rinchen may be the master of breathing when he is awake, but he is a disaster when he is sleeping. Every now and then, his snoring was particularly loud, like he was trying to inhale peanut butter and the three of us would burst out laughing. He would wake up for a second, look around, and ask, "where are we?"

"Ohio, dad," Tripp would respond grinning.

"Oh, okay, wake me up when we get to Akron. We are going to stop there for the night, okay?"

"Yes, dad," said Tripp. Rinchen would be asleep again before he heard Tripp respond to him. There would be a ten minute reprieve from the noise and then the whole cycle would start again. It was actually quite a relief to get to Akron. Poor Tripp, he had to share a room with his dad. Megan and I were next door and we could still hear him snoring through the wall.

In the early evening on the second day, we pulled into a long dirt driveway to an old farm house on a hill. It looked like a pretty typical farm expect there was a ten foot statue of the Buddha in the middle of a garden between the house and the barn. There were cars and vans with license plates from all over the country parked by the barn. We left our bags in the car and walked into the house. There were at least thirty people crammed into various parts of the house and they were all doing chores. Two men and a woman were in the kitchen making a huge pot of some sort of vegetable stew. There were three electric rice cookers on the counter with tiny jets of steam shooting out of them. One of the women was directing the activity in the kitchen. She wore the same kind of red and yellow robes that Lama Jinpa wore. Rinchen waved at her and she smiled while stirring the large pot on the stove, "Rinchen, you made it."

"Yes, we did; it's good to see you again, Zhangmo. Can you put us to work?"

"You could put out the plates, cups and silverware. Otherwise, everything is pretty much in order."

"Where's lama?"

"He's in his room doing his practice, like usual. You can go and get him when the food is ready."

Rinchen walked over to a cupboard and started pulling out stacks of dishes and handing them to Tripp who took the stack into a large room next to the kitchen. It was obvious that they both had been here before because they fell into the natural rhythm of the dinner preparations without anyone having to tell them where anything was. There was not enough room for everyone to gather in any single room in the house, so we began to set up a buffet line on the main table. I stood in line behind Megan to get an armload of cups to take to the next room. It was pretty interesting to see how well everyone worked together. It was kind of like watching an army making camp, but the uniforms were red and yellow instead of camouflage.

When dinner was ready, Rinchen disappeared upstairs to get Lama Jinpa. He did not return for nearly half an hour. Tripp said that this was not unusual. Lama Jinpa would come down when he was ready to come down and everyone was expected to operate on what was called "lama time". He said that his father was one of Lama Jinpa's favorite students and that the two of them could start chatting about almost anything and forget time completely. After a while Zhangmo came up to Tripp and told him to go find his father, in other words, go bug Rinchen and Lama Jinpa to remind them that there were twenty-eight people waiting to eat. After Tripp took off to go upstairs, she turned to me and stuck out her hand, "hi, I am Zhangmo".

"I'm Lhamo," I said shaking her hand.

"Ohhh, *you're* Lhamo, I've heard about you. You know, you were quite right to be concerned about Lama's visit to St. Louis. *He does spit.* It's disgusting and I for one am glad that someone finally confronted him about it." She stood there looking at me without a single facial expression that would indicate that she was anything short of serious.

"Oh, you heard about that. Yeah, well, wow, word really travels far with this group." I said sheepishly.

"It sure does – I'm from Arizona," she said smiling, "it's awesome. All of Lama Jinpa's students now make spit jokes. We love it. You're a celebrity here."

"Oh, great." Suddenly, I was not looking forward to dinner.

"Come on, you can help me get dinner on the table."

Fifteen minutes later Lama Jinpa came down stairs with Rinchen and Tripp trailing behind him. Both Rinchen and Tripp were wearing *katas*, traditional white silk scarves, around their necks. Every Tibetan Buddhist student has a *kata* and offers it to his teacher as a gift. The teacher takes the scarf and thanks the student and then returns the *kata* as a gift for the student. Tripp bought a *kata* for me, but I left it in the minivan. Megan was waiting at the bottom of the stairs with her *kata* out and her head bowed. Lama Jinpa took the *kata* from Megan and said "thank you, Pema Sonam" and returned it to her. Of course, all I had to offer Lama Jinpa as he approached me was a bow. "Jigme Lhamo! How good to see you," he said taking my hands in his and bowing to me. As he made his way through the house, he only called people by the their dharma names and he remembered every single one of them.

We all stood around the buffet table and Lama Jinpa began to chant a prayer in Tibetan. Rinchen explained it to me later. Basically, the food was offered to the deities with a promise that it would only be eaten for fuel and that any merit or benefit derived from the energy of the food was dedicated to all sentient beings. As I stood in line with Megan, I called her by her dharma name, Pema Sonam.

"What does it mean?" I asked.

"'Pema' means 'lotus' and 'Sonam' means 'virtuous'".

"So you're a good little flower, is that what you are trying to say."

"Something like that."

All sarcasm aside, Megan had been a virtuous lotus as far as I was concerned. She had been the person, more than anyone, who had gotten me involved in the *dojo* and started me on the path that I was on. She was one of the main reasons that I was making my way out of the muck.

After dinner, everyone washed their own dishes and returned them to the kitchen. Zhangmo was busy scrubbing down the stove. After that she swept the floor. After that she took out the table scraps and put them in a compost pile. In fact, you almost never saw Zhangmo not working. I followed her outside and helped her shake out a table cloth.

"You seem to do a lot more work around here than anyone else," I said.

She smiled. "Me good squaw, worth many pony," she said curling up her arm and squeezing her own bicep. I had no idea, Buddhists could be so funny. As we folded the table cloth she said, "Chop wood, carry water."

"What does that mean?"

"You haven't heard that expression before? It means that all there ever is to do in life is the task that is in front of you. Chop wood, carry water, eat, sleep, die. People add their own drama to that, of course, but life is pretty much just 'chop wood, carry water'. Why make it more complicated than that?"

"Sounds boring," I said. Zhangmo laughed. "What is boredom?" she asked.

"Doing the same thing over and over again, I guess."

"You breathe over and over again. Do you get bored doing that?"

"No."

"What makes you bored?"

"Waiting for people. Standing in line. The usual things that make people bored."

"What are you waiting for when you get bored."

"Something to happen. Something different or interesting."

"Did it ever occur to you that boredom is your mind being unhappy because it is not being distracted?"

"I never thought of it that way," I said.

"We like to be entertained. It keeps us from having to think. We get addicted to stimulation and start to crave it just like food or sex. We get unhappy when we have to just sit there and be with whatever is. But if we train our minds to be with emptiness; to just sit still. We are never bored again. Routine tasks become opportunities to be one with simple things. You breathe, you chop wood, you carry water, you wash the floor, you live your life. The point is to put yourself into what you are doing and not allow yourself to be unhappy because you wish you were doing something else. If you must scrub the floor, be with the water and the bubbles and the brush. Watch what you do. Listen to the sound of the brush on the floor. Hear the sound of the water when you dip the brush into the bucket. It is every bit as wonderful as staring at garden of flowers or feeling the kiss of that boyfriend of yours."

"I don't know about that, he's a pretty good kisser." I said. Zhangmo laughed. In fact, over the whole time I was at the retreat, Zhangmo was always laughing and working and then laughing some more.

"The point is, there is only one moment in life and that is the one you are in. If you are thinking about the past or the future, you are not in your life. Boredom happens when you let go of what you are doing, the moment you are in, and start wishing you were somewhere else doing something else. But you are not somewhere else, so working yourself into a tizzy over something that is not real or in front of you is a bit insane. You've got to let go of that stuff and be with what you are doing."

"Sounds simple," I said.

"Playing a violin concerto is simple if you practice. "

"Yeah, I have heard that before," I said thinking about the many lessons I had had since joining the *dojo*.

"Well, cool. I am glad we had this little chat. So why don't you grab a broom and sweep the crumbs off of the patio here and try not to think about anything other than sweeping crumbs. You might find that you enjoy it." With that, Zhangmo picked up a broom that had been propped up against the kitchen door and tossed it to me.

I caught it with my left hand and said, "Okay. Chop wood, carry water, got it."

"No, sweep patio. Weren't you listening?" Zhangmo started to laugh again and turned away stepping into the kitchen.

Later in the evening, the group met in the barn to do Chenrezig *puja*. I was relieved that we were going to be doing something that I knew how to do. Unlike the *puja* I had done before at the *dojo*, this *puja* was more elaborate. There was a large table set up in the barn and it had been turned into a shrine. There were copper statues of Chenrezig called *rupas* and two rows of shiny brass bowls. One row of bowls had water in them and the other row of bowls were filled with a variety of things like incense, rice, a kind of candle-like thing called a "butter lamp" and flowers. There was a large painting of Chenrezig called a *thanka* hanging behind the altar.

Unlike the *puja* I do in my room at home, this *puja* lasted an hour and a half. Lama took his time in each section. I have to say that I really liked it. Thirty people chanting at the same time filled the barn with an almost eerie, but inspirational sound. When it was over, my mind was empty and it felt like I had just had a long nap.

There was a building on the property that had at one time been used as a machine shop or something. There was a long wooden work bench still in it and there was a small bathroom with a shower. The group had put up cots in this building and converted into the women's dormitory. The men had a similar arrangement set up in a building attached to the barn. They did not have a bathroom, but there were two portable toilets just outside.

The farmhouse had three bedrooms. Lama Jinpa stayed in the largest one. Rinchen had arranged for Megan and me to stay with Zhangmo in one room and there were two monks that took the last room. He and Tripp slept with the other men in the barn. Some people had brought their own camper trailers and they slept in them. That seemed like the way to go, if you asked me.

Megan and I had gone up to our room about ten o'clock. Everyone was getting up at sunrise to practice before Lama explained the *Nyung Ne* practice that would start the following day. I was told that the practice involved fasting and abstaining from drinking anything as a form of purification. You can't even sneak a candy bar or anything. Just before midnight, I was dozing in my cot when I heard a sound in my room. Zhangmo was gathering some things together as quietly as she could and was leaving.

Megan was in a cot next to mine and I shook her arm to wake her. "Megs, Megs, are you awake?" Megan rolled over and lifted her head. She was not happy. "What do you want, Lhamo?"

"Zhangmo just grabbed a bunch of her stuff and left. What's that about?"

"What time is it?"

"I don't know?"

"Well, look at your watch and tell me where the big hand is and where the little hand is and we'll know."

I turned on the light and nearly blinded Megan. "Holy crap! What are you trying to do to me, Lhamo," Megan yelped pulling her pillow quickly over her eyes.

"Sorry, I can't see my watch. It is eleven-thirty."

"Great, okay, so Zhangmo went to do Chöd. Good night."

"What's Chöd?"

Megan pulled the pillow off of her face and was squinting at me. She took a deep breath and said, "Chöd is a *dakini* practice that is done in the middle of the night. My dad and Lama Jinpa are probably doing it too. I think there is a cemetery near here and that's probably where they are practicing. They are offering themselves to demons and stuff. It is a pretty high practice. Any questions? No? Great. Good night." Megan pulled her pillow over her head and her blanket over the pillow.

"What! So these guys go to a cemetery in the middle of the night and offer themselves to demons? Are they nuts?" Megan gave up trying to sleep. She tossed the pillow on the floor and pulled the blanket off. It had been chilly in the house so she was still in her jeans and sweatshirt. "Come on, get your shoes on. We can go watch."

We stepped out into the night. It was cold, but not freezing. Off in the distance, there was the tap, tap, tap of a drum and the sound of a bell. Megan followed the sound along the ridge of a hill that ended in a grove of trees. There were seven or eight people sitting in what must have been a small family cemetery on the hill. The cemetery was lit up by lanterns and several people, including Zhangmo, were holding round drums that had two small balls hanging from strings that were attached to the rim. I watched as she twisted her wrist back and forth causing the balls to swing back and forth and beat on the skin of the drum. These drums were bigger than the one I had seen Lama Jinpa use in St. Louis. They were chanting in a very beautiful melody. If you could get past the fact that we were in the middle of a cemetery at midnight, it was really quite lovely. At one point, Lama Jinpa blew through an odd looking trumpet that looked like it was made out of a bone. I later learned that this was called a *kangling* and it was made of a real human thigh bone. Rinchen was sitting next to him chanting and playing the same kind of drum that Zhangmo had. Tibetans are seriously fearless people. They look death in the eye and turn their bones into trumpets to calm demons.

We sat in the cold air for nearly an hour until the practice was finished. When everyone got up to walk back to the house and barn, Lama Jinpa asked me what I thought of the Chöd practice. "It's beautiful and creepy at the same time," I said. He chuckled. "Yes, I suppose so. This is a very powerful practice. One has to give up any clinging to his own life to do it. In our visualization we are offering even our own bodies to demons and other beings so that they might find comfort and hopefully someday find enlightenment for themselves. Maybe when you have more experience, you will take this empowerment and do this practice too." I wanted to learn about the practice now, but Rinchen told me the next day that it was not for beginners and that I should stick to what I had been taught. He was not all that crazy about Megan having brought me out to the cemetery. He said that some practices can actually harm people if they do not understand what they are about. They can give observers the wrong idea and it is very important never to do that because it can put a person further away from enlightenment rather than closer to it.

The retreat schedule was rigorous. I volunteered for kitchen duty so that I could spend more time with Zhangmo. She woke me up at five-thirty. It was still dark outside. Every morning, we went downstairs and made hot tea with milk in huge pots. We also made mung bean soup for breakfast. Mung beans are little green beans that look a little bit like a small pea. To make the soup you put rice that was left over from dinner the night before (Zhangmo always deliberately made too much) and then the mung beans that you let soak overnight. You add water to make it soupy, some soy sauce and you are done. Sometimes, Zhangmo would add some chopped green onions and some lemon grass to it for flavor. All you have to do is heat it up. It is kind of the monastic version of oatmeal. Most people eat it with even more soy sauce to make it more flavorful. I have to say, over the course of the week, I actually started to like it. For starters, it was hot and on the chilly mornings hot was a good thing. Zhangmo said that it is good, cheap food. It has both starch and protein to get you going in the morning and it sticks with you until lunch.

The first meditation practice started at six o'clock and lasted two hours. Everyone sat on prayer cushions behind benches that were used as desks to hold the puja texts. Everybody takes a mug of hot tea with them to their bench and sips it to warm up in the cold morning air of the barn. On the first morning of practice. Zhangmo and I carried the big tea pots out to the barn to pour tea before practice. Rinchen, Tripp and Megan were already seated.

Rinchen was wearing robes just like Lama Jinpa and Zhangmo. As we took the pots back to the kitchen I asked Zhangmo about the robes.

"Are you a nun?"

"No."

"Then why do you wear robes?"

"In retreat many of Lama's long time students wear robes. We do not tie them on like monks and nuns do. There is a special way of working pleats into the *shantap*, that's the skirt part of the robe, that indicates that you have a vow of celibacy. We only wear them when we are in retreat and we do observe monastic vows while we are here. Some of us have been through months and months of retreats. I guess you could say we are poser monastics." She laughed and lifted the pot onto the stove.

"Did you ever want to be a nun?" I asked.

"I wanted to be a lama. You know you have to go into retreat for three years and three months to be a lama. You cannot come out once you are in. I was in for two years. Eventually, I got word that my mom was sick so I left to be with her. I didn't have it in me to start over. But, no matter, you can reach enlightenment as a garbage man; you do not need to be a monastic to train in the dharma." She smiled and took the other pot from my hands and hoisted it up onto the stove with the other one.

Then she stopped and looked at me, "why? Do you want to be a nun? You would have to give up that boyfriend of yours. She squeezed my arm. You got some muscles there, sister. You would make a sturdy nun. Who needs guys anyway? Right?" She was clearly messing with me.

It was cold in the mornings and Zhangmo pulled her *zen*, her red shawl, around her torso and over her head. I was wearing a hooded sweatshirt, but ran up to get a jacket before we headed back to the barn. Lama Jinpa started the practice. It was called Green Tara. I did not have this empowerment, but he said that it would be beneficial to chant along anyway. It is more involved than the Chenrezig practice and with all of the senior students in the barn, they were ripping through it. I kept getting lost in the text and had to wait for page changes sometimes to figure out where we were. Green Tara is an awesome yidam. She is a deity of compassion, just like Chenrezig; she is also green in color and sits on a lotus with one foot hanging off. This represents her willingness to step into the affairs of anyone who suffers. She has only two arms, and holds a lotus blossom in either hand symbolizing enlightenment and power. Her left hand is held up in what is called the refuge granting mudra while the other hand is pointed down indicating that she grants wishes for the benefit of beings. She is considered, in a way, the female version of Chenrezig. That is one of the cool things about Tibetan Buddhism, for every male deity, there is a female. Women are considered to be just as big a force for benefit in the world as men.

I sat down at a bench next to Zhangmo and the practice began. Not knowing how it really worked it seemed to take forever. But eventually, we got to the end of it. And no sooner had Lama ended the practice than Zhangmo, with me right behind her, was on her feet and on her way back to the kitchen to heat up the breakfast soup. I helped her carry the big pot of soup out to the buffet table when it was ready. Everyone grabbed a bowl and passed by the pot in a line to get their breakfast. There were also bowls of fresh fruit and I started off my breakfast with a banana.

Lama spent the rest of the day giving everyone practice instructions. In the late afternoon, there was an empowerment, this time for Thousand-Arm Chenrezig. The official practice started the following day. He said that on the first day, we would take only one meal and after that, we would start a fast at noon and would not eat or drink the rest of the day, all the following day and for the first few hours of the third day. We had to promise not to speak except when doing the practice which would be repeated throughout the next three days. There could be no killing, not even mosquitos and no intimate contact like making out with your smoking hot boyfriend.

I had never gone without food and drink for a whole day before and I was concerned that I might not make it. I had visions of me sneaking into the kitchen to raid the refrigerator and getting busted by the dharma police and waking up in a hell realm or something. It is said that this practice will purify any and all past bad karma. After a *Nyung Ne*, you have a clean slate. The *Nyung Ne* practice was developed by a princess in Nepal called Gelongma Palmo. She left her palace to become a nun and was becoming quite accomplished until some negative karma from her past lives started to catch up to her and she was stricken with leprosy. Because of her disease she was shunned and made to live in a straw hut by herself. Her hands fell off and she was very sick. She went to a temple to pray to a statue of Chenrezig, but was not allowed in, so she went to the back of the temple and sat in alignment with Chenrezig and meditated. On the first day, she had breakfast and lunch and then started a fast. For the remainder of the day and all of the following day she did not eat or drink. She recited the Thousand-Arm Chenrezig practice, a practice using a visualization of a white Chenrezig with a thousand arms instead of just four, and repeated the practice over and over. Eventually, she healed her disease and reached full enlightenment.

The Thousand-Arm Chenrezig empowerment was similar to the four-arm Chenrezig empowerment that I had already received. Like my first empowerment, it involved a ritual wherein Lama Jinpa transmitted the practice to the minds of his students via Buddha-net. At a point early on, there was a purification ritual and the students lined up to approach Lama Jinpa with their hands held out and cupped. He poured saffron water into our hands and we put it into their mouths, but did not swallow it. Then we stepped outside of the barn and spit the water out. It is said that our mental impurities are cleared from our being and are cast out in a wad of yellow spit. I noticed that some of the really senior students wiped their wet hands on their hair. I had seen this before. Rinchen told me later that this is done so as to not waste the saffron water and to get extra purification.

The *Nyung Ne* practice started after breakfast the following morning and was repeated throughout the day. There was a break on the first day for lunch, but after that there was no food and water for the rest of the day, all the next day and the early morning of the third day. I remember that first night when we went to sleep, I had vivid dreams. I dreamt of Lama Jinpa, Rinchen and Zhangmo. Lama Jinpa and Rinchen were watching me and smiling, but I was walking through a garden with Zhangmo and she was telling me things. In the center of the garden we came across a bright white light and as we got closer, I could see that it was Chenrezig. He had a crown on his head and a thousand arms spread out like a big fan all around him. It was a beautiful scene; a peaceful scene. In the morning we woke up and went back into the barn to continue the practice. By noon I was getting a little bit thirsty but it was not a really big deal. By night fall I was hungry but, not desperately so. In the morning we practiced some more and then had our breakfast. Mung bean soup never tasted so good.

That night, Rinchen had us put on our *gis* and *hakamas*. We went out onto the lawn and started an *Aikido* class. With only three students, this meant that Rinchen would train. We started with the usual stretching drills and rolling practice, but got down to throwing each other around in pretty short order. A crowd of dharma students formed on the grass and some sat down to watch. Zhangmo brought out a lawn chair and Lama Jinpa joined the crowd. Some of the students could not figure out why Lama was letting us fight in a Buddhist retreat. I heard a couple of people grumble about it pretending that they were whispering, but clearly trying to be heard. Rinchen had us do a round of *randori* practice before we finished for the night. He made Tripp go first. He joined the attack. Tripp did *randori* pretty well in the *dojo*, but with his dad taking part in the attack, he lost his focus and got wiped out pretty quickly. It took him two or three tries to settle down. Even Rinchen took a turn and that was a scary thing. There is no taking Rinchen down. He had the three of us flying all over the lawn and ended his turn by pinning all three of us to the ground at the same time. Lama Jinpa applauded.

After we concluded everyone went inside for tea. Normally, Lama Jinpa would disappear upstairs for his evening private meditation practice, but on that night he stayed downstairs and chatted with the students. One of the students, a middle-aged woman from California, asked him why he allowed combat training during a retreat. She was obviously unhappy about it. Lama Jinpa looked at her and smiled, "these students practice discipline and their art is designed to do as little harm as possible. It is good for their minds and bodies that they do this. Students of Sensei Rinchen's *dojo* are actually much stronger Buddhist practitioners because of it."

"But I thought that the Buddha taught peace and pacifism. How can fighting be consistent with Buddha's teachings." You could tell that she was pushing her point and getting a little bit self-righteous in the process. Lama Jinpa did not budge.

"If a man comes into a store and wants to kill everyone there, wouldn't it be good idea to stop him? He will kill many innocent people and while this not hurt their karma, it hurts *his* karma. He will most certainly be reborn in hell realm. Shouldn't we try to save him from that?"

"But to do so would be to harm him. Worse, you would have to become violent and that would take you off the path to enlightenment."

"What you do then? Let man kill everyone and unleash all that suffering?"

"I would go up to him and try to talk him out of it peacefully. I would try to reason with him."

"And if that failed? What if he shoots you first?"

"Then I die trying to live in peace."

"True. There is no bad karma for you, but not very skillful to stand up and be killed. More skillful to engage hate and violence with antidote. Where is it written that Buddhists are supposed to be sheep sent to slaughter? In every situation there are two things good to have: wisdom and skillful means. Wisdom lets you know that this man going to do great harm. Wisdom make you not be afraid of him. Skillful means would give you ability to stop him from doing harm. Would you not push someone out way of truck if they were about to be killed? Why would you not do the same for this troubled man and the other customers who are in danger of being harmed by his ignorance? Confronting him and getting yourself killed for no reason is fool's compassion. It is like giving money to drug addict. He not going to buy food, he going to buy drugs. By giving him money you have just harmed him. It is important to think these things through. Buddhists seek peace, this is true, but not foolishly."

The woman was still unconvinced. "Fighting seems to betray every teaching of the Buddha," she said defiantly.

"Fighting for a delusion does. Fighting because you think you can conquer another betrays the Buddha. Fighting for greed is worse. But standing up and confronting harm and fighting to avoid harm is high form of practice. It takes skill to leave hate out of it. The idea that Buddhists throw themselves away or do not value their own lives is foolishness. It is not what Buddha taught. You should honor your own life without clinging to it. You should try to cause peace, but sometimes that requires us to take drastic action. It is our intention and our skill that matter and make the karma."

We practiced *Aikido* the next day too, but I noticed, however, that the woman who had debated with Lama Jinpa did not come and watch again. In fact, I think that she left the retreat early after her conversation with him. I asked Zhangmo about it.

"What was that lady's deal who did not like *Aikido?*"

"Who, Darlene? Yeah, well she has some interesting ideas about what Buddhism is."

"To be honest, I thought she kind of had a point at first."

"Buddhists are just like everyone else. There are some who read the teachings and try to follow it like it is a cook book - word for word without interpretation or thought. These people are scared just like the Christians who do that, just like the Muslims who do that, just like anybody else who does that. Some people just want rules to live by. They are afraid that they might get it wrong. Unfortunately, it does not work that way for us. She does not understand the intention of *Aikido*. She sees fighting. She does not see the effort you make to convert hostile energy into something harmless."

"It sounds like you know a thing or two about it."

"Yes, I do. I am a brown belt. I trained for a number of years back when I was just a little bit older than you."

"Really, where did you train?"

"In New Mexico, Santa Fe. But that was a long time ago." Wow. The more I got to know Zhangmo, the more amazing she was. Megan had told me that Lama Jinpa always wanted her to practice Chöd with him because she was so good at it. She knew all of the complicated music that was required by the practice and I remember thinking how beautiful her voice was when I heard it that first night in the cemetery. She was not one of Lama's favorite students like Rinchen was despite her skill, at least according to Megan. Megan's theory was that Lama Jinpa wanted her to finish the lama retreat, but she had not and this disappointed him. This distance did not seem to affect Zhangmo's devotion to Lama Jinpa, one way or the other. I liked her because she did not seem to doubt, or even think about, who she was. She did not care if she pleased others and yet, she was always working hard to contribute. I wanted to be just like her.

After the *Nyung Ne* practice was completed we still had a couple of days before we had to drive back to St. Louis. The retreat was over on Friday at noon giving us a free afternoon and the weekend to get home. Megan went upstairs and packed up her things. Tripp and I decided to take a walk. It was the first time we had had to spend alone since we got there.

We found an old tractor lane that made its way through a line of trees and down a hill that opened into a patchwork of small fields divided by stone fences in some places and trees in others. It was sunny, but chilly and we held hands as we walked. I pulled Tripp's hand into the pocket of my jacket for extra warmth. Eventually, as we made our way to the bottom of the lane and the subject of college came up. We had been more or less avoiding it for months. We needed to make decisions soon, otherwise our places in the schools where we had been accepted would be given to others.

"So are we doing the east coast thing this fall or what?" I asked.

"Yeah, I guess. I really want to go to Parsons in New York, but I really don't want to go to New York without you." The truth was I didn't want him to go to New York without me either.

"Well, don't you think that you should go out on your own for a while?"

"And do what?"

"See the world, meet new people – sow some wild oats, I don't know. Everybody says that we should do our own thing and not take high school with us to college."

"Yeah, well, I don't get that completely. I mean, I understand seeing the world, but why can't I see the world with you? Why do I need to go looking for happiness when it is right here? Am I supposed to spend four years dating and having sex with college chicks so that I get it out of my system? Is there some sort of resume I am supposed to be building here? That's stupid."

"Well, maybe you will meet someone who is better for you than me. I don't know. Don't get me wrong, I am happy with things just the way they are, but it does seem to be the common wisdom that you are better off going out and getting some experience before you settle down."

"But experience at what? Drinking too much so that you can bang sorority girls who have also drank too much? You know, I think the idea that you have to crawl through an orgy and create a long list of bad relationships just so that when you find someone who does not damage you, you can say 'she must be the right one' is a smoking wad of bullshit. Why would someone do that to themselves? Is it so they can go through the rest of their lives comparing their life partner to all the other girls they screwed? Is the point that we go out and trash ourselves so that a mediocre relationship seems like Shangri-La? That seems to be confusing relief with happiness to me -- it's pretty fucked up."

That was the best part of Tripp. He was always taking a stand. He did not talk a lot, but he was very passionate about what he believed in. Like many things, he had thought this through.

"Well, you could do what Ack's parents are planning on doing. You could have your dad arrange something for you."

Tripp stopped walking and pulled me around by the shoulders to face him. "You know that if I asked my dad to do that, he would drive out to your house and sit down with your parents and start working a deal. You know that, right? He really likes you and he really likes the fact that we are an item." I put my head on his chest and hugged him.

"I know. "

"Then why are we having this conversation?"

"I was just making the point that the alternative to combing the world over to choose your own mate is to be married by arrangement and that maybe you would like to see a bit more of what's out there before you stake your claim on a hometown girl."

"First of all, in the end, all marriages, and I don't care if you have a hundred girlfriends that are throwing themselves at you, all marriages are eventually arranged marriages."

"What do you mean by that?" We came along the side of a low stone wall and sat down. Tripp was really getting agitated by this conversation, but I could tell that he had been wanting to have it for a while now.

"What I mean is, that in the beginning relationships start out with attraction or by arrangement. But attraction wears off. I saw this with my own parents. I saw this with Thor and Tracy. Eventually, you have to be in a relationship on some other power than attraction. Arranged marriages at least have the advantage of getting to the point. Beauty fades. People cease to be a mystery to you. At some point, you have to arrange your relationship on something that does not depend on being beautiful and interesting. I have no idea what that is, but I know that if you are going to go the distance, you have to be like my grandpa and grandma. They know each other through and through and no one is going to say that either one of them is a hot property, but they are companions. Their relationship works because they make it work. They argue occasionally, but both of them let their troubles go and reset the relationship back to zero every day. I think that this is the best thing you can hope for. If you are playing for hot and interesting you are going to go through more spouses than a movie star and who the hell wants that?"

"Not me."

"Not me either. Lhamo, we can go to college in different states and we can hook up with other people, but at the end of the day, we are going to be drawing a different face on the same situation. There is no 'right one' out there. That is a big, fat, fucking lie. You don't find a girl who suits your mind, you make your mind suit the girl. Of course, it helps if she is kind of hot and has a motorcycle and can break-fall … I'm just saying. But in the end, you must create your relationship whether you find it in a hookah bar or your parents arrange it for you because at some point you are going it have to make it work one way or the other. Happy relationships, like most of the best things in life, are not accidents – they are art made with awareness and skill."

"How did you figure all of this out. You are starting to sound like my dad. No , strike that, you are starting to sound like *your* dad."

Tripp smiled and started kissing the side of my face working his way to my lips. "Little Bit, I am not my dad. Because if I were, this would be totally disgusting." With that, his lips met mine and he started working them over slowly and methodically. I wanted to pull him into me. I could tell that I was still a long way from enlightenment, because I was all about craving this guy.

They had to send a search party out for us to tell us it was time to leave. Thankfully, it was Megan and Zhangmo and not Rinchen. We were behaving ourselves, but just barely. We heard them coming down the hill and managed to straighten ourselves up before they saw us. Megan was shaking her head when she finally spotted us standing by the stone wall pretending to admire the countryside. The grass at the foot of the wall looked like a couple of cows had taken a nap on it. Megan waved for us to follow. "It's time to go, kids." Having delivered her message, she turned around and started marching back up the hill that she had just walked down. Zhangmo was trying not to smile and turned to follow her. As Megan trudged up the hill she yelled over her shoulder, "and by the way, Lhamo, button your shirt!" I was wearing a hooded sweatshirt. How could she know that my shirt underneath was unbuttoned, which it was. I looked down and about a foot of shirt tail hung out from under my sweatshirt. Oh yeah, that.

Tripp and I walked back to the farmhouse. People were packing cars and loading campers. We went inside to say good-bye. Zhangmo was already back at work mopping the kitchen floor. I said good-bye to Lama Jinpa. He gave me another protection cord. This one was yellow. He tied it around my neck. I offered him my *kata*, which he thanked me for and then gave back to me by placing it around my neck. "Train hard young lady," he said as I was leaving the room. I smiled and bowed.

I slipped out into the kitchen because I wanted to say good-bye to Zhangmo. She was wringing a mop over a bucket with her powerful hands. When she saw me come into the kitchen she wiped her hands on a towel and stepped over the bucket to give me a hug.

"I hope that I will see you again soon, Zhangmo. I really enjoyed hanging out with you this week." Zhangmo smiled. "Me too, Lhamo, me too. Oh, I almost forgot, I have something for you." She dashed upstairs and came back quickly. She was amazingly fast for a woman in her forties. She bounced back into the kitchen holding a roll of brightly colored silk and handed it to me. It was heavier than I had expected. There was something rolled up inside of it. As I unrolled the cloth, I saw that inside was a dark brown dagger. At the end of the handle was a head of some deity and it was ferocious looking.

"What is it?" I asked.

"It is called a *phurba* (pronounced *fur-bah*) in Tibetan, but in Sanskrit they call it a *kila* (pronounced "kee-la"). This one is pretty old," said Zhangmo handing me the dagger with both hands.

"I am pretty sure that this is not a weapon, at least not a normal weapon. What do you do with it?"

"It has a lot of uses. It exorcises demons, strikes down mental affliction, stabilizes the space-time continuum around sacred sites, stuff like that."

"Whoa! Is it loaded?" I asked. Zhangmo laughed.

"In your hands it is something to remind you to never waiver in your commitment to cut through your own bullshit and never shy away from growing yourself into more than you were the day before. When you drive this into the ground, it is your statement to the universe that you are not going to budge from the path. Like, no kidding."

"Chop wood, carry water," I said.

"Yeah, chop wood, carry water," she said smiling at me.

I hugged her and said, "Thank you, Zhangmo. I know it has only been a week, but I am going to miss you."

"We will meet again. But until then, do your best and don't back down."

"Thanks, I will remember." As I walked to the minivan, Rinchen saw me holding the *phurba*.

"Where did you get that?" he asked very surprised to see it.

"Zhangmo gave it to me."

"Well, be careful with that thing. Don't hurt yourself with it. I swear, Lhamo, you have some very interesting karma."

"What do you mean by that?"

"Most people go an entire lifetime without hearing a single teaching of the Buddha. But for you, in less than a year, you have caught the attention of one of the greatest living *Vajra* masters in the United States. Lama Jinpa told me that I am to teach you all that I can. This is unusual. He has never asked me to do that before. Have you noticed how quickly your life is changing? This is not normal either. When you try to teach a teenager who has no prior exposure to *Budo* or dharma, most of what you offer them bounces off. But not with you. It sticks. There isn't a reason in the world that it should, but it does. Think about who you were just two years ago and look at you now. People are handing over three hundred year old sacred daggers to you. For whatever reason, you seem to have a strong relationship to certain elements of the unseen, unspoken dharma world. It seems to be energized by your presence and anyone who knows anything about it feels suddenly compelled to help you."

"I am not sure that I understand."

"I am not sure that *I* understand. Have you ever known somebody that seems to be really lucky. Good fortune just seems to follow him around. He wins the lottery without buying a ticket because he finds one on the street – that kind of guy? This is a form of karma. There is a cause and effect to it, but it is not obvious. In your case, however, you attract teachings and teachers. You stop into an odd storefront by accident one night and learn about floppy fish. Two weeks later, it saves you from great harm. You have learned *Aikido* and *Kenjitsu* faster than nearly anyone I have ever trained. Lama Jinpa noticed you the minute he saw you for the first time. These are subtle things, things that happen only on a level of intuition. And the clearer the mind is that meets you, the more intuition they seem to have about you. It is really quite amazing."

"What are you saying, that I am some kind of chosen one? That's pretty silly."

"No, Lhamo, I am saying quite the opposite. You are not being chosen – *you are doing the choosing*. What is remarkable about you is who and what you are drawn to. There is something in your mind's eye that you are looking for and you are finding it."

Chapter Forty: The Art of Tea

On any given day in April, the weather in St. Louis can do almost anything. Spring can be a rather short season here jumping from slush to sweat-your-butt-off in just a few weeks. It is a month that has a hard time making up its mind. Thunderstorms, especially, thunderstorms that turn into tornadoes are a big part of springtime in Missouri. Eventually, the turbulent season makes a decision, as it always does, and heats up just a degree or two short of OMFG!

For this reason, no young bride in her right mind plans an outdoor wedding here in April. At Westchester High, everyone is more concerned about prom which is always held indoors. Prom pictures, however, are often taken in parks of which the St. Louis area has many. If you lose the weather lottery, however, then all bets are off and you get your picture taken in somebody's living room.

I was heading for prom overkill my senior year because I had a boyfriend that went to a different school than I did which meant that we were going to have to figure out the two-for-one prom experience. When our schools released the schedules, however, both proms were set on the same night. Tripp and I had planned on going to both proms with Megan and Matt, but now things were completely screwed up. Matt really wanted to go to the Metro prom and Megan did not really care if she missed the one in Westchester. Tripp didn't really care about the Metro prom because most of his school friends, except for Matt, had already graduated. I really kind of wanted to go to my prom and this was putting a kink in the idea of us all going together. One night, after training, we all walked down to Terried Sake House for a prom summit. Rinchen, Old Bob and few others from the *dojo* joined the group, but when we got there, the four us gathered at the far end of the plank table. Rinchen and Old Bob sat at their own table next to ours and began talking about a time when Bob was living in Honduras while working for the CIA.

We ordered sushi and tea and got down to business rather quickly. Megan took charge over the conversation almost immediately with an assessment of the situation.

"We have two proms on the same night. The Metro prom will probably be cooler and more fun, but Lhamo will not know hardly anybody there. The Westchester prom will most likely be kind of lame, but Lhamo will know everyone there, but Matt will not and Tripp will only know a couple of people. I personally, would prefer to go to the Metro prom and maybe the Westchester all-night party. The party in Westchester I have heard is quite a bash."

"I'm cool with the Metro Prom. My mom will shit a brick, but what else is new," I said not wanting the plans to be twisted around me.

Tripp raised his hand mocking his sister's assumed authority in the conversation. "Why don't we blow off the prom and do our own thing ..."

"No way!" said Megan and I simultaneously. I frowned at him and slapped him on the shoulder. "You're taking me to one prom or the other, mister. I don't really care which, but my mom has got to have a prom picture for my Baby Book."

"Alrighty then, I guess we're going to the prom." Tripp said holding up his hands in surrender.

"Dude, what were you thinking? I told you that you are not getting out of this," said Matt. Megan and I turned to look at Tripp in complete surprise. I was not really offended by Matt's remark, Tripp was not an overly social guy, but I played the part of the offended girlfriend anyway.

"What a douchebag!" shouted Megan at her brother, "there is no fucking way that we are twins. Mom and dad found your sorry butt in a dumpster or something."

Tripp was looking at Matt with a frown, "thanks bro', way to have my back."

"I am just saying ..." Matt replied shrugging his shoulders.

Megan put her hand on my arm and said, "Lhamo, you still have two weeks, I am sure you can find a perfectly nice guy to take you to the prom. I am truly sorry that my adopted brother here is SUCH A DOUCHEBAG!"

"Holy crap. Alright already." Tripp slid out of his chair and dropped to one knee in the middle of the restaurant, he clasped his hands together and with the most sincere face that he could pull together under pressure he said,

"Madison Lhamo Albright, would you please honor me by being my date to the prom of your choice. Pleeease."

"No." I barked, turning my head away to shun him. "Now you are just being a busted little shit." The sushi lady was bringing some miso soup to Rinchen and Old Bob and Trip turned to her still on his knee and said, "Mrs. Tanaka-san, would you please go to the prom with me, pleeease." The sushi lady was startled and then realizing that this was a joke, hit Tripp on the head with her tray. "You mind your manners or I throw you out." That got everyone in the *sake* house laughing. Tripp crawled back into his seat rubbing his head.

Megan tried to get the conversation back on track. "What do you think, Lhamo, should we split the evening up and do the dance at Metro and the party at Westchester or what?"

"That's fine," I said. I didn't think that I had an opinion when the conversation started, but the more I thought about it, the more I really wanted to go to the Westchester prom. Megan picked up on my lack of enthusiasm for the prom at Metro.

"You want to go to the Westchester dance don't you?"

"Sort of," I said quietly, now embarrassed that I was making things more complicated.

"We don't have to go together," Tripp said. "Lhamo and I can go to Westchester and you and Matt can go to Metro." This was a possibility, but suddenly it didn't sound like it would be all that much fun.

"No dude, that doesn't work. Let's go to the dance at Westchester and the party at Metro. They are doing the Metro party at the City Museum, it will be a good time. I can see everybody there. It will be cool." Matt was being gracious and everybody knew it, but it was an idea that everyone could get behind.

"You're sure" said Megan admiring her boyfriend's generosity.

"Yeah, let's do it. Where are we going to have dinner?"

Matt's question opened a whole new can of worms. St. Louis has some truly great restaurants. In fact, one of the things that you can do very well in that town is eat. The selection is nearly endless. There are a bunch of authentic Italian restaurants, a full spectrum of Asian cuisine; barbeque was out because of the clothing hazard. Of course, there were several really expensive places downtown and in the West End. As we ate our sushi, an idea would be tossed out to the table and it would get shot down or put on the list of possible choices. Megan was actually writing down on a napkin the restaurants that did not get rejected. Finally, Tripp turned to his father and said, "what do you think, dad? Where should we go to dinner on prom night?"

Rinchen thought for a second. I couldn't imagine what a guy like him would suggest. Finally, he said, "what do you want to get out of the evening?" That was exactly a Rinchen kind of thing to say. My immediate thought was "fun" and I blurted it out.

"What does this kind of 'fun' look like to you?" Like many encounters with Rinchen, he was going to make us think through this.

"Well, I guess it means spending a nice evening with each other while we can still be together. You know, before we all go off to college and stuff. I want to spend an evening with my friends enjoying ourselves and loving each other." The table got quiet all of a sudden. Megan was looking into her tea cup and nodding. Tripp squeezed my hand.

Old Bob looked at Rinchen and said, "It sounds like they need a tea ceremony." Rinchen smiled at Old Bob and nodded and then added, "or their own version of it." I didn't get it.

"What's a tea ceremony?" I asked.

Old Bob turned his chair so he could look at me. "In Japan, when you really want to bring people together, like to create the ultimate intimate space, you have tea ceremony. These are typically done in small houses, so small that you cannot stand up in them. This prevents anyone from getting violent. You leave all of your weapons by the door. The master of tea is a person who understands the art of making people feel welcome and appreciated. He might arrange the *tokonoma* in the tea house to present a specially selected piece of art or carefully arranged flowers that will appeal to his guests' specific tastes. He will prepare tea absolutely perfectly and every element of the event, down to how you hold your teacup, will be exact and yet designed to allow all of the people in the room to experience the deepest respect for each other. It is said that you can reach enlightenment in the tea ceremony because it can elevate your consciousness to perfection. Wars were avoided with it and marriages were energized by it. It is the art of paying deep attention to the people you are with in order to be one with them."

"Whoa, sounds like a lot of training goes into this," I said.

"Yes, it takes years and years to be a *Chado* master. There would be no way to have a real tea ceremony here, because I am pretty sure there are no masters around. But what you were saying about wanting to have an evening together where you are really together reminded me of *Chado*, that's all. It was just a thought." Old Bob smiled and re-adjusted his chair to resume his conversation with Rinchen. Rinchen kept his eyes on the four of us as if he was waiting to see how we would react to what we had just been told.

Tripp looked up at me and smiled. "We really should put some thought into this. We should make it very special and intentional." I was happy to hear him say so.

"Yeah, maybe we should do something more private, just the four of us together somewhere," said Megan looking at Matt.

"Do you trust me?" Matt said looking at Megan.

"That depends on what you are talking about. I don't trust you to be anywhere on time, but other than that I probably trust you with my life." She was not sure where he was going with this.

"Why don't the two of you let Tripp and me work the dinner thing out. I have a thought or two about it. But you are going to have to trust us on this." Matt was dead serious. It kind of took Megan by surprise. She looked over at me and said, "well?" I looked at Tripp. He was looking at Matt and thinking this through. They seemed to have to be having some kind of silent conversation on Bro-Net. "Let's see what they come up with, what the heck," I said lifting my tea cup in a toast to the table. The others raised their cups too. "*Kampai!*"

Tripp turned to look at me and asked, "do you happen to have a formal kimono?" Wow! I didn't see that one coming. But he had tipped his hand as to where he and Matt were likely to go with their mysterious dinner plans.

"You know, they were all out of those at Target the last time I was there," I said.

"Hmm. Too bad. Okay, well, it was just a thought." Mrs. Tanaka was standing next to him with the check. We all reached into our pockets and started tossing money into a pile in the center of the table.

As the people filed out of the *sake* house, Mrs. Tanaka tugged on my sleeve. "You come see me sometime this week please. After school, before dinner time, you understand?" She was bowing slightly and smiling. "Uh, okay, I can come before class the day after tomorrow. Does that work?" Mrs. Tanaka smiled and nodded and then said, "And bring Megan too." I was surprised that she knew Megan's name although it made perfect sense. It was embarrassing that I had been to her restaurant so often and was just now learning her name.

A couple of days later, Megan and I went to the *dojo* early to see what Mrs. Tanaka wanted to talk to us about. Terried Sake House was open, but there were no customers. Mrs. Tanaka met us as we walked in and bowed. "Come with me. I have something to show you." She took us to the back of the

333

restaurant and through the kitchen into a small office. There were four or five large rectangular plastic tubs with lids stacked one on top of the other on a work table that was used as a desk. She pulled down a tub from the top of the stack and removed the lid. Inside, neatly folded, was some of the most beautiful material I had ever seen. It was light turquois in color with white egrets rising up from what looked like dark green marsh reeds . The detail was amazing. I turned to look at Mrs. Tanaka not sure why she was showing us what I realized was an extremely nice *kimono*.

"You like?" She said.

"It's beautiful," I replied.

"Perhaps you wear for big party. I heard Megan's brother ask if you have *kimono*. You can wear one of these, if it pleases you." I was stunned. What a nice lady. It was not exactly what I had in mind for prom wear, but I was finding myself in a position where I did not want to turn down her kindness. Megan was holding up the *kimono* carefully and I could see the gears in her mind turning. "It would be a bit over the top," she said, "but we would definitely not have to worry about someone else wearing the same dresses as us to the prom." The idea was starting to sound a bit hokey to me. It was taking the whole adopted-Asian-culture-thing a bit too far.

Mrs. Tanaka opened the other containers. As she removed each lid, she exposed another breathtaking *kimono*. Under each one was a wide belt, an *obi*, that went with the *kimono*. The colors contrasted perfectly. One *kimono* was peach colored with branches of cherry blossoms draped over the shoulders. Another was white with orange chrysanthemum flowers carefully clustered throughout the design of the material. There was no way we could say "no". This was an extraordinary gesture and I was unprepared to insult this nice lady. Megan's attention was drawn to the last tub. Inside was a black silk *kimono* with a pattern of gold and copper color flowers that spiraled from one shoulder to the floor. It had a gold *obi* with raised copper-colored roping running along the center. She tried it on. It was only slightly too short for her, but it was amazing to look at. I liked a grayish-green one that had white stripes swirling through it with orange-red flower blossoms. It looked like a living bouquet. The colors were so delicately matched that it made you just want to stare at it for pleasure and relaxation.

Mrs. Tanaka told us that these *kimono* had belonged to her grandmother. Her grandmother had been rather tall by Japanese standards, but shorter than me by at least three or four inches. She pointed out that the kimono could be let out at the hem and she offered to tailor them herself. We decided that this would be wise because we did not want to be responsible for screwing up these antique treasures. I wasn't even sure that I wanted to wear any of them, especially near food and high school students.

"These have sat in boxes for years. I have two sons, no daughters. It is shame to hide away such beautiful things, no?" Mrs. Tanaka seemed to notice that we were worried about wearing these, but it was getting clearer and clearer that we had to say "yes". She made a few notes about the measurements on a scrap of paper. "You come back Friday, they will be ready," she said even happier than she was just a moment before.

We bowed and bowed to Mrs. Tanaka as we made our way back to the front door. As we headed down the street toward the *dojo*, Megan turned to me to me and said, "Alrighty then." When we got to the *dojo* we told Tripp and Matt what had just happened. Matt looked at Tripp and said, "Cool, this is going to work out."

"What's going to work out?" Megan and I asked in unison.

Tripp smiled and said, "You'll see. But you will want to have those *kimonos* in time for prom night." Tripp and Matt were being very secretive about their plans which made it more interesting provided that you could trust them not to screw it up. At least they were being thoughtful. I was trying to figure out how I was going to break the news to my mom that we were not going to have to go shopping for a prom dress now. She was really looking forward to that. Or course, there would always be time to change into a conventional dress between dinner and the dance. This was starting to look like a good option because I was getting concerned that showing up at the Westchester High School Senior Prom in a century old kimono was going to fail as a fashion statement and turn me into an epic moron in the eyes of my class.

A few days later, my mom told me that a letter had come for me. This was no traditional letter, at least not in our culture. The outer paper was white with leaves and pressed flowers worked into the structure of the paper itself. It looked hand-made and was carefully folded into a self-contained origami envelope that did not use any glue to hold it together. As I unfolded the outer paper, I could see a single piece of white rice paper inside with the most amazing watercolor of a Japanese koi, a goldfish, painted on it. Carefully printed on the bottom of the sheet was:

Your presence is requested for dinner at the Byakuren Tea House.

A car will be sent to pick you up at 6:00 p.m.

Traditional Japanese attire is recommended.

P.S. Parents are invited to take photographs.

Hmmm. Dinner at the *dojo* – how romantic. I immediately called Megan.

"Did you get an invitation for dinner today?" I asked.

"Yeah and before you say anything, I talked to my dad to find out why the hell he allowed these guys to use the *dojo* for a restaurant. My dad is a full conspirator. He has even cancelled classes for Saturday night. He says that we need to trust the guys, but that is, of course, the recommendation of a *guy*, so you have to take it for what it's worth."

If Rinchen was in on the secret, then it couldn't be that bad. "I think we roll with this. Let's see what they come up with. If they screw us over we will make them pay for it for the rest of the summer. What do you think?"

Megan was not sure. "Seriously? We are going to have dinner in a *dojo*? Ahh, the aroma of sweat. How romantic."

"Toughen up buttercup, we're taking one for the team here," I said making an executive decision.

"If you say so, but you will never hear the end of this if these dipshits show up with a couple of Happy Meals and a bottle of Mad Dog."

"Since when did you become such a fairy princess, you douche. It'll be fun ... maybe."

I could hear Megan groaning into the phone. I hung up on her.

Megan's mom took a pass on coming down to the *dojo* for photos. We had found a shop downtown that sold *tabi* socks. These are the traditional white stockings that have the big toe separated from the rest of the toes so that you can wear them with sandals. We decided that the elevated Japanese wooden sandals were a health risk and opted for a substitute that were made out of woven straw and trimmed with black velvet. They weren't authentic, but the Samurai Fashion Police would just have to kiss our butts. Mrs. Tanaka had two white silk inner *kimonos* that were the official underwear of Japanese women back in the day. She had shown us how to wrap the *obis* around our waists and tie them so that they would not fall off. There was no getting out of this garb in a hurry, that was for sure.

We both had American-style dresses that we could wear to the dance, but we were not completely sure that we were going to use them. The *kimonos* were starting to look pretty good although they were clearly not designed for Twenty-first century dancing. On prom night, my mom helped me with my make-up. She had suggested that I pin my hair up in the back to approximate the hair style of a Japanese lady, but I decided against it opting for a simple ponytail tied back with a burnt orange ribbon. When I came downstairs my dad looked shocked. "Wow!" was all he said. I am pretty sure that this is the standard response that they teach at Dad Academy when they prepare fathers for their daughters' proms and weddings. He seemed to actually mean it.

At six o'clock almost to the second, a black limousine pulled down the street. It was not one of those cheezy, stretch Hummers, but a smaller one that was only slightly longer than a large car. The driver held open the rear car door and Megan stepped out decked in her killer black *kimono*. She looked fantastic! She came to the door with the driver following behind her.

"Hello, Mr. and Mrs. Albright" she said, with unusual formality.

"Wow." Said my dad genuinely dazzled by Megan's *kimono*.

"You look lovely, Megan, really you do," my mom added to my dad's elaborate compliment. The driver told my parents that they were invited to come with us and that he would bring them back home while we were having dinner. My mom grabbed her purse and a camera. Tyler was staying over at a friend's house and missed the whole rite of passage.

I had never been in real limousine before. There were two sets of seats facing each other and plenty of room to stretch your legs. This was a good thing because I had not quite figured out how to sit down in traditional silk bondage. All moms live vicariously through their daughters at prom time and my mom was probably more excited than I was as we drove down the freeway to meet our dates.

We had not even come to a stop in front of the *dojo* before it was obvious that Tripp and Matt had really gotten their act together. Even though it would not be dark for an hour, there were paper lanterns hanging from poles on the side of the door and in clusters on the side walk. They even had lit candles in them. This, of course, made no sense given that it was still daylight, but it was thoughtful just the same. But when the driver opened the front door of the *dojo* for us, you could immediately tell that the guys had gone above and beyond. First was the delicate scent of incense that wafted through the door as we entered the foyer. The lights were turned off and there were bunches of paper lanterns flickering with candle light on the *tokonoma* and suspended by fine strings from the ceiling. There were fresh flowers in well thought-out places throughout the room. In the far corner, the sound of a bamboo flute could be heard coming from behind a tall *shoji* screen.

In the center of the room was a small antique table, only about a foot and a half tall, but large enough to serve as a dinner table for four people sitting on the colorful cushions arranged around it. There were four ceramic bowls that were actually an old style of tea cup carefully placed on the table with dark wooden chop sticks complementing the arrangement. To finish off the table setting, the guys had placed a single live orchid rising out of an elegant bronze pot in the center of the table. Next to the table was a rectangular wooden box raised off of the mat on simple wooden blocks. Off to one side was a small stand holding a black iron tea pot. Small wisps of smoke were rising from the box and I realized that there was a small fire burning inside of it.

"Oh, my!" said my mother to herself as she took in the scene.

After no more than a minute, Matt stepped out of the men's dressing room and I could hear Megan say, "holy shit" quietly under her breath. His hair was slicked back and there was just enough length to it that it could be worked into a small ponytail. He was wearing a crisp gray *hakama* with fine white stripes printed into the cloth, a black *kimono* with a white silk undergarment. Over the *kimono* he wore a black silk jacket called a *haori* with the white crests depicting a flower inside of a circle, called a *montsuki*, printed at the shoulders. The *haori* hung open, but was held in place by a bright white cord with a tassel in the center. He had a folded fan tucked into the top of his *hakama*. He looked amazing.

Within a few seconds, Tripp stepped out of the dressing room and my body temperature spiked. Like Matt, he had pulled his hair back. His *hakama* was dark bronze with small flowers printed into the cloth. His *kimono* was clay green with a copper-gold *haori* held in place with a deep burgundy cord and tassel. His *tabi* socks were black. He, too, had a fan tucked into his *hakama*. Both men had left their sandals by the door.

As they made their way around the mat, I could not take my eyes off of Tripp. There was no boy to be found in that *kimono*. They each, in turn, stopped by the small table in the foyer and picked up a bouquet of flowers. They bowed to my parents and then Matt stepped up to Megan and said, "Thank you for coming. I hope you will enjoy yourself tonight. It is my heart's desire." He bowed and gave her the bouquet.

Tripp was slightly more casual, but more emotional when he invited me in. "Hello, Lhamo. You look really pretty this evening. I hope you will be happy with what we have tried to do here." He handed me a small bouquet of white gardenias. Their fragrance was delightful.

"I am very happy and you look absolutely handsome." Tripp smiled and then turned his attention to my parents.

"Mr. and Mrs. Albright, your daughter is in good hands tonight."

"I know she is," said my dad shaking his hand. As he said this, the front door opened from behind us and Rinchen stepped in. He was in street clothes which always seemed slightly strange for him and he was carrying a camera. "Sorry I'm late," he said and then turned to look at his daughter. "Wow!"

The photo opportunity seemed to drag on forever. I was getting impatient to be alone with our samurai and to see what else they had cooked up for us. Rinchen was just as bad as my dad with a camera. There were at least three or four instances of "okay, say cheese, oh damn it, wait a minute, let's try that again". But at last, the photos were taken and the parents had departed. We sat at the small table in the center of the *dojo* and Tripp took the tea cup from my place . He opened a small ceramic jar and with an odd little bamboo scoop removed some green powder from it and shook it into the cup. "Careful dude, that's about twenty bucks of *matcha* there," said Matt as he watched some of the green powder fly past the edge of the bowl and land on the mat.

"What's *matcha*?," I asked.

Megan smirked, "it's a very expensive powdered green tea. I think we are having a tea ceremony." I didn't know what a tea ceremony was supposed to look like, but I was really enjoying watching Tripp preparing tea for us and Megan was crashing my buzz. I smacked her in the thigh. "Be nice."

Tripp poured hot water into the bowl from the iron kettle that had been warming on the *hibachi* and with a bamboo whisk, swished the water around until there was a bright green frothy smoothie sort of mixture in the bowl that could have been confused for swamp algae. He very carefully and deliberately handed me the bowl rotating it as he put it in my hands. "I hope you will like it," he said formally. I took a sip. Despite the tea looking like it should have a taste as overpowering as its bright green color, it was smoother than the green tea that we usually drank and left no trace of bitterness like you sometimes get with cheap tea. I had started drinking tea because nearly everyone in the *dojo* drank it and, while I was not a tea fanatic, I had grown to like it. It was not a blueberry smoothie, but it was relaxing and made me feel warm inside. The *matcha* was surprisingly good for tea. Matt then prepared a bowl for Megan and then two more for Tripp and himself.

As he was pouring the hot water into the last tea bowl, Matt told us a little bit about how they had put together the evening. "Old Bob helped us figure out how to do all of this stuff. We are not going to get it all right, but he said that the most important thing is that we work really hard at trying to show the two of you a good time. It is about paying attention to the experience of your guests, he says, and trying to find ways to stimulate their minds and cause them to enjoy themselves. It is a lot harder than it looks."

"Where did you get the awesome flute music?" I asked, "I would like to get a copy of that CD."

"There is no CD," said Tripp.

"Where is music coming from then?"

"Old Bob is behind the screen. He plays *shakuhachi*. This is a live performance."

Suddenly, the music stopped. "Hi Megan, hi Lhamo" said the familiar voice from behind the *shoji* screen. There was the sound of a deep inhale and the music resumed.

"That is too cool!" said Megan finally dumping her cynicism and getting into the mood of the evening.

I could hear the sound of the office door opening and a tray with two rows of black bowls on it started to make its way into the room. It was Mrs. Tanaka in one of her own *kimonos*. It was a stunning plum color and trimmed with gold and deep green. Her hair was knotted in the back and she had a wooden comb holding it up. She bowed and making very small steps made her way across the mat slowly dropping to her knees to serve the table. She said nothing but smiled at us as she placed four black ceramic bowls of steaming miso soup in front of us. As quietly as she had approached, she then walked backward to the office and disappeared in side.

"No way!" I shouted forgetting my manners entirely.

"Way," said Matt.

"Awesome!" said Megan.

"Yes, we are," said Tripp grinning as he lifted his soup bowl to take a sip.

The music continued throughout dinner and Mrs. Tanaka brought four or five more courses. Some of the food I did not recognize, especially the little bowl of pink chewy stuff. I decided not to ask. I didn't want to know. At the end of the meal, there were small dishes of ice cream made of red beans and green tea. It was delicious. As we sat there together we wandered from topic to topic. There was talk about new motorcycles and the pot stickers served by the ladies at the Buddhist temple in Augusta. There were speculations about college. There were compliments and even a few kisses.

It was getting late and we had to leave to get to the prom on time. It was the custom at my school to lock the doors at nine o'clock and we were going to be pushing it to make it. We decided that we were not going to change our clothes. We knew there would be talk at the dance and maybe even jokes, but we were going to enjoy our evening in the floating world and I, for one, did not want it to end.

We all could be naturally cynical, seeing irony in nearly everything. But the tea and the flute music seemed to destroy all of that. It was real and it was lovely. There is a fine line between cool and fool. If you are going to step outside the lines of what is considered normal, you take a great risk that it will blow the minds of ordinary people. But if they can wrap their minds around what you are trying to do, they might admire you, or, at least, leave you alone. If they can't, well, they might just throw things at you. Showing any sign of weakness when you are taking a chance is usually a really bad idea. If they catch you blinking, they will eat you alive. The secret is not to blink.

The driver had been waiting outside. We put on our sandals and stepped out into the fresh spring air. The sun had gone down and the lantern on the poles by the door and arranged in clusters on the sidewalk flickered in the breeze. It was just so lovely. We slid into the limousine for the ride out to a country club where the dance was being held. The ride was too short. I could have ridden in that car all the way to Kansas with my handsome samurai holding my hand. When we pulled up into the driveway to the clubhouse, there was a line of cars and limos. As we waited for our turn, I leaned back into Tripp's arms and he ran his fingers down the side of my face. There was nothing that I wanted more than this moment. No one cared if we ever got through the front door.

Eventually, we pulled up to the portico, the door opened and we had to step into the chaos.

The music was rocking hard and I could imagine that my classmates were already grinding on the dance floor. We turned more than a few heads as we stepped out onto the driveway. You could see people trying to make up their mind as to whether or not we were really, really cool or the biggest dorks that they had ever seen. Julie Ross and Shana were standing in line waiting to get in. Shana saw us first and tugged on the black lace shawl that Julie had wrapped around her shoulders. Julie looked absolutely glamorous. Under her shawl she wore a long, sleek, black satin gown with spaghetti straps and black satin high-heeled shoes. Her hair was stacked in large curls and she had chosen just the perfect shade of bright red lipstick -- a perfect little burst of color that stood out in waves of black satin and lace. It was hard to imagine that she was still in high school. The long diamond earrings put her whole look over the top. She looked like the essence of feminine energy and elegance. Shana was wearing a black pantsuit that was a play on a man's tuxedo, but looked elegant in its own right. Julie was startled to see us looking like we had just stepped out of a samurai movie, but then she smiled. "Wow, you look terrific!" she said taking her time to admire the detail of the apparel of the four of us. I introduced her to Tripp and Matt and told her briefly about dinner at the *dojo*. "A girl's got to do her own thing and you are doing it really well tonight," she said nodding her approval.

Beth saw us walk through the front door and made her way across the dance floor dragging a boy behind her whom I had never seen before. "Maddie, I mean, Lhamo, you look awesome!" I gave her a long hug.

I looked at her date and asked, "And who is this handsome guy? "

"This is Trent. I met him over spring break. He goes to Kennedy." Trent shook hands with all of us. He seemed nice, maybe even harmless, but you never knew about that sort of thing. Nick Thompson had looked harmless, but he turned out to be anything but.

"You be nice to our friend," I said pretending to be very serious, "you would really not want us to have to come and find you later." I thought it was funny, but Trent looked at Matt and Tripp who were playing along and it looked like he was about to crap his pants. I realized that we were putting him into a panic and I decided that I had gone too far. "I'm kidding, Trent, it's a joke. We really wouldn't come looking for you ... we already know where you live." I couldn't resist. He was kind of a tool and I was starting to feel a little frisky. Later in the evening Tripp and I sat with Beth and Trent for a while. He eventually lightened up and was actually a pretty nice guy when you got to know him.

The big surprise of the night came when we ran into Ack. It took a while to even notice him because he was sitting with his date in a far and poorly lit corner of the room. I had been asking about him all over the place. People said that they had seen him, but he had dropped off the grid. I wouldn't have ever found him if I hadn't heard a girl shout his name. He had his arm around an unidentified female and he was actually making out with her. Tripp and I stood over him for several minutes waiting for him to come up for air. Finally, I was starting to get embarrassed and I cleared my throat to get his attention.

Startled, he spun around to see who was behind him and was immediately confused.

"What the f…"

"Hello Ack."

"Maddie? Holy crap, you guys look awesome! What are you doing here? I heard you were going to the Metro prom." As he moved out of the way, I could see that the object of his affection was Anita Ruiz. I had always liked

342

Anita. She was friendly and really smart. I could see the match almost immediately.

"Are you kidding? And miss your first date?" Ack was suddenly embarrassed, but Anita laughed. She kissed him on the cheek and he felt his confidence return. "So when did you guys hook up? You make an awesome couple, by the way."

"We have been going out for about a month or so. It has been on the down-low. At first my parents thought that she was Indian. She is, I guess, but just from a different continent."

"So what is this going to do to the arranged marriage plans?" Anita suddenly looked concerned. Apparently, Ack had failed to mention this potential problem to her. I realized that I should have kept my mouth shut. Ack, however, seemed oddly at ease about the subject.

"Well, that's not going to happen. As soon as they met Anita, my parents figured out pretty quickly that her family was from Nicaragua and not India. But it turns out that my dad knows Anita's dad and they are business buddies or something like that. They like each other, anyway, so that has been helpful. I had a little chat with my dad and pointed out to him that I am an American now and needed to find my own girls." Anita squeezed his arm and frowned at him. "I mean, girl."

"Dude, I am really happy for both of you."

"I am really happy for both of us, too." It was becoming obvious to Tripp and me that while my reunion with Ack was pleasant for him, he really wanted to get back to catching up on what he had been missing all of these years. I gave him a hug and we turned to head back to the dance floor. Within seconds, they were sucking face again. "Get a room," I said under my breath as we walked away. Tripp chuckled and then asked me to dance.

On the dance floor our samurai guys had the better end of the deal. *Hakamas* are extremely comfortable and you can do anything in them except for pee in a hurry. While *kimonos* could be worse, they are a little more constricting. But if you hike them up a bit, you can get your groove back. We danced and danced, but it started to get hot. There are a lot of layers to this type of clothing and it gets warm. Megan and Matt were off talking to Jason Anderson who, amazingly, was at the prom with his on-again-off-again and highly sadistic girlfriend, Amy. We decided to step out onto the veranda for some cooler air.

As we passed through the tall French doors and stepped into the night, we crossed paths with none other than Rita Montrose. She was just heading inside

343

with her human version of a Ken doll and stopped to examine our clothing. "Didn't you get the memo? Halloween was last semester," she said with considerable smugness. In a flash of thought, I saw thirty-nine techniques that I could use immediately to kick her flabby ass across the dance floor and through the glass on the other side of the ballroom, but just as quickly, I couldn't think of a single reason why I could give a shit.

"Rita, Rita, Rita. Isn't time to get off the hamster wheel? You walk around hating people because you think they hate you and, because you treat them like shit, they usually do hate you. But what if we were to do something different this time?" Rita was trying to think of something really nasty to say. Thankfully, she is a bit of a dipshit and she wasn't coming up with anything.

"You know, that is a really pretty dress you are wearing and you look absolutely lovely in it. I mean it. I am really done looking for your dark side. I hope you have a wonderful evening." With that we slid past her and her date who whispered to Tripp as he passed, "cool clothes, dude." I didn't bother to look back at her. I meant what I said. She did look lovely and I was done looking for her dark side.

All in all, the night didn't suck, not by a long shot. The guys had come through on dinner in a big, big way and they had our undying affection for it -- at least for the next week. The dance actually turned out to be fun and even momentous. After all, Ack broke the curse and had found someone to love him back. We cruised down to the City Museum for the Metro all-night party with a stop-over at Rinchen's loft to change our clothes. We almost blew off the party when Matt and Tripp plopped on the couch and had both nearly fallen asleep. They had been up most of the night before preparing the *dojo* for our dinner party.

The Metro party rocked. Tripp and Matt had some really cool friends at school and it made me even a little bit jealous. By sunrise when they let us out, I had some cool new friends too. It was a night well worth the effort. It was a night well worth the thought that went into it. It was a night that I will never forget.

Chapter Forty-one: My Sweet, Sweet Buddha-boy

Thunderstorms used to scare me to death. I was still crawling into bed with my parents during storms when I was twelve. They started kicking me out when I was thirteen, but I sometimes grabbed a blanket and slept next to their bed.

Missouri doesn't just have thunderstorms, we have tornadoes. And every kid who has ever seen the Wizard of Oz knows that tornadoes are nothing to mess with. St. Louis has an elaborate system to warn people of tornado sightings. We have sirens that blast through large yellow loudspeakers mounted on tall poles that can switch from siren to public address system so as to give you a life-saving message that you can never understand because the acoustics are so bad. When you hear the voice coming through the loudspeaker, however, you don't have to understand the words. Everyone knows what the voice is trying to say: "get your ass to the basement." Of course, most people go to the window to take a look and decide that it is not that bad and usually flop back onto the couch and turn on the news to see whether or not they were wrong to ignore the siren.

While the tornado sirens still creep me out, I started to actually like thunderstorms. There is something kind of cozy about them. It's like they justify crawling under a blanket with a good book and a cup of tea. Who could possibly do homework in a thunderstorm?

A couple of weeks before graduation, I found myself in the unusual situation of being at home on a Saturday night hunkered down under a quilt with my mom talking about my graduation party. The night before, Tripp and Eddie had driven to Columbia to the University of Missouri, fondly referred to

345

as "Mizzou" by Missourians, to stay with some of Eddie's tattoo buddies. Major college campuses are practically Mecca for tattoo artists looking for blank skin to draw on. They said that they were going to catch a tattoo design show that was being held on campus. The guys from the tattoo parlor that Eddie worked for were going to be there, but I suspected that the real draw was the hundreds of nearly naked girls that would be baring more than their souls for the sake of art. They were pretty sure that they would wind up staying over for a second night before making the two hour trip home on Sunday morning. Megan and Matt were having a date night. The crappy weather was just the excuse I needed to spend some quality time with my mom for the first time in months.

It was pouring outside as the lightening flashed through the bay window in the living room. My mom and I were working out graduation logistics. Graduation was on a Saturday evening at six o'clock. Just like prom, school officials do not trust high school students on the night of a big celebration and really do not want drunk driving deaths to mess up the festivities, so they planned an all-night party to lock us down until morning. Graduation was the moment of greatest concern for school administrators, so at our school they pulled out all the stops for this final bash. There would be a live band and raffles for prizes like big-screen TVs and gaming systems. There would be all the food you could eat. The problem was that you had to be there by nine thirty or they locked you out. Of course, if you were there on time, they locked you in. This meant that you pretty much had to go straight from graduation to the party. My graduation party, like everyone else's graduation party, would have to wait until the following Sunday.

This created yet another problem. I wanted to be able to drop in on at least a few select graduation parties for my friends. The short list included Megan, Beth and Ack. This would mean having to duck out of my own party, at least for some portion of it, in order to make the rounds. Fortunately, Metro graduated a week after Westchester so Megan and I were going to be able to give our undivided attention to Tripp and Matt. They, of course, were going to have to be waiting on us hand and foot the week before. The cool thing was that both schools allowed graduates to bring dates to both all-night parties so the four of us were completely booked for the last weekend in May and the first weekend in June.

It was an exciting time. I was definitely ready to get out of high school. Tripp and I had decided to head east for college, but not to the same town and, in fact, not to the same state. He had committed to go to design school in New

York and I had chosen to go to Mount Holyoake in Massachusetts. The good news was that we were only about three hours away from each other and there was cheap bus service between the two locations. We even had a plan B. If the distance proved to be a problem, I was going to transfer to a school in New York City.

At Westchester High School, all of the seniors had been scrambling around getting ready for finals. Ack had dropped off the face of the earth with Anita. I occasionally saw them in the lunchroom, but more often than not they slipped out side for lunch, at least when the weather was good, and found their own private part of the school lawn. Ack said that his dad actually liked Anita and that his relationship was now fully approved.

Beth had gotten into Emory University in Atlanta and was completely stoked about moving there. She was suddenly an encyclopedia of all things Atlanta and even had an Atlanta Braves baseball jersey which is complete sacrilege in a die-hard baseball town like St. Louis. To root for a team other than the Cardinals can get your ass kicked across the Mississippi River.

Julie Roth had been accepted at Yale. This was no real surprise. She smoked the SAT and was proving herself to be a certified genius. I figured we would see her on the United States Supreme Court someday. The big surprise was Tommy Davidson who decided to go to Julliard in New York. He had actually decided to go for the acting thing instead of sports which was probably just as well because the Westchester High football team had won only three of ten games in the fall. His girlfriend, Annie Vega was going to Mizzou with half our graduating class. She had gotten in at New York University, but apparently did not like New York and decided to stay in the Midwest.

After finishing off an entire pot of tea with my mom, there was still plenty of thunderstorm left, but I decided to seek the comfort of my bed. As I crawled under my covers I remembered a story that Rinchen had told me about how storms had saved Japan back in the samurai days. In the Thirteenth Century, the Mongols tried twice to invade Japan. Both times, heavy storms helped the small Japanese army defend their land. In the first attack, thunderstorms assisted 10,000 samurai in inflicting heavy losses on the Mongol force that was over ten times its size. In the second attack, a typhoon wiped out the Mongol fleet before it could reach Japanese shores. The Japanese believed that these winds, like all things in nature, were possessed of *kami*, divine spirits of the Shinto world. When the typhoon wiped out the Mongols, everyone said that it was the *kami* of the wind, the *kamikaze*, that had protected

Japan from invasion. Centuries later, Japan would name their suicidal pilots *kamikazes* after these protective spirits.

Rinchen had told us that the Shinto faith believed that everything had a spirit, trees, water, the sun, everything. These spirits behaved in different ways depending on the nature of the thing. Even rocks had spirits. I listened to the wind beating rain on my bedroom window and I remember thinking to myself that it was the *kami* of rain and wind and that they were hard at work doing something out there. I was pretty sure there were no Mongols.

I slept in late on Sunday. When I finally dragged myself out of bed, I went down stairs and saw that there were broken tree limbs and green leaves all over the lawns along my street. It had been quite a blow. My mom was having coffee at the kitchen table and I had missed breakfast although my dad had left a bowl of pancake batter on the counter and his big black cast iron frying pan was still on the stove. This was his special breakfast pan and was even stored in a different drawer than my mom's stainless steel pots and pans.

I remember going to the refrigerator to pour myself a glass of orange juice when I heard my dad talking to someone in the front yard. The front door opened and he walked in looking like he was about to get sick. There was someone behind him. It was Rinchen.

"Maddie, Rinchen is here to see you and I think you need to sit down." I was suddenly very nervous. This did not sound right. Something was wrong. Why was Rinchen all the way out in Westchester? Why was he at my house? Where was Megan?

Rinchen looked tired. He had bags under his red eyes, but he was perfectly calm as usual. He smiled when he saw me and greeted my mom formally, "Hello Mrs. Albright." I could see the alarm spread over my mother's face. Now I was starting to freak out.

Rinchen did not sit, but my father took a seat next to me. I could hear him take in a deep breath. "Lhamo, I have to tell you something and it is not very good news. Last night, Eddie and Tripp were driving home from Columbia and got caught in the storm. Apparently, there was a small tornado and it blew a road sign through the windshield of Eddie's truck. There was a crash."

"Oh my god, are they alright?" I was starting to panic, but I was holding out for some fragment of hopeful news. There had to be a silver lining, right?

"I am afraid not. No one got to the crash site until after the storm had passed. Eddie was taken by helicopter to Barnes Hospital and is in a coma ..."

"And Tripp? Please *Sensei*, tell me Tripp is okay Please ...." Rinchen took a deep breath and then went icy cold.

"Lhamo, Tripp died last night. The police think that he was killed instantly when the road sign went through the windshield. He's gone, sweetheart. Our boy is gone."

My mother covered her mouth and gasped. My dad put his arm around my shoulders and held me tight. Tears started to roll out of Rinchen's eyes. I did not want to believe him and I fought with myself to deny that what he was saying was true. The news seeped into my mind despite my effort to keep it out.

"What about Megan? I assume she knows by now."

"Yes, Megan and Matt had just gotten home last night when the police called. They both went straight to her mother's house. I am on my way there now, but I wanted you to hear this news from me. I felt that I owed you that."

I was in shock. I couldn't feel anything. It was like someone had just scrambled my brains. I was beginning to feel sick to my stomach. My first thought was of Megan and then Rinchen and then Megan's mom. I jumped up from my chair and ran into the bathroom and threw up. My mother followed me and by the time she had reached the bathroom she had toughened herself and wiped her eyes. There was no time for her to be sad. She had to be a mom.

I could hear my dad walk Rinchen to the door. "I am so sorry, we loved your boy, we really did." I could only hear Rinchen take a few steps outside the door and then he was gone.

No amount of training that I had had before that day could have prepared me for the crush of sadness that fell on me. One minute I would hurt so bad that I wished someone would just kill me and put me out of my misery. After a few minutes, I would go numb, but only for a short while and then the flood of overwhelming sadness would start all over again. I tried to get a grip on myself. I tried to breathe, but it did not work. There was no escape. In just a few sentences containing a few awful words carried on the breath of my master, I had been transported into the worst hell realm that I could imagine.

For the rest of the day, I lay on the couch of the living room with my mom rubbing my back. I can remember myself whimpering and then sobbing and then lying there feeling completely exhausted. What a time to be clear and wide awake. Tripp's death had a direct route into the very core of my mind and there was not enough ignorance or distraction left to even slow down this awful rising awareness. I wanted so much to just go numb. I wanted to die, but in hell you feel all of the pain with no foreseeable end to it. I thought of Eddie lying in the hospital in a coma. He was lucky. When my thoughts turned to Megan, my sadness doubled. She was no longer a twin and worse, her mom for sure had gone off the deep end. She would have to deal with not just a dead twin brother, but would undoubtedly tend to her mother's sorrow along with her own. And poor Rinchen; he was the last samurai standing.

I fell asleep for a few hours, but woke in the middle of the night. I was still on the couch. My parents had not tried to move me to my room. My dad was asleep in the chair next to me, standing guard, watching over his wounded daughter. A sudden thought of admiration filled my mind though it lasted only a second or two before the awareness of my love for the people around me reminded me of the huge hole that the *kami* had torn open in my life. Tripp had been the first to go, but he would not be the last.

The next day was Monday, but I was done with school. I needed to find Megan. I needed to try to be there for her. I called her cellphone, but there was no answer. I did not dare call her mother's house. Finally, I was able to reach Matt. He said he was sitting with her at her mom's house. "Megan says she loves you, but she can't talk to you right now. I love you too, Lhamo. We'll be in touch soon." The phone went dead.

By Tuesday afternoon, I decided that I could not spend another minute more lying around feeling awful. I knew that Tripp's death would be with me for the rest of my life, but I had to make myself useful, if for no better reason than to make myself believe that I was helping those around me instead of being a burden to them. I told my parents that I needed to go downtown to find Rinchen, to see what I could do to help him work through the things that death makes necessary. I had to stand up to this. Not so much for myself, but because I knew that Tripp would never want to be the cause of this much pain. The pain itself, my pain, seemed to me to be an insult to my sweet, sweet Buddha boy.

Both of my parents had taken off work. What a brave thing it is to volunteer to step into the pain and misery of someone you love. Of course, they loved him too and it was their pain as much as it was mine. You hear stories about the effort that parents make to shelter their kids from harm. They tend to remind you of their efforts when you are acting like a jerk and beating them up with your ingratitude. But in those days that followed Tripp's extinction from this world, my parents jumped into the shit pile that had become my life and stood by me with a ferociousness that only people capable of unconditional love can know. It was nothing short of heroic.

On Wednesday evening, my dad and I drove down to the *dojo*. Thor was leading class and said that Rinchen was at home. I was not sure that I was ready to step into the loft. I was more than sure that Tripp's ghost would be all over that place. But I had to take my place in the clan. I had to help. I could not let any of them, not Rinchen, Megan, Matt or my brothers and sisters of the *dojo* face this alone. I have no idea why this became so urgent for me. I do not recall a teaching on this subject. But all that I could think about was the utter selfishness that it would be to think about myself when everyone around me was suffering. I started to lose my sense of me altogether and that was a great relief. When I shook off my sadness and self-pity, my sense of what I had lost and would not recover, all that I could think of was *us* -- the greater sense of *"we"* that I was a part of. You can never feel lonely even when the love of your life has been destroyed, if you know yourself as part of a *we*.

I did not lose my boyfriend to the *kami* in the middle of the night that night. We lost our brother, our lover and our son, our comrade, our friend and one of the finest examples of what a man should be. We will suffer. We will miss him. And we will rise up together and live our lives as better people because he is, and forever will be, *us*.

Chapter Forty-two: Storm Damage

I have heard many stories of the aftermath of great battles. When I finally became conscious enough to know that people really fought and died in the world, I began to wonder what it was like to live through such a horrible thing as war. You can read all the stories about it that you want, but death means nothing to any of us until it is in our house.

My dad and I found Rinchen at home that Wednesday night. We sat with him and shared a pot of tea. He talked about having a memorial training when all the dust settled and when people could come and not be overwhelmed by sadness. Rinchen had arranged to have Tripp cremated as is the Buddhist custom. Cremation has a certain no-nonsense finality to it. It destroys any sense of denial that you might have that might trick your mind into believing that you will see your loved one again. But this is as it should be. Life is really, like no kidding, impermanent. Death is real and it is not just something that happens to some guy on TV. It will happen to you just like it will happen to me. It is nothing to be afraid of, but as a reminder of our impermanence, it is something to be respected. More importantly, death serves to remind us that we need to get busy in this life because now is the only moment in which life actually happens.

Megan came by to see me on Thursday. We both cried our eyes out when we saw each other. We sat on the couch and I mostly listened as she explained how her mother was nearly suicidal with sadness and depression. She needed a break. She needed to have time to herself. She said that her mother's sister had come into town and was staying with her for at least the next week. This would give Megan some room to breathe and to cry her own tears.

We decided that we were both going to go to graduation, but would skip the party afterward. For Megan, the week after our graduation would be the most difficult. She said that she was going to go to the Metro graduation to be there for Matt. I told her that I would go with her and I did.

Our graduation came and went. Rinchen was there and did his best to make it the happiest occasion that he could for his daughter. All four of my grandparents came to St. Louis to watch me graduate. My mom had a small family party for me the day after. Rinchen, Megan and Matt came too. Megan had asked not to have a party, so we made the one at my house a celebration for her too. There were a few tears here and there, but we mostly resolved to be happy and be present to what we had and not to what we had lost.

If we had been close before, we were sisters now. Megan and I found that it helped quite a lot to hang out with each other. Beth had stopped by after school the day after she had heard the news in the hallways at Westchester High. She brought me flowers and sat with me without saying much. Despite the passage of time and our different directions, she is part my *we*.

Not many boyfriends are called upon to stand by their women as they face the loss of a twin brother at the ripe age of eighteen. Matt might look like a biker rock-star, but he is a mountain of strength and kindness. I am proud to call him "brother".

After a couple of weeks, Megan and I decided that it was time to return to training at the *dojo* even if it was only a couple of times a week. Those first few classes were hell to get through, but it did get easier just like it had after my first class and just like it always would when you stand and face your life.

I can see now, why there are so many drunks and drug addicts in the world. If your mind is wide awake, the taste of simple strawberry can fill you with joy greater than any other. The loss of the man you love can hurt more than being burned alive. You give up comfort in exchange for both the strawberry and the fire. Some people just can't handle it. They have never learned to deal with discomfort and medicate themselves as if pain were a disease. It is cowardly, I suppose, but you see it that way only once you have access to strength. Until then, fear and the avoidance of pain is what people do because they do not have the skill to live any other way. I understand this now and have great concern for my generation that has so many ways of sedating itself and is missing the opportunity of this lifetime.

What I have learned from my master and my friends is that someone, somewhere, is always dying while someone else is holding the hand of the person they love the most, while somewhere else someone is crying in a dumpster while another meets her child for the first time. The karma of this world unfolds like the bubbles of a wave crashing on a beach in precisely the only way it can. How you choose to take the next step given the mountain that is yours to climb will determine what happens next. I guess you can surf or be washed out to sea. Ha! And this from a girl who has never seen the ocean.

I know now, through my own experience, why Chenrezig never blinks. I know now why Green Tara is always ready to step into the suffering of this world. They are my *yidams* that tighten my mind and invite me to follow them into the clear light of their example. When you know what real suffering is from your own experience, you know that there is something that you can do about it and ignoring the confusion and pain of the world ceases to be an option.

Om mani padme hung, baby, *om mani padme hung*.

Chapter Forty-three: The Monkey Trap

We live in the delusion that bad things are not supposed to happen. We live in the delusion that natural things like death, are bad. Our clinging minds want to have every meal be ice cream, every day be sunny and every person be happy to see us. Many people on this earth know what it is to lose a lover. Half of every married couple, at least those who go the distance, come to know this experience. But losing a twin, is a mind-fuck of a completely different kind. Megan said that she had spent her whole life thinking of Tripp as half of herself. His death was half a death of her own. She felt dead and alive at the same time.

As the days passed, Megan and I began to sort things out. She said that It may be a blessing to be the first to go and I thought about this over and over. In those first days, I found myself stopping in the middle of *puja* and making the same prayer: "please let me be next; please do not ever let me feel this way again." I told Megan that I had done this and she said that it was a coward's prayer even though she felt the same way. She said that it doesn't matter who goes first. The only difference is that Tripp only had to think about us for a few minutes at most as he died, but that we will have to think about him for the rest of our lives. Either way, for the wide awake person, the remaining minutes in this world, whether they be two or two million, will be filled with life and its turbulence no matter what.

Eventually, we lose everyone. You don't think about this much when you are in high school, but as you get older, one by one, everyone steps out of this life. Nothing makes you clearer about impermanence than having the love of your life destroyed in the blink of an eye. Tripp's death hurt because I was so deeply attached to him. There was no way to want a dead boy so badly and not feel as though the thought of him was tearing your mind to pieces. There you are, sitting in your life staring at the object of your desire in your memory being chased by the reality of his absence in an endless loop that cannot be made into a whole.

After several weeks, Megan asked me to meet her at the *dojo*. She and her father wanted to talk to me about a memorial service. What they really wanted to know was whether or not I could handle such a thing. I met them down there on a Sunday afternoon. It was summer and the day was hot, but beautiful. I rode my motorcycle downtown. The *kami* of the wind was ripping at my clothes and it felt like an old friend.

Rinchen was seated on the mat in meditation facing the *kamidana* when I arrived. He sat there motionless like he had done a thousand times before. I took off my shoes and bowed to the *kamidana* and stepped onto the mat. Both Megan and I sat behind her father and started our own mediation. After a short while, Rinchen bowed to the shrine and turned around to face us. His eyes were as calm as they had ever been. He smiled with the formality that he had when I first met him. His breathing was smooth and intentional. Looking at him, you would have no idea that three weeks ago he had lost his only son.

I bowed to him and thought for a moment that I was sad, but I was not. I was happy. I was home. He looked at me like he was watching the history of my life all at once. For a split second, his eyes watered and like all things to Rinchen, whatever emotion was trying to force its way onto his face had passed through his mind like a floating cloud. His calm was infectious.

"I have been so worried about the two of you. But I can see that you are well and that you are making your way. I am proud of both of you. You are such a credit to this *dojo* and to me. You inspire me." This surprised me – it seemed ironic that I would inspire *him*.

Rinchen continued, "We should consider holding a memorial of some sort for Tripp. He should be honored and we should close the book on our grief even though the thought of him will never leave us. I have been afraid that such a memorial might be overwhelming for the two of you so I am checking in to see if you are ready for us, all of us, as a family, to say our final good-bye to our young man."

Tears started to come to Megan's eyes which was making me sad as well, but I was ready to deal with this. "It's time, *Sensei*. We are ready."

"It is for you to say. It is an opportunity, however, for us to see the clinging nature of our minds and to cut it off in a way. There is a fine line between honoring the dead and dwelling in their lives lost. My concern is that we should think and say what we must in order to honor Tripp but not allow ourselves to turn his memory into a thought of self-pity for us. It would offend his memory to use him as an object of suffering."

"Well, I am definitely suffering," I said, "but I am doing it on my own and he is certainly not the cause."

"Me too, Daddy, me too." This was the first and only time I had ever heard Megan call Rinchen "Daddy". It was startling. He is so many things to so many people, but he is *Daddy* only to Megan.

Rinchen smiled at his daughter and made no visible effort to contain his tears. "So be it," he said softly, "it is time that we step out of the hell of our own making and move on."

"*Hell* is certainly the right word for it," Megan said looking at me.

Rinchen smiled, "Yes, quite literally, it is. Remember what Lama Jinpa taught us about the six realms of existence. These are not places. They are states of mind."

I looked down at the mat, "Sometimes I feel like I will never be happy again."

"You won't as long as you cling to Tripp's life. You are fighting with reality and you are going to lose that fight."

"Yeah, I have been getting my ass kicked for the past several weeks, that's for sure." I was having a hard time looking at either one of them. I was starting to feel sorry for myself and it was pissing me off.

Rinchen decided that it was a good moment for one of his stories. "Did I ever tell you about how certain tribes in Africa hunt monkeys?" Sometimes there seemed to be no logic to the things that ran through Rinchen's mind and I could not for the life of me understand why we were about to start talking about African monkey hunting.

"No, I must have missed that story, *Sensei.*" I said, still looking up at him trying to suppress the sudden need to be sarcastic.

"In Africa, when they want to hunt certain kinds of monkeys, they find or cut a hole in a tree just big enough for a monkey to reach in with his hand. They put some fruit or other bait in the hole and wait for a monkey to come along. The monkey will reach in the hole and grab the bait, but when he does, he holds the bait in his fist making his hand too large to pull out of the hole. He is trapped. He will not let go of the bait because he wants it so much.

Even when the hunters come back, he will hang onto the bait and will not let go even when they start clubbing him to death. We are all like that. We cling to things even if it kills us. We want some things so badly that we never let go. Even if the hunters did not come back, the monkey would die of starvation because it would not occur to him that by letting go, he could be free and possibly find even better food elsewhere. This is the suffering of attachment and clinging."

"What are you saying, that I should just forget about Tripp and move on already? Jesus, *Sensei*, it has only been three weeks!" Rinchen ignored my rudeness. This was not a time to enforce manners. I was startled by his comment because what I thought he was implying was that I needed to find a new boyfriend. I was getting pissed. Doesn't a girl get a chance to grieve?

"That is not what I am saying, Lhamo, not at all. What I am saying is that while Tripp's death is fresh in our minds we might take this moment to notice a few things."

"Like what?"

"Like, what real love is as distinguished from what is merely our hunger for someone." This was one of Rinchen's thunderbolts. I had been having thoughts that were pointed in this direction, but the word "hunger" landed in my mind like a punch in the face. There was no doubt about it. I was dying of hunger for Tripp. Being startled or confused around Rinchen was certainly not new to me, but I knew that I only had to ask and he would help me lift the fog from my thoughts.

"So what do you mean, exactly?" I asked.

"What I mean is that if we look at Tripp in our minds, many, many thoughts rise to the surface. We remember how beautiful he was. We remember his kindness and his strength. We remember his skill and the way he loved us all so well." This was not helping. Megan burst into tears. I was right behind her, but Rinchen held his ground and continued. "These are the things about him that we admired and they do not, by themselves, make us sad, but rather, they make us happy to remember what a fine person he was and to be grateful for all of the joy that he brought into this world. We rejoice in his merit. There is no remorse or pain in these thoughts. But when we start to think about wanting him with us when we know full well it is impossible, when we start to think about a future without him, we get stuck in the monkey trap and we become the source of our own suffering. We think that we are sad for him, but his life is whole and complete and it was wonderful. The living grieve for themselves. His life was his life. It was not one minute longer than it could have been. But we find ourselves wanting just one more day, but for whose benefit? He does not need another day with us. He does not need anything because he is no longer. But we, on the other hand, would offer years of our lives to have him back with us for just one more day – but it would be an offering made by a hungry ghost, a vain attempt to feed our craving and satisfy our own greedy purposes. It is not for him that we would want this. It would only serve our own selfishness."

I understood what he was saying. I had started out by being selfish with my grief. I wanted Tripp back for me. I wanted him to hold me and kiss me like he had done all those times before. And yet, despite what Rinchen had to say, I could not completely get my mind wrapped around how it could be different.

Rinchen pressed on with his teaching. "A tree falls to the ground after two hundred years of stretching to the sky. It rots and becomes part of the soil. Is not its death every bit a part of the arc of its life? It is doing what it is supposed to do. Our thoughts of regret about it are merely self-serving fantasies. If we miss the shade, we are dreaming about something that no longer exists and arises only out of our want to pit our dreams against our reality. You might as well be heartbroken about not being able to flap our arms and fly to the moon. Either way, the object of your heart's desire does not exist. Memory can be quite cruel this way, especially if we use it to fan the fire of our desire and self-pity. The truth is, however, that if we see Tripp's life as perfect, whole and complete, which it is because it cannot be any way other than it was, then his completed life becomes a seed of joy and his memory an inspiration. It seems a shame to ruin our memory of this wonderful life with our thoughts of neediness while wishing that we could reclaim his presence like a drug to make us feel better. He was not a teddy bear. He was a man and as such he did what the best of men do. He lived well and then he died. So be it."

"It's going to take a while for me to get there, *Sensei*," I said. Rinchen smiled.

"Yes," he said, "and that too is as it should be. I am not trying to stop you from feeling sadness. You should cry for him until you have no more tears. But sadness is a powerful opportunity to examine the meaning of lost things. I am merely trying to point out to you what your sadness can mean if you use it well. A young woman who goes through what you and Megan are going through can become lost and damaged forever and that would be a shame. Tripp would never have wanted his life or his death to harm you like that. But he would want you to use both of them to find wisdom, to learn to be happy no matter what happens and to find real peace. He would have gladly given himself over to death well before he did if he knew that it would do that for both of you. All that I am trying to suggest is, as you think about all of this, and you will think about this for years to come, that you use your experience of Tripp, all of it, his life and his death, as an inspiration to love, to care and to be courageous. Don't let your grief and your self-pity defeat you. Do not let it take you off the path. This would be an insult to his life and a great disaster for the two of you. So sit with your pain. Know it for what it is. Let it be your teacher as pain well-used always is."

This was not exactly the hug and shoulder to cry on that I was hoping for. If anything, I now felt worse. But like all things Rinchen, his words were like seeds that started to take root in my mind as I considered the situation over and over and over. His words were like a virus that attached itself to everything that came after what he had to say. After he spoke, every moment of sadness rose in my mind was tainted with the knowledge that it was sadness for myself. My love for Tripp grew stronger than my self-pity. It started to bother me that I would tarnish the memory of such a fine young man with my own self-concern. Over time, I realized, much to my own embarrassment, that my love for Tripp, my real love for him, had been buried in the muck of my hunger for him. At first, it was hard to tell the two things apart. But eventually, my thoughts of Tripp brought smiles not sobs. I could feel him in me. The thought of him influenced how I saw things and what I chose to do about what I saw. I had already realized before Rinchen had told us these things, that I did not want to let Tripp down by tarnishing any of the wonderful things I had learned from him. He became my own personal *yidam*; not a thing to devour, but an example of how to live my life with love, peace and devotion.

On the first day of summer, the longest day, an auspicious day to many of us, the Byakuren Clan gathered to train in the memory of our lost brother one last time. Rinchen put a picture of Tripp on the *tokonoma* under the *kamidana*. The lights were turned off completely and hundreds of tea candles were lit and placed on nearly every flat surface in the *dojo* except for the mat. Rinchen and Megan had divided Tripp's ashes and placed them in three small urns on the *tokonoma* wrapped together with a black belt. Rinchen had promoted Tripp and Megan to the rank of *shodan*, the first rank of the black belts, just before Tripp had died, but had kept it a secret intending to present them with their new belts just before they left for college. Megan was now wearing her black belt having received it without any *dojo* ceremony to mark the occasion.

Every *Aikidoka* in the *dojo* wore a white *hachimaki* , a headband, in the traditional color of death in the *Budo* world. The *dojo* was packed with not only our students, but masters and students from other *dojos* from around the city and beyond. Some came from arts that had no resemblance to *Aikido*, but they were warriors, *Budoka*, just the same. It was an impressive sight. The line of *Budoka* crossed the mat five times. Many had brought flowers or a bottle *sake* as an offering for the shrine. Tracy was there and she wore her *gi* and *hakama* just like she had done so many times in the past.

Eddie Manta had come out of his coma two days after the accident. He had broken his femur along with several ribs in the crash. His father rolled him into the *dojo* in a wheelchair. He was given a white *hachimaki* which he wore along with the rest of us. He still had his hospital bracelet on and a blanket over his legs to conceal the fact that he could not yet wear pants. The truth was that he had not actually been released from the hospital. He managed to talk his doctor into letting him come to gathering for a couple of hours and was taken back to the hospital as soon as the memorial was over.

Only a minute or two after Eddie arrived, my mom and dad came through the front door. My dad wore a suit and tie and my mother was wearing one of her best summer dresses. She had asked me about wearing black, but I had insisted that she wear something more optimistic. Minutes later, Ack and Anita came in followed by Beth and then Julie Ross; Jason Anderson was there too and Tommy Davidson who walked in holding hands with Annie Vega – in all, there were at least a dozen friends from our school who had barely known Tripp. I was stunned. It did not take an enlightened mind to understand that they had come when called as warriors do for Megan and me.

In times of disaster, it is only natural to rally your clan – your whole clan. We think that we live our lives on our own, but this is a lie. We often do not pay enough attention to the pain and suffering of our friends and family because we think it will only add to our burden of living, but the truth is that if we do not open ourselves and take on the hurt and heartache of others, we can never see anything clearly. We can never know the world for what it really is.

This is why empathy is a path to enlightenment. We gather the courage to make the pain of others our pain and transform it into joy to be shared among all of us. In this way, the *we* can say that *we* have gone to war with suffering and have earned some measure of true victory. Sometimes I think that the whole world is so committed to its comfort that it ignores the suffering that can be found at any hour of any day in any place on the planet. But this comfort comes at such high cost. When we seal away our hearts in a cowardly attempt to save ourselves from facing the things that we think might hurt us or piss us off, then we also cut ourselves off from love and communion with the world. This is a very bad bargain. This is the karma of murder and hate; this is the how greed takes over our economy and how every harmful thing on the planet earth takes shape – we simply stop caring. We go blind. And in our ignorance, we bring the evils of the world upon ourselves.

The most important thing that I learned from Tripp, with a lot of help from his father, is that I would rather be burned alive in the funeral fires of a thousand dead loved ones than to miss the opportunity to love my guts out while my friends and family are still with me. To hold their faces in my hands and look deep into their eyes and see every fear and every ache and every doubt just so that I could tell them that I am here for them and that nothing from any of the six realms of existence can make me abandon them. I want to be the one of the many who is willing to stand against harm and delusion and protect the creative evolution of humanity even if I am to be armed with nothing more than my own body and what I can hold in my hands. I want to love like that and no amount of pain or loss is going to stop me.

Tripp's death may have broken my heart, but his life is my inspiration and I will not forsake the memory of such a fine young man simply because it is painful or inconvenient to me. I have come to understand what Rinchen was trying to teach me. To walk on this earth, to really feel the dirt beneath your feet, takes courage. Musashi was right. If you are going to actually be awake in this world, you must have a resolute acceptance of death. Not just your death, but the death of everything around you and everything you love. You have to love in the face of death, impermanence and hurt. You have to love your guts out urgently because of death, impermanence and hurt. And when you put your selfish, self-pitying thoughts behind you, when you give up trying to become a *somebody*, when you walk in the world with concern only for what is outside of you and forget to give yourself a name, then you will really know life. That is what Musashi was trying to say. If there is no *you*, then there is plenty of room for everything else. If you can just pull yourself out of the way, the whole world glows in its own illumination.

The ceremonial practice began when Megan, now the senior student of the *dojo*, rang a small bowl-shaped bell with a little wooden bat. These bells are sometimes used in monasteries to announce the beginning and end of meditation. No one led the warm-up and yet everyone, through force of habit or by the example of a student next to her, moved through the exercises in order as if Tripp were there leading the class. This was done on purpose as a gesture to show that even in death, he is still an influence on us. The leaderless class had a ghostly effect which was exactly the point. Slowly and in unison, the entire group made its way as it always does.

Megan rang the bell again and everyone formed ranks. We sat silently breathing in and out in a single meditation on the shrine. After a while, Rinchen slowly and deliberately stepped up to the *kamiza* and sat before the ashes and the photograph of his dead son. As he bowed, we bowed with him. As he clapped the two thunderous claps, the action and its echo, we clapped with him. When he turned to face the *dojo*, a moment when we would normally greet him with our request to be trained, every *Budoka* in the room bowed in silence. Rinchen rose to his feet and called Megan to be his *uke*. He worked slowly through the first group of techniques and then bowed silently inviting the class to follow his example.

He took his time as was his privilege. The training helped keep my mind off my sorrow, but somewhere deep in my heart I was happy that so many people, so many warriors, had come to pay their respects to my lovely Buddha-boy. There was not a whisper of inappropriate talk or chatter. Every *Budoka* in the room, whether they were from our *dojo* or not, was an example of perfect discipline. Rinchen worked through the five major groups of *Aikido* techniques and then sat down and faced the *kamidana*. He bowed and forming circle with his hands in his lap, slipped into a deep meditation as every *Budoka* in the room followed him in their best attempt at *mushin*.

After a half an hour, Megan rang the bell once more and everyone allowed their minds to find their way back into the room. Rinchen sat up perfectly straight and stared ahead at the three urns bound by what I now realize was his own black belt and the photograph of his son that was to have been Tripp's senior portrait. Rinchen had given up his belt, the record of his training, and had put on crisp new white belt. He had declared himself a beginner again. At last, he made the double clap once again and turned to face his guests. He bowed to them with the deepest sense of reverence and humility. This is how a real warrior says good-bye to his son – among his friends, with a clear mind and a heart full of gratitude for having known such a fine young man – and without as much as a shred of self-pity.

Instead of the normal process of bowing and thanking everyone on the mat, Rinchen stood up and leaving the *kamiza* behind him walked around the *shimoseki* side of the ranks and then behind us finally taking his place as a student in the first position -- the position that for years had been occupied by this son. Again, the ranks bowed to the *kamidana*. Rinchen and Megan while remaining in *seiza*, turned to their guests. Rinchen waved to me as a gesture requesting that I join them in what would become a receiving line of sorts to allow the guests to pay their respects to all three of us individually. On my knees and walking in *shikko*, I made my way to *joseki* and took my place next to Megan. One by one, every master and every student approached Rinchen and bowed and slid sideways to face Megan and bowed again and once more for me. Some could not contain their sadness and tears were flowing down the cheeks of most of them. Matt approached in *shikko* and bowed to Rinchen. He could barely lift his head, he was shaking so badly. He slid a step to the side to face Megan and bowed. He could contain his sorrow no longer and he lost it completely weeping uncontrollably until she slid forward to hold him for moment and steady him. Next came Thor and then Tracy, who broke formality and gave Rinchen a hug. Rinchen greeted each person with a calm smile and a bow as if he was more worried for them than they were for him. He allowed everyone to make any gesture that they needed to make. His calmness helped some of us hold ourselves together as the long line of students and well-wishers passed on their knees.

Megan told me later that her father felt that I should be treated like Tripp's widow even though we were not married. He said that it was important to him that I be honored as a special person of his own family so that we might respect that his son loved me with all of his heart. No matter where my life might take me, regardless of whether or not I might someday marry someone else, Megan said that her father would always and forever consider me to be his daughter.

My parents had sent a large bouquet of flowers to the *dojo* which Rinchen had placed on the *tokonoma*. When I had been called to sit with Rinchen and Megan, I saw my parents sitting in the foyer. It was the one and only time in my entire life, so far, that I can remember ever seeing my father cry. My mom was a mess as they both watched the lines of people pay their respects to Rinchen, then Megan and then me. My mom would never question why I was a member of the *dojo* ever again. She told me later that the whole memorial had been one of the most beautiful things that she had ever seen and that to see those people, most of whom were Americans, behaving with such reverence was deeply inspiring to her. My dad did not speak of it afterwards and did not have a lot to say in general for weeks to come. But he did not pass by me for the rest of the summer without touching me with a hug or kiss or a squeeze of my hand.

As I thought about it afterward, I realized that the less my thoughts were on me and the more that they were on Tripp that it became impossible to see him as the light of my life extinguished. He was and would always be the spark that ignited a bonfire.

Chapter Forty-four: The Difference Between Loneliness And Solitude

After the memorial, life slowly started to return to its old rhythms for most of us. It would be a long time before Rinchen, Megan and I would be able to make it through a day without the sense that something really important was missing. Training resumed in the park. I often found myself sitting by the stream after class watching the water bugs skitter along with no apparent agenda. I could get lost for hours in thoughts and memories, but I was starting to remember what peace was like.

I skipped class one morning, but drove my motorcycle to the park later in the day to seek the comfort of my special spot under the pines by the bank of the stream. As I made my way through the park, I could see our training ground and that there was someone already sitting near my spot. I was disappointed because I had really wanted this place for myself. As I got closer, I realized that it was Rinchen.

As I walked across the grass, I could see that he was meditating, so I sat down near, but not too close, to him and brought my breath into rhythm with his. We sat there for nearly an hour and I wasn't sure if he even knew I was there. My concentration was breaking up and I began to daydream.

Suddenly Rinchen opened his eyes. He turned to me and smiled. "Your concentration is getting better, Lhamo; good for you." He was always saying that: "good for you" like he was generally happy for the success of others.

"Thank you, *Sensei*. I was surprised to see you here."

"Oh, sometimes I need to get away from the *dojo* and the apartment and get a little fresh air. I have always liked this spot. We have been training here since the kids were little." I could see him drift off into a memory of a happy moment with small children that were no more. "You get so attached to them when they are small and you think that you are over that when they start to grow up and carve out their own lives, but it is not true. I am still very, very attached to both of them."

"I miss him still so very much. Just when I think it's getting better, I think about him or find something that he gave me and I feel like I have to start all over again," I said looking around the park trying to take it all in.

"Yes, it seems that it is getting worse for me as well as time passes. I can remember changing their diapers. It was quite a thing having twins. It was a lot of work, but I was so in love with being a dad that I could have raised four of them at a time." I tried to fix in my mind what Tripp looked like when he was a toddler. The image that came to mind was of this little kid in diapers with a big patch of black hair covering one eye. I was pretty sure that he never looked like that.

Rinchen looked out over the stream, "I miss those days. I miss being needed by them. I used to love coming home and having them jump all over me. It is such a pure thing, the love you share with your children. They teach you absolute and unconditional love. They are uncomplicated when they are small. As they grow older they become cynical as they learn that the world is not a fairy tale. And when they decide that they need to be cool, they lose their humanity for a while. But when they are little, they are just little baby Buddhas. I never knew what compassion really was until I had them. They are my most profound teachers."

I was starting to get sad again. This was not like Rinchen to be so emotional. His guard was down and I felt like I had invaded a space that he kept mostly to himself. I started to remember all the daydreams I used to have about Tripp and I getting married and having kids of our own. He would have made an outstanding father. I could feel a deep sense of disappointment rising in me that there was never going to be a Tripp junior. It was almost unbearable. I could feel the tears rolling down my cheeks. I was so sick of tears. When I looked over at Rinchen, he was crying too. This took me by complete surprise. All this time, he had been my rock, the tower of strength that had gotten me and everyone else through so many difficult times.

"I am really worried about Megan," he said. It is bad enough to lose a twin brother, but her mother has not dealt with Tripp's death well at all. Megan feels so much responsibility for taking care of her mom. It is not how things are supposed to work. Parents are supposed to take care of their kids and guide them through times like these. I am afraid that the burden is too much for her."

"I have been talking to her nearly every day," I said. "She is a lot stronger than you think and, yes, I think she takes on way too much with her mom. But nothing you or I can say is going to change that. Megan is intensely loyal to both of you and she would rather die than walk away from either one of you."

"Yes, she is a rare one, that girl. So, what now for you? Please tell me that you are off to college this fall."

"I'm not sure. Things are pretty much up in the air. I was going to go to school out East, but I am not liking that idea now."

"What do you want to learn? Is there something in particular that you would like to study?"

"I am already doing that, *Sensei*; I am already doing that." Rinchen smiled.

"You still need to get out and see the world."

"Yeah, I was thinking about heading West maybe, somewhere near Lama Jinpa so I can learn more from him."

"That would be an excellent idea! In fact, a dear friend of mine, one of my own *Aikido* teachers, in fact, lives in Irvine not too far from Costa Mesa. You might even go to school at University of California, Irvine. His *dojo* is practically on campus. What an experience that would be."

He was right. That would be something. To train with my teacher's teachers would be awesome. But the summer was almost over and I had not applied there. I could feel the beginning of a plan.

"As you know, Megan had actually applied there and was accepted. I think we both know that she is not likely to leave town, at least not this year. It will be a while before she feels that she can leave. It would be great if you could go to UC together. I think it would benefit both of you quite a bit."

"Let me look into it. I doubt that I can get in to any school this late in the game, but I will check it out."

"Do that. I will not enjoy losing you, Lhamo. I have grown quite fond of you, but more important than my fondness is my desire that you learn everything you can to grow wiser as you grow older. These days, it doesn't seem to work like that anymore. People fight like hell not to grow old at all and they are certainly not getting any wiser."

"Well, they say that seventy is the new fifty."

"That's a tragedy."

"Why is that?"

"We are supposed to grow old and die, Lhamo. The older generations have no right to cling to their lives like they do. We are supposed to make room on this planet for our children. We are supposed to face our own deaths. Nowadays, they are even talking about gene therapy that will let people live forever. But most people are not making anything out of the years they already have. What then? Two hundred and fifty years of amusing ourselves? How many movies can you watch in two and a half centuries? How much suffering can you ignore? A single moment fully lived is a far greater thing than the longevity of ignorance and selfishness. Most of these folks are dead already. At least in passing from this world, they have the chance to be reborn in a world of less frivolity. If I were to be honest about it, I fear for this world, Lhamo. I fear that we are slipping into a god realm. Our technology is giving us nearly universal power, but it has not made us any wiser. It has shown us the inner working of our molecules, but not the deepest nature of our consciousness. We cannot seem to free ourselves from our addiction to crude pleasures. I, for one, will not do a thing to extend my own life."

I took his hand in mine. It was tough and calloused from years of training. "Don't die on me yet, *Sensei*, I still have a few things I need to learn from you." He smiled and rubbed my head like I was a little kid. I didn't mind. For a second, I could see the man who used to roll around on this very spot with his twins. I remember doing that with my dad. Where did those days go? Our fathers were toys to us then -- big teddy bears to keep us safe on a stormy night. They try so hard to be our guides in this turbulent world, but somewhere along the line we stop relying on them. I never realized how much my parents worried about me until I saw how much Rinchen had worried about his children. I guess it took finding a second father to teach me how amazing my first one is.

Chapter Forty-five: The Lotus Blossom

Eddie was released from the hospital in early July. The doctors said that he had not suffered any permanent brain damage, but that he would have a steel rod in his left thigh forever. He was going to be stuck in a wheelchair for at least five months with his broken left leg sticking straight out. He was supposed to stay home, but I could certainly understand why after a couple of weeks he felt that he had to go back to the tattoo shop on Washington Avenue, if only to hang out. Being stuck at home reliving the last moments that you can remember spending with your best friend is nobody's idea of a good time. It was hell on Eddie to wake up days after the accident and find out that he would never walk right again and that Tripp's body had already been cremated. Eddie took it very hard at first. I heard that he started to blame himself for the accident. Both Rinchen and Megan visited him at the hospital and reassured him that there was nothing he could have done.

My plan to go to Mount Holyoake in the fall had seemed so solid up until the accident. By mid-summer, I had informed the school that I would not be coming. I knew that there was a waiting list there and I did not want to cheat someone else out of my spot. I spent most of the summer thinking that I would stay in St. Louis, at least for the fall semester. Maybe by winter, Megan would be able to get her life back from her mom and we could go somewhere to school together or just travel for a while. The idea that Rinchen had mentioned of going to California to train with Lama Jinpa was gathering some momentum with me and the idea of training with Rinchen's own *Aikido* teacher made it all the more enticing. As the summer rolled along, I was getting edgy without a plan. Rinchen was right, like always; I really needed to get out of town for a while and go somewhere new.

I got around to cleaning out my closets. All those unused clothes were pissing me off. I didn't need much anymore. I didn't like having a bunch of things to keep track of. I was really getting into simplicity. I packed up four garbage bags of clothes and shoes and took them down to Victoria House and gave them to Sister Constance. She was surprised to see the volume of stuff and said that they did not get many donations that would fit young women who were, of course, her primary customers. I was glad that they would be put to good use.

I took down all the pictures of boys that I had cut out of magazines when I was in seventh grade. There were a few pictures of friends that I actually got framed and hung up on my walls in an attractive arrangement that at first reminded me of my dad's office. I packed up old books that I would never read again saving out the ones, mostly on *Budo* or Buddhism, that I knew were still relevant to my life. I cleaned my shrine and added a set of offering bowls that I filled with water every morning and drained every night.

I trained twice a day, every day. I loved the mornings in the park. Sometimes, I was the most senior student there and Rinchen would ask me to lead the warm up. Later in the summer, Megan started showing up more and more. I started making her go out with me every Wednesday night for a girls' night out. Once, I had even invited Beth along and we had a riot together. Matt had staked out his claim for Saturday nights. Other than those two nights, however, Megan usually stayed at home with her mom. I felt bad for Rinchen because he was mostly alone, but he had told me that day in the park that he was not particularly lonely though I am sure he occasionally lost his battle to turn loneliness into genuine solitude.

While I was cleaning out the desk in my room, I came across the sketch that Tripp had drawn the day after I had been almost killed by the drunk driver in front of my dad. I must have stared at it for an hour. With my finger, I traced the lines of the lotus blossom and the flames floating above it that Tripp had so skillfully arranged. The lotus on fire: it was perfect. The style of the picture was as unique as Tripp's signature. You could feel the aspiration for enlightenment in its petals and flames. At that point in time, it was all I really had to remember him by.

That Thursday afternoon, I jumped on my bike and rode down to Washington Avenue. I pulled up in front of Tattoo 314, the place where Eddie worked when he could work. When I walked into the shop there were two guys I didn't know who, like Eddie, were covered in tattoos. One of them was holding a buzzing device that looked like an old fashioned dentist's drill. Eddie was sitting in his wheel chair at a desk trying to draw out a design.

"Lhamo," he said startled to see me.

"Eddie, you are here. Cool, I need to talk to you."

"Sure, what's going on? How are you holding up?" He was looking at me with genuine concern. This struck me as odd because I was not the one sitting in a wheelchair with a steel rod in my leg.

"I'm good, Eddie. I'm getting there. How's your leg doing?"

"It is still pretty fucked up, but it is still connected so I am not complaining. How's Megs doing?"

"She is getting there too, but her mom is right off the deep end. That girl really, really needs a break."

"Yeah, I bet she does. Her mom is a bit of loon, no disrespect intended."

Mrs. Laskowitz was a nice enough person, I suppose. She looked old for her age. I had only seen her a few times at school functions. I had been warned that she divided the world into "*dojo*" and "not-*dojo*". Eddy was in the "not-*dojo*" category which meant that Mrs. Laskowitz would acknowledge his existence and would even be nice to him. I, on the other hand, was a *dojo* person which meant that she didn't like me without ever having met me. Worse, I had been her son's girlfriend which automatically meant that I was not good enough for him which really meant that I was not good enough for her. I mostly had stayed clear of her which really bothered me because I wanted to be friends with her just like Tripp and Megan were friends with my parents. I got my wish with Rinchen and that was more than enough for me.

"So what did you want to talk to me about, Lhamo? I am pretty sure that you are not here for a tattoo," he said trying to lighten the conversation with a little humor.

I reached into the back pocket of my jeans and pulled out the sketch of the flaming lotus blossom. "Well, actually Eddie, I am here for a tattoo."

Eddy took the sketch and stared at it intently. "Tripp drew that. You can tell his work a mile way." Eddie was starting to get sad. The sides of his mouth were drooping and his chin started to quiver.

"He drew it that day that you guys came out to see if I wanted to go to the monastery. That was the day after I had the near miss, remember?"

"Yeah, I remember " he said quietly.

"I want you to draw this on me, Eddie." Eddie looked up at me and said nothing at first but nodded slowly and then more rapidly as the idea of it began to take over his mind. "Yeah, we should do this. Awesome. When do you want to come in?"

Before I could answer him, he turned to one of the burly tattoo artists who was working on a client and said, "Hey Bo, I got a tatt here that I need to do myself. Is that going to be a problem?" Eddie was an apprentice and was normally limited to working out designs. The guy, who I assumed was his boss, put down his needle gun and walked over to look at the sketch. "The lines are pretty straightforward and wide except for the flame detail. Two colors on the flower, but those flames are shaded, that's some tricky stuff there dude, I am not sure you are quite ready for that."

"But I want him to do it," I said, interrupting their conversation, "you gotta let him do it." Bo looked up at me and could tell that there was more to this than was being said. He thought about it for a second and then he handed the sketch back to Eddie and said, "Just to be perfectly clear here, I *don't gotta* let him do it, but I'm *gonna* let him do it." Turning to Eddie he said, "She is going to have to sign a release. I'm not going to guarantee that you won't fuck this up, but if she does that, you are good to go. But you don't do this tatt without me or Mitchell being here. If something starts to go south, you're going to let us know about it before you screw up this pretty little lady's arm, you got that?" Eddie nodded. He was starting to actually get excited about this.

"I am not getting this tattoo on my arm," I said. This startled Eddie and caused Bo to stop in his tracks and turn around to look at me. "What did you have in mind, little sister?" Bo asked.

"Over my heart center. I want this over my heart."

"Okay," said Bo, "that's actually easier to do than an arm." With that he turned away and went back to work on his client.

"Damn, Lhamo, you know these things don't rub off, right? I can do a practice one in henna that wears off in a month so that you can make sure that you like it." I couldn't tell if Eddie was nervous because he was going to do his first tattoo or if he was nervous because he was probably going to see my boobs. It was probably a little of both.

"We are doing this, Eddie. When can you work me in?"

"I need a day to work out the stencil which I can get to work on this afternoon. Tomorrow or Saturday, I suppose." He paused. "Are you sure about this, Lhamo?"

I started to laugh. When he had first teased me about drawing on my arms months ago, who would have thought that I would have to kick him in the ass to get him actually put a tattoo on me for real. "Chill, Eddie, chill. It'll be a piece of cake. I'll see you Saturday morning, okay?"

"Yeah, Lhamo, sure thing, yeah… I'm good. It's all good."

As I turned to leave, a thought crossed my mind. "What exactly do you wear to a tattooing," I asked. Without turning around, Bo shouted out, "A thong and a wet T-shirt works for me." Eddie was mortified. "Shut the fuck up you asshole, this is my friend you are talking to." Bo was only mildly embarrassed and made a half-assed apology. I thought it was hilarious.

"Alrighty then, a thong and wet T-shirt it is. I'll see you guys on Saturday." And with that I walked out of the shop and fired up my bike. As I rode back out to Westchester I wondered to myself, "What do you wear when you get your first tattoo?"

When Saturday came, I thought I would be nervous, but I was really kind of excited. I wondered if my mom would take a picture of my new tattoo and put it in my Baby Book Maybe she would – right after she crapped her pants. I was hardly the first girl in Westchester to get one. There were unicorns on ankles and roses or daisies just above the bikini lines on many a Westchester girl. Eddie was the only one who knew that I was doing this. I figured by the time anyone started to give me shit about it, it would be too late.

It was a hot, muggy St. Louis summer day as I rode into town to meet Eddie at the shop. I had decided on a button up shirt because I figured I could expose the part of my chest that was going to become art without having to take off my top. I didn't really care. I was pretty sure these guys had seen a boob or two before and probably had drawn all over them.

I parked my bike in front of the shop and walked in. Eddie was looking over the stencil of Tripp's sketch that would become my new tattoo. It looked just like the original except he had made it smaller. There were papers to fill out including a two-page document that said that if Eddie screwed up I couldn't sue the shop. This was not encouraging, but I trusted him and I was not going to change my mind. There were no other customers yet, so Eddie pointed to a chair that looked like it was stolen from a dentist's office and I took a seat. There was even an adjustable dentisty looking light hanging over the chair. There was a curtain that wrapped around the work area and provided some privacy. Eddie had his tools and some small vials of ink set out on a table next to the chair. He was really nervous. He asked me to unbutton my shirt, which I did. After a few minutes, it was pretty clear that the shirt was going to be in the way, so I just took it off and removed my bra. This made

Eddie even more nervous and I was starting to get concerned that he was going to scribble all over me or something.

He washed my skin with rubbing alcohol and then took a disposable razor and shaved all the tiny little hairs off of his work space. He said that the surface had to be perfectly smooth. Then he took a stick of deodorant and rubbed it all over the newly shaved skin to help the stencil transfer better. Next, he placed the stencil on my chest and rubbed it. He was wearing surgical gloves and was very careful to make sure that the entire design stuck. When he pulled the paper away, he moved a mirror attached to a swinging arm over me so that I could see what it was going to look like. I smiled. There was Tripp's lotus blossom about to become a permanent part of me.

Eddy had poured several colors of ink into little cups on his work table. He opened a sealed package and took out a needle that he then placed into the gun. He even wore a face mask and magnifying glasses which made him look a little bit like a surgeon in a wheel chair. He was ready.

"I can rub you down with some lidocaine cream. It will make this nearly painless."

I smiled at him. "No Eddie, we are going to do this old school. I want to feel it -- all of it. I am only going to do this once and I want to remember the day that you poked Tripp's lotus blossom into my skin. Go ahead and let it burn. Let's do this thing."

"You're the boss." With that Eddie turned on his gun and it started to buzz. The first poke stung and I winced a little because I had not known what to expect. He moved the gun along the lines of the stencil slowly filling in the color that formed the outline of the lotus and the flames. When he got the outline in, he called Bo into the little operating room behind the curtain and asked him to check his work. Bo was huge and bald with a stubbly beard. He poked his head through the curtain and put on a pair of magnifying glasses and looked very intently at Eddie's work. "Not bad, rookie, not bad. Do the upper flame pieces first. Yellow first, orange second, red last. You can cover a goof in yellow with red, but not vice versa. The secret is not to goof up in the first place. You got that?" Eddie nodded. Bo winked at me and disappeared behind the curtain.

Eddie took his time, poking little drops of color into the flames. After hours of this, my chest was just one big sore spot and I hardly noticed the needle popping in and out of my skin anymore. Toward the end, Eddie would stop and cock his head one way and then the other checking his work. He wasn't nervous anymore and, in fact, it was like I wasn't even there. All there was for him was the design and he was taking great care to get it exactly right. Finally, he put in the last little touch. "That's it," he said, swinging the mirror over me so I could see his work.

Though my skin was red and already pretty swollen, he had done a wonderful job. There, over my heart center, was Tripp's flaming lotus – a perfect copy of a little piece of my Buddha-boy's mind cut into my skin. There it was, the lotus blossom, the symbol of my clan, the object of my training, my hope for the future and my promise for the benefit of all sentient beings. I smiled at Eddie and said, "You done good. Tripp would be very happy with your work." Eddie smiled and nodded.

He rubbed some antiseptic on my tattoo and then started to put a large square bandage over it. From the other side of the curtain, Bo called out, "Hey, Eddie don't forget to take a picture. It's your first tatt, man, and you are going to want to remember it." Eddy looked at me not knowing what to do. He was certainly not going to force the issue. I had already slipped my shirt back on. The bra was not going to happen anyway because it was going to rub on a very sore chest. "Get your camera," I said to him leaving my shirt unbuttoned. Eddy wheeled himself backward toward the desk and returned in few seconds with a small digital camera. I held my shirt open to expose the tattoo and he took the picture. He showed it to me on the camera screen. You couldn't tell it was me, but you sure as shit knew who had drawn the lotus blossom.

As I buttoned up my shirt, he told me that I needed to keep "the wound clean" and let it air out every day. "It's going to take at least a week or more for everything to heal," he said sounding like my doctor.

"I think we both know that it is going to take much longer than that," I replied. He looked down at his leg and then back at me. "Yeah, that's a fact."

I tried to pay him, but he wouldn't take my money. He did the whole thing sitting in his wheel chair trying to keep his leg out of the way the entire time. He looked exhausted, but happy. It had to have hurt him to sit bent over his leg like that for so long, but he never once complained. Finally, it was time for me to head home and explain the bandage on my chest to my parents.

"See you Eddie, thank you so much!" I bent over and hugged him around the neck.

"Anytime, Lhamo. Come and see me when you are ready for your next one."

I chuckled. A few hours ago, there could not have been a next one. But as I walked out of the shop, I wasn't so sure.

It had been hot when I came to the tattoo shop, too hot for a jacket, so I had made the ride wearing just a shirt. It was even hotter when I left. As I leaned over my gas tank flying down the freeway, the wind beat down my shirt and the flapping cloth made the lotus blossom burn. That's how life works. You take a stand for something and then commit yourself to it with pain and sweat. It's a small price you pay to be truly alive.

Epilogue: A Meteor Over Kansas

August 15, Boulder, Colorado. I have been riding for two days. It is lovely here in the state park where I am spending the night. There are tall pine trees everywhere and even in the dark of night, you can still see the outline of the mountains. I stopped by a Tibetan dharma center tonight and did Chenrezig *puja* with the group there. It is a Shambala Center. It would take a whole new diary to explain what that is. Let's just say that the Shambala practitioners are warriors of a whole different kind and I may have to look into that for myself in due time.

I decided, after all, to go to college at the University of California, Irvine and it took a whole lot of pleading and exaggerating of my circumstance to get me in. Ultimately, they more or less let me take Megan's place. It was not where I thought that I would wind up when I first applied to colleges. The conversation that Tripp and I had at the retreat that was supposed to have decided our future is still fresh in my mind. I thought, then, that when this moment came that I would be driving with my parents to Massachusetts. Of course, all that changed when the *kami* took Tripp away.

I am heading to the other coast now because there are important teachers there and I have never seen the ocean. I am going to train with two of Rinchen's own teachers. One I already know and the other I do not. As a matter of formality and good manners, Rinchen has written letters of introduction to both of these masters and I am carrying them with me now. One of these teachers is a legendary *Aikido* master who teaches in Irvine and the other is Lama Jinpa in Costa Mesa. Rinchen says that I will be in good hands, but I am pretty sure that I will be in my own hands.

I think I cried all the way across Kansas. I have not been out of Missouri much. You can't tell the difference between Kansas City, Missouri and Kansas City, Kansas other than by the license plates. That all changes when you leave the city and head out onto the prairie. It is the flattest place I have ever seen. You can drive for miles and miles and barely see a tree. The fields look like large carpets stretching to the horizon.

The thing that knocks you down about Kansas is the night sky. It is jet black and there are more stars scattered in it than I had ever thought possible. Last night, I camped in a cluster of trees in a hay field that ran along a side road. The GPS in my phone had said that there was a campground nearby. When I got there, it was overgrown and had not seen campers in years. I decided that it would be safer to camp near people, so I rode back toward the freeway and found this small grove that was within shouting distance of a convenience store near the on-ramp. The store was dimly lit and stayed open all night and I could see the people coming and going from the grove.

My bike and my camp were hidden from view and no one, not even my parents, knew where I was. I was scared shit-less at first. I have never done much real camping and I have never slept outside by myself, let alone miles from home. I wanted to be scared. Rinchen always taught us that fear is a mind killer. It is not your friend. The way to defeat fear is it to face it. So last night, as I sat down to meditate, I took the *phurba* that Zhangmo had given me out of its silk wrapper and drove it into the ground. This is where I was spending the night, come what may. This was the center of my experience. As I sat in meditation in that dark grove, I invited my fear to come and eat me alive, if it could.

To be honest about it, once I stopped being creeped out, it was a truly amazing night. There was a meteor shower last night over Kansas and in that black sky you could see it like it was fireworks. I saw one meteor fly across most of the sky leaving a vapor trail that glowed green for a minute or two after the meteor was gone. That flaming rock shot across the sky and exploded. I could even hear it pop. I understand now why ancient people would see such things and think that they were witnesses to gods and angels. That meteor-god went to war with the night sky last night and it was beautiful. You don't see that on the Disney Channel.

While I sobbed my way down the freeway yesterday, it felt like there was this rope tied to everything that I knew and loved in St. Louis at one end and to my heart at the other. The further I drove, the harder it pulled. I know that this is just my own attachment to these things and that this suffering is made by me. But I want to suffer a little bit. I want it to hurt. I want these things that I love to burn in me. I am not afraid of pain. It is my friend. It is the proof of my existence in this world. I am like that meteor flying across the prairie. Someday my vapor trail will glow its last and I will be gone, with or without a pop.

The sunrise this morning was amazing. In the early morning, the black sky turns to gray and then purple just before it bursts open with sunlight. I freshened up in the bathroom at the convenience store, grabbed a couple donuts and an energy drink and hit the highway.

My parents begged me to let them take me to Irvine. When I told them I was riding solo they had a fit. But ever since Tripp died, they have been worried about me and they know this wound is going to take a lifetime to heal. I told them I needed some time alone and the trip to California would be perfect. My dad finally broke down and let me go so long as I called in twice a day, which I have done. He even bought me some saddle bags for my motorcycle. They look a little funny and the guy at the shop had a difficult time getting them to fit. Crotch rockets are not made to carry saddlebags. For one thing, they really screw up your aerodynamics. I have a small bivouac tent and a sleeping bag that I strap to the back of my seat with bungee cords. Isn't that funny? I used to have closets full of crap at home, but everything I really need in this life fits on a motorcycle.

Leaving the *dojo* was nearly unbearable. Rinchen made a big deal out of my last practice. He sat me down in front of the class and instructed me as to what would be expected of me in my new *dojo* and how I should pay respects to my new teachers. Even in departure, there is training. But I nearly died when he handed me one of the small urns with some of Tripp's ashes in it that had been resting on the *tokonoma* since the memorial practice. There were three urns altogether. One would rest on the shrine at Byakuren for as long as there was a *dojo* there. One was given to Megan's mom. Rinchen and Megan decided that I should get the third one. What a mind fuck! There has been nothing in my experience that could prepare me for that. But as I sit in camp tonight with the urn wrapped in a silk altar cloth tucked safely in one of my saddle bags, it is an odd comfort to me. I told Rinchen that I had no idea what to do with the ashes, but he simply said that I would figure that out, just like I would figure out what to do with my memory of Tripp. So be it. I am deeply honored that he gave them to me.

Rinchen gave me something else that was equally mind-blowing. He had planned to give both Tripp and Megan authentic Japanese *katanas* from his personal collection as graduation presents. Megan had showed me hers when she got it earlier in the summer. It was beautiful. It is hard to believe that something so elegant could kill someone. It was made in the Sixteenth Century by a very reputable smith. It was sheathed in a black lacquer *saya* and decorated with gold trim pieces. As we sat in the *dojo* for what would be the last time for a while, Rinchen, sitting in *seiza*, turned to the *tokonoma* and lifted a long black-sheathed *katana* from the rack that had been sitting there since Tripp died. He said, "This was to be a gift for my son, but he has no use for it now, so I wish to give this to you, my other daughter, if you would be so kind to honor me by accepting it." He was bowing much lower than me with the sword held out in front of him in both hands. I burst into tears. I was shaking with sadness. Finally, I took a deep inhale and composed myself and made the wild horse lie down. I took the sword from him and bowed, "*Domo arigato gozaimasu, Sensei.*" My tears splattered like drops of rain on the perfectly polished *saya* that protected the blade.

It is funny what objects we choose to give us comfort. Ten years ago it would have been a stuffed animal or a doll. Two years ago it might have been new clothes or a cellphone. On that day, it was a four hundred and fifty year old sword. No one ever owns a sword like that. It outlives you. Over the centuries, it has had many owners who lived and died passing the care of this weapon, this object of beauty and death, on to the next custodian. It was my turn, but I will not be the last.

Before the ceremony ended, Megan approached the front of the class and sat next to her father. The two of them sitting side by side immediately suggested to my mind that part of the picture was missing. Once again my sadness rose up to overpower my eyes with tears. She bowed to me and said, "When you came here, you were an idiot, but no one has ever learned faster than you. You are my *kohai*, my best friend, my sister and I love you more than you will ever know." She reached into her *gi* and pulled out her prayer beads. "This is my *mala*, my most sacred possession; the tool I use to find my inner Buddha, the symbol of everything I believe in and want for this world. But I do not want these things just for me. I want them for all sentient beings, especially my favorite sentient being – *you*." And with that she bowed and offered me the *mala*. I had seen these beads wrapped around her wrist since I had known her. They were made of lotus seeds and while newer looking than the ones on Rinchen's *mala*, they were worn and shiny from being passed between her thumb and forefinger countless times. I was dumbstruck. I couldn't breathe. This was too much. I was shaking so hard that I thought that my mind was going to shut down and that I would faint right there on the mat. I leapt at her and held her in my arms squeezing her so hard that I am sure that she had difficulty breathing. I sobbed into the collar of her *gi*. She sobbed into mine. When I started to come to my senses, I could see tears rolling down Rinchen's cheeks. I placed the urn and the sword back on the *tokonoma* for safe keeping while we finished the ritual that brings all classes to an end. I bowed to the *kamidana* and to both Rinchen and Megan in turn. Then, I pivoted on my knee and took my place among my brothers and sisters. Every eye in the room was full of tears.

I clutched the *mala* in my hand and held it to my lips and kissed it and then I slipped it into the fold of my *gi*. I straightened myself and cleared my mind. I started to breathe in harmony with my clan. Thoughts slipped in and out of my mind like passing clouds. I never knew. I never knew how much beauty there is all around me, all the time.

As sad as yesterday was in Kansas, today in Colorado is filled with joy. As I got closer to the western half of the state, the Rocky Mountains came into view. I had never seen real mountains before. I had seen them in pictures, but pictures do very little to prepare you for seeing such a thing with your own eyes. I stopped for a late lunch along the freeway and just stared at the jagged horizon off in the west. A couple of hours later they were even larger and I had to stop again to take it all in. They are so beautiful. I guess it takes something as enormous as these mountains to overcome my fear of new places and flush from my heart the sadness of what I have left behind. I know that in time, things will get easier and that my heart will, once again, sit still for a single drop of rain.

I will camp in the desert in Nevada tomorrow and be in California the day after. I plan to drive straight to the ocean. I promised Megan that I would spit in the Pacific for her when I get there. Then I will make my way down the coastal highway to Costa Mesa and on to Irvine.

Megan is going to stay in St. Louis for the fall, but is planning to come out to California for a visit and check out the university and my new *dojo*. She says that if she likes it there that she might move out to Irvine too. Her mom is still not doing so well and Megan, ever her mother's guardian angel, will not abandon her until she thinks that the time is right. She may never come to California at all, but I will be back in St. Louis for Christmas, so we will have to live on email and phone calls until then.

My dad has shipped a few boxes of clothes and things to California and is flying out with my mom to meet me when I get there. This was the compromise that we struck when I told them that I needed to ride to California by myself. Tyler is coming too. They have promised him a trip to Disney Land. He needs to find a *dojo*.

When you ride a motorcycle cross-country you have a lot of time to think. How did this all happen? What collision of cosmic forces propelled me out of my old world and into this new one? Rinchen says that, for whatever reason, I am a person of extraordinary karma. I wonder. One minute you are in a tanning salon servicing your appearance and the next minute you are in a tattoo parlor having a fragment of your dead lover's mind forever etched between your tits. And yet here I am, a thousand miles from home; a young woman racing across the prairie, over mountains and through the desert on a motorcycle with a sleeping bag strapped to the seat, an ancient *katana* in a red silk bag tied to her back carrying her boyfriend's ashes to the sea. And like Joshu's dog, there is nothing that you can say about it that means a god damned thing.

I used to hate my name, until I came to realize that I don't really have one. But people have to know you as somebody from somewhere. Otherwise, it makes them nervous. Well, I guess, Rinchen has solved that problem for me. I am Lhamo of the Byakuren Clan. The purpose of my life is to chop wood and carry water. And tomorrow when the sun rises, I am going to ride hard and love my guts out.

About The Author

D. M. Kenyon is an author, a father of four, a husband, a lawyer, an entrepreneur, a community builder, an inventor, a Tibetan Buddhist, a martial artist and a teacher. He began the odyssey of his most unusual life in southern Michigan where he grew up on his family's farm. From there, his adventures took him to college where he earned a degree in English and then on to law school in St. Louis, Missouri where he took up residency and practiced law for over twenty years. During this time, he trained under the direction of a Tibetan Buddhist lama of the Kagyu lineage for seventeen years and studied martial arts for over a decade with some of the world's greatest masters. A man deeply committed to conscientious living, Kenyon has started several companies that went on to employ dozens of people, many of whom had been chronically unemployed. He helped found the multi-ethnic St. Louis Buddhist Council and is currently helping to form a green-tech sustainability consortium of companies, educational institutions and labor unions that use environmental responsibility as a form of economic development.

Kenyon wrote *The Lotus Blossom* for children, particularly his daughters, after he observed the difficulty that his wife and other professional women had in managing confrontation and competition in the business environment. Concerned that women do not always have access to the same training opportunities as men and that the injustice of gender double standards persist in our culture, he has committed himself to raising the issue of consciousness training and committed living not just for women, but for everyone, as a way to cultivate compassion and fairness in the face of the dehumanizing effects of the Information Age.

You can learn more about the world of *The Lotus Blossom* and follow D. M. Kenyon's articles and essays on culture and consciousness at *The Lotus Blossom* website at www.blog.lotusblossombook.com.

Glossary

Aikido (/ˌīkēˈdō/): (Japanese) A martial art of Japanese origin devoted to the principle of non-aggression that manipulates the energy of an attack against the harmful intention of the attacker. The word *Aikido* is a composite of three Japanese words. "*Ai*" suggests harmony; "*ki*" is the essential energy that flows through living things and "*do*" is a word suggesting a path or a way to understanding. Roughly translated, the word *Aikido* means "a way to enlightenment by harmonizing energy."

aikidoka (/ˌīkēˈdōˌkä/): (Japanese) A person who practices the art of *Aikido*.

bokken (/bō-kən/): (Japanese) A wooden practice sword, usually made out of white oak, that is carved to approximate the shape of a Japanese *katana* and used for practicing sword movement and sometimes for sparring.

Buddha (/ˈboodə/): (Sanskrit) Buddha is the name used to refer to Siddhartha Gautama of the Śākya clan who lived in what is now Nepal. Because he came from the Śākyas, he is sometimes referred to as Śākyamuni Buddha. Buddha as an ordinary human being and is not associated with any supernatural abilities although his insight into the nature of reality and the human condition is considered absolute. It is said that he reached enlightenment when he was around thirty-three years old and lived and taught until he was eighty. His long teaching career is one of the many reasons why there is a rather large degree of friendliness and cooperation between the various Buddhist sects to this day.

budoka (/ˈbuːdəʊˌkä/): (Japanese) A person who practices the art of *Budo*.

Budo (/ˈbuːdəʊ/): (Japanese) The way, method or path of war usually referring to a training methodology. *Budo* can be a general term that encompasses all martial arts or any other practices involved with the study of conflict.

bushido (/ˈbooSHēdō/): (Japanese) Literally, "the way of the warrior," *bushido* can indicate the general manner of living attributed to the samurai or the actual code of conduct that they lived by.

chado (/CHädō/): (Japanese) A highly refined practice of heightening consciousness by use of a tea ceremony. *Cha* is the Japanese word for "tea" and *do* is the Japanese word for a path or method of understanding that leads to enlightenment. *Chado* is considered a path to enlightenment and is as difficult to learn and master as any martial art.

Chenrezig (/CHən͵rä͵zē/): (Tibetan) Chenrezig is the Tibetan name for Avalokitesvara or "the lord who watches". This is a manifestation of the Buddhist compassion in a symbolic form. His Holiness the Dalai Lama is considered to be a living manifestation of Chenrezig.

Chöd (/CHood/): (Tibetan) Chöd practice is based on the *Prajnaparamita*, the latter being referred to as The Heart of Perfect Wisdom Sutra, that explains the emptiness teachings of the Buddha. The main emphasis of the teaching is to confront death and impermanence, visualize compassion in order to destroy the mental construct of *self*. It is often practiced in a cemetery at night. A highly musical practice, it is based, in part, on the visualization of offering oneself as food to a wide array of beings including demons so that they might transcend suffering and reach enlightenment. Chöd practice originated with the great female practitioner of the Eleventh Century, Machig Labdrön, and uses her image in the form of a *dakini*, an enlightened female being, as part of its visualization practice.

dakini (/ˈdokˈēˈnē/) (Tibetan) A tantric deity described as a female embodiment of enlightened energy. In the Tibetan language, *dakini* is rendered as *khandroma* which means "she who traverses the sky" or "she who moves in space". Dakinis are considered to be quite powerful and actively engaged in human activity.

dharma (/ˈdärmə/): (Japanese) Often translated as "the way" or "the law" it might be best to think of *dharma* as meaning the natural essence of how something works. The word *dharma* by itself has no Buddhist connotation. There are many *dharmas*. There is the *dharma* of baseball that would include the rules and the skills necessary to play the game. *Dharma*, however, is often used as a short form of the term *Buddha-dharma* or "the way Buddhism works." When the word is used without any other reference, this usage is often assumed.

dojo (/dōjō /): (Japanese) A training hall or school, usually dedicated to martial arts or meditation practice. The term, however, can be associated with a place of study for other arts.

Dokkōdō (/dəˈkōtō/): (Japanese) The name of a set of precepts that outline the expected behavior and attitude of samurai. Written in the 16th Century by Miyamoto Musashi, the *Dokkōdō* is said to establish the samurai ideal.

domo arigato gozaimasu (/dōmō-arē'gatō-gōzī'masoo̅ /): (Japanese) A formal way of saying "thank you very much".

dorje (/'dôr'jā/) (Tibetan) *See: vajra.*

eubidori (/yoo'bē-dôr,ē/): (Japanese) An *Aikido* technique whereby the *nage* takes hold of one or more fingers as an attacker is trying to grab. By bending the fingers backward, the tendons of the hand are extended causing extreme pain for the attacker if he proceeds with the attack.

gi (/gē/): (Japanese) Originally, a *gi* was a thin kimono that was worn under an outer kimono, hence the description of a *gi* as *underwear*. Sometimes referred to as a *do-gi* in *dojos*, a *gi* is usually a white cotton duck or a thicker *Judo weave* of cotton that is used in martial arts uniforms. *Gis* are durable and allow for a full range of motion.

Green Tara (/grēn 'tɑːrə/): (English) Known as *Jetsun Dolma* in Tibetan, Green Tara is the female manifestation of compassion and is considered to be the tantric consort of Chenrezig. While it is said that Green Tara watches the suffering of the world, she is depicted with her foot stepping off of the lotus on which she traditionally sits indicating that she actively intervenes in the suffering of beings.

hibachi (/hə'bäCHē/): (Japanese) A box lined with metal for holding hot coals that is used as a cooking stove in traditional Japanese homes.

hachimaki ('hätCHē,mäkē/): (Japanese) A headband made from a piece of cloth that is rolled into a rope-like shape and tied around the head, usually with the a half knot on the forehead. Used sometimes simply to absorb sweat, it has ceremonial uses as well.

hai (/'hī /): (Japanese) Yes.

hajime (/'ha'jim'mā/): (Japanese) Literally means "begin". Used in *dojos* as a word for *go* or *start*.

hakama (/'hakəmə/): (Japanese) Technically, a *hakama* is a pair of pants although the blousy legs appear to Western eyes to look like a skirt. There are five pleats in the front of a *hakama* and two in the back representing the seven virtues of *bushido*. These include, benevolence, honor and justice, courtesy or etiquette, wisdom, sincerity, loyalty and piety.

hara (/'har,rə/): (Japanese) The center of gravity in the human body. *Hara* is the center of mass in the human body said to be located a few inches below the navel. In martial arts practice, *hara* is the point from which the greatest strength can come, but it is also a point of orientation meaning that a swordsman can only strike objects that are in front of his hara. Locations not in front of the hara are considered "dead angles". See, *shikaku*.

haori (/ˈhəˈourē/): (Japanese) A jacket, usually made of silk, with wide sleeves typically worn by men over a *kimono*. Traditional *haori* often had pictures of various scenes or animals printed in the lining that would be shown when the garment was removed and hung up.

himo (/ˈhēmō/): (Japanese) Literally, "string". *Himo* are laces that are woven over the gripping surfaces of swords, used to tie on *hakama* or *Kendo* helmets.

ikkyo (/ˈēkˌyō/): (Japanese) Literally means "first technique" or "first category of techniques". *Ikkyo* techniques are characterized by intercepting strikes and redirecting the force in order to take balance. Contrast to trapping a strike in a joint lock.

irmi nage (/ˈirēmē-ˈnägā/): (Japanese) *Irimi* means "to enter" and *nage* means "to throw", hence *irimi nage* means "entering throw". In this type of technique, the *nage* will step into her attacker's energy to redirect the power of the attack. This often results in a very sudden a violent redirection of energy that leave the attacker on the ground.

jo (/jō/): (Japanese) A wooden staff, usually made of white oak, that is approximately four feet long and an inch or more in diameter. It is contrasted to the "*bo*," the long staff, that is six feet or longer. Staff fighting uses many of the same movements and principles as sword fighting. Students are trained at first by learning *kata*, or forms, that are a sequences of movements that help the student learn individual techniques and the flow of motion between them.

joseki (/ˈjōˈsekē/): (Japanese) Related to the word *joza* or "upper seat," *joseki* indicates the higher ranking portion of a line or the most important side of a room. Similar to *kamiza* and *shimoza* (high seat, low seat) which in a *dojo* would be the front and back of the *dojo* respectively, *joseki* is the right side of the *dojo* when facing the *kamiza* or *kamidana*. It is the side reserved for those of the highest rank.

kami (/ˈkämē/): (Japanese) A divine force or being in the Shinto religion. In the Shinto religion it is believed that all natural things have a *kami*, or a spiritual force. A divine wind, similar to the typhoon that destroyed the fleet of the Kublai Khan in the Thirteenth Century is called a *kami-kaze*.

kamidana (/ˈkämēˈdänə/): (Japanese) Literally means "spirit altar" and is a small, Shinto-styled shrine, often no more than a picture frame with a shelf underneath it, that hangs on a wall. *Kamidana* hang in homes as well as *dojos*.

kamiza (/ˈkämēˌsə/): (Japanese) Literally meaning "top seat," it is the place of honor usually closet to a shrine in a room or the head of a table. In a *dojo*, the *kamiza* is usually a place on the mat nearest the shrine though the person sitting in the *kamiza* is expected to have his back to the shrine and usually facing the door. The *kamiza* was traditionally placed farthest from the door because it was the warmest part of a room and the safest place in the event of an attack.

kampai (/kämˈpī/): (Japanese) A salutation used when making a toast. Similar to the English use of "Cheers!"

kanling (/ˈkonˈliNG/): (Tibetan) A ceremonial trumpet made of the upper portion of a human femur, usually from a young girl who died in child birth. In Tibet, it is not unusual for some parts of deceased people to be donated to make certain ceremonial items including *kanlings*. *Kanlings* are now prohibited from being exported from most Asian countries because of the rise of the black market that supports grave robbers, often of Islamic cemeteries, who create false *kanlings* for the Western market.

Karate-do (/kəˈrätē-dō/): A way to enlightenment fighting with the hands and feet. *Karate* is a martial art form developed in Okinawa by peasants who were not allowed to own weapons. One the of the principle concepts in *Karate* is to use human limbs as swords, staffs and pikes.

karma (/ˈkärmə/): The chain of cause and effect. Often confused for a notion of fate, *karma* is really the logical progression or chain of events and their consequences that are understood to be interdependent.

kata (/ˈkätə/): 1. (Japanese) A series of motions performed in sequence that teaches a student how to execute various strikes, blocks and stances and the transitions from one to the other. 2. (Tibetan) A ceremonial scarf made of white silk that is offered to teachers and others as a sign of devotion and respect.

katana (/kəˈtänə/): (Japanese) A Japanese sword that is between two and three feet long usually with a slight curve to the blade. *Katana* were usually part of a two-sword set, the other sword being the shorter *wakasashi*. While most *Budoka* are trained to use the *katana* with two hands, it is light enough to be used with one hand. The famous swordsman, Miyamoto Musashi, often fought with two *katana*; one in each hand.

Kendo (/ˈkenˌdō/): (Japanese) Literally, "the way of the sword", but in recent times has come to mean the sport of Japanese fencing. While *Kendo* earned its right to be considered a path to enlightenment, it is rarely practiced in its deadly form in modern times.

kenjitsu (/ˈkenˌjitsoo/): (Japanese) Literally means "sword technique". Unlike *Kendo, Kenjitsu* is not an entire art of sword, but rather training techniques designed to teach correct movement and power in sword movement.

kila (/kēlə/): (Sanskrit) See *phurba*.

kiai (/kēˌī/): (Japanese) A short syllable shouted during an exhale of breath that helps compress the breath in the thorax to make the body hard while striking or being struck.

kohai (/ˈkōˌhī/): (Japanese) A term a person who is of relative junior rank. Used similarly to the English term "junior". A *kohai* is a junior student relative to a *sempai* in a *dojo.*

mala (/malə/): (unknown origin) A strand of beads, similar to a Catholic rosary, used to count mantra recitations during certain meditation practices. Buddhist *malas* have 108 counting beads, exactly the same number as Catholic rosaries. The counting beads are divided by a large *guru bead*. This bead represents a practitioner's teacher and is never crossed, meaning that as the meditator counts beads and arrives at the guru bead, the *mala* is flipped around and the counting resumes in the opposite direction.

matcha (/mäCHə/): (Japanese) A very high quality, finely powdered green tea used in tea ceremonies.

menuki (/menōōkē/): (Japanese) A charm, usually made of iron or precious metals, that can depict nearly anything from birds to boat oars that are placed under the braided laces of the handle of a Japanese sword, called a *tsuka. Menuki* typically had artistic or ritualistic meaning and usually were selected to fit into a theme of decoration of Japanese swords.

montsuki (/ˈmänˈsōōkē/): (Japanese) A emblem, usually depicted with an image inside a ring, that symbolizes a clan or family. Every noble family in the samurai era had a *montsuki* that was used in the same way as the European coat of arms.

mu (/mōō/): (Japanese) This term is untranslatable and indefinable. It denotes the notion of emptiness of all concept or idea. *Mu* is a state of mind that is fully aware, but absent of concept or thought.

nage (/ˈnägā/): The person who is executing a throwing technique. Compare to *uke.*

nikkyo (/ˈnēkˌyō/): Literally means "second technique" or "second category of techniques". *Nikkyo* techniques are characterized by trapping appendages and locking out the critical joints forcing the joint into flexion. Contrast to trapping a strike in a joint lock that forces extension.

Nyung Ne (/NyooNG ˈnā/): (Tibetan) A two and a half day practice which involves complete fasting for the last day and a half. Based on the visualization practice of Thousand Arm Chenrezig, the practice is undertaken as a method of karmic purification and to develop compassion. It is said that the *Nyung Ne* practice can purify all negative *karma* from this and past lives.

obi (/ˈōbē/): (Japanese) Literally, "belt". An *obi* is a type of flat cloth used to hold closed a *gi* or *kimono*. *Gi obi* are usually two inches wide and made of very strong cotton webbing. *Kimono obi,* especially for women, are usually much wider, made of silk and can bear some decoration.

phurba (/ˈfərbə/): (Tibetan) A ceremonial three-edged dagger with the head of a deity at the pummel. Used for a variety of ceremonial purposes, *phurbas* are said to exorcise demons and stabilize the space-time continuum.

randori (/ˈränˌdorē/): (Japanese) Literally means "creating order out of chaos." In a *dojo, randori* is a free style practice where attackers converge on usually a single defender using any form of attack that pleases them. The defender must rise to the occasion of this multi-attack freestyle melée designed to simulate real combat.

rinpoche (/ˈrinˈpäCHˈā/): (Tibetan) Literally, "precious one". A title often used in association with Tibetan Buddhist lamas.

Samsara (/Saṃsāra/): (Sanskrit) Meaning "continuous flow" in Sanskrit, *Samsara* is often referred to as the "ocean of suffering". This is the continuous flow of delusion, attachment and mental affliction that causes conscious experience to estranged from the natural state of enlightenment.

saya (/sīˈyə /): (Japanese) The scabbard of a Japanese sword often coated in black lacquer, but can be many different colors.

sangha (/ˈsəNG(g)ə/): (Sanskrit) Originally, a term meaning a community of ordained monks or nuns, it has come to be used as a more general term for any community of Buddhists.

sankyo (/ˈSäNGkˌyō/): (Japanese) Literally means "third technique" or "third category of techniques". *Sankkyo* techniques are characterized by trapping appendages and locking out their critical joints by forcing the joint into extension. Contrast to trapping a strike in a joint lock that forces flexion.

sempai (/ˈsempī/): (Japanese) A term of relative seniority. Used similarly to the English term "senior". A *sempai* is a student of senior rank and responsibility in a *dojo*.

sensei (/ˈsenˈsā/): (Japanese) Literally, "a person who is born before another". The term is widely used to mean an elder teacher. A student generally has only one teacher, thereby giving the word the implication of "root teacher" or "primary teacher".

shantap (/ˈSHanˈtap/): (Tibetan) A skirt like garment that is used as part of monastic robes in the Tibetan Buddhist tradition. Typically made of red cotton or wool, the *shantap* is wrapped around the waist with pleats folded at the waist in a specific configuration indicating monastic vows. The *shantap* is held on with a cord, similar to rope, that is often orange in color.

shakuhachi (/ˈSHākoōˈhäCHē/): (Japanese) A bamboo flute with a haunting sound that is the woodwind instrument of preference in a large body of traditional Japanese music.

shikaku (/SHēˌkäˈkoō/): (Japanese) Literally, "dead angle". This is a relative location near an attacker where he does not have the ability to see or reach. For example, if one is standing behind an attacker's shoulder blade, he can neither see or reach that spot. *Shikaku* is sometimes erroneously translated as "the eye of the hurricane" because of how it functions in martial arts, but this is an inaccurate translation.

shikko (/SHēkˌō/): (Japanese) The practice of walking on one's knees practiced in a *dojo* to accommodate relocation without standing up. *Shikko* is not merely shuffling across the floor on one's knees, but rather a very fast and deliberate form of ambulation that can be performed without allowing the practitioner's head to rise up and down while in motion.

shimoseki (/SHēmōˈsekē/): (Japanese) Related to the word *shimoza* or "lower seat," *shimoseki* indicates the lower ranking portion of a line or the least important side of a room. Similar to *kamiza* and *shimoza* (high seat, low seat) which in a *dojo* would be the front and back of the *dojo* respectively, *shimoseki* is the left side of the *dojo* when facing the *kamiza* or *kamidana*. It is the side reserved for those of the lowest rank.

shinai (/Shinˌnī/): (Japanese) A practice sword made of sliced bamboo cut to the approximate the length of a *katana* and used in the practice of *Kendo*. A *shinai* is considerably lighter than a real sword and, therefore, practice for real sword training tends to rely on the heavier *bokken*. A *shinai* is strong, but does not deliver the same shock when striking another in practice or competition.

shomen (/ˈSHŌmən/): (Japanese) Literally means "head," but is used in a variety of ways including as a short form of the word "*shomenuchi*". *Shomen* is also the term for a *Kendo* helmet and can be used to refer to the top of something.

shomenuchi (/ˈSHŌmənˌooCHē/): (Japanese) A sword cut that is performed by raising a sword with both hands over the head and cutting straight down.

shugyo (/ˈSHoōgˌyō/): (Japanese) Literally, "conducting oneself in a way that inspires mastery." In *dojos*, *shugyo* can also be interpreted as the suffering one does to develop oneself.

tame shigiri (/ˈtamā-SHeˈgērē/): (Japanese) A method of practicing real cutting with a sword usually done by cutting rolled-up mats of bamboo stalks that have been soaked in water to simulate the density of flesh.

taifu no me (/tīˌfoō ʾnō ʾmā/): (Japanese) Literally, "the eye of the typhoon or eye of the storm."

thanka (/ˈtäNGkə/): (Tibetan) Literally, "a thing that is rolled up". *Thankas* are ceremonial paintings that follow rigorous rules of construction and are usually blessed by various *Vajrayanna* processes. *Thankas* are painted on paper, but sewn into silk frames that are weighed down at the bottom by a wooden rod and have a silk flap that covers the painting when it is rolled up. *Thankas* are designed to be rolled up for storage and to make them portable.

tokonoma (/tōkəˈnōmə/): (Japanese) A recessed portion of a wall or alcove that is used to display objects of art or special interest. *Tokonomas* are common in tea houses and often seen in *dojos*. While merely designating a display area, the term is often misused in the West to mean a shrine in a *dojo*.

tsuka (/ˈtsoōkə/): (Japanese) The pummel or handle of a Japanese sword. A *tsuka* has a core of magnolia wood wrapped in the skin of a manta ray. Ray skin has a rough texture that enhances grip. The *tsuka* is usually, but not always, wrapped in flat cotton or silk cords called *himo* that are braided over the surface of the *tsuka* to act as the primary grip surface. *Menuki* are often placed under the *himo* to create bulges that enhance grip as well.

tsuba (/ˈtsoōbə/): (Japanese) The hand guard on a Japanese sword. *Tsubas* can be either very plain or extremely decorative and are collected even without the sword as works of art.

uke (/ˈooˈkā/): (Japanese) A person designated to be the attacker in a training exercise. This term is used primarily by *Aikidoka* and *Judo*.

ukemi (/ˈooˈkemˌē/): (Japanese) Sometimes referred to as "the art of falling down," *ukemi* it the art of simulating attack and withstanding the martial technique that responds to the attack. The term is used primarily in *Aikido* and *Judo* where throwing techniques are the predominant techniques of those arts.

Vajra (/ˈvəjrə/): Sometimes translated as "thunderbolt" or "diamond light", a *vajra* a sudden burst of illumination in consciousness that brings about immediate awareness and enlightenment itself.

Vajrayanna (/ˌvəjrəˈyänə/): (Sanskrit) The Sanskrit word *vajra* has no direct English translation, but conveys the notion of a sudden, clear awareness compared to a lightning strike that immediately provokes enlightened awareness. Yana is often translated as "vehicle," but its actual Sanskrit meaning is "raft" implying that it is a tool to be used to cross the ocean of suffering. *Vajrayanna* Buddhism is practiced extensively in Tibet and to a lesser extent in parts of Japan. It uses visualizations to speed up the process of enlightenment by avoiding the mental meandering that some students experience while trying contemplate emptiness alone.

zen (/zen/): (Tibetan) A long shawl that is part of the robes of a monk, nun or lama. Zens are usually long enough to be wrapped at least three times around the shoulders, but are usually worn wrapped around the shoulders only once with the excess material folded ritualistically and carried on the right arm.

Zen (/zen/): (Japanese) A form of Buddhism widely practiced in China and Japan that uses the principle practice of meditating on emptiness. *Zen* is known for its simplicity and the direct approach it takes to experiencing enlightenment.

wakazashi (/wäkēˈzäSHē/): (Japanese) A Japanese sword that is between one and two feet long usually with a slight curve to the blade. *Wakasashi* were usually part of a two-sword set, the other sword being the longer *katana*.

yankyo (/ˈyänkˌyō/): (Japanese) Literally means "fourth technique" or "fourth category of techniques". *Yankkyo* techniques are characterized by manipulating attackers by applying pressure on nerve meridians to cause pain. Contrast to trapping a strike in a joint lock that forces flexion.

yidam (/ˈyidˌdam/): (Tibetan) Literally "tight mind". A *yidam* is a deity with a specific set of qualities and characteristics that is used as a visualization object in meditation. *Yidams* are understood to exist in consciousness and are not necessarily treated as "real" divine entities as they might be in other religions. They focal points of consciousness that are part of a very effective practice methodology. This is not to say that they are not real, but rather, begs the question what is *real*.